RACHEL HOWZELL HALL

"A fresh voice in crime fiction."

—Lee Child

"Devilishly clever . . . Hall's writing sizzles and pops."

—Meg Gardiner

"Hall slips from funny to darkly frightening with elegant ease."

—*Publishers Weekly*

PRAISE FOR *WHAT FIRE BRINGS*

"Rachel Howzell Hall is a master of the psychological suspense thriller. *What Fire Brings* delivers shocking secrets, surprises on every page, and a killer twist that will leave you breathless. A must-read!"

—Melinda Leigh, #1 *Wall Street Journal* bestselling author

"This one will keep you guessing! Hall's considerable talent is on full display as she expertly deploys misdirection and subterfuge in a riveting tale of intrigue and suspense where nothing is as it seems. The past collides with the present to forever alter the future while the twists keep coming until the final shocking reveal. If you love an intricate plot with well-crafted prose, incisive insight, and complex characters, do not miss this propulsive mystery by a superb storyteller!"

—Isabella Maldonado, *Wall Street Journal* bestselling author

"Crackling wildfires, dark secrets, and a serial killer on the loose. Rachel Howzell Hall's *What Fire Brings* is a captivating and creepy thrill ride through the California canyons, right up to the final and fiery twisty end."

—Wanda M. Morris, award-winning author of *All Her Little Secrets* and *Anywhere You Run*

"Rachel Howzell Hall is simply one of the finest crime writers of her generation, and *What Fire Brings* is her most assured novel yet . . . and one that hits a little close to home for everyone who puts pen to paper or finger to keyboard. Tense, illuminating, and filled with surprises on every page. A masterwork that will leave you flipping pages to see what you might have missed."

—Tod Goldberg, *New York Times* bestselling author

PRAISE FOR *WHAT NEVER HAPPENED*

"Rachel Howzell Hall does it again. *What Never Happened* blends blade-sharp writing and indelible characters with a suspenseful story that pulls you in and won't let go, as a seeming paradise grows dark with storms, suspicion, and murder. I couldn't put it down."

—Meg Gardiner, #1 *New York Times* bestselling author

"*What Never Happened* opens with a gut punch and doesn't let up from there. Rachel Howzell Hall's twist on the you-can't-go-home-again story is smart, dizzying, and thrilling. She not only handles the mystery elements expertly, but she honors the grief and rage of our past and present."

—Paul Tremblay, bestselling author of *The Cabin at the End of the World* and *The Pallbearers Club*

"Rachel Howzell Hall has crafted her own genre of slow-boiling, powerfully emotional thrillers. Her realistic characters are ordinary people, haunted by past horrors that won't stay buried, forcing them to face pure evil to find their own redemption."

—Lee Goldberg, #1 *New York Times* bestselling author

"In *What Never Happened*, Rachel Howzell Hall seamlessly weaves together the past and the present, decorating her breakneck plot with dark secrets and unexpected reveals that glitter like jewels. I couldn't turn the pages fast enough."

—Jess Lourey, Amazon Charts bestselling author of *The Quarry Girls*

"*What Never Happened* is superb. Beautifully and smartly written, it is an engrossing thriller with an ending that will leave your head spinning. It is deliciously creepy and perfectly crafted. In a word, stunning! Don't miss this one!"

—Lisa Regan, *USA Today* and *Wall Street Journal* bestselling author

"Rachel Howzell Hall's *What Never Happened* is a spine-tingling twist of a roller coaster that keeps you on the edge of your seat to the very last page and will have you saying 'Thanks a lot, Rachel, for my lack of sleep.'"

—Yasmin Angoe, award-winning author of the critically acclaimed Nena Knight series, *Her Name Is Knight* and *They Come at Knight*

PRAISE FOR *WE LIE HERE*

"*We Lie Here* is another fast and surprisingly funny thriller from Rachel Howzell Hall. I was on the edge of my seat through all the revelations, twists, and turns in a fast-paced third act. Get this book and relax with the knowledge that you are in the hands of a fantastic crime novelist."

—Adrian McKinty, Edgar Award–winning author of the Sean Duffy series

"In *We Lie Here*, Rachel Howzell Hall gives us a tight, lean, eye-level look at the Gibson family—flawed, normal, abnormal, and each affected by a deadly secret left buried for years—while weaving a page-turning tapestry of dread, cold-blooded murder, and nail-biting tension. What a ride. What a wonderful writer. More, please."

—Tracy Clark, author of the Chicago Mystery series

"*We Lie Here* is definitive proof that it's impossible to be disappointed by Rachel Howzell Hall, who just gets better and better with each book. She has tools and tricks to spare as she pulls you to the edge of your seat with her razor-sharp plotting and keen eye for the darker side of human behavior that's too easily obscured by the California sunshine."

—Ivy Pochoda, author of *These Women*, a *New York Times* Best Thriller of 2020

"Loaded with surprises and shocking secrets, and propelled by Rachel Howzell Hall's magnificent prose, *We Lie Here* is a captivating thriller that I couldn't put down. It's very clear to me that Hall is one of the best crime writers working today, and she keeps getting better. *We Lie Here* is a can't-miss book."

—Alex Segura, acclaimed author of *Secret Identity*, *Star Wars Poe Dameron: Free Fall*, and *Blackout*

"Rachel Howzell Hall continues to prove why she's one of crime fiction's leading writers. *We Lie Here* is a psychological-suspense fan's dream with both a heroine you'll want to root for and a story you'll want to keep reading late into the night. A must-read!"

—Kellye Garrett, Agatha, Anthony, and Lefty Award–winning author of *Like a Sister*

PRAISE FOR *THESE TOXIC THINGS*

An Amazon Best Book of the Month: Mystery, Thriller & Suspense

"This cleverly plotted, surprise-filled novel offers well-drawn and original characters, lively dialogue, and a refreshing take on the serial killer theme. Hall continues to impress."

—*Publishers Weekly* (starred review)

"A mystery/thriller/coming-of-age story you won't be able to put down till the final revelation."

—*Kirkus Reviews*

"Tense and pacey, with an appealing central character, this is a coming-of-age story as well as a gripping mystery."

—*The Guardian*

"The mystery plots are twisty and grabby, but also worth noting is the realistic rendering of a Black LA neighborhood locked in a battle over gentrification."

—*Los Angeles Times*

"Rachel Howzell Hall . . . just gets better and better with each book."

—CrimeReads

"Rachel Howzell Hall continues to shatter the boundaries of crime fiction through the sheer force of her indomitable talent. *These Toxic Things* is a master class in tension and suspense. You think you are ready for it. But. You. Are. Not."

—S. A. Cosby, author of *Blacktop Wasteland*

"*These Toxic Things* is taut and terrifying, packed with page-turning suspense and breathtaking reveals. But what I loved most is the mother-daughter relationship at the heart of this gripping thriller. Plan on reading it twice: once because you won't be able to stop, and the second time to savor the razor's edge balance of plot and poetry that only Rachel Howzell Hall can pull off."

—Jess Lourey, Amazon Charts bestselling author of *Unspeakable Things*

"The brilliant Rachel Howzell Hall becomes the queen of mind games with this twisty and thought-provoking cat-and-mouse thriller. Where memories are weaponized, keepsakes are deadly, and the past gets ugly when you disturb it. As original, compelling, and sinister as a story can be, with a message that will haunt you long after you race through the pages."

—Hank Phillippi Ryan, *USA Today* bestselling author of *Her Perfect Life*

PRAISE FOR *AND NOW SHE'S GONE*

"It's a feat to keep high humor and crushing sorrow in plausible equilibrium in a mystery novel, and few writers are as adept at it as Rachel Howzell Hall."

—*Washington Post*

"One of the best books of the year . . . whip-smart and emotionally deep, *And Now She's Gone* is a deceptively straightforward mystery, blending a fledgling PI's first 'woman is missing' case with underlying stories about racial identity, domestic abuse, and rank evil."

—*Los Angeles Times*

"Smart, razor-sharp . . . Full of wry, dark humor, this nuanced tale of two extraordinary women is un-put-downable."

—*Publishers Weekly* (starred review)

"Smart, packed with dialogue that sings on the page, Hall's novel turns the tables on our expectations at every turn, bringing us closer to truth than if it were forced on us in school."

—Walter Mosley

"A fierce PI running from her own dark past chases a missing woman around buzzy LA. Breathlessly suspenseful, as glamorous as the city itself, *And Now She's Gone* should be at the top of your must-read list."

—Michele Campbell, bestselling author of *A Stranger on the Beach*

"One of crime fiction's leading writers at her very best. The final twist will make you want to immediately turn back to page one and read it all over again. *And Now She's Gone* is a perfect blend of PI novel and psychological suspense that will have readers wanting more."

—Kellye Garrett, Anthony, Agatha, and Lefty Award–winning author of *Hollywood Homicide* and *Hollywood Ending*

"Sharp, witty, and perfectly paced, *And Now She's Gone* is one hell of a read!"

—Wendy Walker, bestselling author of *The Night Before*

"Hall once again proves to be an accomplished maestro who has composed a symphony of increasing tension and near-unbearable suspense. Rachel brilliantly reveals the bone and soul of our shared humanity and the struggle to contain the nightmares of human faults and failings. I am a fan, pure and simple."

—Stephen Mack Jones, award-winning author of the August Snow thrillers

"Heartfelt and gripping . . . I'm a perennial member of the Rachel Howzell Hall fan club, and her latest is a winning display of her wit and compassion and mastery of suspense."

—Steph Cha, award-winning author of *Your House Will Pay*

"An entertainingly twisty plot, a rich and layered sense of place, and most of all, a main character who pops off the page. Gray Sykes is hugely engaging and deeply complex, a descendant of Philip Marlowe and Easy Rawlins who is also definitely, absolutely her own woman."

—Lou Berney, award-winning author of *November Road*

"A deeply human protagonist, an intricate and twisty plot, and sentences that make me swoon with jealousy . . . Rachel Howzell Hall will flip every expectation you have—this is a magic trick of a book."

—Rob Hart, author of *The Warehouse*

"*And Now She's Gone* has all the mystery of a classic whodunit, with an undeniably fresh and clever voice. Hall exemplifies the best of the modern PI novel."

—Alafair Burke, *New York Times* bestselling author

PRAISE FOR *THEY ALL FALL DOWN*

"A riotous and wild ride."

—Attica Locke

"Dramatic, thrilling, and even compulsive."

—James Patterson

"An intense, feverish novel with riveting plot twists."

—Sara Paretsky

"Hall is beyond able and ready to take her place among the ranks of contemporary crime fiction's best and brightest."

—*Strand Magazine*

FOG AND FURY

OTHER TITLES BY RACHEL HOWZELL HALL

The Last One
What Fire Brings
What Never Happened
We Lie Here
These Toxic Things
And Now She's Gone
They All Fall Down
City of Saviors
Trail of Echoes
Skies of Ash
Land of Shadows

FOG AND FURY

A THRILLER

RACHEL HOWZELL HALL

THOMAS & MERCER

Published by Thomas & Mercer, Seattle

www.apub.com

EU product safety contact:
Amazon Media EU S. à r.l.
38, avenue John F. Kennedy, L-1855 Luxembourg
amazonpublishing-gpsr@amazon.com

ISBN-13: 9781662522840 (hardcover)
ISBN-13: 9781662522857 (paperback)
ISBN-13: 9781662522833 (digital)

Cover design by Caroline Teagle Johnson
Cover image: © Jiojio / Getty

Printed in the United States of America

First edition

This one's for me . . .

Life begins on the other side of despair.

—Jean-Paul Sartre

PART I

Big Trouble off Highway 1

August 1, 2023
6:15 a.m.

This forest smells like dead things.

Like old shoes stuffed with dying roses or a locker room in the middle of a candle store.

Terpenes—organic compounds from the pine trees. Geosmins—compounds made by the bacteria in the soil. Dead things like dried leaves and twigs, squirrels and shit. For real. Shit.

Oakland smelled like dead things too. My old neighborhood is surrounded by pine trees and smells like Christmas. The Oakland Zoo is a mile away, and I could smell elephants because of the wind and humidity trapping odor molecules. In West Oakland? Where some of my friends live? I smelled weed, spilled beer, burgers . . .

I miss the stink of elephants.

Ha. Never thought I'd say that.

Back in December, after football practice, me, Keenan, and Trystan cut through the alley behind Happy Sunshine Market to buy some Red Bulls, Takis, and Flamin' Hot CHEETOS. Trystan said, "You smell that?" and I took a breath cuz Trystan was always saying, "You smell that," and the smell was always smoked barbecue. Dude was always hungry. This time, though, we smelled Homeless Joe. Not his name, whatever, but we found him behind this big dumpster with his fucked-up feet sticking out from under all these trash bags. He smelled like old steak meat, rotten cabbage, shit, and old eggs. What dead people smell like.

Dying cells with no nutrients and oxygen. Microbial invasions of multiplying bacteria.

Cuz Homeless Joe was dead.

My stomach churned as I called 911, but the police treated me and my boys like *we* killed Homeless Joe, and then they fuckin' *handcuffed* me and Keenan. *Technically*, I wasn't even supposed to *be* in Acorn, but I had been tutoring Keenan, who lived in the Moore Houses. Keenan was the best linebacker at Bishop—six feet six and 220 pounds—but he sucked at chemistry and I was low-key a beast in AP Chem and AP Physics.

Okay. Not low-key. Everybody knew.

Homeless Joe was the sixth murder near the Acorn projects that month, and some asshole said, "Two Black teenagers went running thataway." Trystan was Ecuadorian or something like that. But me and Keenan, we were Black teenagers. Almost *every* teenager in that neighborhood was Black, but for some reason, OPD had a hard-on for me. Probably cuz one of 'em went to Oakland Tech or something. "Why were you in the alley?" and "Do you know the victim?" and "You far from home, Sequoyah-boy."

A few hours later, OPD caught the real murderers, but it was too late for me.

Blood in the water.

Mom—still wearing her waders and straw hat—cried as she drove us home from the police station. She'd come from a lagoon somewhere and smelled like grass and dead fish. She didn't even yell at me for hanging out in the projects. Too tired after discovering more ways humans were fucking up the planet. Later, though, after they thought I was sleeping, she and Dad started whispering about Oakland being too dangerous. If it wasn't the guns and the gangs, weed and fentanyl, it was cops and friends "who lived over there."

"Prayer ain't working," she snapped at Dad.

"STEM ain't either," Dad clapped back.

I couldn't sleep, not with my chest squeezing, making it hard to breathe.

Days later, once my parents said the fucked-up part aloud—*We're moving to Haven over the summer*—I kinda exhaled cuz I thought we were moving up to wherever-the-fuck-Haven-is next year after I graduated from high school and left for UCLA.

Nope.

"It's less dangerous," Dad said.

"Their science program is nothing like Bishop's but it's . . . well . . . ," Mrs. Nguyen, my science teacher, said that next morning.

"Their football program is nothing like Bishop's, but it's okay," Coach said at practice that night.

"I said what I said," Mom said. "What good is physics or football if you're dead or in jail? We're moving to Haven."

I'd committed to play for UCLA, and even though it was dead period, I attended some practices a few weeks ago—unofficially, at a friend of a friend's house. At the same time, I had also attended a summer session on electrodynamics and how electric currents and magnets interacted with each other. Totally legit. Maybe I should've skipped practice the afternoon I caught this one *sick* pass because I overreached and came down hard, and I heard my right ankle pop, and it hurt like *fuckkkkk, what did I do?*

Physics, that's what my stupid ass did—Newton's third law of motion. *For every action, there is an equal and opposite reaction.* The turf pushed back at my feet, and I landed as stiff as a board. My ligaments weren't doing their job to keep me stable, but then I fucked up by landing off-center and . . .

Physics.

Boo-yah.

The Bruins coach leading the practice said, "Just a sprain," cuz I'm a running back and we're always rolling our ankles. He told me to ice it.

Done.

Dad picked me up from practice and drove me to the emergency room, all of me shaking like a bitch since I already knew I'd have to sit out for a few practices. Then I'd be back on the field because I *had* to be back on the field.

If my stats dropped because I didn't start that next season, the Bruins could've rescinded the offer, especially since I hadn't signed any paper yet. If my ankle kept being a punk, my high school football career would be over—my college football career nonexistent. It takes six weeks for a fracture to heal, but this is bullshit because it really takes a year. But Wolff's law states that bones get stronger and more dense in response to increased loads and weaker and less dense with decreased loads. The best approach to fixing my ankle would be to run and lift weights, and not baby it. I'd still be a Bruin, even if rehab failed; my scholarship wasn't only because I could run the forty-yard dash in 4.6 seconds, but because *I'm smart.*

Physics, a crazy choice since I know what football does to the body. But I am who I am. This accident is my origin story. Just like Victor Stone, high school football star until a tragic accident led to his transformation.

It's all Gucci—that's what I kept telling myself, fingers numb, lips numb, all of me numb as I limped to the Honda on crutches, wearing a soft cast on my ankle. No biggie. That's what physical therapy was for.

As Dad pulled out of the hospital parking lot, he took a breath and asked, "What do you want for dinner?"

"El Pollo Loco."

"Cool."

Then he took another breath and said, "There's good news and there's bad news. The bad news: Coach can't start you this year—"

"It's just a stupid fracture," I shouted, exploding before Dad could even finish his sentence. "I hurt my ankles all the time, and I always come back stronger than ever." Near tears, I asked, "What's the good news, then?"

"If you recover a bit more," Dad said, "they'll start you on the Bobcats."

"Who the fuck—"

"Excuse me?"

"Who in the world are the Bobcats?" I asked, my neck getting hot.

"The football team in Haven," Dad said, gripping the steering wheel. "You keep your stats up, and you'll stand out even more because you're you. It's not a big deal." He smiled, then added, "It's all Gucci. Did I say that right?" But he knew that something more than anointing oil and prayer circles was needed this time. He became a disciple of Wolff's law: weight-bearing exercises to stimulate bone remodeling in the day and at night, immobilization in a soft cast to decrease stress but not so much that it made my ankle weak.

It's been two months now, and my ankle still hurts. Like, knives carving my muscles hurt. Not that anyone knows I'm still in pain. I can't transfer to Haven High and lead this wack-ass team if I'm already on the injured list. I've made excuses to skip drills with my new squad.

"Gotta complete some stuff for the Caltech thing." That lie is for Geochemist Mom, who is already anti–contact football.

"I'm volunteering at the food bank." That lie is for Pastor Dad, who loves football but also wants me to keep doing good for others.

The few drills I *do* attend over at school are throwing the ball around. I don't run, though, and Coach Wes is cool with that. "Don't want some freak accident taking you out," he said. "Just keep up your leg strength."

That's why I'm running. Four miles each morning, from five thirty to six fifteen in the—

"Hey, X!"

My knees are getting weak and stupid because she's near. How am I hearing her with my earbuds in? We're like penguins. Me, I'm like Happy Feet hearing his girl's cry. I'd know her voice in a thunderstorm. Basic law of universal gravitation. Objects with mass attracting each other.

There she is, all smiles and freshness, curves and bright eyes. Yeah, this forest smells like dead things, but she makes it smell like vanilla and flowers and honey. And pheromones, the OG chemical. All of it makes me all tingly and shit. I'd take vanilla in the forest over elephant ass, weed, beer, and dead Homeless Joes back in Oakland.

She runs beside me, listening to Future, and I'm listening to Kendrick Lamar, one of the greatest lyricists ever—so good, he won a Pulitzer. And this morning, my ankle doesn't hurt so much—a four on the scale of ten, drowsy and loose, a pink cloud instead of fire-truck red.

I'm less pressed about Haven now, probably cuz of her. I'll be the big fish in a small town. I'll run the ball and make Bobcats' history. I'll win their science awards and be valedictorian at graduation and figure out how to make bionic ankles, and I'll keep fucking her as many times as she wants, which is all the time. She likes using that word for what we do. *Fuck.* "Makes it . . . sexier," she says.

I use that word another way.

Fuck them dads who get pissed their sons will be redshirted because of Haven's new running back. *Fuck* their angry phone calls; I'll win them their first championship, *and* I'll get college recruiters down here to not only try to woo me away from UCLA but to also watch the Bobcats' wack-ass team. Betas like Justin, who trips over his feet just doing side shuffles and eats every french fry placed before him. Harvey, his playa-hater dad, has the balls to be the loudest—

I stumble over a tree root—"Shit!"—and my ankle explodes with new pain.

She laughs. "You're gonna break your neck on a redwood tree."

"Funny." I walk it off, heat burning through my legs, purposely dropping an earbud to the trail to win more recovery time. Breathless, I slant away from her, avoiding eye contact. If she offers those painkillers again, I'm gonna tell her no. Shit makes me dizzy, and I always wanna sleep.

And anyway, it isn't my neck that's broken. No one in Haven knows that my ankle still hurts. I'll keep that secret until I sign for

UCLA—maybe until I retire from playing ten seasons with the 49ers. Then I'll reveal my bionic ankle, my patented built-in repair tech for injuries, and another system that protects against concussions—which'll please Mom—and I'll make millions, being sure to give away 10 percent of everything to make Dad happy.

Yeah. Can't wait to see my name all up in the newspapers.

Football and physics. Heisman Trophy and Nobel Prize.

Cuz there's nobody like me out there.

I'm un-fucking-forgettable.

1.

The fog kept me blind.

My scalp prickled with worry-sweat as I crept along Pearl Way, the least twisty road in Haven, with the headlights of FaB, my 1970 Ford Bronco, pushing through the mist only to find more mist, driving to my first day as a private investigator in a town of one thousand people, terrified that I'd end up warped and wrapped around a redwood tree. I'd crept through fog before—and in the same truck with the same headlights—but that was in Los Angeles, more than five hundred miles south of here. Here in Haven, I could've driven off a cliff, hit a deer, or slammed into a logging truck. I'd have never seen my end come.

Yeah, I may just die here.

Too early in the day to be thinking such thoughts but this fog and this highway . . .

Weather was making me hyperbolic.

At the same time . . . Was it so strange that a woman who'd chased a homicidal rapist into the fog and come out of that fog alive but with a bullet in her shoulder was acting a little fidgety?

In the last two years, I'd clenched FaB's mahogany-wood steering wheel so tight, my hands had damn near whittled the wheel into an embroidering hoop.

"Stress," Dr. Tess Molina had diagnosed.

"Hell yeah," I'd said.

"It's Los Angeles," she'd added.

"The fuck it ain't," I'd said then. Because there I was, driving through a town three square miles big—ocean on one side, forests on the other—*still* clenching.

My cell phone buzzed from the cup holder, but I didn't take my eyes off the road, not until I stopped at one of the seven traffic signals in Haven.

You starting today?
A million years to drive a mile?

I tapped a response.

You want me there walking or riding in a pine box?

Fog getting to you?

Yeah

Take your time

Not like I was still a homicide detective rushing to a crime scene. Not like there was a cooling body waiting for me to figure out whodunit and why. Not like I was driving to notify a family that the worst thing that could ever happen *had* happened—and had happened to *them*. I no longer had to experience any of this, not anymore.

I dropped the phone back into the cup holder and looked to my left—no cars heading northbound on Highway 1—and to my right—no cars heading southbound. Except for the waves of fog, the two-lane highway looked clear, and if I wanted, I could've buzzed through that red light, easy peasy. Just my luck, though . . . *Bam!* T-boned by a train.

A thick cloud rolled around my gut, making me dizzy, but I couldn't close my eyes. My breath grew shallow and fast as my eyes flicked at the rearview and side mirrors. Not that I 100 percent believed the Suarez family had followed me up here from Los Angeles. Not that I 100 percent believed their threats. *You'll never take another deep breath again.* But 9 percent believing is a helluva lot, and I'd watched members of that clan drive slow circles around my car in parking lots and the streets around my apartment building. There was nothing stopping them from harvesting the power of fog to reap my breath for the lost breath of their loved one, Autumn.

The traffic signal turned green.

Weary of monster fog and an angry, grieving family hiding in it, I looked left and right again before spurring the Bronco through the intersection. Once I safely reached the other side of Highway 1, once I saw that no one had pulled up behind me, my damp hands relaxed.

Yeah, I may just die here . . .

Travel blogs had nicknamed this village "Mayberry by the Sea." On my first trip, downtown Haven and Seaview Way, especially, had made me go *"Aahhh,"* and my eyebrows had crumpled, and I imagined living full-time in such a charming, walkable town. No buildings over three stories in Haven but plenty of craft stores, bookstores, real estate offices, art galleries, and boutiques that outfitted your inner Stevie Nicks or Jack Nicklaus. No bare asses hung out in Haven, and nothing popped or dropped here, either, not with old couples shuffling to Roll-Roll-Roll-Your-Dough Diner over there, and over there, young parents posted at tables outside a coffee shop named Deegan's with one leash clipped to their dogs and the other leash clipped to their toddlers. No twerking allowed in the Victorian-era buildings soon to be designated as National Historic Landmarks.

I rolled west on Seaview Way, and like a sheriff on her horse, I slipped into a parking space, stopping before my bumper tapped the polished wood rail. Made it. One more glance in the Bronco's mirrors—still alone—and my hands finally released the wheel. In front of me, through the windows of the repurposed Victorian with gray clapboards and white gingerbread trim, I spotted Ivan Poole at a bank of file cabinets with his sleeves rolled up and his lips and brows rolled down. Half

Robert De Niro and half polar bear, Ivan was a former LAPD Missing Persons detective, now the sole proprietor of Poole Investigations. He was my godfather, and now he was my boss.

A plastic tub of office desk trinkets sat in the Bronco's cargo area, stuffed with a framed picture of Ivan standing on my left and my father, Al, standing on my right, both men with an arm wrapped around my shoulders. They were my sword and shield. Once Dad died, though, my right side had been left vulnerable. That's when the wolves started their hunt.

Husky, German shepherd, golden retriever, poodle, mastiff . . .

Lungs tight in my chest, I took a deep, calming breath in, thankful that I was wearing a good bra that didn't dig into my ribs, a gray silk shirt that breathed and dried quickly, jeans that boasted a stretchy waistband, and gray Nikes fitted with cushiony insoles.

I wasn't a crime virgin—for ten years, I'd worked in a city of four million people, stepping in blood that looked like chocolate pudding, examining bodies that resembled beef jerky. I'd been blasted in the face with bear spray by a twelve-year-old drug dealer who'd pimped his methed-out mother since his eighth birthday. On both sides of my left shoulder blade, I wore two surgery scars from that homicidal rapist's .22-caliber bullet. That incident had been the first successful wolf attack after my father's death.

Haven didn't have *shit* on Los Angeles.

If that were true . . .

Why was I sitting in my daddy's Bronco then, fighting the nausea burning up my throat?

Well, it was because my alleged poor judgment was costing me thousands of dollars.

Because I was now second-guessing my aptitude as a cop.

Because I needed to prove that they were wrong about me. *They* were the wolves who'd demanded my badge and gun. *They* were the wolves who'd dragged me on social media and knew not a got-dam thing about anything but knew all the fuck everything after the three hours they'd spent on YouTube Police Academy and late-night binge-watching *Cops*.

If it wasn't the fog or the Suarez family keeping my hands clenched, it was hearing "You should've done . . ." and "Why didn't you . . . ?" and "If it was me . . ." over and over again.

Labrador retriever, Pomeranian, dalmatian, French bulldog . . .

Sufficiently damp and clammy, I grabbed the plastic tub of office bits and bobs from the cargo hold. As I walked the twelve steps to the office, the fog parted and quickly swirled to close behind me.

Like I was never there.

I opened the door to Poole Investigations.

Above me, a brass bell tinkled.

"Sonny's here!" Ivan shouted.

"Yay!" I shouted back.

"Welcome to your new life, sweetheart!"

"You threatening me?" I stepped over the threshold and into an office with a reception desk with no receptionist and three dime candy machines filled with Skittles, bubble gum balls, and chocolate-covered almonds. Lots of light spilled through the windows and from the fluorescent light panels overhead. A mute flat-screen TV hung from the wall of a small waiting area with two empty chairs and a love seat. Contestants on *The Price Is Right* were bidding on a pair of twenty-four-carat gold earrings.

This place already smelled like home. Not "home" as in my apartment in downtown LA, or even the cottage I now leased here in Haven, but *home* as in my office at LAPD's Pacific Division Station. "Home" was the scent of Ivan's cologne—moss and fire—and old paper and rusty file cabinets. "Home" was coffee, thick and black, two hours old, and perfume—orange blossom and cedar that sometimes caused chaos in the testosterone soup found in male-dominated spaces like police stations.

Ivan lumbered over to take my plastic tub, his black tactical Oxfords-meets-Skechers scuffing the gray Berber carpet. "I was about to send out a code three but realized there ain't no patrol units with sirens in Haven." His twice-broken nose looked redder than before; his head of thick black hair was now completely gray. "You're back here, next to me. We share a wall."

Ivan and I reached the hallway and turned right. At the end of that hallway, we took another right and reached an office with two north-facing windows and a dark wood desk. A mason jar of yellow tulips sat between the landline phone and computer monitor. There was a forty-inch television on the wall to my left, maps of Haven and Northern California, and an empty corkboard to my right. File cabinets, short and tall, everywhere.

"You good?" he asked, eyebrow cocked.

"Yep. I'm great."

"You're lying."

"Of course I am." I opened the desk drawers to find sticky notes, pens and markers, empty binders, and a whiteboard. My confidence sloshed around my heart. I prayed Ivan couldn't hear it.

He flicked his arm to peep at his watch. "We don't have a lot of time before—"

"You're finally wearing it." I tapped the thick black solar smartwatch on his wrist.

He grunted and scratched his forearm tat of a bearded god. My father had worn the same tat. "The heart rate bullshit comes in handy," Ivan said. "Respiration and oxygen too. My doctor's pleased I give a fuck now."

I snorted. "Thank you for joining us."

"I still think you paid too much for it," he said. "And this solar shit . . . Next, you're gonna tell me that birds exist. Anyway, lemme give you a quick tour before your first client comes."

"First client already?"

"You were supposed to be here an hour ago."

No excuses. I just didn't want to *be* here an hour ago.

Ivan beckoned me, and I followed him back down the hall and up a flight of stairs.

The second floor boasted two intake offices, a bedroom, a full bathroom with a shower, a conference room, and a lounge with old leather armchairs and a sofa with mismatched pillows that somehow matched. There was a K-Cup coffee maker on a side table, two boxes of name-brand tissue, and windows with a view of the Pacific Ocean lost behind a bank of white.

"Most times," he said, "I conduct interviews up here. More comfy, you know? Something about these pillows brings out honesty. I've watched a grown man cry in that chair, and just this morning, I listened to a preacher cuss on that couch."

I wandered over to the coffee maker and browsed the pod collection. "A lovely place to hear that your husband has been cheating on you with his cousin. Maybe it's the view."

Ivan pointed at the couch. "The pillows were Belle's idea."

Ivan's wife, Auntie Anabelle, a retired court reporter turned interior designer, may her memory be a blessing. The smartwatch had actually been her idea, another attempt to steer Ivan away from cardiac arrest. Last year, she'd caught COVID-19 on holiday in Bali. I didn't know she'd passed until after the funeral—my mother never told me that Belle was sick. She still hasn't.

"Elliott get you and Val all settled?" Ivan asked.

Elliott was my new landlord.

"Almost. He's helping Mom unpack this morning, and then he'll take her to the bakery. And thanks again for the referral. I'm sure they're not charging me as much as they could. I really appreciate it."

He squeezed my shoulder. "You're the closest I'll ever have as a daughter. Can't let you just flail around, you know?" He chuckled. "Don't want Al or Belle asking me why I didn't do my job when I see them again."

I tapped his hand. "I don't know whose foot would be up your ass more."

He said, "Ha," then ruffled my hair and lumbered over to the stairs.

I peered out a window, certain that another thirty-five-year-old on the other side of the fogbank was also staring out a window and wondering, *What the hell happened?* Disappointment, an everlasting poke in the ribs.

Back on the first floor, Ivan led me to his office. His windows looked out to the Pacific Ocean. The same maps and TV that were in my office hung on his walls, but his file cabinets were all wood. There were pictures: Ivan and Belle on their wedding day and vacationing in Palm Springs and Turkey; pictures of Ivan and my dad in uniform and smoking cigars; of Ivan holding newborn me, and then cop me beside my paper shooting target with perfect center-mass bullet holes. A red-and-black Fender guitar sat on a stand in the office's eastern corner, and commendations from his days leading Missing Persons hung and sat in any available space. His desk was a riot of sticky notes, manila folders, and clipped papers, a banana, a vase of fresh tulips, and a box of Cohiba cigars.

I took a deep whiff: white sage, the last holdover from Auntie Belle, a registered member of the Santa Ynez Band of Chumash Indians. In the picture on his desk, she wore a two-piece deerskin dress with a blue shawl embroidered with a butterfly. She smiled directly at the photographer, smoky eyes, full face, larger than the big blue sky behind her. What meshuggaas had Ivan smudging and praying?

Ivan and I stood there, both silent, our eyes burning with tears. I never had the chance to say goodbye . . .

Finally, I cleared my throat and said, "I'll go settle in."

Not that I had much to unpack. A box of latex gloves and an unopened pack of evidence collection paper bags. A "History of Psychology" desk calendar. A framed photo of Mom and Dad at Benihana. A photo of Dad and me standing in front of the Bronco before its Sonny makeover. Another picture of Dad standing beside me after I'd received my detective stripe. Last, and encased in plexiglass, the bullet that tore through my left shoulder—a gift from Ivan, who'd also been shot in his left shoulder, same location.

"Shit happens for a reason," Ivan said from my office door.

I looked back at him. "Out with the old shit to make room for the new shit?"

He handed me a folder. "You don't know what random thing will bring you answers, bring you closure. Even if it seems like a waste of time, even if it's painful and unrelated, you gotta keep an open mind." He dropped the folder on my desk. "If you do, you'll learn a lot of shit about who you are."

"I used to know who I was . . ." I sounded ridiculous in my head as I placed a shaky hand on the desk. "That bitch was great. Iconic. A legend in homicide detective shit. There were stories, Uncle Ivan. Statues being built—"

"Stop being a smart-ass, all right?" Ivan said, chuckling. "I'm only saying don't freak out, not that you do, at least in front of people. And trust your gut. I'm not telling you anything you don't know—you're a Virgo—but with everything that's been happening over the last year . . . I'm a little worried that you don't believe in anything anymore."

I blinked at him. I *didn't* believe in anything anymore. I peeked inside the folder: blank retainer of services forms and a printed email sent to the Poole Investigations website.

"After your meeting, I gotta head out," Ivan said. "A seventeen-year-old kid was found dead this morning. That cussing preacher I mentioned? That was the boy's father."

My eyebrows lifted. "Is that my first case?"

He frowned. "Nope." He squinted out the window to Seaview Way. "Your clients just pulled up. Black Maserati."

"In *this* town? I thought Northern Californians didn't care about such crass displays of wealth like Italian sports cars." I stood beside my boss and looked out to Seaview Way.

Two women—both white, both pretty—were climbing out of the Maserati. The younger one leaving the passenger's seat had long chestnut hair parted in the middle, dark eyebrows, and full lips collapsed into a frown. She carried a giant Louis Vuitton satchel in one hand and a giant pink travel mug in the other. Wearing that blue oversize sweatshirt, those black leggings, and black UGGs, she looked nineteen or twenty.

The driver, middle-aged, tall, and tanned, wore a blond bob and a bright smile. She had a Pilates body and wore a pink lululemon set—never ever LuLaRoe. This chick would die before wearing anything with a print pattern.

"Ugh. Good luck with those two," Ivan grumbled, rolling his eyes.

I peered at my boss. "It's like that in humble Haven?"

He headed over to the door. "Kid, there's no place like Haven."

2.

The bell above the front door jangled, and two new scents—earthy juniper for the brunette, vanilla and leather for the blond—surfed into Poole Investigations.

"Good morning, ladies," Ivan said. "Glad you could make it. Sorry that you needed to."

The younger woman swiveled her bloodshot gaze toward me, and her coffee-brown eyes widened, like she'd been caught off guard. She swiped at her red nose with a tired tissue and pushed out a shaky breath.

"Mackenzie, London," Ivan said, then motioned to me, "this is Alyson Rush, my new investigator. Ten years with the LAPD, five of them in homicide. The best of the best, and I'm not saying that just cuz she's my goddaughter. Sonny, this young lady is Mackenzie Sutton, and that's her mother, London."

"The *old* lady," London snarked.

I blinked at the women, and my stomach dropped. *Sutton. Shit. Really?*

"Your bestie is at home," London said to Ivan. "He may stop by later. Something about a vandal tagging a redwood. I stopped listening but call Coop when you can."

At home? As in *Haven* at home? Or San Francisco at home? Or—

Had to be.

"Sonny," Ivan barked, leading the Suttons to the hallway, "we'll head up. Grab the forms, and we'll meet you up there."

"You're from *LA* LA?" Mackenzie asked me as she backed down the hall. "Not, like the Valley or Anaheim?" Her voice was husky, like she sang sad songs at her grandpa's café after working two shifts in a steel mill to support her dying mother.

"Yep. The one, the only—*LA* LA, *for real* for real," I said, my legs feeling like they'd been stung a million times by hornets and shredded afterward by thorns. *Because why were they living here in Haven?*

"It's Los Angeles, Mackie," London whispered as they climbed the stairs. "Not Jupiter."

I ducked into my office, grabbed the forms from my desk with trembling hands, and squeezed shut my eyes and forced my thoughts to slow. My anxiety tasted like red clay and salt.

Stop freaking out. Do your job.

By the time I joined my clients, Ivan had already made cups of coffee. London stood at the window, her hard gaze willing blue sky from the mist. "This is almost as nice a view as from our house," she said to no one. "Coop would be pissed if it was."

"Coop's been up here plenty of times," Ivan said.

Mackenzie pulled a glittery folio from her Neverfull and set the satchel on the carpet.

My heartbeat quickened. *Bad luck to put your purse on the floor.*

Junior year in college, at a sorority brunch, I placed my fake Dooney & Bourke purse on the floor *one time* for three minutes, and *now* look at me.

Ivan caught my eye and said, "You ready?"

"Yep." I settled in an armchair, its brown leather gray in some places, dark and greasy in others. The cushions were soft and smelled of baby powder.

"Miss Rush," London said over her shoulder, "did you drive up Highway 128 to the 1?"

"Mm-hmm." I exaggerated a shiver. "I've never been so scared to drive in my entire life. Every curve threatened the thing I cherish the most."

"Your life?"

"Control."

"It's an absolutely beautiful route," London agreed, "and hella vindictive."

Two hours of one curve after the next on a two-lane highway through the forest. That afternoon, once we'd reached the cottage, I'd gulped a finger of bourbon as soon as I found the bottle packed in the box labeled BOOZE.

London quirked a smile. "Highway 128, also known as Damascus. You become a believer on that road. Some people just relocated to Haven because they refused to do that drive again." She chuckled. "I've petitioned the state to straighten out Highway 128."

Ivan said, "Ha," and placed a cup of coffee on the table before me, then lumbered to the landing. "Sonny, call if you need me."

Mackenzie tapped on her phone as London and I sipped from our cups.

The stairs creaked beneath Ivan's weight. Once the doorbell chimed, the office settled into silence.

London said, "You're very lucky, Miss Rush."

"Please call me Alyson." Still shaky, I flipped to the first clean page of my legal pad. "And why am I lucky?"

London stared into her cup. "You're now living in the most beautiful place in the world and compared to LA, working a cushy PI job. I thought Ivan was crazy to open an agency here. Because what kind of *real* crime happens in a town with a thousand people?" Awed, the blond shook her head. "But now that he's hired you . . . He must know something that I don't." As she nestled in the nicest of the two armchairs, she pushed off her lilac-colored Nikes and curled her feet beneath her, comfortable in this space. "Why did you come to Haven of all places? Did Highway 128 trap you too?"

"Yes, and also, opportunity," I said, calmer now. *And love.* "Ivan was my father's best friend, and, yep, he's my godfather. He taught me how to look at the world as an investigator. Vouched for me when the testosterone in the room was too thick to punch through. When my father died, he made sure my mother was safe, that no one gave her the runaround in the pensions department. Ivan knew that I needed a change, and so he offered me a chance to do what I loved in a place smaller than LA."

Mackenzie cleared her throat. "Can we . . . ?" Her eyes clouded with tears, and her hands shook as she brought the travel mug to her lips.

"How can I help?" I asked, ready to hear about a cheating boyfriend or girlfriend.

A teardrop slid down Mackenzie's cheek. "I can't find Figgy," she said, her busker's voice quivering.

My pen paused on the notepad. "Figgy?"

"My baby," Mackenzie said, nodding.

"*Fur* baby," London clarified. "Our goldendoodle. Will you take a breath, Mackie, and communicate, please?"

Mackenzie broke into a sob.

I pushed the tissue box toward Mackenzie.

Sniffling, the young woman plucked a few tissues from the box. "We've searched everywhere for her."

I scribbled on my legal pad:

FIGGY—LOST GOLDENDOODLE—REALLY??

Mackenzie slipped off her UGGs and, like her mother, tucked her feet beneath her. "I know it's just a missing dog—"

"No, Mackenzie," I interrupted, my eyes soft, my mouth softer. "She's family. Don't ever apologize for loving her."

"My father got her for me," Mackenzie continued.

"Six years ago," London interjected.

When she had her appendix taken out.

"When I had my appendix taken out," Mackenzie said.

"And he brought Figgy to the parking lot of the hospital," London continued, nodding and smiling. "He'd visit every day and Mack would wave from the room. I admit that was kind of him. My husband—"

Ex-husband.

"—isn't one for big gestures of love and sentimentality, but this time . . ."

Wrong. Cooper made *lots* of big gestures of love.

My throat tightened, and every word stuck in my windpipe. The same windpipe beneath a diamond *C* pendant, one of his biggest gestures of love and sentimentality.

"Figgy helped me heal in so many other ways, and I don't know how—" Mackenzie grabbed a pillow and hid her face.

With her face and eyes flat, London watched her daughter's shoulders shake.

Poor girl. I let Mackenzie cry and let London brood as a surge of adrenaline coursed through my veins. Sorrow hit me like a well-deserved sip of Maker's Mark, and I leaned forward and whispered, "It's okay," each time Mackenzie apologized for her tears.

London also leaned forward and touched Mackenzie's knee. "We'll find her, Mackie."

Two million dogs were stolen across the country last year, with French bulldogs being the most common breed of dog stolen. Only 20 percent of those dogs were found.

Back in LA, I'd worked cases that had started with a search for some starlet's teacup poodle but had ended in the murder of that same starlet. A group of masked thieves had stolen purebred dogs worth half a mil and sold them back to the owner. From puppy-breeding mills and earning cash for returned dogs and dogs used for research to stealing pooches for dog-fighting clubs, the main driver of these thefts was always greed.

Mackenzie pulled a paper from her glittery folio. "We've put these everywhere . . ."

Thick bright-white paper with a red-block header and bold white letters:

****MISSING DOG****
****HELP US FIND OUR LOVED ONE****

"We're not sharing that her collar is Versace," Mackenzie said, "or that . . ." She tapped the rump of the dog pictured. "There's a dark patch on the other side of her butt."

"Her birthmark," London said, showing me another picture of Figgy on her phone.

A wine-colored spot that stood out against the lighter hair on the dog's rump.

"It's fig-colored and fig-shaped," London said. "That's how I came up with her name."

I nodded. "Cute."

"Even if someone shaved her there," London said, "the mark would still be on her skin."

"Good to know," I said.

Back to the flyer. "A thousand dollars is a helluva reward," I said.

"But we've heard nothing," London said, "even with that much money."

Mackenzie had torn pieces of the damp tissue until they resembled sprinkled snow on the couch cushions. "And then I got this text yesterday—" She showed me her phone screen.

I GOT YOUR BITCH

The attached picture showed Figgy dangling over a bluff with churning water slamming into the coastline.

"What the hell?" I exclaimed, hands tingling, ready to fight. "Please forward this to me." I didn't *plan* to seek out bloody violence over a dog but if I gotta do some dangling, then . . . I rattled off my cell phone number.

"Whatever they want," Mackenzie said, "I'll give it to them."

My phone pinged with the forwarded message and picture.

"Why not just return the dog and collect the reward?" London wondered, stretching out her legs. "Why haven't they asked for ransom? Why haven't they just called to say, 'We found your dog'?"

"I don't know," I replied, though I had my suspicions. "But anyone who can do that—" I pointed to Mackenzie's phone.

Mackenzie handed me a lined sheet of notebook paper. "I made a list of people who could've taken her."

Audrey Lujan, Harvey Parrish, Keely Butler.

The stairs creaked as Ivan climbed the steps. He appeared at the landing with a calculator in one hand and a notepad in the other. "Time to talk about how much all this is gonna cost."

I left them to it and returned to my office, stronger than I was last time I stood in this spot, almost excited to start my search for Figgy the goldendoodle. Worried, though, that Cooper would play a part in my first investigation in Haven. This was a small town—I'd have to get used to smaller social circles, an overlapping love life that meant being friends with another friend's ex. Knowing that London Sutton and I weren't friends . . .

"Shit happens for a reason."

Before leaving, London and Mackenzie stopped by my office to thank me. "Ivan speaks highly of you," London said, "so we're expecting great results. No pressure." She paused, smiled, and said, "That was a lie."

I said, "Ha," and stood with Ivan to watch the Sutton women exit the building.

"This case is all bullshit and mirrors," Ivan remarked as the mother and daughter returned to the black Maserati.

I studied the MISSING DOG flyer in my hand. "You don't think someone dognapped Figgy?"

He grinned as he backed away from the window. "Someone *did.* And you just met her."

3.

Of all the private detective agencies in town, they had to walk into mine. The daughter and ex-wife of Cooper Sutton.

A year ago, Cooper and I had stood across from each other at an art gallery in Santa Monica, both admiring a mutual friend's installation piece of hanging tattered umbrellas titled *Acid Rain*. Cooper was tall, naturally tanned—his mother's mother had been Creole—and dark-haired, movie-star handsome but accessible, a guy who, according to him, transformed "abandoned pieces of land into mixed-use opportunities, strip malls into shopping experiences." After the show, we walked to the Santa Monica Pier, shared corn dogs, took pictures in a photo booth, and made out on the Ferris wheel. Just thinking about him made me weak.

Cooper, the man who'd made millions as a developer, told me that his ex-wife was moving up to San Francisco—she'd tired of small-town living, and since their daughter would soon be twenty-one, she could relocate. Cooper, who'd shared my bed just two weeks ago, had shown me the divorce papers, which had taken months to complete—land, retirement, stock, rich people shit. Later that night, he kissed me on the Ferris wheel just as he had a year ago, but this time, he told me that he was in love with me and that he could breathe and just *be* with me, and all of this left me feeling light and bright eyed, and I'd imagined visiting Santa Monica once a year as an anniversary, maybe even taking engagement pictures in our gray Ferris wheel car. He'd called Haven one of his favorite places, and once Ivan offered me the job in Haven, I decided to start my new life closer to the man I loved. London would be 150 miles away from Haven, but by the way she talked this afternoon . . . Mr. and Mrs. Cooper Sutton didn't sound past tense, nor did it sound like she lived in San Francisco. In fact, she sounded very present tense, living in the same house, still married.

Last year, Cooper told me, "I just ended a long relationship." There was no reason for me to translate that as *I'm still married and have a daughter*. There was no tan line on his ring finger. He never took his phone into the bathroom; he didn't take phone calls out of earshot. Sometimes, he stayed with me for a weekend; sometimes, he'd stay a week. He never rushed back home and always took his time with me like a single man would. And he spent money on me like a single man would. And he dreamed with me like a single man would.

But now . . . Bile rose in my throat, and I pushed it back down. No reason to freak out yet. A misunderstanding, yes. Co-parenting in a turbulent, post-pandemic moment as this. London had probably stayed the weekend once the dog disappeared. Yeah. My stomach writhed, knowing and recognizing the truth my heart wanted to deny.

Cooper had lied to me.

But I saw the divorce papers . . . *right*?

Before Ivan could further explain his "And you just met her" remark about one of the Sutton women dognapping their own goldendoodle, the bell over the front door jangled again.

"Anybody here?" a woman shouted.

Ivan shouted back, "I'm here, Renee."

I followed my uncle to the reception area.

A petite, silver-haired mail carrier tapped that day's mail against the reception desk.

Ivan introduced me to Renee.

I smiled with numb lips—numb because my new place of work still smelled of London Sutton's perfume and my legs still felt like damp tissue paper, which came from staring at a MISSING DOG flyer announcing a reward to find the goldendoodle of my boyfriend's daughter—a flyer that smelled of my boyfriend's daughter's perfume. Nauseated, I lifted my head once Renee called my name.

"How are you two related?" Renee asked, smiling at me. "Can't be by blood because, Alyson, you're so pretty." She turned to Ivan. "And you, my friend . . ."

Ivan wagged his thick finger at Renee. "Okay, young lady."

Flirting.

"My dad and Ivan were partners for forty-five years," I said. "In many ways, yeah, we're closer than blood."

"And you left all that excitement of LA to come live up here?" Renee asked.

"C'mon, Renee," Ivan complained.

I shrugged and smiled. "Yeah, well . . ." A sharp pang of shame drove into my right eye.

I didn't fool with dogs unless somehow they led me to the dead—like Queso. Two years ago, he was found wandering the neighborhood. A Good Samaritan discovered that the Labrador retriever had belonged to Janet Worton and had been trained to alert someone if his person, Janet, ever collapsed, and Janet, a person with diabetes, had collapsed . . . and not naturally. That's when my team of murder police were called.

Ivan and Renee returned to their discussion about the upcoming community meeting.

I said "Nice to meet you" to Renee and retreated upstairs to text Cooper.

Dude

I just met your fucking ex-wife

She talks like she still lives here

Tell me that I'm tripping

Tell me that you're a liar

Tell me SOMETHING!!!!

There I was again, breathing fast, wanting to scream while clutching my elbows to keep it together. I stared out at the now-blue sky and drank more K-Cup coffee while waiting for his reply. The brew wasn't bitter, nor did it burn my tongue or hint at a future bout of heartburn. But it had no personality or soul. Tragedies abounded in Haven, and drinking an apathetic, apolitical cup of coffee while investigating those tragedies was yet another.

The bell above the front door clattered—Renee had left the building.

No response from Cooper.

Ivan called me to come down.

"So, what did you mean by 'and you just met her'?" I asked Ivan, settling in a guest chair at his desk.

"Meaning," Ivan said, sifting through the mail, "Mackenzie Sutton has lost that dog twice. Also, her car's been stolen three times. And someone vandalized her little boutique down the street. And she's been stalked twice, neither person spotted nor arrested."

"Is she acting out because of her parents' relationship?" I asked. "You know how kids get when dealing with divorce or—"

"Coop and London aren't divorced," Ivan said, "and Mack's not a kid."

Coop and London aren't divorced.

"Mackenzie Sutton is a spoiled rich kid who wants the world to pay attention to her, and if they don't, then she goes nuclear." He plucked a cigar from the box and offered it to me. "You would've hated her back in college."

I ran the Cohiba above my upper lip and said, "She's a perpetual victim, then?"

Aren't divorced.

I accepted the Hillshire Farms catalog Ivan was handing me, recalling London's facial response while her daughter spoke—she'd gone through this before with Mackenzie.

"Anything to make her daddy pay attention," Ivan said, "and to make her mother care. But you know what? Sutton checks don't bounce and shit resolves itself without any effort from me." His cell phone rang from his shirt pocket.

My eyes filled with burning tears as I dog-eared the first page of summer sausages. Because I was one of her daddy's distractions. "So . . . should I not look for Figgy?"

"Look for the dog," Ivan said, plucking out his phone, "but don't expect to find her. Anyway, it'll be good for you to meet the people of Haven. Maybe you'll find your *why*."

As a child, I'd simply wanted to be a good person. After my Frisbee hit a neighbor's already-cracked plate glass window, I'd paid for repairs with my allowance. I bagged care packages for women's shelters because the thought of someone's mom not having sanitary napkins horrified me.

I always asked, "Why?" which drove my mother to snap, "*Because.* That's why."

Her response never satisfied my ten-year-old curiosity.

Because *why* was this mother hiding out with her kid in a women's shelter?

Why would an adult blame a child for breaking something already broken?

Why would someone walk into a school and just start shooting people?

My bachelor's degrees in history and sociology helped answer some of my *whys*, and my master's degree in psychology answered a few more. But I wanted a career that didn't require years of research and data to bear out answers. I wanted that time crunch, to quickly figure out *why*, to immediately fix the problem.

My mother, dismayed and distraught that I'd chosen the LAPD over a PhD, had asked, "Why, Alyson?"

I'd smirked and said, "*Because*, Mom. That's why."

Historically: fuck the patriarchy, man.

Psychologically: to help and defend those in need.

Sociologically: that pension.

Reality: all the above and more.

By choosing the LAPD, I met women who'd hidden in those shelters, but most times, I would end up standing over their corpses. I took pictures of plate glass windows shattered by bullets instead of Frisbees, their journeys ending in the soft stomachs and thighs of grandpas watching *Wheel of Fortune*. For too many Angelenos, murder was the solution. *Why?* Wives who wanted the divorce because he was cheating—murdered. College coeds who'd rejected creepy admirers in dive bars and at pool parties—murdered. Schoolkids who could no longer keep the secret their fathers' best friends made them keep—murdered. *Why?*

I was not a cookie maker, a masseuse, or a pastor. People never sought me out to perform baby blessings or to offer shoulder rubs. Families met me because the worst thing ever had happened. Blood had been spilled and armchairs left vacant.

The *whys* in Haven wouldn't be any different from the *whys* in Los Angeles. Haven just made more fog.

Sounded bad but . . . I wanted a real case. The transient murdered in her encampment. The jogger shot and killed by someone in a car. But those weren't the cases I'd be handling—and may never handle in Haven. People amazed me, though.

Patience, Sonny. Patience.

After finding Figgy, maybe I'd pick up something more interesting. Catfishing gone wrong. Workers' comp fraud. Finding somebody's babydaddy.

"The Search for the Missing Goldendoodle" would give me something I needed: money. At that time in my life, I shouldn't have minded clients who cried wolf and were willing to pay for expertise that required my bare minimum.

I'd reached Haven yesterday and hadn't explored the town—and now the Suttons would be paying for my tour. Maybe Haven was bigger than it seemed. Maybe a thousand people was more than it sounded. Maybe I wouldn't run into London, because she *did* live in San Francisco and she was now on the road to becoming a merry divorcée. Hopefully, when she visited on the weekends, she frequented one coffee shop in town—I'd avoid that one out of respect.

Anything to make her daddy pay attention and to make her mother care. That's what Ivan said about Mackenzie Sutton. That was some sad shit.

But what if Ivan was wrong this time, and Figgy actually *was* missing?

Shit happened for a reason.

I closed the door to my office and pulled the laptop from my bag.

First things first: Who was Mackenzie Sutton?

According to the internet, Mackenzie Sutton, a Leo, was a self-centered fashionista. She was a travel influencer on Instagram, a romantasy book reviewer on TikTok, and a small business owner on LinkedIn. She lived on 1 Pearl Way, owned Food Desert Vintage Clothing, and donated enough money to have her name included in the ASPCA's annual report. Three years ago, she'd graduated from Haven High School with honors and as Most Likely to Survive the Hunger Games.

Images showed Mackenzie standing beside Cooper at the annual Haven Founders' Day. There was ten-year-old Mackenzie leading the annual Fourth of July parade. There she was, bleary-eyed and disheveled, after driving erratically on Highway 1 and getting charged with the first of two DUIs. And finally, there she was with Figgy, both of them dressed in vintage Chanel.

A quick search on PeopleFinder told me that London Sutton still lived at 1 Pearl Way, that there were zero divorce records available on California online dockets. No case number, no filing date, no list of pleadings.

I grabbed my phone, texted YOU LYING BITCH to Cooper, covered my face with the crook of my elbow, and screamed.

Little did I know while driving the treachery known as Highway 128 that I would already have an ex-boyfriend in Haven.

Life came at you quick—quicker than a neon-orange Frisbee.

4.

Redwoods and ocean. Blue skies beneath the fog. No police helicopters or fire truck sirens. Space to breathe. Space to think and plan. That morning's drive from my new home to downtown Haven had taken only four minutes, with two of those minutes spent waiting at that lonely traffic light. "Not that I'm complaining," I said as Ivan resumed the tour of the office, "but why do people living in a place named Haven need *two* private investigators?"

I'd splashed my face with cold water, dropped Visine into my eyes, and turned off my phone. No idea when my new T-shirt, the one with the scarlet *A*, would arrive.

"Because no matter where you are," Ivan said, "people are people. They steal and cheat and lie, and then they disappear into the night. We also have had tourists running from warrants and their spouses, a few runaways . . ." He led me down the hallway, passing a copier machine, a small bathroom, a tiny kitchen, and a closed door behind the staircase. He pulled a set of keys from his pants pocket. "This room stays locked—we keep confidential reports in here."

On the far wall of the office stood three tall bookcases stuffed with thick black binders. Local maps of Haven and regional maps of Sonoma County hung beside a corkboard filled with MOST WANTED flyers. An unopened box of expandable file folders sat atop a desk lit now with two lamps. A trash bin and shredder were the only other technology in the space.

"Client information," Ivan said. "Closed cases. Active cases. General information that I've collected since opening up three years ago. Keep this door locked even if you're going in and out. Prop it open with . . ." He pointed to the floor and a rubber doorstop wedge. "Because I've made certain the door won't stay open." He tapped a speaker near the doorframe. "Intercom in case you somehow get stuck—"

"Stuck?" I asked, my breathing tight. "Is this a death trap?"

"Yes." His eyes flitted around the narrow room as he handed me a key. "Explosive shit in here. Protect it with your life. Our clients trust that we keep their private shit private, got it?"

"Got it." I eased the key onto my own ring. "What's up with you and the mail lady?"

Ivan blushed. "Nothing." He looked sad saying that.

I tugged his earlobe. "Auntie Belle wouldn't want you eating mayo and onion sandwiches until you shuffled off this mortal coil."

He nodded his big bear head, not believing it. "And it's mayo and banana sandwiches."

"Equally disgusting," I said, circling the key ring around my index finger.

"If I haven't said it to you recently," Ivan said, watching me lock the door, "that was bullshit what they did to you. Wagner knew it was bullshit too. He'd just pinned the fucking Preservation of Life medal on your shoulder—and not the shoulder that got shot up. He awards you for saving a life, but then he penalizes you for showing mercy to a poor woman who boosted milk and Wonder Bread to feed her toddler? All bullshit."

"But showing Royalty Miller mercy got Autumn Suarez dead," I countered.

There was a framed picture in the plastic tub on my desk of Chief Philip Wagner pinning the blue-and-gold Preservation of Life medal on the dress uniform I'd rarely worn since my promotion to detective. During the packing, I'd thought about tossing that picture but chose to keep it as proof that, once upon a time, I'd been beloved and honored.

"If we could all tell the future," Ivan said, heading back toward his office.

I pulled from the box my picture of Dad and Ivan receiving the Medal of Valor after they'd rescued an unconscious woman and her baby girl from a burning car.

"I still think you're ace," Ivan said. "Brava, kid."

My face warmed. How could one incident produce two different outcomes?

"Anyway," Ivan said, "wander around Haven and look for the damned dog. Here, though, it's gonna take you twenty minutes to find your way around instead of twenty years, so relax."

"What's that word, 'relax'?"

He dropped his head and crossed his arms. "Val still won't see me?"

"She's defrosting. Give it a week."

"I know she still blames me—"

"Dad lifted the whiskey glass to his lips," I interrupted, heat creeping up my neck. "He was a grown-ass man with free will. I really don't understand why it's so hard for her to believe he drank himself to death. Cops do it all the time."

Even cops with loving wives and daughters.

"You carrying?" Ivan asked, changing the subject.

"They're both locked up," I said, "but do I need to?"

"Yeah," Ivan said. "We're still in tourist season. And didn't you tell me that Autumn's family won't leave you alone?"

I waggled my head and sighed. "Fine."

I preferred not to carry my Glock—as a patrol officer, I'd shot it less than twenty times during my ten-year career. As a homicide detective, I'd held my gun on a few suspects, but as a detective, I'd never squeezed the trigger. I hoped to continue that streak here in Haven. Then again, with this much fog . . .

On the other side of my office window, couples walked their dogs and their kids, old people shuffled in and out of Roll-Roll-Roll-Your-Dough, and selfie-takers posed over on the bluffs. A Black man and woman stood near a blue Honda Accord parked a few spaces from my truck. The slack-jawed woman with high cheekbones and Michelle Obama hair swiped at her tear-filled eyes. The man holding her elbow was round and short with elf-like ears and a neat goatee. He stood over her, stiff-backed, his gaze frozen on the gravel.

"The two standing at the Honda," I said, nodding at the couple. "You know them?"

Ivan peered past the blinds. "They're the parents of the dead kid I mentioned this morning. A jogger found their boy, Xander, out on a hiking trail . . ."

Neat Goatee was now helping Crying Woman climb into the passenger seat of the Honda.

Before I could open my mouth, Ivan said, "No foul play, so calm down, Supercop. Xander had a heart condition or something."

"Or something." I tossed him a look, a sour taste in my mouth. "It always starts as 'or something.'" I paused, then added, "And don't talk to me like I'm some blue falcon—"

"I'd never—"

"I'm not interested in busting someone's head just to make myself look good."

Ivan held up his hands. "I've never thought of you like that. Sorry if it sounded like it."

Skin still prickling, I nodded. "Who's working the case, other than you?"

"Mendocino County Sheriff's Department," Ivan said. "They're an okay group of guys. They'll give you some good-natured ribbing once they find out you're ex-LAPD. And you lookin' like you do, they'll be strutting around with their dicks out, hoping you'll choose one."

I'd never dated a cop and wasn't intending to start.

"I'll switch you," I said, crooked grin in place. "You take the dog; I take the kid?"

"You don't know anyone here," Ivan said.

"I didn't know any of my victims and their families, and yet, I had an eighty-five percent clearance rate." I paused, then added, "'Shit happens for a reason,' remember? Maybe I'm in Haven because this death is bigger than a kid with an undiagnosed heart condition 'or something' going on a hike."

I couldn't tear my eyes away from the grieving couple. I'd comforted parents who all wore that same hollowed-out gaze, swiped those same swollen eyes, and all wore tight mouths to keep from wailing and cursing the skies. I'd comforted Benito and Magdalena Suarez, too, until I received a text two days after Autumn's murder:

Vete a la mierda!!
JODETE!
WATCH YOUR BACK!

Unlike the other threats I'd received over my career, the Suarezes' hit different.

My bladder pressed against my ribs—here was that hollowed-out, tight-lipped look again, this time, in a town of a thousand. "I'll be back," I said.

"Where are you—"

But I was already heading toward the front door.

Crying Woman saw me first, and her eyes widened like she'd just seen a wolverine. The man gaped at me and stiffened as I joined them on the passenger side of the Honda.

"Hi," I said, holding out my hand. "Alyson Rush."

He hesitated before taking my hand.

"I just moved to Haven yesterday," I shared.

"To do *what*?" the woman asked, breathless.

"I'm a new private investigator working with Poole Investigations." I thumbed back to the gray Victorian.

The couple exchanged looks before she held out her hand. "I'm Lori Monroe."

"Devon Monroe," he said.

Lori's face hardened. "Did Ivan tell you that someone killed our son?"

"He told me that Xander had a heart condition."

"What?" Lori said.

"If we need your help," Devon said to me.

"If?" Lori scoffed.

"Would you be available?" Devon continued. "Just to consult. We'd pay you."

"Because they're not taking this seriously," Lori added, her eyes skipping around a town filled with *they*.

Families eating pizza. Joggers making their way down to the beach. Baristas, real estate agents, salesclerks. So far, I'd seen no other people here that looked like the three of us. The fourth was now cooling on a mortician's steel table; the fifth, my mother, was unpacking boxes she'd brought from Los Angeles; and the one-eighth, Cooper, was somewhere hiding from me.

"Will you help us?" Devon asked.

I nodded. "Of course I will. Give me a moment to catch up. Really—I *did* just get here yesterday. Let's exchange contact info, and I'll see what's what."

I had to help—a requirement in the *We Black Together* handbook.

The happy, laughing people. The cute dogs on leashes. Selfies and sunsets and sand and sauvignon blanc.

What did a kid do to die in a town like this?

Ivan met me at the front door of the agency. His creased brow and frown didn't soften the hard-on I had for the Monroe case. The buzzing across my skin would lessen whatever blow Ivan was about to send my way.

"Stop feeling like a stud," Ivan said. "This case ain't ours to solve. I'm only consulting."

"Didn't say I was solving it," I countered. "I'm just offering advice from a *cultural* perspective if and when they need it. Community policing, Haven-style."

"You gotta stay in your lane up here. We need the deputies to trust us, especially since they toss me cases all the time. They'll solve it, Sonny. They'll bring the Monroes justice. You're not the only one who can do that, you know?"

"Of course I know that," I said, glowering at him. "And I also know that Black families don't always receive the care and attention they deserve."

Even though Black folks had a nuanced and often complicated relationship with police, they still deserved fairness and safety—and to interact with officers who understood the struggles they faced. Even Ivan, who'd had a Black best friend and a Black play niece. He's never completely understood how meaningful it was to be helped by an officer who looked like you.

I would not let Ivan kill my vibe.

My cell phone rang—Mom's number.

I answered. "Yes, Mother?"

"Alyson?" This caller—a man—was not Val Rush.

My pulse kicked into panic mode. "This is Alyson. What's wrong?"

"Your mother."

5.

On watery legs, I hopped into the Bronco with Ivan shouting, "Let me know if you need me. Don't wanna make her more upset." Before turning the truck's ignition, I took several shaky breaths and started my calming lists:

Alabama, Alaska, Arizona, Arkansas, California, Colorado . . .

At *Hawaii*, I'd steadied myself enough to grip the steering wheel and calmly back out of the parking space.

At first, I hated the idea of grounding techniques—sounded like some movie shit made up on social media—but my therapist, Dr. Molina, said it would help me do the emotional work of healing. Stress kept me from completing that work—and the lists would help alleviate that stress. So, yeah, this movie-therapy shit worked, and now, as I drove, the fuzzies crept back over me. I fought back with the fifty states of the Union.

Idaho, Illinois, Indiana, Iowa, Kansas . . .

She's okay. Breathe. She's okay. After Dad died, Mom took karate lessons with me because of all the weight gain from grief and from eating all the desserts she cooked. She ranked up to a green belt. And before I took it from her back in April, she'd been an eagle eye with the SIG SAUER before Dad even bought her one.

Before she married, Val Moody had baked cream puffs, but she wasn't one. She and her brother Vincent grew up in Watts, specifically Nickerson Gardens, the largest public housing project west of the

Mississippi. Never boring; friendly, if you're not coming in crazy; gangs, but gangs existed everywhere. Her cousins' names had been painted on The Wall alongside other dead friends and family members. While cooking broke her out of that cycle of poverty, Val Moody also knew how to fight—Uncle Vin and his crew of Bounty Hunter Bloods made sure of that while earmarking some of their drug-dealing money to send her to culinary school. He never saw her march across the stage to receive her degree—he'd died of a heart attack from an undiagnosed murmur—but she named her famous peach cobbler cake Vin's Jam.

In other words, my mother was no shrinking violet. Did she remember that?

Despite the revving in my head, I kept the Bronco steady at forty miles per hour and did not manic-drive like LAPD Sonny, who'd weave from one lane to the next, blowing traffic lights after a blurp of the sedan's siren.

There I was, in one of the most beautiful places in the state, surrounded by redwoods and coastal oaks and the ocean . . . and I couldn't see any of it because of the curvy roads.

Damascus—that's what London had likened these highways to. Saul saw the bright light and heard the voice of Jesus on that road, which led to his sudden conversion. Humbling came quick in the presence of God. He'd been transformed.

I'd loved driving—that is, until I was faced with Highway 128 in the fog.

Damascus.

A tailgater wanted me to go faster. Why? So I could slide into a ditch and my undercarriage would spark and start a fire just so that Mr. "Knows This Highway Like the Back of His Hand" could get home in time to see the Oakland A's lose?

"Sir, it's only three thirty," I shouted as the Subaru sped past me.

South Dakota, Tennessee, Texas . . .

At a roadside lighthouse-shaped mailbox marking Summer Way, I made a right and another quick right, rumbling down the gravel road toward the two-story, cedar-shingled, big-windowed beauty with a wraparound deck. Nestled among the redwoods, that house belonged to Elliott Frye and his partner, Giovanni Espinoza. Mom and I were renting the miniature version behind it. The cottage boasted the same brown shingles but a smaller wraparound deck, two bedrooms instead of four, no big windows but windows big enough.

Utah, West Virginia, Wyoming . . .

Elliott paced in front of the cottage, his brown ponytail escaping the elastic.

"Thanks for calling me," I said, hopping out of the truck.

"I came back to check on her," he said, "and the front door was open."

With stars spotting my vision, my gaze skipped from that still-open door to the dense forest around me. "Shit, shit, shit."

Elliott's face crumpled. "I'm so—"

I held up a hand. "No, Elliott. *I'm* sorry. It's not your job to look after her." I pulled out my phone and opened the app that tracked the AirTag hidden inside Mom's sneakers.

Elliott pointed north. "I think she headed that way. Fortunately, there's fencing and barbed wire to keep her from going deeper into the woods." He started walking in that direction.

I said, "Wait," stopping him. "Could you stay here in case she returns? Sorry for all this."

Twenty-four hours as tenants and the Rush women were already assholes.

I looked down at my phone: Mom's icon had stopped about .2 miles away.

Valerie Rush was only sixty-seven years old and still had agency and vigor. That meant that I was looking at spending several thousands of dollars in rent, most likely, over twenty years for memory-care facilities. In the last three weeks, she'd made sea-salt caramel macarons to prove that my concern about her diminishing memory was an overreaction. "And we can't afford it anyway," she'd added. "It's not like that motherfucker left me enough money." Mom sometimes forgot to act like the devastated widow of the dearly departed Sergeant Saint Albert Rush . . . unless she wasn't forgetting, and it was what it was.

"There would have been a time for such a word . . ."

Sunlight pulsed through the thick redwood canopy, making a glare on the phone. Once I heard crying, I stopped walking. According to the app, Mom stood .1 miles away.

All I wanted was for her to be healthy again—or to be sick all the way. All I wanted was for her to live safely with me or live in a place that provided the help she required. All I wanted was for her care to cost less than the $8,000 a regular American was expected to pay each month. Who had that much money just *sitting around*?

"Tomorrow and tomorrow and tomorrow . . ."

Holding a bottle of Diet Cherry Vanilla Dr Pepper, Mom stood at fencing that disappeared into the trees. Short, brown, and round, and wearing her shiny purple tracksuit, she looked like a Holiday Hershey's Kiss. Her perfume—Shalimar—fit in with the earthy scents of moss and redwoods . . . and me reciting *Macbeth*.

After pushing out a sigh, I stood beside her. "Hey, Mom."

The memory of saying this—"Hey, Mom"—too many times at the end of treks like this chilled me.

"Creeps in this petty pace from day to day . . ."

"I know what you're gonna say." Mom's bottom lip quivered, and her brown eyes shone with tears that wouldn't fall now that I was here. "You're gonna say . . ."

Why are you out here?

Did you realize you were headed in the wrong direction?

What happened before Elliott found the front door open?

"We should go home," I said, willing the cramps in my stomach to loosen some.

Without a word, Mom pivoted and stomped toward the cottage, head high. What dessert would she make tonight to prove all was well?

Did I really feel like arguing?

Every time I tried to bring up her memory, Mom resisted.

I don't wanna talk about it.

We'll just agree to disagree.

I would never agree that getting lost in the woods was the same as forgetting to buy unsalted butter. And Mom would never concede that vitamins, supplements, and yoga couldn't halt and reverse the deterioration of her memory.

She looked back at me now. "You're making a mole out of a mountaintop. You're standing there trying to tell me I've lost my way. *I'm* not lost. *You're* lost."

Hell yeah, I was lost as *fuck*. But because I was a Virgo, I was now the manager of the gift shop Lost as Fuck, open all day except on Election Day.

I said, "And the saying is 'make a mountain out of a molehill.'" This was no accidental transposition of a cliché.

"Out, out, brief candle!"

Nostrils flared, Mom peeped over her shoulder again, fear thrumming in her bright eyes. She was forgetting—and she hadn't forgotten that.

Back at the cottage, she made it a point to greet Elliott, now standing on the deck with his hands cupping his elbows. "Didn't mean to scare you, sweetie. It gets dark out here quick, don't it? *Dark* dark."

Elliott offered a smile. "Nighttime does not play around in Northern California." Once she disappeared into the house, he locked eyes with me and whispered, "Will she be okay here?"

I tossed a quick grin and whispered, "I'll put a latch on the top of the doors to keep her from getting out so easily, and I'll install the security system by end of day tomorrow." My cheeks burned—frustration and embarrassment.

All good—or as good as it was gonna get.

Mom had changed out of her tracksuit into a pink-and-purple housedress. "I don't wanna live up here. It's too dark. Too many trees and . . . and . . . I'm moving back home."

Anger blazed through my gut. "Moving back home? With what money? Your Social Security check of a thousand dollars a month? Or with Dad's pension that he borrowed on without telling you? And are you moving back to my apartment or to the house with the reverse mortgage, the same bank-owned house that no longer has electricity or gas because no one paid the bills—the bills you wouldn't let me handle because you're not 'some imbecile' since you 'ran a bakery for thirty years'? That house?"

She marched back to her bedroom. "You'll just have to help me out financially, then."

"Oh, okay," I snapped. "Let me grab a few stacks of money from my shoebox—"

She slammed the bedroom door in my face.

Instead of screaming at her, I backed away and trudged to the kitchen—splashed cold water from the sink onto my face, my lungs pinching in response to her Marie Antoinette-ing around our *rented* cottage.

She'd turned on the TV—the theme music to *Murder, She Wrote* drifted from behind the door. Just two days ago, she'd been so excited to move to a town just like the village in her favorite TV show.

I blew out my cheeks, thought about grabbing that bottle of Maker's Mark. Instead, I grabbed the bundles of mail I'd brought with me from Los Angeles. Phone bill, subscription notice, LA Mission . . . The stub of my last unemployment check showed that $450 had been deposited into my checking account. I'd also received the monthly settlement statement.

Your account ending in -3896 has been debited $700. Balance remaining: $97,210.

It would take nearly nine years for me to zero out this balance. Right then, I had $8,000 in my checking account. Bills, including rent, cost $2,500 a month. Doing the math, I had three months of income available. Ivan couldn't pay me what I'd earned as a homicide detective back in Los Angeles, but something was certainly more than zero.

Sadness swelled in me, making my body too heavy. I grabbed a dish towel from the oven door and sank to the floor. There, I squeezed my eyes shut, hid my face in the towel, and wept quietly, privately, believing in nothing—not anymore.

Except for maybe the power of Maker's Mark.

Life begins on the other side of despair. Sartre had said that.

Agreeing with Sartre didn't make my life any easier.

Because what if this *was* the other side?

Before Despair
South Los Angeles

I stopped at Amir's Liquor, enjoying a quiet day off duty. No plans, not even pawing through closets and doing laundry. The store smelled of hot dogs and coffee, but I didn't want either. I came for water and CHEETOS, my reward for jogging three miles today at the park.

A young woman with tawny skin and blue-and-black box braids stood in the aisle behind me. She was thin and hunched over as she slipped a loaf of Wonder Bread from the shelf and smashed it into a baby carrier, where an infant slept. A pack of bologna and a jar of baby food were already hidden in the makeshift shopping bag.

The sight tugged at my heartstrings—this wasn't just petty theft; it was desperation.

Duty told me to intervene, but empathy . . . I remembered Mom's tales about her childhood growing up poor in Nickerson Gardens—her brothers and cousins stealing food, toilet paper, and Tylenol, praying for miracles but needing to live as those miracles manifested. My conflict wasn't just about the law or remembering my legacy of poverty—it was also my off day, and arresting someone meant going into the station and completing paperwork.

"Don't you move!" Amir, the grim-faced store owner, wore a black Netflix cap as he aimed a gun at the young woman. His brown eyes were wild, his finger twitchy on the trigger.

Other customers cried out and shuddered. Fear shrouded the store like dank mist.

I already tasted gunpowder that hadn't even exploded from Amir's gun. I stood there in the narrow aisle between shelves lined with loaves of bread and cases of cold drinks, my heart hammering in my chest.

The young mother with the blue-and-black box braids stood frozen in place, her hands held high.

The baby sensed her mother's distress and started to wail.

"Calling the cops now," Amir said, his free hand plucking the phone from his waistband. "You're gonna pay for this."

The baby's cry pierced the tension, a high-pitched scream that amplified the desperation of the moment.

The young woman's eyes brimmed with tears, her voice shaky as she pleaded, "Please, don't. We're just so hungry."

I stepped forward and said, "Amir, please put the gun down." He knew that I was a detective—he'd offered me free coffee and doughnuts for weeks until he finally understood I'd take neither without paying. I turned to the young woman. "I'm a cop, and yeah, you were stealing."

The young mother's face crumpled. "We ain't had nothing to eat. I lost my job at Big Lots last week and . . . and Heavenly—she needs to eat."

I turned back to Amir. "Please?"

Amir lowered the gun.

I felt the weight of every pair of eyes in that store.

"What's your name?" I asked the young woman.

"Royalty Miller." Her eyes were flooded with the kind of fear that eats away dignity.

"Listen carefully, Royalty," I said. "I need you to promise me that this is the last time. You can't do this again—it's no kind of life for you or Heavenly."

Royalty, clutching her baby closer, sniffled and nodded, her voice barely a whisper as she replied, "I swear on my life, I'll never do this again. I just . . . I didn't know what else to do."

I believed the sincerity etched across the young woman's face. Trusting her was a gamble, but I'd always been one to play my hunches. I walked to the store counter and pulled my debit card from my phone case. I glanced back at Royalty. "Need anything else?"

Royalty paused, understood my question, and grabbed more baby food, diapers, bananas, deodorant, and packs of Top Ramen.

I paid for all of it, including my original needs of water and CHEETOS.

Amir squinted at me, and then he looked at Royalty, his eyes hard and unforgiving. With a smartphone in his hand, he snapped a photo of Royalty, ensuring her face was clear in the frame. "Never step foot in here again," he warned, his tone brooking no argument. "Consider yourself lucky today, but if I see you around my store, it'll be the cops first, questions later."

Royalty's shoulders slumped, a silent acceptance of the terms.

I grabbed my CHEETOS and water, nodded to Amir, and walked Royalty out of the store. "Take care of Heavenly." My words were more than a farewell; they were a directive. Bad shit would happen if she didn't think of her daughter beyond diapers and jars of baby food.

By the time I arrived at my desk the next day, my simple act of charity and the lack of desire to work on my off day had morphed into *She's a hero*. Community members had seen me act and appreciated my calm thinking and compassion. My actions, according to Captain Wagner, didn't just keep a poor, desperate woman out of jail and a baby out of the system; my actions had helped heal a rift in the community.

True community policing. Compassion and practicality. Helping a citizen in dire need. Preventing an escalation. There were nods of acknowledgment, soft smiles from weathered faces. The Black community, often suspicious of the badge and what it represented, now offered me a silent ovation—all for that one small act of kindness.

6.

A medical examiner for Mendocino County, India Laster, MD, noticed everything—from the smallest abrasion found on the back of a dead man's ear to the mismatched serial numbers of a dead stripper's newest breast implants. Tonight, we settled in chairs by the firepit behind the cottage and opened a bottle of Bengtsson Cabernet Sauvignon and a bag of puffed CHEETOS. India's coffee-colored skin danced in the dying light of crackling flames. Even after cutting into dead people all day while dealing with her own Jerry Springer marriage, she had no wrinkles from grimacing, no extra weight from eating more bags of CHEETOS than necessary, and no bleary eyes from weeping. She was a dream in a pink slouchy sweater and black leggings.

Those big brown eyes had seen enough of the past to predict a future most of us couldn't. She wasn't about the *why* like I was. No, she was all about the *how*. Tonight, though, I'd hoped that a long, hot shower would bring about my rebirth or a change in my emotions, and I'd also thought my childhood friend would somehow miss noticing my puffy eyes.

I felt cleaner—that was good. I smelled of Black Opium—that was good too. And I greeted my friend with vigor that I truly *did* feel. But none of this—the shower and the scent—could change the effects of crying for twenty minutes on the kitchen floor. That is, after crying at work in my office about Cooper. Puffy eyes, tissue-flecked nose, hitching voice.

India had seen me at my worst since our days in fifth grade.

Now, thousands of years later, I forced down residual tears brewing from my heart. The worst kind of heartburn. No antacids or over-the-counter remedies for this kind of indigestion.

Tonight, the redwood trees gave way to black sky that gave way to coastal oaks that highlighted the moon only to be hidden by drifting gray clouds.

"To new beginnings," India said, lifting her wineglass.

"To life after despair," I added.

We toasted, and India kept her gaze on me as she pushed off her clogs.

I kept my gaze on India's left finger. Her cushion-cut wedding ring wasn't burning with firelight, because that finger was now bare. "Who's going first?" I asked, smirking.

"In the movie versions of our lives," India said, twisting her dreadlocks into two Princess Leia buns, "we're at the 'all is lost' beat of our lives. But that also means that hope is on the horizon." She paused, then added, "Tyler pretended that he has custody of the kids, but the judge saw through that bullshit and denied his request for support. Hope, indeed, is a comin'."

I rolled my eyes. "Why should you have to pay for him, his mistress, and their baby?"

"You mean little Brigadoon?"

"Brita*jeen*, India," I said.

"What the fuck ever kind of name is that?"

"New World Roman Arabic?"

"He had the nerve to call me and say—" She lowered her chin to imitate her soon-to-be-ex-husband. "'How could you treat a baby like that?' I'm, like, bitch, how could you treat Brooke and Sam like this?"

"Indy, he's always been a fucking disaster."

She sighed and said, "I should've listened to you. He has a *what* . . . ?"

"An undiagnosed and therefore untreated oppositional defiant disorder. Always angry, always argumentative, doing the opposite of what he's been told to do—"

"And totally vindictive," she completed. "Which totally inflames his—"

"Premature ejaculation," I said. "But again, you knew that back in high school."

India sucked her teeth. "I thought it was because he was young and inexperienced. I guess he got it in quick enough to knock up—"

"The *worship leader*?" I said, grimacing.

She squinted at me. "How does one go from singing 'I Will Magnify the Lord' praise songs, then after the potluck, roll around naked in the fellowship hall storage closet?"

Yeah, that had happened.

"And now *I'm* supposed to support their sin baby?" India screeched. She chomped a cheese curl. "At least we'll always have CHEETOS."

"CHEETOS remain unproblematic," I said, smiling.

"Especially now that our chances of dying after licking the cheese dust off our fingers has decreased by .5 percent."

We toasted to post-pandemic CHEETOS and stared into the flames.

"Mom got lost again today," I whispered, my face to the sky. Sorrow popped in my chest, and tears popped in my eyes.

India thumbed back toward the cottage. "Does that explain the peach cornmeal upside-down cake for dessert tonight?"

"Absolutely. And it was delicious proof that she still remembers."

"I'm sorry."

"Yeah, me too."

The last time Mom had wandered away from home, I'd found her six miles away from my apartment at a grocery store in West Hollywood. "I meant to do that," she'd claimed once I wrangled her to the car.

"She still doesn't know about the AirTags?" India asked now.

I shook my head. "And the security system and all of that comes tomorrow."

India drained her glass. "You know . . . This was supposed to be a celebratory evening—this bottle of wine cost seventy dollars."

"Girl, I'm trying," I said, laughing.

"Try harder."

I lifted my hands and shouted, "Woo-hoo!" I grinned and said, "How was that?"

India sank into the deck chair. "You can't even fake joy anymore. But then, owing the entire world thousands of dollars can affect the libido. Let's put a pin in it for 2032."

I took a gulp of wine, then added, "It's not like I'm asking to go back to the days of spending a fortune on a purse—"

"Or more crazy-ass renovations on the truck. Or eating at restaurants with sommeliers. Buying whole wheels of Parmesan cheese—"

"I've never bought whole wheels—"

"That one time in Florence."

I flicked my hand. "I just wanna go into the grocery store and not have to do math or look at my bank balance without holding my breath." Sorrow spilled into frustration, and now my throat burned with bile.

"You thought more about buying half the business from Ivan?" India asked. "You'd have access to more money."

"I've thought about it," I said, "but he'd make me prove my worth first. By the way, I already have a case." I gave India the high-level version of Figgy the kidnapped goldendoodle, leaving out names of the players involved. "I want *Ivan's* case, though. You hear about the Black kid found on a hiking trail somewhere around here?"

India grabbed the wine bottle and said, "Mm-hmm."

"I met his parents today," I said. "Didn't get to talk long, but I told them I'd help in any way I could."

India said, "Mmm," again and poured wine into her glass.

I squinted at her, then said, "You're working on this kid, aren't you?"

India reached for the CHEETOS. "Mmm."

"You do the autopsy yet?"

"Thursday."

My mouth lifted into a small grin. "So, the goldendoodle I'm looking for belongs to London Sutton."

India's eyebrows scrunched. "As in ex-wife to Damn-Near-Perfect Boyfriend Cooper?"

"Yep. Damn-Near-Perfect Boyfriend Cooper."

"First of all," India said, "I didn't know Coop had a dog. Second, the thief stole London's dog in San Francisco and brought it down to *Haven*?"

"No." I shook my head. "London still lives here in Haven, Indy."

"I thought you said she moved after their—"

"Divorce? Yeah, well . . . She still lives here—with her husband, Cooper, and their twenty-one-year-old daughter, Mackenzie." My head hurt.

India sat up, knocking the bag of cheese curls to the ground. Then she smiled at me. "Don't play like that, Alyson. Not funny, dude. Not . . ." But she saw no humor in my eyes, and her smile dimmed. "I thought . . . You saw the . . . He told you . . . Did you . . . ? When did you . . . ? How . . . ? No. Don't say that."

I shook my head. "Believe me, I don't want to say any of this. I didn't know he was still married. Two weeks ago, yes, I saw the filing, but as of today . . . He didn't tell me. He *still* hasn't told me. That's one reason my eyes were swollen—from crying about it."

India gaped at me, gagged. "Not only is he passing as a total white man, he's passing as a single man too?" She whooped to the sky. "On the next episode of *Jerry Springer* . . ."

Just thinking about the lie felt like a knife twisting into my navel.

Together, we sat, sipped, and crunched cheese curls. Both stunned, we listened to the wood crackle and pop, to the glug of me pouring more red wine into my glass. Crickets chirped as other insects *zzhed*. Leaves rustled, not because of the wind but from creatures I didn't want to imagine. Like Benito Suarez, his face painted camo green, blade clenched between his teeth, creeping through the ferns, closer . . . closer . . .

I looked over my shoulder at the dark brush and gulped a breath.

"So, let me . . ." India shifted in her chair. "Coop flew down to LA on business and to see you every month. He'd drop his *g*'s, you'd go out to dinner; he'd pull the hot sauce out of his bag, and then y'all would go see a Madea play; or afterward, you'd go back to his hotel and have sex with Luther playing on the stereo and talk about your hopes and dreams, then fall asleep in each other's arms. Before leaving you, he'd pick those *g*'s back up, switch the soundtrack to Maroon 5, and present you with a high-priced bauble—"

"All of which will soon be listed on some website—"

"Then, miserable, he flies back home, files for divorce," India continued, "but still lives with his wife and kid *but then changes his mind without telling you that he's changed his mind*."

I waggled my eyebrows. "Un-fucking-believable, right?"

"C'mon, Coop." India muttered something else, and then she glugged the wine in her glass. "What are you going to do about that?"

I shook my head and shrugged.

India and Cooper had played *Animal Crossing* and *Words with Friends*. On my birthday, they had coordinated a mystery date scavenger hunt that started in San Diego wine country and ended on a secluded trail in Big Sur. He'd even helped India find a new place for her and the kids after her breakup with Tyler. Me losing a boyfriend also meant her losing a friend.

India pointed at me. "And you told him that you were moving, right?"

I sank into my chair. "I told him, but that was a month ago. He wanted to pay for everything, and I didn't want that, so I kept it vague. I wanted to surprise him once I got here."

India scrunched her nose and waggled her hands, and together we said, "Surprise!"

On his last visit to LA, I'd stayed at his hotel room, and he never saw the packed boxes, the Bubble Wrap, my entire life in disarray. Maybe if he had . . .

"He's rich," India said.

"He is."

India's gaze burned the side of my face. "And you're not. Rich, that is."

"Far from."

The fire crackled. A dog barked. In the distance, an engine growled, then popped.

"Are you done with him?" India asked, finally looking to the stars above us.

"Yes." I glared into the flames, my skin burning but not from the fire.

"You're still wearing *C* around your neck."

I tapped the diamond charm.

"Take it off," she said.

My fingers couldn't leave that *C*.

"Answer my question," she demanded. "Are you done?"

"Yes," I said, tugging at the necklace but not hard enough to break off the charm. "I texted him, but he hasn't responded." I leaned back and shoved cheese puff crumbs from the bag into my mouth to keep from crying.

"Remember those times when we never failed at shit?" India asked. "Wanna know why you're failing at shit now? It's because your therapist, Dr. Molina, forced you to stop using my very perfect Christmas gift to you."

"My color-coded 'No Failures or Lapses in Judgment' wall calendar." I laughed.

India did not.

"What's wrong?" I asked.

"I need two things from you," she whispered. "First . . ." She held out her hand.

I stared at her palm.

"Alyson—"

"I'm gonna sell it."

Her hand remained outstretched.

I said, "Fuck," then unclasped the pendant and dropped it into her hand. "And what's the second thing?"

"Be careful," she said. "Men get stupid and dangerous when they're cornered."

"I'm a cop, Indy." I poked my cheek with my tongue, lifted the bottle of cabernet to my lips, and drank. "Three women woke up today, and only two will wake up tomorrow. I'm aware of the threat."

Above us, the moon glowed, her soft pearly light whispering the promise of life after despair. Not because the daystar would come out tomorrow. But because she, the night star, pushed the tides in and out—out went the old, in came the new.

With a shaky hand, I grabbed the unopened CHEETOS from the shopping bag at my feet. "Once I can keep a hundred dollars in my hand, I think we should invest in Frito-Lay—"

Someone knocked on the side of the house.

"Sorry if we're being too loud, Mom." I looked over my shoulder. "Shit."

India looked over her shoulder. "Nuh-uh."

Cooper.

7.

Cooper Sutton, my liar/lover, wore the vintage Body Glove sweatshirt I bought him, his favorite Dodgers baseball cap, and the soft joggers that I'd threatened to steal. He looked as though he'd gone out to pick up milk, cigarettes, and the *Sunday Times* at 7-Eleven.

Did London buy those joggers I coveted? Did she buy the green-and-black flannel shirt packed in one of my boxes? Was it her eye for casual fashion that helped me fall in love with him?

I wanted to shoot Cooper and leave him to die right there in the leaves, the cicada husks, and the fog. But I kept my hands in my jacket pockets and my face neutral, hyperaware of his effect on me, my white-hot anger at him, the proximity of my gun. After India slipped inside the cottage, Cooper plopped into her chair by the firepit.

I looked everywhere except at my newest ex. After listening to the flames chew at the wood, I shot him a glare and said, "I want to push you into this firepit."

He opened his mouth, then closed it again, pushed out a breath, then said, "And after I'm burned to a crisp, you need to leave Haven—you can't stay here."

Those blue eyes—I wanted to poke them out. Those lips—I wanted to lop them off. That strong nose—so . . . *breakable*. Cooper inspired violence in me like ballet dancers inspired Degas, like Maine inspired Stephen King, and now I found myself laughing instead of raging, gaping at him instead of scowling. "I need to . . . *what*? I can't . . . *huh*?

Such extreme statements. Maybe you should've been this definite when I asked you a year ago—"

"I wasn't lying," he said, holding up a hand. "Things changed. But ask me if I regret us."

"I'm not asking you *shit*."

He squeezed the bridge of that breakable nose and said, "I don't regret us, Alyson. You are the love of my life—"

I dragged my hand across the sky. "'You are my heart, my life, my one and only thought.' Arthur Conan Doyle wrote it, but you said that so many times to me, I almost had it tattooed on my forehead." I took a pull of red wine from the bottle. "But then I sobered up."

"But it's true," Cooper said, his face flushed. "Every moment we spent together—every conversation we had, every quiet moment—I savored because I couldn't get enough of you. I was ready to pay off the settlement for you—"

"I don't need your help—"

"—and I wouldn't have even *considered* that if I didn't love you."

"You told me that she lived in San Francisco," I said, sipping from the wine bottle. "That you two were done. So, not only am I tripping off the *marriage* lie but finding out this afternoon that you both still live *here*? In the same *house*?"

"Sonny," he said, "you kept going back and forth on whether you were moving because of your mom, so I didn't worry because it's expensive up here. More than LA." He leaned forward, his face glowing with fire. "Honestly, I wish you would've been more direct and told—"

I gripped the neck of the wine bottle tighter, *this close* to bashing it against his head. "You're fucking kidding right now. You *must* be on some good shit right now."

"I'm sorry," Cooper said. "Believe it or not, but I am. And yes, I still love you and as much as I miss you, as much as I'll miss us—miss our field trips and our shared silence, soul food Wednesdays, and cupcakes . . ." He held his hands to his face, prayer-style. "Haven's too small for both of us."

Blood filling my face, I clenched the bottle so tight, it would soon shatter from the pressure. "I'm not going anywhere right now. My mother isn't doing well, and I'm now being paid to look for your *daughter's* dog. I didn't even rock the boat and bust you out as a cheater and a liar—and nor do I plan to. London seems like a nice lady just trying to live her life, even though her husband keeps lovers up and down the coast—"

"Lovers?" He blinked at me in awe. "You think that—"

"That I'm not your only girlfriend?" I scoffed. "Not when there's Central California needing a rep. Where is she? In Fresno? Goleta? Watsonville?"

"There's no one else—"

"Except your *wife*."

He pulled in a shallow breath before saying, "Except London, yes."

"I can't believe I fell for the old loveless marriage / about-to-divorce speech."

He shook his head, slumped his shoulders. "Not a lie."

"Then what was it?"

He sat silent, chewing the inside of his cheek. He didn't know what it was—because he never planned to divorce London. Because he still loved her.

All this time, Cooper Sutton was never mine. He'd never be.

"Tell me about your wife. Am I anything like her?" I grinned without humor. "She's a bad boss bitch—I could tell that the moment she walked into my life."

He glared at his hands.

"I really thought you were an incredible human being, Cooper," I said, my brain fizzling. "You've been so supportive of me and so generous during the worst year of my life. I would've done anything for you."

"Then do this one thing for me," he whispered, his eyes cold and desperate.

I leaned toward him and extended my middle finger. Hot tears threatened to roll down my cheeks, but I blinked them back, refusing to let them show my hurt.

"Your life. My life. Our lives will be torn apart if you stay," he said, quieter now. "And I do love you, but . . . this ain't gonna work. I promise you this, though. I'll help take care of your mother. I'm not asking you to go all the way back to LA but move up to Sableport. I own property there. There's also a beautiful memory-care facility less than a mile away from the condo. Fifteen-minute drive to San Francisco. I know you don't wanna uproot her again. You know that I know what you're going through."

His own mother, Sophia, drove alone 100 miles east of Palm Desert. She'd been found dead behind the wheel of her Prius by the California Highway Patrol on the most desolate road in the Mojave.

So, yes, he knew my anguish. Still . . .

"That's all you care about," I whispered, my breath hitching. "Making sure that your perfect little life in Haven and the life you led in LA with your whore—"

"That's not who you are—"

"I warned you a year ago," I said, pointing to him.

"That my life would never be the same." He chuckled, then added, "That you'd give me heartburn as the main meal but never as the side dish."

"And yet, I *still* became the side chick. I'm as dumb as a brick of cheese."

"I'm sorry." His gaze burned into mine, and for a moment, I saw a flicker of the man I thought I knew. He reached for my face with a trembling hand.

Air left my lungs—his skin smelled like clean laundry and lemons, and I loved that scent, and right then, it stirred a Pavlovian response deep within me.

"Sonny," he whispered, his breath so warm on my cheek as he leaned in to kiss me.

I wanted to give in—to feel his nose nuzzling my neck, to lose myself in him just one more time.

But this was a trap.

"No," I spat, standing from my chair and reeling away from him. "Now that I know the truth, I can't be a liar with you." I wished that I could unlearn that truth. I wished that I could hate him completely and never deal with him again.

But that was a trap too.

This time, a single teardrop, hot as lava, escaped down my cheek.

"I thought . . . ," I said, my voice breaking, "I thought you would ask me to marry you and that we'd live in a place like this. I thought . . ."

Kids and Christmas trees and Friday night dinners and soccer camp and love, lots of love.

"And I wish that I could give you that." He stared at me for a long moment. "Right now, I can't. This—you—it's not frivolous. I'm not into drama. You aren't either. I . . . I'm sorry, Alyson."

Stuck between *fuck you* and *I wanna fuck you*, I crossed my arms and lifted my face to the sky, my breath coming in shallow and quick.

Washington, Adams, Jefferson, Madison . . .

My breathing slowed, and my palms stung from my fingernails digging into them. I kept my eyes closed and said, "Figgy. When was the last time you saw your dog?" I plucked the phone from my pocket and opened the Notes app.

Monroe, Adams, Jackson . . .

He gaped at me. "Seriously?" When I didn't respond: "July twenty-eighth. Friday morning."

"And where were you?" I asked, tapping his responses into the app.

"At home. You need my address?"

"No," I said. "Your wife gave it to me earlier today."

He twitched and clenched his teeth to remain on simmer.

"By the way," I said, "it was very cute how you'd bring Figgy to the hospital. You also told me about her appendix bursting, and today, Mackenzie cried as she told me how you'd shown up with the dog and . . ."

My desire for violence toggled to love, and now, just a teeny-tiny bit, I understood the people who committed some of those heat-of-the-moment murders. No one had ever made me want to kill. Cooper Sutton would be my first and only affair—and my first and only homicide.

"I love my daughter," he said now, hands spread, "and I wish . . ." He stared into the flames, his lips still parted, his words stuck there.

"If needed, I'll request your help in further understanding Haven's citizens, people who could've stolen your daughter's dog. Here's who she and London named as suspects." I handed him the phone.

He scanned the list, his eyebrows dipping. He rubbed his bottom lip, then said, "You wanna know who *I* think did it?"

"I'm not interested in anything you have to say beyond what I've asked."

His eyes flashed with anger.

"Does the list look complete to you?" I asked. "Did we leave someone off?"

Cooper shook his head and handed me the phone. "When are you starting interviews?"

"Tomorrow." I paused, then added, "I've learned that Figgy's been lost before."

"Yes. Mackenzie gets distracted sometimes."

"I've also learned that she's had two DUIs."

His nostrils flared. "What does *that* have to do with anything?"

"Everything has to do with everything," I said.

"These people aren't gonna talk to a stranger," he said, his voice laced with impatience.

"Well, then, I'll just rely on my newest ex-boyfriend to make the introductions."

He peered at me with stormy eyes.

Simmering.

"You stay out of my way," I said, "and I'll stay out of yours."

"Haven ain't what it seems," Cooper said, standing from the chair, his anger moments away from bubbling over. "People do bad shit up here."

"Yeah." I huffed. "I've been fucking one of their villains for a year now."

"You'll regret this," he said, his voice low, cold.

I squinted at him. "You're threatening me?"

"No. I'm warning you that this place ain't LA."

I tensed. "Okay. I'll consider that as I rub scar cream on the shoulder still fucked up by a .22-caliber bullet shot from the hot gun of a monster who raped and killed four women, the monster I chased through the city on a day it hit 110 degrees during fire season. But thanks for the warning. I think I got it, though."

Cooper could make living in Haven difficult for me—he had played rough in his business. He'd personally shown me that he'd do whatever he needed (lie) to get what he wanted (me).

But I was also used to rough play. As a cop in a male-dominated field, I'd learned to keep my balance and hold fast as the boys tried to manspread all over my cases. After being shot, though, I had something most of them didn't have: a battle scar. I'd literally lost blood for the blue. No one could ever tell me that I didn't belong. No one could ever tell me that I wasn't tough enough. That I couldn't survive.

Without speaking another word, Cooper turned on his heel and disappeared into the shadows. A moment later, his Porsche's engine growled—sounding like the engine I'd heard popping on a nearby road—and tires smashed against the gravel and then . . .

Silence.

Except for the crackling fire, the whispering wind, and my thundering heartbeat.

I stood there, still, my mind loose from the wine, my shoulders tight from ending my happily ever after with Cooper Sutton. What now? My phone vibrated in my hand.

Sonny

What, Cooper?

Ellipses bubbled on the screen and stopped. Bubbled and stopped.

By the time I walked back into the cottage, Cooper still hadn't finished his response. He was always a slow texter. I sighed, tired of waiting for him, and composed my own message.

You've offered to take care of my mother

Maybe I'll take you up on that offer

Once she settles in we can revisit this conversation and my plans for the future

What would I do?
I didn't know.
Which meant Cooper didn't know what I'd do either.
The hair on the back of my neck stood on end.
A dangerous game.

You said you'd help pay off the settlement

Maybe I'll take that help too

I'll find your daughter's dog

I won't give you any problems

I won't expose you

I hit "Send." This wasn't blackmail. It was the least he—*the adulterer*—could do.

And Cooper *had* made those offers—I was just taking him up on it since, yes, I *did* need help. Since he couldn't provide me with love . . .

Just two days ago, he'd declared his enduring love for me over thirty text messages. Those declarations were supposed to play a part in the love story I'd tell our children.

I'd kept every text and letter he'd sent me. And I'd kept every dick pic he'd sent me too. All of them sat in the cloud.

Waiting.

8.

I follow the light of the moon, its glow a flashlight through the redwoods.

Someone follows me, hidden in the ferns and the darkness.

I hurry in my step and hide behind a log, holding my breath and listening for the cracks of twigs beneath his boots.

I shiver as the sound of his approach grows louder. I can't stay here. My legs cramp as I crouch, and my left shoulder aches from the damp cold. No matter how much I want to, how much I need to, my legs won't carry me deeper into the woods. No, they quickly numb and that prickly thudding eases up my thighs to my abdomen, splitting at my arms.

There he is, his face in shadow, his shotgun bright with moonlight. He stops in his step.

I hold my breath.

He cants his head.

Nightcrawlers push out of the damp earth and coil around my ankles. No, not worms. Snakes. Red ones and black ones, writhing around me like the sea.

But I can't move. My feet . . . Where are my feet?

He hears the hissing and my growing terror, my quickened breathing, and he cocks that beautiful gun, and he lifts it until it rests against his shoulder.

Our eyes meet.

My mouth opens wide, ready to scream, but my jawbone cracks, and no sound comes, and the snakes see an opening and slither up my arms and sink into my mouth and . . .

On Wednesday morning, the world beyond the kitchen windows hid behind fog. My nightmare had pulled me from sleep, and I lay in bed, listening to India snore, wondering if I'd be in this bed next month this time.

Two hours later, I checked the locks of the doors, peeked in on Mom—still sleeping—and padded to the kitchen. I watched my reflection quietly unpack boxes of Mom's favorite things: the yellow Dutch oven, the blue stand mixer, the seasoned cast-iron pots and pans, and the block of Japanese knives. She'd grown aggravated last night as she searched for bakeware that would help prove that she was still Val Rush, queen of the Cuisinart. While she slept, I tried to arrange the cottage's kitchen just like Mom's back in Los Angeles. We'd keep her most important belongings, like the items in these boxes, while other high-end, high-volume items—hand mixers and serving/display platters and stands—would be sold online or at thrift stores around Mendocino County. The cottage didn't have as much space as the house down in Los Angeles, but it had more space than my apartment.

I also owned sellable things. The clothes that used to belong to Cooper but also baubles he gave me in turquoise boxes: a charm bracelet to match the charm necklace in India's possession, diamond studs, high-end handbags (though I would not be relinquishing my Birkin—fuck *that* noise). Luxury consignment shops would take these pieces, and I'd budget that money for expenses.

All night, I'd thought about London Sutton. Who was she? Did she know Cooper was having an affair? Maybe they had an open marriage? Maybe London was stepping out too?

"Doesn't matter," India said. She dusted spilled coffee grounds from the vest of her denim jumpsuit into the sink.

I kept clicking around London's LinkedIn page.

The woman in this profile had a rounder face and softer hair. She'd earned her medical degree from UC San Francisco. "Child/adolescent psychiatrist dedicated to improving the quality of whole-patient health care," I read aloud. "I already feel that I need to tell her everything."

"Don't," India said, tapping "Brew" on the coffee maker. "You don't know her. You don't know what their marriage is like. You don't know how she'd react. Confessing to her ain't your responsibility."

"I hate messy shit." I stroked the patch of skin left bare without that diamond *C*, panting as though I'd just finished cardio.

"Were *you* married to her?" India asked, eyebrow arched. "No, you weren't. You aren't obligated to do *shit* except stop fucking her husband." She grabbed two mugs from the undercabinet hooks and peered at me with soft eyes. "It's messed up, I know, but I'm telling you—that lady doesn't want the other woman telling her *jack*. At least, not until she needs a witness in divorce court."

It had all been so romantic. Gale—my artist friend who created the art installation with the tattered umbrellas, *Acid Rain*—had been so proud that he'd brought Cooper and me together that night in Santa Monica. "Who would've thought acid rain would be a good thing?" When would I tell Gale that my relationship with Cooper had indeed corroded and that acid lies had done what acid rain couldn't?

Over coffee and slices of peach cornmeal upside-down cake, India and I studied her Bumble matches:

A dentist with great hair and—

"Lowercase teeth and uppercase gums?" India said, nodding.

An ex-pro lacrosse player (*That was a thing?*) looking for a "God-fearing female."

A middle school English teacher who'd used "your" instead of "you're" and whose personal statement began with, "So, I don't really follow politics . . ."

India groaned and said, “Guess I’m having a threesome with Sam Malone and Homer Simpson tonight.” She squinted into the distance. “And to think I was married to a man with a PhD in forensic anthropology.”

I walked my best friend to her olive-green Fiat, a roly-poly parked behind my mastodon Bronco. The cold air smelled of pine and peat, and the fog swallowed the chirps of morning birds and the shapes of the trees. The sun was an egg yolk lost in milk. That creeping anxiety pressed against my chest as I clutched my elbows and watched India back out the driveway. She shouted, “Get dressed,” before disappearing into the mist.

Too soon to change out of my boxers and T-shirt, though. I needed to make more important decisions first, like: Was I staying in Haven, yes or no?

Working for Ivan, I’d taken a fifteen-thousand-dollar pay cut, but I’d save on gas, clothes, twenty-dollar cocktails, and car repairs. Before I knew the truth about Cooper, I figured he’d provide me with as much as I needed. He’d basically agreed to do the same last night, but only if Mom and I left Haven.

Maybe I should’ve negotiated more with Ivan over my pay. Maybe I could ask Ivan for a raise, even though I hadn’t even worked a full week.

My phone buzzed from the kitchen counter—a text from Cooper.

The ground rolled beneath me, and I leaned against the counter before reading:

Hey

This is the place in Sableport

Pictures of a two-bed, two-bath, two-story condo overlooking the Pacific. Marble countertops and Viking kitchen appliances. Wood floors. Walk-in closet.

Just say the word and it’s yours

That panoramic ocean view. That beautiful kitchen.

I want a written agreement from you stating the terms

And HOA covered

My finger hovered over "Send."

What more could I demand?

Everything.

And why couldn't I have everything?

Everything had been promised to me since my very beginnings. In church: Do good, and the windows of Heaven will open and pour out a blessing. At school: Study hard, and you'll land the best job. In the United States: Work hard, and you'll live the American dream. From the LAPD: Protect and serve, and you'll receive a great pension. From The Man: Stay open and communicative, be sexy and a good cook, be the Madonna *and* the whore, and you'll die peacefully in the arms of your beloved on your hundredth birthday.

Bullshit.

I'd been good, and yet, here I was with the opposite of *everything*.

Nothing.

I should've been waking up this morning in Los Angeles, racing west on Manchester Boulevard with a box of Randy's Donuts in the back seat, ready to search for spent cartridges on bloody blacktops, and then, afterward, picking up dinner from Fresh & Meaty Burgers and returning to Pacific Station for a night of making copies for my newest murder book.

And yet . . .

I'd find Figgy because I promised I would, because I was getting paid to find her, because the goldendoodle was cute and deserved to be found. I'd move past life's disappointments just so that I could breathe. I'd tell Ivan that I needed a better case—I wanted to find the truth about poor Xander Monroe and help his parents heal . . . and that I needed a little bit more money than what he was paying me. I needed to find a therapist, not one in Haven, though, but up the highway—someone who knew what it meant to work hard for shit to *still* not work out, a therapist with real-life experience of extraordinary disappointment and . . .

Was I staying in Haven after all?

Just as I rolled into a parking space near the office, my phone chimed again—a text from Lori Monroe.

Hope you haven't changed your mind
Will you still help us?
I just need answers
Please

Uncertain of my response, I sat frozen in the driver's seat, so tense I twitched.

The phone rang, and I yelped, almost dropping the phone.

"You don't even know what you're helping us with." Lori sounded stronger today than she had yesterday.

"You're right." I grabbed a pen and the folio from my bag. "How old was Xander?"

"Seventeen."

According to Lori, her son had been found around nine o'clock yesterday morning on Seabreeze Trail. Strung along the coast, Seabreeze was a popular trail, and Xander jogged that spot every morning at the crack of dawn. "He usually has the trail to himself," Lori shared.

A man named Jairo had been walking the same trail with his black Lab, Ace. The dog had bounded ahead of him, returning with a black size 13 Nike Pegasus in his mouth. Alarmed, Jairo had rushed ahead, his eyes sweeping the dirty trail until stopping at a patch of poison oak.

"Xander wasn't breathing," Lori whispered. "He was in great physical condition—he'd been cross-training, preparing for football season. Let me send you a picture . . ."

Xander Monroe had that perfect American smile—Cam Newton meets Deion Sanders—flawless brown skin, and a diamond stud in his left earlobe. Cocky and adorable. In another photograph, he wore that same smile in his black-and-gold football uniform—number five. Yeah, I'd root for this kid.

"This morning," Lori said, "the detectives found a suicide note in his shorts pocket. A suicide note but Xander wasn't . . . He wasn't on the verge like that. He'd just received an acceptance from JPL for this virtual internship, and we were planning to celebrate this weekend."

"JPL, as in Jet Propulsion Laboratory?" I said, awed.

"Football and physics. Make it make sense."

Genius athletes: Kareem Abdul-Jabbar, Marion Bartoli, Wladimir Klitschko.

"Did the detectives tell you what the note said?" I asked.

Lori texted me another picture.

A steno book–size piece of blue paper with five words written in black marker:

A beautiful place to die

"Is this his handwriting?" I asked, throat tight.

Silence, then: "Yes."

"And where did they find it?"

"In his right pocket."

"Was he working on a school project? Did he write poetry? Could there be some other explanation of why he'd write a line like that?"

Silence.

"Did the investigators tell you exactly where he was found on the trail?" I asked.

"No," Lori said, "but when he didn't come home at his usual time, I used Find My."

This screenshot was a map with a small circular picture of Xander above a blue dot.

"I know my son," she said, "and he wasn't depressed. They haven't told me how he supposedly took his life, but it doesn't matter to me. I know that he didn't."

I needed to visit Seabreeze Trail.

Not that I was working the Monroe case. I was just curious and needed to familiarize myself with Haven, the environment, and the people who lived—*and died*—here.

After ending my call with Lori, I swiped to Messages and reread my message to Cooper.

I'd want a written agreement from you stating the terms

And HOA covered

I couldn't take Cooper's money. Even if we were together, $97,000 was a lot of money. Yeah, he could afford it, but I didn't want to owe anyone. I'd never taken a bribe in all of my days working as a cop. My parents taught me to be self-sufficient and to never allow *anyone* to hold something over me—even a box of Randy's Donuts.

If it took me twenty years to pay off the balance to the Suarez family, then . . .

My arm tingled—was I having a heart attack?

I wouldn't regret this decision. It would all work out, even though Mom and I had just arrived in Haven. I hadn't even started life in Haven yet.

A beautiful place to die.

In a town as beautiful as Haven, why would Xander Monroe end his life? Then again, in a town as beautiful as Haven, why would someone take it from him?

9.

Facebook–Audrey Lujun looked like a nice lady with her pearls and a smile that belonged to every saint who'd directed twelve-year-old Sonny Rush to the stacks of Jackie Collins, Sidney Sheldon, and V.C. Andrews library books—nice ladies with their graying blond hair parted in the middle and curled at the ends wore that same warm smile as they smothered their husbands with pillows, slipped antifreeze into their son-in-law's protein shakes, and lobbed axes at their tenants' heads for Social Security checks. Lujun owned A Page Turned, the bookstore on Sea Rose Way. She volunteered at Haven's only Catholic church and won open houses and garden shows because of her gorgeous mauve Barbra Streisand hybrid tea roses.

Mom had tried to grow roses during her fresh flower baking phase. Every Sunday, she'd pull on gloves, grab shears, and work in the garden, spending hours tending pink-edged garden roses and pale-yellow miniature roses. She didn't realize aphids would attack her garden and that she'd have to use pesticides to kill those pests. Then she realized that she couldn't put toxic flowers on her cakes. "All that effort," she'd cried, "and I don't even *like* roses."

On Sunday, as we drove up Highway 128, Mom had wondered aloud if she should try fresh roses on cakes again. "Or maybe I should just stick with edible flowers. Pansies are pretty. You think they have places in Haven that sell them?" Before I could respond, though, she'd shifted in the passenger seat and slipped back to sleep. Once I stopped to fill the gas tank in Los Banos, she'd sat up, blinking, forgetting that we'd left Los Angeles. "I'm not leaving LA," she'd said arms crossed and didn't speak to me for the rest of the trip. As though I also wouldn't miss the city where I'd kissed a boy for the first time (Griffith Observatory) and learned how to drive (Forum stadium parking lot)—the city where I'd put my body between bad guys and citizens for a decade.

And now, just two days later, I parked in front of a tan Craftsman house across the street from an off-leash dog area of Cranston Park. Which was worse: the smell of dog pee in the air or the nonstop barking? It was all bad, and that made me smile. I slipped my keys into the pocket of my denim maxi skirt, then whispered, "I'm back."

White rosebushes lined the walkway that led to the porch. A dusty-violet Subaru was parked in the driveway. A light burned in the dining room.

Instead of ringing the doorbell, I closed my fist and knocked.

Almost immediately, the front door opened.

Those four hard and sharp raps brought people, even innocent ones, to the door.

After I introduced herself, Audrey Lujan breathed a relieved sigh, then asked, "Would you like a pop?"

I blinked. "A . . . *what*?"

"Sorry. Soda," Audrey said, eyeing my caramel-colored heeled boots. "I've lived in Haven for thirty years, but I'm from the East Coast. In Buffalo, we call it *pop*. Funny—thirty years later and I still call it *pop*. Aren't you hot in those?" She nodded at my boots.

I smiled without looking down at my feet. "I'm good. Thanks for your concern. So, I'm here about a dog—"

"Let me guess: Figgy?"

"She's missing."

"Again?" She rolled her eyes.

I pushed up the left sleeve of my blue cable-knit sweater. "I've learned that Figgy's—"

"Been a nuisance?" Audrey asked, rubbing her temples. "She killed my flowers. Do you want to see them?"

I followed the book lady to the backyard. The stench of dog pee had replaced the strong fragrance of roses, grapefruits, cloves, and jasmine. The color mauve on the internet couldn't capture the beauty of the large dusty purplish-blue flowers with their glossy green leaves and giant thorns like falcon talons. Hummingbirds and butterflies of every color buzzed and fluttered from one bloom to the next.

"These are gorgeous," I said, tapping a velvety petal.

"I love dogs," Audrey said, plucking a pair of shears from a nearby basket. "I chose to live across the street from a dog park. I absolutely love them. Anyway . . ."

She clipped a bloom. "I couldn't understand why my roses were dying. One day, I saw Figgy run from across the street at the park and right into my yard. Then she stopped—" Audrey crouched in place with her hands out. "—and she sniffed." Audrey wiggled her nose. "—and she ran over to the roses and peed." Audrey stood upright. "After that, I put a security camera—"

The woman pointed to the eaves of the house and the small security cameras on each corner. "Figgy's come back to relieve herself six more times. And she pees only on the Streisand roses. *Six times.* Maybe she's a Cher fan."

Audrey pointed to a spot where the leaves had lost their green and the soil looked pale and sick. "That's where Figgy pees."

I took pictures of the dying shrubs and poisoned soil.

She opened an app on her phone and found the video of Figgy relieving herself.

"Once I caught Mackenzie leaving my yard, and I showed her the video of Figgy peeing. Did Mackenzie apologize or offer to compensate me for her dog killing my roses? Of course she didn't. She's special, you see, and she doesn't *have* to do the right thing." She handed the clipped rose to me.

I accepted the rose. "Did you file a formal complaint?"

"Of course I did," Audrey said, "and nothing happened. I've spent twenty years cultivating these roses. They're very particular and so, I'm vigilant. I worry, worry, worry. About water stress, about rose beetles, about making sure the soil drains, about making sure they get enough sun. And Figgy, bless her heart, she's just a dog, but she comes running over here, damn the thorns, and she tramples everything and pees on everything, just like the Suttons have trampled and peed on everything in Haven." She paused, then added, "Not literally peeing—"

"I understand," I said, rose to my nose.

Because another Sutton had peed on me, not literally, I wasn't into that, even with a hot rich guy like Cooper. But now I knew, for the Suttons, disrespect was a feature, not a bug.

"What do you mean the Suttons trample on everything?" When Audrey didn't respond, I added, "I'm new here—"

"Of course you are," Audrey said, chuckling. "You stand out. It's the sweater and the boots. You're probably the only one in Haven wearing either."

"Cuz it's cold," I said, laughing.

"Don't go undercover, then," she said, face bright. "The bad guy will know you're the one who's not supposed to be there."

Great advice, Audrey Lujan.

"And since I'm new here," I continued, "I don't know everything that I should—including who holds the keys to the kingdom here in Haven. Do you think you're being set up?" A purposefully vague question.

"Is that what's happening?" Audrey asked, eyes bugged.

I shrugged. "I don't know, especially since I don't know the psychology of the people I'm dealing with, including my clients. I mean . . . we just met, you and I, and it's obvious that you're not the dognapping type. But you were the first name they gave me. Why do you think they included you?"

Audrey pushed back her hair with a shaky hand. "It's because they—"

"Who is 'they'?"

"The Haven Chamber of Commerce," she said. "Cooper Sutton is the chair of the board of directors. They want anyone with a business to do facelifts to their storefronts. New paint. New lighting. Plants. New electrical. And yes, my bookstore looks a little tatty, but facelifts take money. My store is two thousand square feet, and at forty dollars per square feet . . . That's eighty thousand dollars. *I don't have eighty thousand dollars.* They're giving out these small business loans, but the interest rate is twelve percent."

My jaw dropped. "That's almost ten thousand dollars in interest."

"Exactly," Audrey said, twisting the wedding band on her ring finger. "And so I said, 'Heck no!' I'll slap on a new coat of paint and some varnish and call it a day."

The book lady snorted. "But that isn't enough for the hoi polloi of Haven, who want to make Haven into some fancy tourist destination, like Pismo Beach. But I'm not going into hock to line somebody else's pockets, especially the Suttons."

Audrey glared out at the dog park. "Blaming me for stealing a dog. Like I'd use an animal for revenge. I wouldn't even do that to a snake, and I *hate* snakes." The book lady smiled at me again. "Sure you don't want a pop?"

10.

I returned to downtown Haven and parked at a yellow Craftsman-style supermarket with white trim and a yellow awning. Good Pickings, a smaller version of Whole Foods, was priced just as high and sold every variety of olive and sparkling water. And like Whole Foods, there were no Black hair-care products like Pink Lotion or black castor oil conditioner on the shelves. There were no bottles of Crystal or Red Rooster hot sauces but at least there was seasoned salt and Tabasco pepper sauce. I'd either order my other essentials online or drive to San Francisco.

Tanned, blank-faced white women wearing wash-and-go hair, store-brand yoga sets, and Skechers crammed the aisles alongside tanned and grumpy white men wearing baseball caps, khakis, and cargo shorts. In Good Pickings, everyone knew everybody, and either they openly stared at me or ignored me as I roamed the store's tight aisles.

I blamed my blue sweater.

According to PeopleFinder, Harvey Parrish struck a man with a pole fifteen years ago. His second wife, Elizabeth, had been found dead in their bathtub during the early days of COVID-19. He also torched his ex-girlfriend's Acura Integra. He remarried his first wife, Ruthie, just a year ago.

Harvey Parrish lorded over the meat and seafood department counters. He was a sequoia of jowls, raisin eyes, and hands bigger than boulders. Harvey joked with an old lady about the price of short ribs and chuck roast, which cost about three dollars more up here than at the fancy butcher shops down in Los Angeles. High prices didn't quell the long line of waiting customers, though. It quelled me but not because of the expensive meat. I couldn't meaningfully interview Parrish about the dog he allegedly hated.

Keely Butler owned Rise & Grind, located down the block from Good Pickings. The small Craftsman-style café needed a new coat of mustard-colored paint for its wood planks and turquoise paint for its frames. *That would be forty dollars a square foot!* With a gluten-free, vegan, and organic menu, Rise & Grind didn't have many customers lined up for jackfruit crab cakes and jackfruit carnitas. No one stood at the distressed wood counter or fixed up their hot drinks at the coffee bar.

The brown-haired woman I wanted to talk to was taking a phone order. I stood at the counter studying the receipt of my order scribbled by Keely. Rushed and right-slanted print, the *C* for chili could've also been an *L* or a left parentheses.

Mackenzie Sutton walked outside past the café. In tears, she clutched an empty dog leash in one hand and a sheath of MISSING DOG flyers in the other. With her face splotchy and red, she wasn't faking her sorrow. Figgy was truly gone.

According to PeopleFinder, Keely Butler had lived in Haven all forty-four years of her life. She'd inherited Rise & Grind from her parents, Gordon and Rebecca Butler, who'd served burgers and meatloaf, fried green tomatoes, and bacon on everything. Keely had dabbled in town politics, in particular, crime and law enforcement because her only child, daughter Honor Butler, was missing and Keely's husband, Javier, deported back to Jalisco, Mexico.

Keely ended the call, ripped away the order, and slapped it down on the pass to the cook. She scowled at me and said, "This really isn't a good time. Lunch rush."

One customer seated at a table tapped at his laptop and nursed a foamy orange beverage.

Suspect Number Three led me to a back table.

Arms crossed, Keely asked, "What's this about Figgy?" She scratched at her left bicep and a paw-print tattoo with *Bella* scripted beneath it.

"She went missing on Friday," I said, "and your name was given as someone to talk to."

"Why?"

I shrugged, then smiled. "But I'm also taking a moment to meet my new neighbors. I just arrived in Haven."

Keely squinted, making her small eyes even smaller. "Aren't you hot in that sweater?"

I chuckled. "No. I'm from Los Angeles."

She grunted. "No wonder." She paused, then asked, "Did you move here for the so-called revitalization of Haven? To buy up property before real estate prices skyrocket?"

I opened my folio and flipped to a clean page of notebook paper. "I'm here because Ivan Poole asked if I'd like to work for him and because I needed a change of scenery. I told him, 'Yeah, as long as I can bring my summer sweater collection.'"

Keely smirked. "Oh. So, you'll also *not look* for my daughter, then. Awesome."

I blinked at the woman simmering across from me. "Ma'am, whatever's between you and Ivan is between you and Ivan. I'm here about—"

"The dog. Right. Searching for a dog instead of Honor. Got it."

A server slipped a bottle of water and a bowl of chili in front of me.

I prayed for the patience needed to talk with an angry and frustrated parent scared for her child. Finding Honor, though, wasn't my job—at least, not yet.

Keely pointed at the bowl of chili. "You should probably eat that before it gets cold. It's no good if it's cold. The vegan cheddar cheese becomes . . . *weird*."

I moved the wooden spoon through the dark soup to help the fake cheese mix in and melt a little bit more. And then I took a bite of the vegan black bean chili and . . . tasted just like what it was named—nothing more, nothing less.

Keely's dark eyes darted down to my boots. "Don't your feet hurt in those?"

A frown flashed across my lips. "They're more comfortable than they look."

Will she poke my brown skin and ask, "Is that more painful than it looks?" And then will she tug my hair, and wonder, *How does it do that?*

I asked, "Why would Mackenzie Sutton think that you could've taken Figgy?"

"Because Figgy belongs to my greatest political rival," Keely said. "Not Mackenzie. *London*, her mother. We're both running for mayor in the next election. I'm for change, and London's for gentrification, which means making Haven into a featureless, busy hellhole with expensive cocktails and eyewear boutiques. I wanna help small business owners fix up their existing shops, improve the infrastructure, bring in more visitors. Invest in Haven *thoughtfully*."

I nodded. "Honestly, your plans sound no different than London's. Just differences in taste. Moving furniture around Haven's living room."

Keely glared at me. "But my mission is coming from a different place. I know what it means to struggle, to lose it all. My husband. My daughter . . . I want to make families whole, and I don't want anyone to go through what I've experienced firsthand.

"London's never lost anything," Keely continued. "She has a husband, a daughter, a big house on a bluff, and money to hire a detective to find a dog. Who has that kind of money? The average salary in Haven is eighty thousand dollars, and soon, there will be more old people here than young. The heart of this village resembles me and my family and so should the leadership."

I tapped my pen against the pad. "And Figgy?"

Keely scratched at her paw-print tattoo. "What about Figgy?"

"You never answered my question. Did you take the dog?"

Keely rolled her eyes and fished in her pocket for a business card. "Order nine times and on your tenth visit, you get complimentary smashed avocado toast." She slid the card across the table. "If I wanted to get back at Cooper Sutton, I wouldn't take his dog. I'd just put some ex-lax into the green juice smoothie he orders almost every day. And to specifically answer your question: No, I didn't steal Figgy. I know what it is to lose loved ones and wouldn't wish that on *anyone*, not even the family I hate. Figgy is the only living creature that London's ever had taken from her. Tell her to lose her husband and daughter, and *then* get back to me."

11.

I thought about Keely Butler as I walked to my car—about her loss, her anger, that chili. None of it was good. Little did she know, London had been close to also having her husband taken away.

You are my heart, my life, my one and only thought.

Incorrect. Cooper wasn't leaving his wife, not anymore, and though I didn't know London, I doubted she'd *want* to leave him. But then again, Cooper ordered a green juice smoothie each morning from a woman who could've stolen his dog and mentioned ex-lax as revenge. So . . .

The two suspects I'd talked to loathed Figgy's people more than they loathed the goldendoodle. I understood the anxiety and the anger, and really, I could see either the book lady or the café owner acting rash one afternoon and luring Cooper, London, and Mackenzie Sutton into the back seats of their cars and dropping them off in the desert. But I couldn't see them doing the same to Figgy.

Yeah, Haven was nastier than I thought—Cooper had warned me. He knew this because the few people I'd talked to hated him. They resented his efforts to polish Haven into one of California's shiny seashells. Who else resented Cooper and London for similar reasons?

Haven High School, home of the Bobcats, sat on a hill with views of the Pacific Ocean on one side and California oaks on the other side. The digital sign on the front lawn announced that August 28 was the first day of school as workers slapped new paint on the buildings and gardeners drove lawn mowers on the grass near the parking lot and gymnasium. The Bobcats' football field wasn't the most impressive—nothing like Los Angeles stadiums—but the lights looked new and so did the turf.

In the parking lot, Figgy's MISSING DOG flyers had been taped, tied, and stapled to gates and walls. A few flyers had been slipped beneath windshield wipers on parked cars. A couple were being swept by the wind to the surrounding field. Young men wearing white football practice jerseys and shoulder pads huddled around a player holding a cell phone. Some were red-faced, pacing and pushing their sweaty hair from their foreheads. I wanted to walk over to the group and ask them what was up—what had upset them, what was on the cell phone, and what did they know about Xander's death. Had the coach or school administrators called a special meeting? Had investigators from the Mendocino County Sheriff's Department talked to them?

I found a parking space as close to the players as possible—not too close since I couldn't let them see my sharp teeth.

My phone vibrated from the cup holder.

A text from Mom.

I whispered, "Shit," and held my breath as I tapped the message.

All unpacked 👋🥰🍾🥂

I released the breath I'd been holding and flexed my hands, which had lost their feeling.

Mom was okay. Maybe her condition wasn't as severe as I thought. Maybe the noise of Los Angeles had worsened her condition. Maybe I'd actually be able to focus on improving my life and jump-starting the "Before the Wolves Came" version of Sonny Rush.

A football player in the huddle threw his shoulder pads into the air. Another shouted, "Calm the fuck down." A few walked off, heads dropped, shoulders pad-free, spirits slumped.

Was this about Xander Monroe? Did they know him enough to be upset? Did they know him enough to have wanted him dead?

A linebacker-big Black kid stood beside me. He wore shoulder-length dreadlocks with bleached tips that brushed the shoulders of his black-and-yellow Bishop O'Dowd hoodie. His swollen eyes told me that he'd been crying. "They don't look upset, do they?" he asked, nodding toward the players on the field.

I looked back at the young men on the field and shrugged. "I won't assume." A pause, then, "What's your name?"

"Keenan."

"Alyson, hi. You played with Xander?"

Keenan nodded. "I'm the reason his pops moved him up here." Then he told me about his life in Oakland. Acorn Projects. Finding a transient he and his friends had named Homeless Joe dead in an alley. Lori and Devon's freak-out. The move to Haven.

Tears welled in his eyes, and the young man swiped his face. "As soon as I heard they found him on that trail . . ." He chewed on his bottom lip. "You the detective they hired?"

"Basically."

A teardrop rolled down the teen's cheek. "He wasn't depressed, not like that—not to, you know . . . Like some people said what happened. He had shit going on, but it wasn't that."

"What other shit?" I prodded, eyebrow raised. When Keenan didn't speak, I cocked my head. "School shit? Family shit? Girl shit?"

Keenan shifted uncomfortably as a light flashed in his eyes. "He wouldn't tell me a lot about her. Just that folks would be pissed if they knew he was with her." He waved to the football field. "I don't think it has anything to do with this bullshit. He's a Black boy in a place where there ain't no Black girls. He gotta kick it with somebody, right? And her daddy probably wasn't gonna be happy with shit like that, no matter how many degrees the Monroes got."

I squinted at him. "Someone's father may have . . . ?"

Keenan shrugged and swiped his hand across his mouth. He pushed out a sigh and muttered, "This is fucked up."

I looked back over my shoulder at the players huddled on the field. "Yeah. Truly."

Shaking his head, Keenan backed away from me. "How you gon' live in Oakland for seventeen fucking years and in the two months living here . . . ? Like . . . he shoulda got vaccinated against this place. Nah. He shoulda stayed in the Oakland bubble. That's on his parents." He glared out at the football field, then said, "Fucked up."

I let out a breath. Before I could ask another question, Keenan was already climbing into the driver's seat of his gold Dodge Challenger. "If I have more questions," I shouted as he revved the engine.

"Doc Monroe know how to reach me," Keenan shouted over the rumbling, then peeled out of the parking lot, leaving behind a rancid cloud of burned rubber.

I watched the Bobcats longer, wanting to know the answers to my questions—old and new, including the mystery white girl who may have gotten Xander killed. Since I'd started work on the missing goldendoodle case, what would be the harm in taking a moment to help the Monroes navigate their new world of pain and anguish?

Hi Lori, I texted.

I just talked with Keenan

He's heartbroken

Anything new come in?

The Bobcats, still huddled in the parking lot, were laughing now.

He's angry with us
I can't blame him
Here's the police report

I'd helped parents whose children had perished by their own hands or someone else's. Ultimately, the method didn't matter. The place in their hearts would remain forever desolate, and even if they received answers or witnessed that deadly needle sliding into the ropy veins of their child's murderer, nothing would ever grow in those barren places again.

The police report had been completed by Deputy Rip Gilmore.

August 1, 2023, at 8:55 a.m.: Jairo Hood called 911 asking for help. Call answered by the Mendocino County Department of Emergency Communications.

On the call, Mr. Hood sounded panicked and seemed to have trouble speaking. Mr. Hood was able to provide an approximate address to the dispatcher, who then transferred the call to the Mendocino County Department of Emergency Communications (MCDEC). While on the phone with the dispatcher, Mr. Hood said that the decedent looked as though he was sleeping, that there was no blood but there was also no pulse.

While trying to articulate what happened, Mr. Hood said he had been jogging with his dog Ace who had run ahead on the trail. The dog returned with a black Nike athletic shoe.

Realizing that the shoe was newer, Mr. Hood ran ahead on the trail and spotted the decedent on Seabreeze Trail. The decedent appeared to be sleeping and Mr. Hood tried to rouse the decedent with no success and could not find a pulse. He called 911. Mr. Hood expressed concern over emergency personnel not being able to find his location on the trail. Mr. Hood stayed on the phone with 911 until members of Mendocino County Sheriff's Department (MCSD) arrived.

MCSD Deputies Rip Gilmore and Mitchell Castaneda arrived to Seabreeze Trail at 9:12 a.m. and found Mr. Hood. Deps. Gilmore and Castaneda saw the decedent lying in the poison oak off the trail, not breathing with no apparent injuries. Dep. Gilmore radioed, "Male down."

Case Status: Further Investigation by MCSD

What now?

I'd met Lori Monroe and her husband in their Honda parked yards away from Poole Investigations. I knew nothing of their life or their son's and yet, I'd promised to—

My phone vibrated—Lori Monroe again.

What do you think?

"Extra crispy with seasoned salt." Ivan dropped the bag of french fries on my desk beside the bud vase of Barbra Streisand roses on my desk. "Pretty. Audrey's?"

I dug into the bag. "Yep, and thanks for the fries. I tried eating Keely Butler's vegan chili and my taste buds . . . The scream they scrumpt after that first bite."

"Her folks used to cook good food," he said. "After Gordon and Beck died a few years ago, Keely threw out anything that tasted good and started cooking leaves and acorns." Ivan's face contorted. "As long as you work for me, and as your godfather, I'm telling you—don't ever eat that crap again. I can speak for Val, Belle, and Al when I say that we believe in salt, pepper, and onion powder in this family. You could pay me a million dollars to find flavor in that food shack of Keely's, and I'd find fuckin' Jimmy Hoffa first."

My phone vibrated and I grabbed it, frowned, and sighed. "The security stuff for the cottage just got delivered. I thought it was Lori Monroe—"

Shit.

"What did I tell you?" he said, pointing at me.

"You're not my dad!" I shouted, smiling.

He scowled.

"I'm not a child," I said, mouth filled with fries, "and I'm not some teenager who took your car without permission. You and your tone really got me—"

"I'm not paying you to investigate a case already being investigated—"

"The Monroes don't want me to investigate—"

"Bullshit."

I bristled. "They want me to make sure they're being listened to and respected."

Ivan rolled his eyes and stormed out of my office.

I grabbed my fries before following him next door. A bigger, greasier bag of food and a sweating cup of iced sweet tea sat on the credenza.

"Even in perfect Haven—" I said, plopping into his guest chair.

Ivan held up a finger, his face stern. "I'm not saying Haven is perfect and that there isn't racism here. And I'm saying this is as a guy with an invitation to the picnic—"

"You of all people should know then," I said, pointing two fries at my boss, "don't eat everybody's potato salad, don't eat pumpkin pie when there's a perfectly delicious sweet potato pie right over there, don't ever underbid while playing spades, and always remember that Negroes hook each other up, especially when there are only six of us in a town of a thousand—and one of us is dead."

"Six?" Ivan started counting on his fingers.

"One drop rule."

"Oh. Him." Ivan's face reddened as he rubbed his crooked nose and the half-moon circles under his eyes. Haven hadn't given him that nose or those bags. Both came courtesy of the drunks, thugs, and monsters he'd chased for over thirty years all around South Los Angeles—and from eating supreme burritos at Pepe's Tacos every afternoon and drinking vodka tonics at Loosey's every Friday night.

"I'm not sayin' fuck them, all right?" he said, his hands up, his tone clipped like a perturbed vice principal talking to a teacher about reading *Beloved* to her class. "I'm sayin' . . . Don't go out of your way to be Superdick, especially for free. Your focus—"

"Is on finding the lost dog you said wasn't lost because her owner wants attention."

"But said attention-seeker is the one paying you, not the Monroes. As lovely as they are, as tragic as Xander's suicide—"

"Suicide?" My eyebrows crumpled. "You still believe that?"

The phone on his desk rang. "The kid was troubled. Preachers' kids always are. And preachers and their wives never want to see the trouble even when it's too late."

Because suicide was impossible if a person was full of the Holy Ghost and righteous in His blood. Because if a preacher couldn't save their own kid, how the hell were they gonna save someone else's?

My phone vibrated again—Lori Monroe had tired of waiting for a response.

Thank you for your help

We slept better knowing that we have you on our side

We're praying for you

The Monroes weren't blessing me with money. No, they were blessing me with blessings.

Ivan was holding the receiver between his ear and shoulder, taking notes on a battered legal pad.

My fingernails dug into my wrist, restraining me from swiping the sweet tea off the credenza. Instead, I jammed more fries into my mouth.

The medical examiner working Xander's case was my best friend. I could persuade India to talk to me off the record. If I continued on this path, I'd be doing what Ivan wanted me to do—getting to know the people of Haven. Could I help that the medical examiner was another Black woman twenty-five miles away but still committed to bringing the families of Haven a sense of closure through her discoveries?

My body knew the truth, and I pulled it along, kicking and screaming toward duplicity. *I'm a superdick again, gallbladder. Better get used to it.*

My vibrating phone sounded like a growling tiger.

Another text from Lori:

This came in the mail 10 minutes ago

A picture of a typewritten note:

Lori

This note is for YOUR benefit. You need to know that Xander did not commit suicide. They may tell you that he did but we know that this isn't true. We can't tell you who is responsible but it was NOT Xander. We think you should not take the word of the officers if they tell you that Xander took his own life. We knew your son and HE WOULDN'T DO THAT. Beware of who you talk to about this case. QUESTION EVERYTHING.

Anonymous notes were never good. Messages of *don't believe*, *do not trust*, and *question everything* have always led to another path of discovery. My gut told me so, and right now, that feeling was nestled around my belly button, ready to squeeze me until I sagged, breathless.

This case was now officially dirty.

En route to the bathroom, I spotted the new stack of mail left on the reception desk. Among the catalog of meats and cheeses, sale circulars, and bills: today's edition of *Haven Voice*.

I dumped my near-empty bag of fries into the waste can and grabbed the newspaper.

"Good idea," Ivan said, strolling into the waiting room with his briefcase. "The *Voice* ain't the *LA Times*, but they got a good editor. I'm headed to take pictures of an adulterer."

"Personal trainer or real estate agent?" I asked, heading back to my office.

"Personal trainer. You good?"

"Always," I said, then tossed him a wave as the bell above the door sounded.

Haven Voice covered news here in town as well as some news in surrounding communities, including Sableport.

Back behind my desk, I skipped past the front page: "The State of Homelessness" above the fold. "National Lighthouse Day—Upcoming Events" and "Haven Launches Beautiful HeAVEN Initiative" below the fold.

On the next sheet:

"Deputies Respond to a Loud Music Call at High School."

"Golf Cart Stolen from Couple's Driveway."

Did the boys at practice this afternoon trespass on school grounds after hours and throw a raucous party ending in deputies shutting everything down? Did one of them snitch about stealing the golf cart?

The next stories:

"Hundreds of Plants Destroyed in Water Main Break."

"Drunk Couple Jailed for Skinny-Dipping."

Hmm.

One of the best football players Haven High would've ever had—who was also the only son of a prominent community member—was found dead in the redwood forest a stone's throw from the Pacific Ocean, and there was no mention of his death on the front page of *Haven Voice* or even in the section that included "Man Throws Fries at Wife in Drunken Tirade." Couldn't be because of timing—that skinny-dipping couple happened at nearly midnight last night and *still* made this edition.

The doorbell tinkled again. "Forgot my phone," Ivan shouted, then trudged down the hall to his office.

"Uncle Ivan," I shouted.

A moment later, he stood in my doorway.

"May I ask what may possibly be my last Xander Monroe–related question of the day?" I lifted the newspaper. "It's not in here."

"What's not?" he asked.

"Xander's death."

Ivan scrunched his eyebrows.

I waggled the paper. "See for yourself."

"Not every crime gets covered," he said.

"Skinny-dipping and loud music calls make it in but a dead Black kid found on a trail—"

"Sonny—"

"Fine—a *dead* kid. Black, white, or what's the other color? Purple? The purple kid doesn't get 120 words in the town's only newspaper?"

Ivan's eyes narrowed as he backed into the hallway. "Okay. You're right. It's odd. But—"

"I know." I tossed the paper on my desk. "Figgy."

"Figgy."

The shadows in his eyes and the tightness of his lips told me that he didn't like the way this case was starting to smell. He said nothing else, though. Just tossed me a wave and plodded to the waiting room.

The doorbell sounded again.

I found a tub of lip balm in my bag, and the burn of the camphor added to my discomfort. I crossed my arms over my chest and studied *Haven Voice*'s crime blotter—and its conspicuous lack of a dead teenager. This gap twinkled like fireflies in the dark—or as I imagined fireflies to twinkle since I'd never seen one firefly in real life. If I had, though, a bunch of them would gather in a blank space that should've been filled with Xander Monroe updates.

Why wasn't he in the paper today? Was it because Pastor Monroe was ashamed his son may have taken his own life? Was it because readers didn't think Xander's death mattered? Was it because the sheriff of Mendocino Country had forbidden the editor from mentioning it?

Or all the above?

Finding Figgy the lost / unlost goldendoodle was my priority, my bread and butter, my way into meeting the people of Haven. If I was lucky, Figgy would also lead me to the bullshit I sensed piling up around Xander Monroe's ending.

"Beware of who you talk to about this case."

That's what the note to Lori Monroe advised.

"QUESTION EVERYTHING."

No need to tell me twice.

PART II

The Jackal of Seaview Way

My Origin Story Idea

Title: The Birth of PhizX

—

Page 1:

Panel 1: A bright sunny day. Xander is on the football field surrounded by his teammates. He's wearing his football uniform, #5.

Caption: That's me, Xander Carpenter, star running back of Saint A. High School and physics prodigy.

Panel 2: Xander, in the classroom, at the whiteboard, solving a complex physics equation. His classmates watch in awe.

Caption: Balancing sports and academics, my life was a perfect blend of brains and brawn.

—

Page 2:

Panel 1: Xander, in his room at night, studying quantum mechanics. His desk is cluttered with textbooks and papers.

Caption: Always pushing the boundaries of my knowledge, I dreamed of unlocking the secrets of the universe.

Panel 2: A shadowy figure peeks through Xander's window, watching him.

Caption: But someone else noticed my extraordinary mind . . .

Panel 3: The shadowy figure steps back, revealing a sinister grin.

Caption: And they had plans of their own.

—

Page 3:

Panel 1: On a hot summer day, Xander is training with his football team. Sweat pours down his face as he pushes through intense drills.

Caption: During an intense summer training session, disaster struck.

Panel 2: Xander collapses on the field, clutching his chest. His teammates panic and rush to his side.

Caption: My heart stopped.

Panel 3: Xander's vision fades as he sees paramedics rushing toward him.

Caption: And that's when I died.

—

Page 4:

Panel 1: Darkness. Xander's lifeless body is seen on a hospital bed, surrounded by powered-down machines.

Caption: But death was only the beginning.

Panel 2: Xander's body is surrounded by a bright, electric blue light. The machines around him go haywire.

Caption: A mysterious energy filled the room, infusing my body with unimaginable power.

Panel 3: Xander's eyes snap open, now glowing with a brilliant blue hue.

Caption: I was reborn, not as a mere mortal but as something more.

—

Page 5:

Panel 1: Xander stands, his body now crackling with blue energy. His hospital gown is torn, revealing a new sleek suit beneath.

Caption: I was no longer just a football star or a physics genius.

Panel 2: Xander raises his hand, and a bolt of energy shoots from his fingertips, lighting up the room.

Caption: I was PhizX, who now had the power to manipulate physics itself.

Panel 3: PhizX stands tall, the Oakland skyline visible through the hospital window behind him.

Caption: With the power to bend the laws of the universe, I, PhizX, am ready to protect the world from those who would seek to exploit it.

—

Page 6:

Panel 1: PhizX flies over the city, leaving a trail of blue energy.

Caption: From the ashes of tragedy, a new hero arose.

Panel 2: He swoops down to stop a robbery in progress, his energy blasts disarming the criminals.

Caption: A hero who uses his knowledge and power to fight for justice.

Panel 3: PhizX stands victorious, the criminals at his feet. In the distance, the shadowy figure watches from a rooftop.

Caption: But as I start my journey, shadows from my past lurk in the corners, waiting for their moment.

Panel 4: A close-up of PhizX's determined face.

Caption: I'm ready.

12.

Why wasn't Xander Monroe's death mentioned in the print edition of *Haven Voice*?

I clicked on the website and scrolled . . .

"City Council OKs New Lease on . . ."

"Haven's Boys' Volleyball Team Captures Tourney . . ."

I typed "Xander Monroe" into the search bar.

Nothing about the star high school running back from Oakland moving to Haven and playing on the Haven Bobcats. Nothing about the pastor, his geochemist wife, and his JPL-intern son becoming new residents of this town or about Devon Monroe, former pastor of one of Oakland's historic Black churches, serving as the new pastor of Haven Methodist Church. Okay, so the Monroes weren't the Kennedys, but how much more excellent did they need to be for a mention alongside this year's winner of the cherry-pit-spitting champion? Xander's presence on the Bobcats would've brought scouts to a place that wasn't on the radar of high school football recruiters. Remarkably, in less than four months, Black excellence had found its way into Haven on the backs of five people—including Mom and me, of course.

My hands trembled—I was already nervous about what I wasn't seeing. The print blurred as I scanned pages for a story that wasn't there. Frustrated, I whipped through the newspaper a fourth time. Obituaries, classifieds, local events, letters to the editor, ocean activities, public notices—each section in neat columns, each column important to at least one of the thousand people living in Haven. But wasn't Xander Monroe more important than "*Our Town* Production Returns to Stage After COVID-19 Cancellations"? Just like they know the hours of the upcoming flea market, shouldn't people know that a kid was found yesterday on a trail that many of them have probably walked? Shouldn't those who didn't know about Xander's death learn that he'd died?

The football star and his death had been swallowed by silence.

The omission gnawed at me and itched at the back of my mind, and I didn't want to scratch it. No, I wanted it to make me so miserable that I had to learn at least that answer—*why*—in order to be sated. This made no sense, especially in a town like Haven where even the smallest disturbance—"Haven Eatery Under New Ownership"—rippled across the town's consciousness.

Unless I was wrong. And I'd been wrong before, which was why I was here in Haven.

I pushed out a breath and shoved my chair away from my desk. Out on the other side of the window, the village bopped along as though nothing horrible had happened just a day ago. Not every person walking and chatting and licking ice-cream cones was a tourist who didn't have the privilege of living the Haven dream. Some of these folks paid taxes here, prayed here—preyed here—cheered on Bobcats Volleyball here.

With clammy hands, I tapped the space bar to wake up my laptop.

Haven Voice's internet home page was as cluttered as a junk drawer. Instead of old batteries, old keys, and expired health insurance cards, the web page held a jumble of mismatched fonts and spacing, chaotic color schemes, and a barrage of pop-up ads that I manically clicked like I was playing Whac-A-Mole. Each click led to more hyperlinks, each more confounding than the last. This was a maze with no exit, and I shouted, "Okay, guys. Stop playing."

I found more news articles that mirrored the stories in the print edition.

Community bake sale. High school chess tournament victory. Dead florist. New florist. The mundane was a security blanket here, a reassurance that Haven was Heaven.

A paywall. Fine. After purchasing a $200 yearly subscription, I searched Xander's name again.

No search results.

Haven may have been fooling these people, but it wasn't fooling me. I knew there was bullshit hiding in the back of this town's closet. Ivan made a living here, and those secrets lived inside his locked file room—and Cooper more than hinted at it.

"Haven ain't what it seems. People do bad shit up here."

I knew there was one unreported death. How many unreported deaths were there—deaths that weren't "Former School Principal Paula Moore Passes After Long Sickness"? And who made the call to keep Haven in the dark?

"Who runs this freaking . . . ?" I found the masthead and saw Tanner Orr's name beneath *Editor-in-Chief.* I pushed my hands through my hair, my gut churning with suspicion of Tanner Orr and unease with his disastrous editorial direction. I scrolled more, clicking, scrutinizing, hoping that I was wrong—that I'd missed a mere mention of the kid from Oakland, maybe lost beneath an ad for Haven Vacation Rentals. But hope waned with each click.

Out there, on the other side of the glass, Haven's spiders were spinning more secrets, sticky and obstructive, doing everything to hide the fly.

There was something there, and I'd have to pull its cold hand from the swamp and push it into the town square.

Ivan wouldn't be happy. That meant before I pissed him off, *I needed to be sure.*

A recycling bin filled with old newspapers, crumpled soda cans, and empty water bottles sat near Ivan's desk. I grabbed the old newspapers, wincing as flat Coke dribbled from a can onto my hand. I sat on the carpet and scanned past chronicles of life in Mayberry by the Sea.

"Local Scout Troop Holds Successful Bake Sale for First Responders"

"Celebrating International Day of Happiness, Haven-Style"

"Annual Surf Contest Rescheduled"

Newsprint dirtied my fingers, but I didn't stop searching for anything with teeth and bite—but I only found sweet tales of charity raffles, the birth of the kindergarten teacher's triplets, and tomatoes falling off a truck on Highway 128. No scabby knees or elbows in this town.

Back in Los Angeles, I'd visited the downtown and El Segundo newsrooms of the *Los Angeles Times* often over my ten-year career as a cop. There had been reporters typing frantically on computers seated beneath the harsh glares of fluorescent lights, reporters hidden behind stacks of newsprint and surrounded by chaos that infiltrated break rooms and elevators. Awards, certificates, and commendations everywhere, lauding the best and brightest journalists who questioned everything, including crime, cops, and my homeboys fucking me over.

The newsroom of *Haven Voice* was located in a slate-blue and white building at the end of Sea Star Street, closest to Highway 1. Desks were cluttered with circulars, pens and pencils, and coffee mugs. A MISSING DOG flyer of Figgy had been tacked to a corkboard with other announcements about music festivals and carpet cleaners. Cell phones chirped, and the copier and desktop printers droned and whined. I counted five people—four more than I'd expected—and headed to the gray-haired woman seated at the desk closest to the front door.

I introduced myself.

Her penciled-in eyebrows lifted, and her scallop-colored lips made the O of surprise. "And how may I help you?"

"I'd like to talk to Tanner Orr." My eyes skipped around the room.

The green pair of eyes behind the designer eyeglass frames widened, and their owner, a thin man with thinning brown hair, said, "I'm Tanner."

I headed toward the editor in chief of the *Haven Voice* and introduced myself again.

Tanner led me into an office stuffed with fat cabinets and fatter binders. He sat in his squeaky desk chair, his nervous hand wiping his mouth. "How may I help you, Miss Rush?"

"Sonny, please." Adrenaline pushed through my fingers and made me sweat, and I took a deep breath to take my time. "I'm here about Xander Monroe."

His eyes guarded, Orr said, "Okay."

"Do you know who I'm talking about?"

He nodded. "What do you want to know?"

Irritation pushed away adrenaline, and I hoped that he sensed that my deliberate pause was a warning to not fuck with me. "He was found dead yesterday," I said, "so why wasn't his death reported in either the print or digital edition?"

Tanner Orr's chair squeaked as he leaned forward with his hands steepled beneath his chin. "We report on what matters to our readers, Miss Rush."

My nostrils flared. "And it doesn't matter that a seventeen-year-old boy who'd just moved here from Oakland was found dead on Seabreeze Trail yesterday?"

Tanner Orr held his poker face . . . until something almost imperceptible flickered in those eyes. He knew what I meant. "Miss Rush, sometimes stories are more complex than they appear, and sometimes, there are stories that aren't ours to tell—"

"Stop," I said, holding up my hand. "You're about to try and bullshit a former LAPD homicide detective. You're also about to piss off a woman who's already pissed off that she's sitting here, asking this question. Do you really want to go there with me? Do you wanna play

today, Mr. Orr? Cuz I got time." I knew how hard my face had become, how tight my lips looked, how flared my nose was.

The bone in Tanner Orr's throat bobbed and his skin flushed. He sank in his chair but not a lot. Enough, though, that he dropped his gaze.

"Let's start again," I said, "because I've obviously mistaken your intent when you said that the death of a child wouldn't matter to this town. I *know* you didn't say that." I stared at him, waiting, my silence a challenge and a threat. "Yes?"

"Are we off the record?" he whispered.

"If we need to be, then yes." I crossed my legs and offered him an unperturbed smile.

He cleared his throat and then exhaled. "We don't do violent crime in Haven."

"Meaning?"

"There are no robberies in Haven. No sexual assaults. No domestic abuse. Definitely no homicides. Haven is Heaven."

"Says . . ."

"Says the mayor. Says the Chamber of Commerce. Says anybody who hopes to turn this village into a destination." Tanner Orr faded into his skin's real color of pink ice. His face relaxed as though he was finally talking to someone who understood.

"Before coming here," he said, "I was a newsman in San Jose. The *Mercury News* with a readership of nearly four hundred thousand in a city with more than five thousand violent crimes annually and an almost thirteen percent increase in homicides. I covered the crime and public safety beat for thirty years. Shoot-outs and gangs and drugs, and I loved it for those first ten years. The last twenty? Three ulcers. A friend of a friend was the editor of *Haven Voice*, ready to retire and drive across the country with his wife, and he didn't want to hand the keys to just anyone. So, he asked me to do it. And after talking with my wife about it, I said, 'Yes.'"

He twisted in his chair and shook his head. "The first weekend I'm here, I covered two drunk driving arrests that turned violent, a Pride flag being burned, and a swimmer drowned after getting caught in a riptide. And I wrote about it, ready to pull the string on the flag burning in particular. That is, until Boomer Levy—"

"Who's Boomer Levy?" I interrupted.

"The owner of the paper. He paid me a visit. He was so pissed his face turned purple, and he stood over me, foaming at the mouth, cursing at me like I'd killed his dog.

"'We don't do violent crime in Haven.' That's what they told me." Tanner Orr considered the piles of paper on his desk. "And then Boomer said if I didn't like that, then I could take my sorry ass back to San Jose. That was three years ago, and Haven is Heaven; we're so blessed; we're protected by good people and good air; there's no place like Haven, blah blah blah . . ." He rubbed his eyes beneath his glasses and looked at me, weary. "I'm sure someone out there is telling Boomer right now that I'm talking to the new PI in town."

I grunted again and nodded. "Probably." I leaned forward. "Who is 'they'? The ones who told you that there's no violent crime in Haven?"

He didn't speak.

I grinned. "Barrel maker?"

He thought about it and coughed.

Money—and the promise of more of it if Haven remained unblemished. Which meant that no matter how I felt about him and his lies, I couldn't avoid talking to Cooper. Not if I was pulling the truth from the back of Haven's closet. If I wanted to know how Xander got dead, then I needed to pull out that truth.

I said, "Xander's autopsy is being performed tomorrow morning."

Tanner Orr waited for me to say more.

I wouldn't. That was fine—I was driving up there anyway.

"My heart broke hearing about Xander," he said. "He was a good kid, and I was looking forward to building up our sports section with all the excitement he would've brought to the game here, in both football and cross-country. If I was still a newsman in San Jose, there would've been six articles written already about his death, from the first story of him being found to the last when they sentenced whoever the fuck did it to life in prison. But . . ."

"You can't," I said, nodding.

His eyes gleamed with tears. "No."

"So, you believe he was murdered," I said. "You just said 'whoever the fuck did it.'"

Tanner swallowed again and didn't speak.

I placed my chin in my hand. "Do you get weekly stats from the sheriff's office?"

He nodded.

"Do those stats include every call, including crime? Not just Gary Failed to Register for Upcoming Haven Car Show but also fentanyl and rape and stabbings and all that? Could you get documents like warrant requests, incident reports?"

He paused before nodding again.

"Could you send me those reports? Doesn't matter if they're relevant or not. I don't need you to curate—just forward. I'm asking you to be my CI, Tanner." I grinned as though I'd asked him to the prom.

He rubbed his lips. "And if I decline?"

I wagged my finger at him. "You wouldn't. You miss this shit. I see it in your eyes." I leaned forward and squinted at him. "Yep, there it is. The guy who likes the real shit."

Another flicker. "I don't want to cause trouble."

I sat back. "Of course not. That's my job."

"Are you investigating Xander's death?"

"Officially? No. Officially, I'm investigating the disappearance of Figgy Sutton the goldendoodle." I tossed him a smile. "I'm in the information-gathering stage since I hear one of Figgy's favorite places was Seabreeze Trail, the same trail where Xander Monroe was found." I paused, then added, "Isn't that a coincidence?" And a lie. "I know that in real places, I'd be *your* CI. But Haven is not a real place, and so, our roles are reversed. You're gonna be my guide through each level of hell here, and I'm really looking forward to being your secret friend."

I stood from the chair. "The people of this town need to know what the fuck's going on outside their doors, even if they don't want to. If that means one family deciding not to move down here because their kid might get dead, then that's enough for me. Are we clear?"

Tanner stood, too, his face pulling on the mask of irritation again. "Yes." Louder, he said, "I can't help you, Miss Rush."

Behind me, the door opened, and a young woman with a fiery-red ponytail poked her head in. "Cooper Sutton's on line one." Her eyes lingered on mine before darting back to Tanner's.

Did someone tell Cooper that I was there, asking questions?

"Thanks, Faith." To me, he said, "I wish I would've been able to help you, Miss Rush."

Faith looked like the type of woman who'd vote against her own best interests for validation and acceptance, the pick-me bitch who ran to powerful men anxious to hobble powerful women. She'd be dismayed to learn I had legs that she couldn't even see.

"If you change your mind," I said, looking back at Tanner Orr, "I'm over on Seaview."

The newsman said nothing before picking up the receiver. "Cooper, hey!"

Faith walked me to the front door. Neither of us had anything to say. Not even goodbye. Her eyes burned the back of my neck and shoulder blades. Good.

That burn meant that I was alive.

And that was the worst possible news for Haven.

13.

I tore open the boxes of the security system bundle I'd ordered before leaving Los Angeles. With three sensors—front door, kitchen door, and Mom's bedroom window—and two doorbell cameras, it didn't take long for me to install the system. We'd use the same passcode as the house back in Ladera Heights, and I'd download the app onto Mom's phone tonight. Using a dining room chair as a ladder, I screwed in one of the swing-bar door guards on the front door—just out of Mom's reach—and did the same with a second latch on the kitchen door. If she wanted to get out, she'd need a chair and gumption.

The scent of fresh-baked bread wafting throughout Sweetlife made me think of childhood: The Isley Brothers singing "Footsteps in the Dark" from the kitchen radio; me watching my videotape of *The Lion King* on our den's big-screen TV; Mom in her Tommy Hilfiger sweatshirt and biker shorts, phone receiver caught between her ear and shoulder; Dad snoring from the bedroom, exhausted from his late-night shift. We were happy then.

We couldn't be the same kind of happy, not with Dad gone, but Mom could enjoy something close. That scent of fresh-baked bread may not have come from her kitchen, but she still smiled as we entered Sweetlife, the bakery run by Elliott and Giovanni. The cashmere-soft lighting, the easy-on-the-eyes dirty-blond hardwood floors, and banquettes instead of tiny tables and chairs made this space more comfortable than Keely's Rise & Grind.

"You're here!" Elliott shouted, dusting off his flour-covered hands on his apron.

Mom's eyes drifted from the seafoam-and-sea-blue floral walls to the light-blue menu boards, the empty display cases, and empty cushioned chairs. "No customers?" she asked.

Giovanni's thick black eyebrows lifted in surprise. "We have customers—it's just that we close at six to get ready for the next day." He grinned, his white teeth bright against his Mayan copper skin. He was the kind of handsome that made every sex turn their heads. Thick black eyelashes. Thicker black hair kept in a wavy fade. Short but with a *body-ody-ody* from all the kneading and pushing dough. "We're so happy you're gonna help us out, Miss Valerie. I know El has told you many times, but we're fans."

Mom blushed and said, "I'm ready to get my hands dusty."

Elliott tossed me a spotless red apron to protect my gray sweatshirt and black leggings. Giovanni helped Mom into a white one with red embroidered letters, Head Baker. Not that she cared about mucking up her pink Val's branded T-shirt. Mom scanned the organized chaos of the bakery, her eyes gleaming with nostalgia. Powerful stand mixers and stainless steel worktables, short towers of mixing bowls, cooling racks holding sheets of raspberry-colored macarons. A moment later, she was kneading dough.

Staying out of the way, I greased sheets and pans as my mind wandered back to my visit with Tanner Orr over at the *Haven Voice*.

Mom grinned as Tina Turner sang about private dancers from the bakery's stereo system. "Brings back memories. She was a badass on stage; I was a badass in a kitchen. A mic for her, a whisk for me. Don't fuck with neither of us. Move, bitch, or get out the way."

"That's the one hip-hop song she likes," I added.

The boys said, "Ooh, Miss Val," and "I heard that."

Mom cocked her chin. "Sonny tell you that I used to bake for some important people back home? Cakes, cookies, pies . . . You name it, I baked it. One actress—who shall remain nameless—asked me to make sweet potato cupcakes but without sugar, butter, or white flour. They tasted like shit to me, but she was happy. And no matter how much she got on my nerves, there was something so satisfying about seeing her face light up when she tasted those pieces of baked—whatever that I still refuse to call cupcakes."

"C'mon, Miss Val," Giovanni said, "tell us who she was." Bright eyed, he'd stopped paring lemon peels to lean forward.

"She made me sign one of those nondisclosure agreements," Mom said.

I cackled. "Well, *I* didn't sign anything—"

"Sonny," Mom said, smiling.

I rolled my eyes. "You may know her from a show about high school kids."

Giovanni laughed. "That could be anybody."

"She sings," I added.

"That's enough." Mom chuckled and started to croon with Tina.

She was okay right now, her hands remembering to knead more for a finer crumb and knead less for a coarser crumb. Like wet dough, some things just stick with you.

As she worked, Mom shared her hacks to make baking quicker and tastier—placing a piping bag into a tall glass for easier filling, dropping a cake onto the worktable for a flatter top, ripening bananas for banana bread using an oven instead of waiting for days. "I have one for brown sugar not hardening, but if I tell you, I'll have to shove you in that ocean behind us."

The trio turned their attention to six pans of chilled yellow cake. Mom started a batch of royal icing, sifting powdered sugar into a mixing bowl first and adding egg whites. After confectioners' sugar, vanilla, and soft-blue gel food coloring, Elliott dipped a knife into the bowl and his eyes rolled to the back of his head. "Ohmigod. Gio. Taste." He dipped a clean knife into the batch, handed it to Giovanni, and puckered his lips. "How did you make it so smooth?"

"She put the same ingredients in that you do," Giovanni said, licking the knife.

Mom smirked. "Did I?"

Dad's death and his lack of preparation took the bakery from her. But Sweetlife offered Mom a fresh start, a chance to be part of a community that cared about one another. She wouldn't let her anger at my father define her any longer. For both of us, it was time to focus on the present and the future we both wanted to build here in Haven, together.

Giovanni swatted his hands against his apron and surveyed the sheet of croissants. "Let's get these in the oven. Then we'll make cookie dough for the morning and call it a day."

"But first . . ." Elliott pulled a bottle of rosé from the fridge.

"I love it here." Mom squeezed my shoulders. "It's fancier than my place back home."

"I'm glad you like it," Giovanni said. "Some people think it doesn't look like Haven."

"They wanted knotted wood and seagulls and hard-ass cupcakes," Elliott said, pouring wine into Sweetlife-branded glasses.

"Doing their absolute un-best with flour, sugar, and butter," Giovanni said. "How is that even possible? How do you fuck up butter? Rhetorical. I've tasted fucked-up butter."

"Sweetlife does not do driftwood and seashells," Elliott said. "Cry harder."

"Happy bakers make sweeter treats," Mom said, accepting a glass of rosé. Her eyes misted as she took in the tower of white coffee cups with aquamarine cup holders and their matching plates. "Thank you for inviting me to work with you two."

"We're grateful." Giovanni raised his glass. "Here's to a sweeter life for Sweetlife."

The rosé chased any lingering doubts from my mind. This woman may have struggled some with memory problems, but I blamed Los Angeles and all its noise. I blamed my small apartment with her stuff piled beside mine, not being able to move without bumping into things.

But then the door to Sweetlife swung open, and my stomach dropped, and *he* walked in with banks of fog rolling behind him. Cooper wore stonewashed jeans, a white Levi's T-shirt, a flannel shirt tied around his waist, and maroon Vans. He was wearing the ALPHA rottweiler baseball cap I'd brought him from Greece. Did those designers make a donkey cap that said ASS?

"We're closed," Elliott sang, "even for you, Coop."

Cooper didn't respond—he was now gaping at me.

Shit. Mom didn't know that Cooper and I were no more, that Cooper was still a married man with a family. She smiled at him but kept busy with icing the cake.

Hydrogen, helium, lithium, beryllium . . .

"Sonny," Giovanni said, coming over to me, "this is Cooper Sutton. Coop, this is Sonny Rush. She just moved to town—"

Cooper finally blinked. "We've met. She stands out."

"I wore a sweater today," I told Elliott and Giovanni, "and almost started a riot."

Boron, carbon, nitrogen . . .

"You met here in Haven?" Giovanni asked.

"Down in Los Angeles," Cooper said. "Someone told me about a bakery named Val's. Said she made the best lemon bars in the city, and so, I went, and Sonny was there." He'd visited Mom's three shops in the year we'd been together.

Elliott pushed his boyfriend. "I told you—she's looking for Mackie's dog."

Giovanni's eyes widened. "Oh, that's right!"

"Coop brought us here," Giovanni shared with me. "Fortunately? Unfortunately?"

"Stop," Elliott said, frowning.

"Anyway," Giovanni continued, "Cooper came into our shop three years ago."

"San Jose," Elliott said. "High rent. Completely miserable—"

"And then," Giovanni said, waving at Cooper, "he tasted our lemon bars—"

"I like lemon bars," Cooper said to me, knowing that I already knew that since Mom always made him lemon bars on each visit.

"And," Elliott said, "he saw just how miserable we were—"

"We?" Giovanni cocked an eyebrow.

Elliott flushed, and his smile faltered. "And he invited *us* to move up to Haven, saying he was building it into something bigger, something special."

Giovanni said nothing—finished now with his role—and sipped wine in steely silence.

Hmm.

"And when he flew us over and showed us the shop," Elliott said, his smile back again, "I felt so much peace. I knew we were home."

"But we're still closed," Giovanni said, forcing a smile, "angel investor or no."

Mom rolled the cart with the cake over to the counter. *"Et voilà."*

"Miss Val," Elliott said, "have you also met Cooper Sutton?"

Cooper's eyes darted to mine. *Shit.*

Mom offered Cooper her hand. "Val Rush. I'm this one's mother." She touched my back.

Was she pretending for our sake?

Cooper paused, then said, "Pleasure to meet you. Welcome to Haven." He paused again, then said to Elliott and Giovanni, "I'm actually here to give you a heads-up."

Mom tottered off to the closest banquette with her glass of wine and a vacant look in her eyes. She wasn't pretending.

Relief washed over me, thankful—this time—that she didn't remember us.

Giovanni handed him a lemon bar and a to-go cup of coffee. "What's going on?"

Cooper took a bite of pastry, his lips now dusted with powdered sugar. "I'm leading an important tour Friday. Big-time business owners interested in expanding to Haven. Bob Lee, the vintner over in the Valley. Reginald West—"

"For a gym?" Giovanni asked, gasping.

"Oh, so you're happy now?" Elliott said, eyebrows high as he sipped wine.

Cooper said, "Tracy Louise—"

"She wants a boutique *in Haven*?" Elliott asked. "Ohmigod. This is fantastic!"

Cooper smiled. "I'm working hard, guys, and this is only the beginning. I know this isn't San Jose"—he said this to Giovanni, who was focusing on the last sip of wine—"but I appreciate your patience. I'll bring the group here, of course. This bakery is probably the prettiest business in town—Tracy's seen it on Instagram."

Elliott placed his hand to his forehead, faking a swoon.

Giovanni caught my gaze and rolled his eyes.

What was going on between these two?

"If you guys could talk about how great life is for small business owners," Cooper said, "I'd appreciate it. Be prepared to offer them something delicious, which won't be hard to do—"

"Especially with Miss Val over there helping us," Elliott said, nodding to my mother.

"She is?" Cooper said, his eyes jumping over to me.

"We're Val stans," Giovanni said, "and now she's here, and she's ours, and I'm happy about *that*. She'll be helping out a few days a week. And she and Sonny are renting the cottage."

Cooper and I pretending that we didn't have a past felt like swimming against a strong current during a winter storm. I didn't have the energy to be haunted by two specters of shame—being an ex-cop and an ex-mistress was pretty jacked up. How could I attain inner peace when the shame of past mistakes kept pulling me beneath the surface?

"Awesome," Cooper said, his neck flushed. "So, Friday."

Giovanni said, "We'll make sure they leave impressed."

"Everything will be *perfect*," Elliott said, clapping his hands together. "Fingers crossed that you'll have good news."

Elliott was pro-development—eager to impress, eager to make Cooper happy. Giovanni was . . . *pissed*. At Elliott for dragging him over the hill and up the coast? Or . . . ? This was a future conversation between two brown people. Still, I understood Elliott's excitement, his loyalty, and gratitude. More business meant a chance for growth, both professionally and personally. Cooper would make that happen.

At the same time, Cooper was part of the reason the newspaper hadn't reported Xander Monroe's death. He didn't want one of these businesspeople reading about a possible homicide in Heavenly Haven.

"Thanks, guys," Cooper said now. To me, he nodded. "And nice seeing you again."

I forced myself to smile.

He waited a beat for my response. Once he figured I wasn't saying *shit*, he said, "I'll see you all Friday."

As the door closed behind Cooper, I had the strongest urge to hop in my Bronco and run over him. Then set him on fire. Then run over his ashes.

"Lord, forgive me for I have sinned," Elliott said, flapping napkins at his face.

"He's El's hall pass," Giovanni said to me, finally laughing.

"Also, he is so straight and so married," Elliott responded.

So married. *Really?*

"But by the way he looked at Miss Sonny over there . . ." Elliott smiled.

"Danger," Giovanni said, waggling his finger. "Look but don't touch, or his wife will throw you off a cliff. She is the Scooby-Doo villain of Haven."

"She is *not*," Elliott said. "That would be Joelle What's-Her-Face over at Deegan's. I hear Joelle believes hepatitis A is a government construct and that if you get sick eating her food, then you're going to hell. London is more . . . Claire from *House of Cards*—no! Brienne of Tarth or . . . or . . . Hermione—"

"Don't ever eat at Deegan's," Giovanni said, head cocked. "Not if you like both your large and small intestines."

I chuckled. "I wouldn't dare." Eat at Deegan's or cross London Claire-Brienne-Hermione Sutton. But I *was* gonna force this town to see Xander Monroe, who would be actively ignored while Tracy Whoever and Reginald Who-the-Fuck-Cares snarfed down macarons and cookies dipped in aquamarine royal icing.

What was the point of living in a small town if you were still being ignored? The *East Bay Times*, even with all the shit that was happening up there, would've dedicated *at least* two paragraphs to the Monroes and this tragedy.

The town needed justice more than it needed a gym.

14.

The outside buildings that comprised the substation housing the Coroner's Division of the Mendocino County Sheriff's Department were painted a creamy tan with brown trim. On this Thursday morning, the air smelled of ocean, wildflowers, and wood fire. Had there not been an adjoining jail, this spot could've been a tranquil, slow-paced spot to eat lunch and catch up on some Colleen Hoover shenanigans. A different vibe than the coroner's office down in Los Angeles.

But the surrounding landscape—that's where the differences ended.

Just like in LA, the dead awaited discovery in autopsy suites behind double doors that never squeaked, that boasted cold sterility and stainless steel tables. Like the inside of Las Vegas casinos, if it weren't for the clocks on the wall, no one would ever know the time of day or night in those suites. Time stopped here—but not really. Bodies held time-stamped secrets, and the quicker the revelation, the clearer their truths. Today, there were three bodies in this cold, clinical space, mysteries beneath white sheets. Housewife? Construction worker? Teacher? We all looked the same beneath plain white sheets.

Wearing borrowed scrubs, a face mask, and goggles, I stood on the other side of that stainless steel table across from my best friend, India. This was my twenty-third autopsy, not that I was counting. Since my first, modern science had moved from swipes of eucalyptus oil and Noxzema beneath the nostrils as a combatant against the smell of death to a shea butter stick invented by an emergency room nurse. I had both in FaB's glove compartment, and this time, I used the stick.

India used nothing—fighting the smell of death would be pointless, like a lifeguard using a towel to dry off.

Beside me stood Lieutenant Detective Brady Kwon, a meticulously groomed, middle-aged Black-Korean man with tired eyes and an annoying tendency to sigh. The gatekeeper of the investigation into Xander's death wore a paper gown over his blue suit that would never be the same again . . . unless this was the suit he always wore to autopsies. I knew the weight he bore in his official capacity—I was now a private investigator, and this death pressed down on me like all the planets in the galaxy. He considered me with lifted eyebrows, waiting for me to explain my presence. I would tell him but only if needed.

My gaze lingered on the sterile tiles of the autopsy room, its clinical gleam so familiar to me. Goose pimples on my arms made me shiver—not because the room was chilly but because memories were clawing up my spine. *Los Angeles.* Those sunbaked streets. Those echoes of sirens and helicopters and—sometimes—gunshots. Eyes sweeping, never stopping. Always looking for the guy I saw on a MOST WANTED flyer pinned on the break room's corkboard. Always searching for the blue-and-white Hyundai Sonata that had been stolen with a baby in the back seat. All of it gone because of a bad decision that didn't seem bad at the time. *What if—*

No. I wasn't doing that right now. I couldn't doubt myself at the moment I was representing the Monroes. But I was now addicted to guilt, a junkie for self-hate. At my sides, my hands curled into fists, and my nails dug into my palms—a self-inflicted reminder to focus on the now, to put down the pipe and pay attention. "Stay present," I whispered. But this *right now* was fucked up. The white sheet covering a dead kid on a cold steel table and the empty blue body bag tagged XANDER MONROE placed on a neighboring table by India's assistant, Troy, told me so.

"Where's Will?" India asked Kwon as she pulled on blue nitrile gloves.

"Being a baby cop," he said, his voice brooding, deep.

"What did he eat?" I asked.

"Rooty Tooty Fresh 'N Fruity," Kwon said.

"Blueberry?"

"Yep. It's always blueberry."

Tools of the trade lay on a table beside India: scoopers, cutters, pokers, and pluckers. Like speculums, primal tools, never fancy, always cold, forever obtrusive. Eternally agnostic. Scales hung from the ceiling. Tubes with different colored tops held different fluids. A dry-erase board filled with words in a sequence only known to medical examiners. DANGER FORMALDEHYDE signs taped to walls and paper towel dispensers. Orange buckets.

I spread my feet and kept my knees soft. Sure, I'd done this before, but even though I considered myself an expert in this macabre dance of determining the cause of death—keeping my stomach empty, bringing a change of clothes and dry shampoo—life came fast, and I could possibly find myself face down on the tiled floor.

India pressed the foot pedal, and a gear clicked, and she peered at the digital clock hanging behind me. "9:12 a.m. August 3, 2023. Joining me: assistant to the medical examiner, Troy Kirby, Lieutenant Detective Brady Kwon of the Mendocino County Sheriff's Investigation Services, and private investigator Alyson Rush."

Kwon's head snapped in my direction.

I wasn't required to acknowledge him, so I didn't.

Troy gently pulled away the sheet covering Xander Monroe.

The same punch to the gut. The same damp sorrow. The same, "My God."

Naked now, Xander's limbs were no longer stiff. He'd been dead for forty-nine hours, and his brown skin had turned gray, his nail beds were tinged blue, the tattoo on his right bicep—#5—had lost definition. No bullet holes. No blade marks.

India's sharp eyes were ready to trace every inch, to seek the hidden narrative. "Weather back on Tuesday?" she asked.

"Forty-nine degrees low, sixty-three degrees high," Kwon offered. "Around nine a.m., it was about fifty-five when he was found."

"And foggy." My hands had strangled the steering wheel driving that one mile to work.

Seventy-four inches tall, 190 pounds, black hair braided into cornrows, brown eyes. With a penlight, she peered into Xander's left eye and then his right. Both dilated. His lips—also tinged blue—crusted with dried froth. No puncture wounds or track marks on his arms, legs, or feet. Pulmonary edema: fluid in his lungs. He couldn't breathe. Distended bladder: abnormally enlarged and filled with urine. Possibly conscious before he died. Cerebral edema: fluid in the brain, swollen and heavier than normal. Could mean anything—from stroke to head injury, meningitis, or medication. A healthy liver looked reddish brown, but Xander's looked a bit paler. Could mean something; could mean nothing at all.

India collected blood in the gray stoppered tubes and gently turned them upside down, mixing the anticoagulant and blood preservative. No clots. No degradation. Then she captured urine in a collection cup.

Scars: everywhere.

"He played football and ran cross-country," Kwon said.

Broken bones: possibly.

"Again," Kwon offered. "He was a running back."

"X-ray required." India glimpsed Xander's left ankle and then, his right. "Swollen right ankle." She pressed the skin there.

"Pretty early for bloating?" Kwon asked, the puffiness unmistakable to trained eyes.

"Possible fracture," India said.

Did this injury come before the last breath or after?

I focused on that ankle, storing the detail away for later thought.

India said nothing for several more moments. Neither Brady Kwon nor I spoke or moved. We stood still as though India had become an easily spooked cat.

"You said he was found in poison oak?" she finally asked.

Kwon nodded. "We took clippings of the plants."

I peered closely at Xander's arms. "What was he wearing when he was found?"

Kwon showed me a picture of Xander, face down in the poison oak. He wore a black short-sleeved T-shirt, gold gym shorts, and black Nike running shoes. His hands were now protected in brown paper bags.

I looked back at the part of Xander's arms beneath his elbow. "Dead skin can't react to poison oak. You need an immune system, right? If you aren't alive, your immune system isn't alive, which means it can't respond."

India said, "Correct."

"Did he die before he landed in the poison oak?" Kwon asked.

Or was he dropped there after he died?

As I cleaned up in India's personal bathroom with its yellow duck shower curtain and cakes of French-milled lavender soap, I thought about Xander Monroe's final moments alive. If he had died before dropping into the underbrush, that may have meant a quick death. Did he stagger over to the side of the trail? Did he brush his hand against the log to steady himself? Maybe the skin on his hands was riddled with shards of wood.

Before returning to the chaos on the other side of India's office, I grabbed my phone and texted the editor of *Haven Voice*.

Tanner!

Just checking in

May swing by later with a few questions

No ellipses to show he was responding.

"Don't make me be a bitch, Tanner," I said, typing those words.

I enjoy it too much which means I'll never stop

India was waiting for me in her office, and her eyes pecked at me—from my dry-shampooed hair now swept over one shoulder to my antelope-colored chinos and brown cuffed T-shirt. "All you're missing is a gold badge," she said.

My detective shield sat in the drawer of some administrative clerk, the keeper of busted careers and shattered dreams. My gaze had lingered on Kwon's star on his lapel. Badge envy.

"So, are you officially working with Ivan on this?" India asked.

"I'm more of a comforter to the Monroes. Keeping them updated on Xander's case."

"I don't need you telling everybody about what's been found—" India said.

My head swiveled. "I'm not an idiot, Dr. Laster. My clearance rate was eighty-five percent with four cases a month back in LA. That's forty-eight cases a year for me to solve alone, not me and another detective. That happened because I was smart, and I knew when to keep my mouth shut." I blinked at India, then said, "Lori told me there was a note found in Xander's pocket."

India nodded. "Any thoughts on that?" She peered at my phone screen and the photo of the note found in his pocket.

A beautiful place to die.

"Could mean anything," I said. "Pretty poetic."

India's office door opened, and her assistant said, "Okay. Ready."

India sighed, then said to me, "I'll call you later. Gotta hop on this call before finishing up." One last wave and she was gone.

15.

The *rup-rup-rup* of the Bronco's tires against the blacktop had always comforted me as a child. My parents would drive me around Los Angeles to calm me down—as a newborn with breaking, irritated gums; as an angry teenager after "the phone call" breakup with either a boyfriend or a best friend; from the disappointment of placing third in debate; to not getting into Berkeley, even though two of my dearest—and dumbest—friends had.

Even after I'd stopped relying on the Bronco's tires or the sticky tire *cluck-cluck-click* of Mom's minivan, driving allowed me the space I needed to restart.

Easier to do in Los Angeles with miles of wide streets and freeways—the comfort of sitting in traffic staring at the Goodyear Blimp floating over me or a car accident happening before my very eyes. Here in Haven, I'd never lose myself because of all the freakin' trees on both sides of twisty-ass Highway 1, which either sent you off the cliff and into the Pacific, careening into a logging truck in the opposing lane of traffic, or racing into a cliff wall or gorge or ancient redwood and killing yourself.

But this twisty-ass freeway was my only choice. And it was okay that I'd blatantly disregarded Ivan's directive about investigating the Monroe case. Attending Xander Monroe's autopsy benefited Poole Investigations.

Ivan had not seen the benefit of my involvement or friendship with India. In fact, his knuckles were bright white as they clenched the steering wheel of his black Toyota Tundra.

Because, after surviving my drive from Sableport and parking the Bronco in front of Poole Investigations, Ivan grabbed his keys and told me to get in the front passenger seat of his truck.

"Where are we going?" I asked.

"To Moonview Bluffs," he said, "where that picture of Figgy was taken."

We listened to the Eagles on the truck's stereo, and for a few bars, we sang harmony on "Hotel California" as my hand hung out the open window to catch the wind.

Just like he did every time it played, Ivan hit "Off" at "Best of My Love." Grumbling, he made a right into a parking lot of a beachy vantage point. "We can't work like this if you won't listen to me," he said, staring ahead. "I texted you a bunch of times, and you ignored me—"

"I was driving a highway that scares the shit out of me," I said. "And right now, you sound like a jealous boyfriend instead of my godfather."

"What if something had happened to Val? What if something broke in the Sutton case?"

"Then," I said, "I would've responded right after prying my hands from around the steering wheel. Look." I shifted in my seat to face him. "I've talked to two of the three suspects in the dog case—and that doesn't even include Cooper Sutton. And I also told you that the Monroes needed an advocate who also spoke their language."

"Brady Kwon is a good cop," he said.

"He probably is," I said, nodding, "but he's also babysitting some kid who ate IHOP before an autopsy. And secretly? I think Kwon's happy that I'm on this too. I made some very important observations." I told him about the poison oak.

Ivan grumbled some more, then left the car.

I pushed open the truck's door and ocean mist immediately slicked my face. "You don't want Kwon mad at you," I said. "You've built this relationship with him and the other investigators up there, and I'm fucking it up. Am I right?"

Ivan scratched the bearded man tattoo on his left forearm. The outline of the god's profile was made up of letters. Ivan had sworn he wasn't associated with any police gang, and with my father having the same tattoo, I chose to believe them, although I knew it was bullshit. Those letters spelling SUTULP did not stand for Sanctified Unique Talent Unity Leadership Principles. What they meant—I wasn't ready to drill further, not with the sting of my father's death still tender.

Mist pebbled in Ivan's gray hair, and he ran his hand over his head. "Haven's not Los Angeles, Sonny—"

"I know—"

"You *don't* know, sweetie," he interrupted. "You gotta blend in here—"

"Hard to do for me, easy for you to say," I spat. "In five years from now, my house in Haven could be part of the garden tour, with me as chief float maker for the annual Founders' Day parade, but I will always stand apart, even if it's just my physical appearance."

I paused, then added, "And don't give me that 'I don't see color' bullshit. There's nothing wrong with my color. I just need you to acknowledge that this place is ninety percent white and that I'll never blend in. And since I can't—and frankly, *won't*—I can do the shit that *you* can't because you're too busy blending in. Let them shoot their arrows at me while you do the thing you do."

He spun away from me and stomped toward the cliffs.

I followed him to the sand and rocks.

"Wanna be a lightning rod?" he asked, his chin to his chest. "You want that in your life?"

"I've *been* that in my life."

"Well, I didn't bring you up here to be a fucking lightning rod, Alyson."

I swiped my damp cheek, my blush smearing on my damp hand. "If I have to be a distraction here in Haven, so be it. Just as long as—"

"Justice is served," Ivan said, rubbing his eyes. "Yeah, yeah."

"I was gonna say, 'as long as I get paid,'" I said, eyebrow high. "Justice is a given."

He climbed one in a series of sandstone boulders that were wider than they looked. "The bastard stood here."

I hopped up to join him. My gaze trailed over to the dark rocks being eaten away by the pounding waves and over to driftwood that used to be trees.

Who'd stood here—dog in one hand, phone in the other—to take that picture? Visitors were pulling in and out of the parking lot—someone had to see Figgy and the stranger. Someone's heart had to race when they saw the stranger holding a dog over the rocks . . . *Right?*

Ivan was telling me about his start here, how Haven had saved him, how congestive heart failure *something, something*—shit I already knew because I'd visited him in the hospital and had walked the trails at Kenneth Hahn Park afterward with him and Dad. Then he told me about Haven's charm and its growth and that once more people moved here, I'd have the opportunity to work a variety of cases. "Right now," he said, "I need you to relax, Sonny, and I need you to listen to me. Trust me—I know what I'm talking about, okay? I've been doing this for as long as you've been alive."

Ivan had experience, but I had instinct. I flexed my shaking hands and quieted my core, upset with his admonitions but more upset by the cold, hard reality of it all—a kid was gone too soon, someone else had made him gone too soon, and one of the two investigators working this kid's case had no experience.

"These people are now your neighbors," Ivan said. "Show more respect—"

"Respect?" I frowned. "I've been nothing but respectful. Who's saying that I'm not?"

"Keely Butler."

"Because I didn't finish eating her nasty-ass chili? The same nasty-ass chili you told me to never eat again?" I gaped at him. "And anyway, I wasn't disrespectful."

He shrugged. "According to her—"

"You're taking her word over mine?"

"It's not a matter of who I believe, hon," Ivan said. "Just remember: everybody knows everybody here. So be careful with what you say and who you say it to. One wrong word and you could spook someone—or worse, the whole town. Don't act like you've never failed."

"Ouch."

He shrugged and poked my arm. "I had to say it because I need for you to get your fucking nose out of the air, all right? And even though, yeah, she's batshit crazy, she may also become the mayor, and I don't want her pissed off at me because she's pissed off at you."

"Even though she may have kidnapped my client's dog?"

"Disrespectful."

"How was I disrespect . . . Don't answer that. I already know. *You* already know." I hopped off the boulders and started back to Ivan's truck.

Black girls were born women. We all had attitudes, and if we spoke with too much confidence, we'd be called disrespectful. I knew the rules, and remembering them made my eyes burn, and hot air from my nose made my upper lip sweat.

Did this prejudice result in Haven's only Black kid lying on India's stainless steel table?

In my mind's eye, I saw that handsome kid and his smooth, dark skin. His cornrows, now flecked with leaves, were exquisite and had been braided with the accuracy of a cartographer—our ancestors would have successfully escaped to freedom if they'd followed Xander's hair.

"Maybe she should stop stealing people's dogs," I said, finding the loyalty card from Rise & Grind in my wallet.

"You find proof of that?" Ivan asked. "Her stealing people's dogs?"

"Yep." I tore the card into tiny pieces and tossed it in the trash can. "She's evil. And if she wants me to be disrespectful, well, then who am I to deny her?"

"Alyson."

"'To protect and serve' was old Alyson," I said, with a tight smile. "Today's version means I'll serve her bitch all day if she keeps fucking with me."

My phone rang. It was India.

"This is a professional call," she said.

"Good. Ivan's right here."

Ivan and I returned to sit inside the truck. Once Ivan and India caught up, she said, "Sonny, once you and Kwon left, I did another sweep of Xander's body. And I found this stuck on the back of his tongue."

My phone vibrated with a picture: a plastic tub held a gold metal object that could've been a bracelet charm shaped like a . . .

"What *is* that?" Ivan peered closer at the picture.

"Don't know," India admitted.

"Jewelry?" I asked, squinting.

It was circular with small protrusions around that circle. Were those legs and arms?

"Like a person with Einstein hair running," Ivan said.

"Why was it in his mouth?" I wondered.

India says, "That's for you to . . . Actually, it *isn't* your job to find out. Ivan, that's for *you* and Brady to find out."

A chill lurked along my spine—this seemed familiar to me. I'd seen this shape before. When? And what had been the circumstances?

"I found something else," India said. "Almost missed it but going over his body with a flashlight helped me catch it."

The phone vibrated again with another picture of a swatch of dark skin behind an ear.

"I'm assuming that's Xander's ear," Ivan said.

"His left ear," she said. "Look closer."

I took in a breath. "Is that a small puncture wound?"

"Yes, it is," India said.

"Did it happen before or after he died?" I asked.

"Before," she said.

"A needle?" Ivan asked. "Filled with what?"

"Not sure yet," India said. "But it's possible that this wound and whatever made it could possibly shift the case, wouldn't you say?"

I whispered, "Yeah. Were there other wounds?"

"After finding this one, Troy and I went over the body again. Nothing."

"Someone could argue that it was self-administered," Ivan said, shrugging. "If he OD'd, it wasn't because he was shooting up on a regular basis."

"This one time, then," I asked, eyes narrowed. "He shoots shit directly into his carotid artery? One precise puncture for a kid who, looking at his arms, has never used a needle before?"

"Are you asking me or . . . ?" India said.

"Thinking out loud." I turned to Ivan. "Do you know if CSI found any needles nearby?"

Ivan scribbled into his pad. "No, but I'll check."

"Off the record," India said, "Xander doesn't look like your typical heroin user. I see no signs of that, meth, nor cocaine."

"Maybe he was doing a tester shot," Ivan suggested.

"What would he have shot up?" I asked.

"Tox results will tell us," India said, "but you know how long that may take."

"We'll rely on our eyes," I said to Ivan, "and learn more about his behavior."

And look in his bags and bedroom for baggies, syringes, squares of aluminum foil . . .

"Let's hope Kwon and McCann don't wait for breadcrumbs to fall into their laps," I said, the dragon within me stirring—hungry for the gold, ready to burn through the heavenly veneer of this charming seaside town and expose the truths lurking beneath.

Pearly fog barreled in from the ocean and over the Tundra. The sun still shone even though the world now—for the Monroes, for Haven, even for me—was less bright than before.

16.

The afternoon sun slid across the skies over Haven, and even though it wasn't the golden hour yet, that soft, golden glow made this town look as perfect as it pretended to be. Elliott and Giovanni promised that Mom would be fine alone with their bakery staff. "They wanna give you more tea," Mom said, "and not the kind that comes from a kettle." Her eyes sparkled as she tied the laces of her apron. Then she moseyed toward the kitchen. There, at the gleaming stainless steel worktable, a cloth-covered bowl of dough awaited. She dumped it onto the table, and her hands kneaded the dough with the expertise of a lifetime spent in the kitchen. Muscle memory.

I cherished moments like this—I'd moved us here to keep Mom safe, to preserve these glimmers for as long as possible. "She'll be safe," Elliott said. "I promise."

"And we're not walking far," Giovanni added.

With Mom engrossed in her bread making, I turned my gaze to the tranquil main street lined with repurposed Victorian homes and Craftsman-style storefront windows. Living here three days now, and I'd only seen a leisurely pace in Haven, people ambling by with nods and smiles, unhurried by the racing doom-clock that sometimes dictated life in Los Angeles.

Behind this idyllic facade, though, evil lurked. The death of a seventeen-year-old high school student found in poison oak with a needle mark behind his ear . . . Shit like that didn't just happen. That shadow had to have existed even beneath Haven's sunny veneer. His loss was a crack in this town's picture-perfect surface—not that anyone beyond this zip code knew cracks existed. No, the visitors here couldn't sense the riptides beneath the serene, cheery faces of Haven's baristas and bakers, merchants and tour guides.

But Haven's vibe was obviously working for Elliott—and maybe even for Giovanni. In fact, neither man had mentioned Xander's death at all. Did they know?

We paused to stand on the sidewalks.

"Smell that," Giovanni said, eyes closed, mouth falling hard into a smile.

The scent of cinnamon, fresh breads, and cakes wafted from the bakery and sweetened air that smelled of sea and salt.

"That scent convinces me to stay," Giovanni said.

"Will you stop with that?" Elliott snapped, eyebrows furrowed.

"It's the truth," Giovanni snapped back.

Elliott lifted his arm toward me. "She just got here."

Giovanni rolled his eyes. "You don't think she knows this place has fucked-up ways? Ohmigod, really?"

Elliott glared at his partner, his cheeks vibrating with anger and frustration. He yanked up the long sleeves of his Sweetlife T-shirt and pushed out a cleansing breath.

"San Jose wasn't kind to us," Elliott said to me, his voice tinged with a hardness. He rubbed the tattoos of whisks, chef knives, and a cupcake topped with colorful berries running along his forearms and smiled at tourists inside a craft store making candles flecked with seaweed and driftwood. "Cooper painted a picture of Haven that we—*I*—couldn't resist.

"He showed us that there's life beyond looking over your shoulder." Elliott's eyebrows flicked with an emotion that wasn't cheer. He smiled at me, but I sensed his tension.

"No homophobes in Haven?" I asked.

"I didn't say *that*," Elliott said. "When we first got here, we hung a Pride flag outside our house. Someone stole it and burned it in the middle of the road."

"What?" I screeched. "I heard about that. That was *you*?"

"That was us." Giovanni groaned and rubbed his temples. "Just remembering that night . . ."

Even Elliott flushed. "Yeah . . . We . . ." He folded his arms and peered toward the coast.

No one spoke for a moment until: "But you decided to stay," I said.

Both men nodded, Elliott more vigorously than his partner. "I went back to therapy," he said, trying to smile. "Talking it out made it better."

"I did a half IRONMAN," Giovanni said. "Instead of eating, my old way of handling shit."

I dropped my head, the sadness of simply surviving living weighing on my neck.

"Bookstore Audrey brought us roses," Elliott added, smiling now.

"But Haven carried on," Giovanni pointed out, "as though nothing had happened."

"That was terrifying," Elliott said, nodding. "I promised Gio if something else out of pocket happened again, we'd leave. We haven't had any problems, thank goodness."

Another squint from Giovanni and Elliott shook his head. "There were *less* problems—"

"Because Haven is not heaven," I said.

Giovanni grabbed Elliott's hand and kissed it. "Cooper hired Ivan to find out who did it. And Ivan found the guy, and it never happened again. June came—"

"And Coop hung a Pride flag outside his offices," Elliott said. "Not that anyone could *see* it since it's at the very end of the bluff but still. He also encouraged them to fly a flag outside of City Hall. It stayed up the entire month."

"No one's fucked with us since," Giovanni said. "At least, not about our sexual orientation. Now, we *do* have haters who can't stand our bakery."

"They've left awful reviews on Yelp," Elliott said. "I wish Cooper and Ivan could find out who those people are—"

"Who says they're not looking?" Giovanni said, chuckling. "Anyway, we're now the official pastry providers for Mason's, the new restaurant down—" He pointed west toward the pier. "And that happened because of Mr. Sutton."

"He's got his hands in everything but all for the good of Haven." Elliott peered at me. "You talk to him yet? He seemed fond of you. I know, he didn't say much, but it was all here." He gestured wildly at his face.

I tugged my earlobe, my cheeks warm. "I haven't. Didn't you tell me that he's married?"

"Leave Nancy Drew alone, El. She's not interested in going to hell or being run over in the middle of the night by London's broom." Giovanni leaned closer to me and quickly nodded to the floral shop across the street. Four MISSING DOG flyers had been made into a larger square and taped into the corner of her picture window. "So, Marge Henley over there? Cooper helped her out of a bind when the bank threatened foreclosure. Which explains the Figgy flyers."

"And then there's Old Pete, the store owner," Elliott added. "He was an awful man. His little knickknacks store was . . ." He narrowed his eyes as he turned, turned . . . and pointed toward Highway 1. "He was actually running a pawnshop. He was also a loan shark. And you know what happens to a neighborhood when there's both."

Pawnshops encouraged burglary and theft. Trading in people's iPads for forty dollars. Stealing Grammy's antique diamond brooch for a hundred. Cops wouldn't track down an iPad, and rarely did pawnbrokers turn away diamonds and tech for the good of the community.

"First of all," Giovanni said, "he didn't have a permit to operate a pawnshop. Second, high school kids started stealing shit from lockers and bringing it to Old Pete. Cooper and Ivan shut that down *real* quick."

Orin over there had started a moonshine operation deep in the woods. Swatted down.

Brynn and her husband, originally from Vegas, had key parties. "Swinging wasn't bad," Elliott said. "People leaving their house drunk—*that* was bad. Michael and Genesis, who you'll never meet, left drunk as a skunk last year and hit two hikers and a deer. Both were arrested and charged with manslaughter, and then Michael and Genesis tried to sue Brynn and Ronny—"

"Because they'd hosted the key party," I added.

Both men nodded, and Giovanni said, "That shit was *also* shut down *real* quick."

"Seems like Cooper is Haven's guardian angel," I said, half jesting. "With Ivan as muscle. And the sheriff's office—"

"Since Haven isn't the squeaky wheel," Elliott said, "he only has one patrol car with one deputy earmarked for us."

I frowned. "Cops do more than just arrest people." I paused, then added. "You guys do know about the dead kid they found—"

Elliott grinned and pointed ahead of us. "Isn't that beautiful?"

The sky had melted into the sea. I'd never seen a horizon like that. Never visited a town dedicated to the facade, killing crime in a way I'd never seen.

"Cooper isn't paying Ivan to be the secret police or anything like that," Elliott clarified. "The guy runs a PI business—he's not interested in folks being perfect. But they both just want Haven to stay as safe as possible for as *long* as possible. That's why you don't see lots of cops or see any fights until tourist season. We're like . . . bonsai trees in Haven, and I'm here for it."

I gaped at him. "Bonsai? Someone else having control of your destiny? The shape you take? Really?"

"Maybe not *bonsai*," Elliott said, flicking his hand. "Don't be so literal. I *mean* . . . Working with the powers that be to let the bad guys know they can't fuck with the people here and get away with it."

My stomach yawed as Elliott's gaze bore into mine. "Understood." I chewed on my bottom lip, remembering that I used to be a part of the powers-that-be machinery.

The unspoken words hung in the air between Elliott and me—*don't come here and fuck things up for us*. But things were already fucked up. Again, three days in and I'd already stumbled across a dead kid and needed to find a dog either stolen by someone who hated the family or not stolen because the owner needed her dad's attention but her dad was too busy being an adulterer around the state of California. The secrets of Haven were deep currents beneath calm waters—unseen but powerful, capable of pulling anyone under if they weren't careful.

"*I'm* not okay being a bonsai tree," Giovanni said, "but right now, my opinion—"

"It *does* matter," Elliott interrupted. "It's not helpful—that's what I meant." My landlord's focus flitted to me. "Sorry about this."

Giovanni chuckled and folded his arms. "It's fine."

It was not fine.

"And," Giovanni said, "we know about Xander. He reminded me of my baby cousin, with his supernova kind of personality. We talked sometimes—I was on the gymnastics team at William and Mary until I ripped off my kneecap and . . . fuck, I don't miss that pain. Xander was dealing with his ankle."

Swollen ankle, possible fracture.

"He loved our caramel marshmallow treats," Giovanni said with a sad smile. "We're making a batch for Lori."

Elliott shook his head. "After his funeral, we're gonna name them after him and donate those proceeds to a suicide prevention center."

Giovanni quirked an eyebrow—the gesture of a skeptic.

We had a lot to talk about, Giovanni and me. Because people believed that's how Xander died. Was I—along with his parents and the gymnast-turned-baker—the only one who thought different?

There was so much here in Haven, layers of stories like Old Pete's and the swingers'. Elliott and Giovanni just hadn't heard about them yet. Haven held its cards close, and I knew it would take time for the truth to be revealed. If Cooper wanted the town to grow, then that truth would immediately be pushed into the dark . . . until businesses came and then? Let Haven be Haven, and whatever happened, happened. The sheriff would send more deputies, but Haven would still be remembered as a gem before it had been destroyed by outsiders.

Yeah, that was the play, the long game. I wouldn't disappoint Elliott—this town and its godfathers had saved him and Giovanni from the worst, and he was grateful. So, I simply listened, filing away each morsel of information like evidence to be examined when it was time.

"And you're good with that forty dollars a square foot upgrade?" I asked.

Giovanni shrugged. "We don't have to pay it—Sweetlife is already a sexy motherfucker."

"If your shop is crumbling and moldy and not safe for customers?" Elliott said. "Then yes, you should have to paint, spackle, and follow building codes from the late twentieth century. Why do we even have to explain why earthquakes are bad and buildings falling on people during a six-point-five earthquake is something we should all avoid?"

"What if folks can't afford it?" I asked.

"Speak to the manager, honey," Elliott said, laughing. "That's above my pay grade."

Back at Sweetlife, I curled my fingers around the warm mug, and the steam from my latte slinked from the cup to my nose. Every now and then, the bell above the door jingled, and a visiting couple purchased the last slice of tiramisu or old couples shuffled in for half-priced, end-of-the-day breads. I watched Mom concentrate as she measured out flour to start a rum cake.

"Mom, you remember to level it off?" I said, concerned and encouraging.

"Mm-hm." Mom nodded without looking up, her movements deliberate but shaky.

I sipped my coffee and watched Mom's hands shake as she now tapped vanilla into a measuring spoon. The weight of my past pressed down on me. Los Angeles didn't get hurricanes, but the liquor store shooting had torn through the lives of Autumn's family, Royalty's family—and it had left my career in tatters. Fucked Up Things.

I closed my eyes for a moment, summoning the tranquility that the ocean outside promised. But even that was fucked up. The violence of waves crashing against the shore and rocks, eating away at the coast, making big rocks into sand—even if it took hundreds of years. To the rock, it was just a matter of time until the Pacific Ocean won the battle, and children would make sandcastles and bury each other in what were their mighty slate and sandstone bodies. Fucked Up Things, even for the non-sentient.

Fine.

If I could find perfect peace in Haven, I'd find redemption and a new start. Solving Xander's case would bring me both.

"Everything okay, Sonny?" Elliott's voice broke through my wonderings.

"Fine, just . . ." I fixed a smile that didn't quite reach my eyes. "Enjoying the quiet."

"You'll do that a lot here," he said, grinning. "There's nothing but quiet in Haven."

Depended on your definition of quiet.

17.

Ivan's office was dark, the desk chair empty. From his windows, I could see the day was fading, the sky becoming Lakers colors but a paler gold and purple that glinted off the framed Preservation of Life medal hanging on the wall. No fog rolling in yet, and I hoped that mist would stay offshore until it was time to pick Mom up from Sweetlife at six o'clock.

After turning on the waiting room television to *The People's Court*, I plopped into the armchair and opened a new spreadsheet to capture my notes from Xander Monroe's autopsy—Ivan didn't have official software *yet.* One new column—*Personnel*—tracked those involved. India, yes, but also Brady Kwon and Will McCann.

The digital edition of the *Haven Voice* still hadn't mentioned the death of Xander Monroe. Now that I'd met Tanner Orr, though, I knew that the editor in chief would never post such an alarming update that didn't jibe with the narrative.

My watch vibrated with a text message, but I'd left my phone on my office desk beneath printouts and newsprint.

A text from Cooper:

Hey we need to talk

Was it a giant leap to characterize Cooper as one of the most dangerous men in Haven? Not at all. My father always told me, "If you lie, you'll cheat. If you cheat, you'll steal. If you steal, you'll kill." Cooper had committed two of these three sins. He was a Taurus—he'd never leave any task incomplete.

I stared at that text and scrawled a message on my watch's tiny trackpad:

Checked account today

Less in there than yesterday

Why?

??

You know what the fuck I'm talking about

Ellipses and then nothing.

I retreated to my office, those dual question marks draining my battery.

Cooper was probably slumped in his seat, barely breathing, squinting at the phone, tapping his finger against his lip—his tic anytime he needed to think deeper than normal. He didn't need to scroll up to remember my demands: *Take care of my mother. Help pay off the settlement. No problems. No exposure.*

The bell above the front door jangled. A moment later, footsteps headed in my direction.

"Ivan?" a woman shouted.

I shuffled over to my doorway. "He's—"

Startled, Keely Butler whirled around.

"Sorry," I said, hands up. "Ivan's gone for the day."

She gave me the up and down. "You're the one looking for Figgy."

No longer wearing a branded Rise & Grind T-shirt, Keely wore a hot pink tank top that stuck to her like plaque on teeth. Her skinny jeans couldn't hold a thought and the stitches along her inner thigh had busted enough to show some skin. I could see my bemused expression in her mirrored sunglasses before she pushed them up to hold back her hair.

I backed into my office as she moseyed in my direction to invade my space.

Her eyes landed on my desk and skidded into a MISSING DOG flyer covered with sticky notes. "Looking for dogs while my daughter might be lying dead somewhere." She swung her purse and knocked over my bullet trophy, sending it onto the floor.

I chewed my inner cheek. *Disrespectful.*

She snapped up the case and dropped it flat on my desk.

I set the glass case upright and back in its spot with great intention. "May I help you with something, Ms. Butler?"

On cue, her eyes filled with worry and her trembling hand clutched at her purse strap. "Ivan's supposed to be handling my daughter's disappearance. Maybe he'll give the case to you since it seems like he doesn't give a fuck."

"Sure, let's talk," I said, grabbing my binder and pen.

Keely followed me to the loft and asked for green tea. There were plenty of those pods, and I imagined that Ivan had purchased those just for Keely. She settled on the couch, and I settled in the same armchair with graying brown leather. I flipped in my notepad past my Figgy notes and my Xander Monroe autopsy notes and said, "Let's start at the beginning, okay?"

Keely's daughter, Honor, had last been seen leaving a cross-country track meet back in April. Her gray Honda Civic hatchback hadn't moved from Haven High School's parking lot that day or that following week. Nothing had been vandalized or stolen—her earbuds were still in the cup holder with a pair of Dior sunglasses. Her two pairs of expensive, custom-built running shoes still sat in the passenger seat.

"She was wearing her favorite red hoodie over her running uniform," Keely said. "When I texted her, she told me that she was going to Deegan's after the meet to hang out. When I texted her again asking how she placed, she didn't answer my texts. She was just . . . *gone*."

"And you reported her disappearance to the sheriff's department," I said, nodding.

"Not at first," she said.

That made me look up from my pad. "Why not?"

"Because she sometimes disappeared without any explanation," Keely said, shrugging. "And I knew that the cops would say that to me. That she ran away just like she ran away back at Christmas and before that, during summer break."

"Those prior times," I said, writing, "how long did she stay away?"

Keely sipped her tea. "Two weeks. But back in April, once those two weeks went by without a word, I reported it, and then I hired Ivan to find her."

"Honor's phone," I said. "Was it left in the Civic?"

"No. Her phone is gone."

"Back in April, May, was it still on?" I asked. "Is it still on now?"

Keely flushed and blinked at me. "Like . . . does it still work?"

"Yes. Is it still bouncing off towers? Maybe someone is using it to make calls?"

"I didn't . . . I don't . . ." Keely's eyes flicked from her phone to the cup of green tea.

"Okay," I said, "what about her bank card? Any strange charges?"

Keely shook her head and chewed her lower lip. "I check that every Friday. The last time she used it was in April, on the morning of the track meet. She bought a chocolate croissant and protein shake from Sweetlife. Elliott sent Ivan that clip from their security camera. Saturday, April fifteenth, at eight o'clock, as soon as they opened."

"Did she run that day?"

"I didn't go to this meet. I had to work. There were visitors from out of town who'd come for the meet. Some kids say that she ran; other kids say that she didn't. I just know that she didn't come home that night."

"The meet was . . . where?"

"They started at the lighthouse," Keely said, "and ran through the Point Arena State Reserve. So, that includes Dannon's Trail, Dewdrop Trail, Seabreeze Trail—"

Seabreeze Trail—that's where Xander had been found.

Keely noticed that I'd stopped writing. "Is . . . ? Is that important? Those trails?"

I tossed her a quick smile. "Not sure yet. I'm not familiar with your case, but it's a very good detail. Was she in any pictures that day?"

Keely cocked her head. "I don't understand."

"This generation can't go five minutes without taking selfies and group shots for social media. Did you see her in any pictures?" When she didn't respond, I said, "She was meeting her friends after the meet. Even if they didn't go, someone still would've posted something like *Honor is a badass*, or *Having pound cake after the meet*, or something like that."

Keely frowned. "Honor wasn't big on social media."

I waggled my head. "That doesn't mean she wasn't in pictures for a friend who was."

"You've had months to look for her," Keely said, "and what? You're asking me about social media and pictures, even though it's been almost four months and you have nothing to show for it?" Keely's gaze narrowed on me. "It seems like laziness to me."

"Ma'am," I said, "I just got here three days ago. I'm trying to help, okay?"

But this was deflection. This was grasping for control. This was something helpless people did when faced with the unthinkable—blaming the person seated across from them. Even those trying to help were part of The System. The "you," a royal you. I represented Ivan, the sheriff's office, the town protectors . . . and even Keely, who was also supposed to protect her daughter but had failed alongside The System.

Knowing this still didn't stop the heat rising in my cheeks, my heartbeat a steady drumming in my ears. Because there was something else at play here too. *Lazy,* which now joined "disrespectful." Every day of my life, I fought against both labels. Joining the LAPD, I'd moved mountains in cases less complicated than this, and here this bitch was, intentionally lobbing this new word at me.

Keely Butler was a mother on the edge. Her daughter was missing. *Give her grace,* I told myself. But grace didn't mean she had the privilege to verbally abuse me. I didn't take an oath to serve and protect her—no swear-ins at Poole Investigations.

"I need more to go on than a hoodie and a chocolate croissant," I said, taking a deep breath. "You want results? I need details."

She rolled her eyes, then saw the tea dripping from her cup to the carpet.

I bristled at the spilled tea. Was she gonna wipe that up?

"It's like you all don't care about working-class people of color, and yet, you're moving heaven and earth to help the Suttons' case and the Monroes' case but my girl—"

"Last time I checked, the Monroes were Black." I pointedly looked at Keely with her freckles and green veins running beneath pale hands . . .

"Keely's father is Mexican," she snapped.

I blinked at her. "So, Honor's half white, then. Did she present as white, or was she more brown? Another important detail I need. If people I ask are thinking *white girl* in their remembering, then . . ." I paused, and said, "Do you have a recent picture of her?"

"On me? No, I don't." She held my gaze, not backing down. "There's one in her file."

"Great. And you are Latino as well? *Butler*—is that your married name since it's not a . . . *traditional* Mexican surname?"

Still refusing to be ashamed of her statement, Keely's eyes flickered with fire. "Haven isn't just some quaint coastal town; it's a battleground for the future. You've got the old families clinging to their legacies like survivors on the *Titanic*. Then there are the white boys like Elliott and Giovanni with deep pockets, trying to mold Haven into a playground for the rich."

"Giovanni isn't a white—"

"What does it matter? His rich lover is—who wants to pretend he's persecuted."

This woman. Keely had the fervor of a fire and brimstone preacher. Her hands sliced the air, carving out the lines of division within the community. Yeah, I was coming to understand how tightly this village clutched its secrets, but she needed to calm the fuck down.

"Nobody cares," Keely continued, her voice tinged with bitterness. "It's easier to pretend everything's fine in this town than to face the ugliness beneath the surface. Feuds. Vendettas. Deals made and broken in the dead of night. That's the *real* Haven."

"I'm sure Ivan's trying hard," I said, closing my notebook, tired of her antics. "I know him and he's—"

"An ass kisser just like the rest of these people." She flicked her eyes up and down at me again. "And it won't be long until you will be kissing Cooper Sutton's ass too."

I chuckled—if she only knew what parts of Cooper I'd kissed.

"Sit there and smirk," she said, slamming her cup down on the coffee table and splashing more green tea before standing. "When I run this town, I'm coming for you all first."

I raised my eyebrows but I refused to stand. "You *threatening* me?" I asked, my voice as calm as the Dead Sea. "I certainly hope you're not."

Keely colored—yay, for three seconds, she became what she'd claimed to be—then stomped down the stairs and marched to the door, the bell alerting me that she'd exited.

I glared at the wet spots on the table and carpet and tried to quiet the clanging in my head. The office around me expanded, as if it had been holding its breath too.

After wiping up Keely Butler's mess, I returned to my office, dropped into my chair, and rubbed my temples to conjure up my next move.

My cell phone dinged. A text. Another ding. Another text.

Anything new on Xander?

Lori Monroe.

Let's catch up this weekend

Cooper Sutton.

I turned back to my laptop, and my fingers hovered over the keyboard. I clicked into Google and typed in Keely's and Honor's names. The search yielded blog posts from Keely's vegan café, local news snippets featuring Honor as a high school athlete, and social media pages frozen in time.

But this wasn't my case. And I didn't like Keely Butler. No free labor.

When I run this town?

Tha fuck?

Red Birkin—keep.

Tiffany multistone filigree heart pendant necklace—sell. No, keep. No . . .

I kicked away a box filled with marvelous things—from silk scarves and designer handbags to sparkling jewelry. Each box had its own unique aroma—from the musky leather of a vintage purse to the lingering floral scent of a designer scarf—and I wanted to keep every wrapped and curated item around me. Frustrated, I ran my hands through my hair and lay on my back in the middle of my bedroom, and made a snow angel in luxury Fucked Up Things. My gaze drifted up to the wooden beams on the ceiling as my heel caressed the second cashmere throw that I'd decided to keep. I'd done good so far, photographing a few items and uploading them onto The RealReal, like:

Square-cut diamond earrings—rhodium-plated 14k white gold. Carat weight: 1.78 Excellent condition.

Cashmere throw—gray, white, and multicolor cashmere. Horse motif at center. Includes box. Excellent condition.

Mirrored aviator sunglasses—gold-tone metal. Includes case. Pristine condition.

He'd gifted me thousands of dollars' worth of gifts. Yet, all I wanted was one thing.

The heart of Cooper Sutton: ten ounces. Red-blooded American. A limited edition. Visible signs of use. Fair condition. Will be returned after one year.

18.

The clock on my phone told me that it was almost eight o'clock on this Friday morning. The headlights of the Bronco barely penetrated the clouds of rolling fog. The mist's chilled breath crept through the truck's half-open window, prickling my neck as I drove Highway 1—the devil's highway—to reach Seabreeze Trail.

Dawn had supposedly come, but there was no sun, no moon, nothing that told me I still existed on the third rock from the sun. But I wanted to experience a morning similar to Xander's last morning alive. Back on Tuesday morning, it had been fifty-five degrees and foggy like this.

How many miles were there between this trail and the Monroes' house? How were Lori and Devon okay letting Xander run in the forest alone even earlier than eight in the morning? Was that the danger-danger-everywhere LA cop in me talking?

I pulled into the parking lot closest to the start of Seabreeze Trail. Behind me, the sun tried to push past the mist, casting a pale glow too weak to survive. Funny how mist made the most powerful star in our galaxy into a feckless fleck of dust. I stared out at stunted redwoods whose roots had touched too much salt water. No one ran past me as I sat there. Was it too early? Did runners know that one of their tribe had been found dead here?

My pulse quickened, a metronome ticking in my head. Despite the ten years I'd worn a badge, despite my experience facing down the worst in the city with nothing but a Glock and a vest made of Kevlar, my breath and my memory stuttered. In addition to Keely Butler's threat—"I'm coming for you"—bad things hid in the fog. That was true in Los Angeles, and it was proven to be true in Haven just three days ago. Despite the gun nestled in my hip holster, I needed something beyond bullets, metal, and polymer to push me out of this car—something that offered assurance I would return to my truck safe and uninjured.

Heebie-jeebies—even hard-asses get them.

Piano . . . pizza . . . panda . . . pride . . . pimento . . .

At *pancetta*, I pried my hands from the steering wheel. At *patio*, I opened the driver's side door and plucked latex gloves and a few evidence bags from my repurposed dick kit. My left shoulder ached—the damp somehow penetrating my fleece and thermal shirt to push against my allegedly healed wound. At *precipice*, I reached the gravel trail that would lead me to the site where Xander Monroe had been found by a black Lab named Ace.

Somewhere in the early-morning fog, a woodpecker tapped into a tree trunk. Somewhere in the fog, a hawk cried out, an alert that morning breakfast had been found.

My breath puffed around my face.

Picture . . . polo . . . panini . . .

The crunch of dried leaves beneath my boots joined the bark of seals and the everlasting roar of the Pacific Ocean.

Lori's first instruction: *Walk past the brown sign announcing Seabreeze Trail.*

Fog curled around the tops of the Douglas firs. A lizard scampered across the trail.

Walk past the fallen, twisted tree trunks.

The mix of pine- and redwood scents mixed with the smell of salty ocean air.

Cross the small bridge over the creek bed.

Beneath that bridge, nothing but fern and moss.

Walk twenty paces and look over to the right.

I counted aloud, my eyes fixed on the leaf clusters of three. At twenty, I dropped into silence, respectful of Xander's resting place. I shivered—not entirely from the chill—then took in the world around me.

The natural chaos of foliage was even more chaotic because of makeshift memorials left by those who mourned the young man's death. Spent candles rested on the trail's edge along with photographs of Xander—some with friends, solo shots in his football jersey, leaning against a Ferrari, arm around the shoulder of Bay Area native Marshawn Lynch, who'd made it in the NFL. Strangely, my soul lifted—there were those who acknowledged that a young man had departed this world and would be missed.

Who'd left the white cross? Who'd left the football? How many times had Lori and Devon visited this place? Would they ever return? Would they even remain in Haven now?

A teddy bear, its fur damp with the morning dew, lay against the tree trunk—its glassy eyes staring ahead. Colorful notes protected in plastic sleeves and attached to branches and twigs by string fluttered gently in the morning breeze, each a testament to the void left by Xander's untimely departure. I resisted the urge to read these notes, knowing each word would weigh down my already heavy heart.

Using my phone, I took pictures of the memorials—from the flowers to the running shoe. I took close-ups of the dirt and patch of poison oak that had cushioned his body. My eyes swept over every detail, committing each to memory—taking pictures, though, so I didn't have to rely on that memory later today or for however long it would take to solve this puzzle and bring justice to Xander, his parents, and to those who sympathized. Right now, I didn't care if this case was Ivan's or mine. The need to bring truth to light was as much a part of me as the blood coursing through my veins.

Ten minutes past the hour and still not one runner or hiker had passed by.

If Xander had tripped as he'd jogged, he wouldn't have fallen into the brambles and scalloped leaves. Had he been standing off the side of the trail when he collapsed? Had he known that he was standing in poison oak?

I pulled on the latex gloves, keeping a wary eye on those scalloped leaves. I stooped and moved aside some of the memorials to reach the brush.

Xander had fallen into this nest, his immune system already dimmed before he'd landed.

I zoomed in on the plants. Ferns there. Poison oak there. Moss-covered log there. I ran my hands over the leaves, then parted the toxic plant.

Had the sheriff's department forensics team gone over this?

No signs that a village of one thousand people lived nearby—the forest was that dense. The air felt heavier here—warm but with icy eyebrows that brushed against my cheek. All of me felt slippery as trickles of sweat slid from beneath my breasts to dampen my bra and down the small of my back to the waistband of my—

What was that?

I sat back on my heels and looked back over my shoulder. Tried to hear past the sloppy thumping of my heartbeat. But I saw only branches clutching at each other and gobbling the sky. Dirt too soft to crunch, fallen leaves too soft to crunch.

I shivered—was about to reach for my gun but paused before touching the Glock's smooth polymer.

One more look back over my shoulder—*no one there, you're good, it's all—*

There it was again.

A creak. Almost imaginary.

I slowly pulled the Glock from its holster and aimed at the sound and—

A squirrel leaped from one tree branch to another, and the leaves rustled, and the squirrel peered at me, and I whispered, "Shit, squirrel,

I almost shot you." Once the critter scurried off, I slipped the gun back into the holster and turned my attention back to the earth before me.

I ran my gloved hands over the dirt and . . . a glimmer in the dark earth. I pulled at a gold . . . *chain.* I held it to the light to see . . . *nothing remarkable. Just a rose gold chain. A chain this light and delicate, probably a woman's chain.* Even after being left in the dirt, it hadn't dulled. Actually, the chain looked new even though the clasp was broken like it had been snatched off. There was a bent link in the middle of the chain that may have held . . .

The charm found in Xander's mouth. Did it come off this chain?

I reached into my pocket and pulled a small paper bag from the bunch. I dropped in the chain and marked the bag with where I'd found it, and the date I'd found it.

The leaves rustled in the gentle breeze—a *You did good,* from Mother Nature.

I stared at the trail. Too many people—including me—had traversed this path, and so it was impossible to tell if the drag marks in the dirt had been made by the toes of his sneakers. Deadweight—whoever was with Xander had been strong enough to pull him off the trail. *Could I pull nearly two hundred pounds of deadweight six feet?*

I pushed my hands through the soil again. Nothing more in this patch. I circled the tree, searching for something, anything, violating the leaves and earth. The land dropped some and right before that edge of land declined . . .

"What the . . . ?" I whispered.

A syringe not even covered by dirt—as though it had been thrown but hit tree limbs before it dropped here.

I placed a greeting card from the memorial beside the syringe for scale, then took pictures.

Why hadn't Kwon, McCann, or their team discovered this? Even if it ultimately wasn't a part of the Monroe case, all evidence needed to be examined before being dismissed.

"Someone there?" A man's voice cut through the quiet.

I shouted, "One minute," and dropped the syringe into another paper bag and marked it.

Back on the trail, a guy with a brown ponytail paced as a black Lab sat and panted.

I said, "Hi."

The man startled and eyed the bag in my hand. "Are you working the case?"

I started to say no, but I wasn't crawling around the forest for shits and giggles. "Yes. Not for the sheriff's department, though. I'm investigating on behalf of the family."

The man nodded, then said, "I'm Jairo, the guy who found their son."

"If you're Jairo . . ." I pointed to the dog and smiled. "Then this good boy must be Ace. Have you remembered something more to tell the detectives?"

He frowned. "The detectives haven't talked to me since that first time on Tuesday."

I cocked my head as Ace sniffed my hand. "Really?"

"I came by later that morning," Jairo said, "because I wanted to take pictures of the CSI team working, but no one was here." He pushed his hands through his hair. "I was hoping that you were one of the detectives. This sucks."

"Yeah." I held up a hand. "Give me a moment? Let me finish up and we'll talk?"

Jairo pointed at the paper bags. "Did you find something?"

"No idea."

I returned to that incline. After snapping more pictures, I returned to Jairo and Ace. I plucked off the gloves—turning them inside out—and dropped them into a third paper bag. "Could you start at the beginning? And would you mind if I recorded this? I don't have my notepad with me."

Jairo shifted his weight from one foot to the other, flushed and jittery. "Sure. Okay, so . . . Ace and I got here, like we do every morning.

It's usually quiet, you know? Peaceful." He cast a glance toward the clustered memorials. "But that day, I saw him, Xander, lying there—so still, covered in leaves and—" He paused, swallowing hard.

"Did you touch anything? See anyone else?"

"No, no, I knew not to mess with a crime scene. Called nine-one-one right away. But—" He shook his head. "I always saw him on the trail a few times a week."

"Yeah?" I said.

"Great athlete. We never spoke—just nodded to each other. He'd have his earbuds in, and I'd have mine in, you know?" He paused, then said, "One morning, last week, though . . . He was running but he wasn't alone. A white female was running beside him."

"Old or young? Blond hair? Skinny? Athletic?"

"Umm . . ." He tugged back his hair. "I don't know. Nice sneaks. Like, expensive. Not for cross-country. More for road runs. She was tall—not as tall as him but maybe your height."

I was five-seven. "The sneakers. What did they look like?"

"Orange . . . umm . . . Nike . . ." Jairo bit his lip as he thought more, then shook his head.

That was that.

We exchanged numbers as the dog sniffed my boots. "Any detail, no matter how small."

As Jairo and Ace trudged back toward the parking lot, my mind crackled. Xander's companion being white was no help—everyone in Haven was white. *Those shoes . . .*

Orange Nike running shoes, not for terrain but for roads.

Fit. Not poor. Confident—wearing orange shoes, she had to be.

Had a female also joined Xander on Tuesday morning's run? A girlfriend? Was she wearing a chain? Maybe they'd stopped here to make out. Maybe his lips were on her neck, and she jabbed him with a needle, and frightened, he bit off the charm—accidental or intentional, his last act before being poisoned. But why would a love interest jab him with a needle?

Maybe it had been a delivery method for pain medication—choosing a less obvious spot to receive treatment instead of his forearms or the webbing between his toes? Maybe he knew she was going to inject him; he'd wanted her to—*just make it stop hurting*—but she fucked up and hit the wrong spot accidentally, and she freaked out, panicked, left him there and . . .

Maybe whatever was in that needle made him convulse and froth at the mouth. How long had he suffered? Did she watch? If he staggered, though . . . No. He fell back from the trail and had been dragged into the bushes. Contusion on the back of his head—the braids back there had been filled with dirt and leaves.

I turned to the vegetation and the jagged contours of poison oak leaves surrounding the gnarled tree. *Leaves of three, let them be.* The sun was out now, and early-morning light cast long shadows over the trail. I dropped back to the ground, convinced that I'd missed something. Wearing no gloves, I grabbed a strong twig and pushed aside the leaves.

That's when I spotted it—a single pill, half buried beneath disturbed earth near the base of the tree. I stared at it, hoping that it wasn't a mirage. The familiar thrill of discovery pulsed through me, convincing me that I *was* seeing what I was seeing. I used the stick to roll the pill into the last brown paper bag I'd brought from the truck. My breath left my chest, and I wobbled some. From surprise. From anger. *Why haven't they sent a team out here?*

Suicide—that's what they said, all because they'd found a note in Xander's pocket.

A beautiful place to die.

Didn't matter if it wasn't related to Xander's case, this pill and that syringe should've been in someone's lab right now.

Why were they in my possession instead?

19.

I was headed back to the office and driving north on Highway 1 when necessity overcame anxiety. Harvey Parrish, Suspect Number Three, was speeding south in his big-ass red Dodge Ram. Where was he going, and was this my chance to finally talk to him without distraction?

At the turnout, muscle memory overtook anxiety, and I made a three-point turn to follow him.

Parrish made a right into the same parking lot at Moonview Bluffs where I'd sat with Ivan just yesterday. By the time I parked FaB three spots over, Parrish was already ambling along the edge of the bluffs. The butcher was tall and thick—a middle-aged hockey player's body—his gait surprisingly nimble and casually arrogant despite that perilous drop to the ocean.

Whoever had kidnapped Figgy had stood on this very precipice and held an innocent dog out over the void. The photo—a ghastly image of the pooch's wide, fearful eyes against the backdrop of open air—had seared into my memory, even though it hadn't been splashed across the front page of *Haven Voice*. Even the text message—WE GOT YOUR BITCH—made me clench my jaw and ball my hands into fists.

I killed the engine, pulled my fleece over my thermal T-shirt, and opened the driver's side door, remembering this time to bring a small notepad and pen. I aimed to stay on the side of solid ground, closest to the parking lot.

"Mr. Parrish," I called out, my voice one of nonchalance I'd honed over my ten years as a cop. "I didn't expect to find you here. I was planning to try the market again." I approached him with measured steps, the crunch of gravel beneath my black Dr. Martens marking my approach. "I stopped by on Wednesday, but you had a lot of customers."

The ocean breeze tousled the butcher's thick, dark hair. His wide, round face reminded me of that actor, the big guy who always took his small roles playing jerks and made them lovable. His face flushed with a surprise that didn't reach his cool blue eyes. "I know you?"

I held out my hand. "You don't, but now you do. Sonny Rush of Poole Investigations."

He cut his eyes at my hand, but we still shook. "What does Ivan want with me this time?"

This time? Which meant that Harvey had a folder locked away in the office file cabinets.

"We're looking for a dog," I said. "Her name's Figgy. She belongs to the Suttons."

He blinked at me. "And what's that gotta do with me?"

"Well," I said, pulling out my notebook and pen, "you were mentioned as someone who had a problem with the family and their dog."

A smirk danced on his lips. "Well, I think they're ridiculous people."

I shrugged. "I'm sure you're not the only person with that opinion. Why do you think the Suttons are ridiculous people? Why would they think you'd want to harm their dog?"

He chuckled and looked out toward the gray ocean.

I stood still and studied him. The nervous flicker of his gaze. The way his hands patted the pockets of his Green Bay Packers windbreaker. He was more nervous talking to me than mincing his way across the edge of this cliff.

"You a real detective or are you pretending?" he asked.

"Ten years with the LAPD, five as a homicide detective."

"Homicide?" He raised his eyebrows in surprise. "No shit?"

"Mm-hm." I waited a beat, then said, "Tell me about your relationship with the Suttons."

Even though I hadn't moved, the breeze still made me nervous. There was something about the way the wind tugged at my collar, the way I couldn't see this man's hands one minute and then only the backs of those large hands crisscrossed with pearly scars the next. He would have no problems grabbing me and flinging me into the Pacific.

"Business," Harvey replied curtly, his gaze drifting toward the horizon. "I give 'em all the protein for any Haven events and every Sutton whoop-de-do. Cooper Sutton wants me to bring in some fancy shit like wag-yoo bone-in rib-eye roast and venison steaks and pheasants. Do you know how much pheasants cost? Who eats fucking pheasants in Haven? And then he wants me to season some of the meat with rubs and shit. I'm not a fucking cook, all right? Just because him and his rich friends eat razor clams up in San Francisco every other day don't mean that regular people down here in Haven can afford to or would want to if they could."

"You're mad because . . ." I looked up from the pad. "Cooper Sutton wants to appeal to a broader customer base? Because he wants to meet the needs of customers? I'm sure people who've eaten foie gras also enjoy breakfast sausage and roasted chicken—and would pay for all those things, especially if they're preseasoned. And they'd purchase all of that at Good Pickings since it's the only grocery store in Haven."

He shoved his hands deeper into his pockets. "This place is just changing too much too quickly. He's pushing us out and bringing strangers in."

"Strangers like . . . ?"

"Them gay boys and their bakery, for starters." He shook his head. "Before they flounced here over the hill, my grandma had a bakery in that same spot. Sold coffee cake and cinnamon rolls. French apple pie, if you wanted something fancy. With a dollar, you'd leave with a bag of sugar cookies and some doughnuts. Fresh-brewed coffee. Strong shit. Not no European bullshit.

"But now? At—what is it called?—Sweetlife? You need to take out a loan just to afford the bullshit they call cake. What the fuck is a beignet and naan, and what the fuck kinda macaroons don't have coconut?"

"My mother's a baker there now," I said. "She owned three shops down in LA. Retired but wanted to still make sticky toffee cake. It's delicious. You should try it."

He growled, "No thanks. I'll stick to my regular coffee cake and coffee. You shouldn't have to pay more than five dollars for cake and coffee. My wife went once, and she came back with croissants that cost thirty dollars. They're seven dollars for a dozen at my store."

I squinted into the distance, at that flat gray ocean and its never-ending roar. This vista point's proximity to Seabreeze Trail: less than half a mile from Xander Monroe's death site.

"These rocks," I said. "This is where Figgy was last seen before she disappeared. Well, she was actually held closer to the edge. Where you were just standing a moment ago."

A flicker of unease crossed Harvey's face, quickly masked with a swipe of his hand across his mouth. Too late, though—I'd already caught it. I toed the gravel with my right boot and asked, "You come here often?"

The man's eyes jumped to the churning waves below before meeting my gaze again. He looked calm, but then so did I. All a trick—a veneer temporarily plastered over our faces, like movie posters on construction planks.

"Just taking in the view," he replied, shrugging. "What does it matter to you? I'm not breaking no laws, not that you can even arrest me if I was."

"It matters because," I said, narrowing my eyes, "this is more than just a scenic overlook. Whoever took Figgy took a picture of her being dangled over that cliff."

"Ah. And here I am, a suspect, standing in this same spot. Returning to the scene of the crime." He chuckled. "Is this the moment I twirl my mustache, Miss Rush?" He smiled and shrugged. "Just a coincidence. I like this place. I come here all the time to find some peace, especially away from those idiots demanding that I stock octopus tentacles and ostrich filets."

"I'm told that you refused to grind sirloin because they fed it to their dog."

"Starving people in the world," he said, "and they're serving their fucking dog—"

"Meat that they bought?" I said. "Meat that they'd otherwise eat in ways you wouldn't know about unless they told you? Why do you care what they buy and who consumes it?"

My question was wrought with frustration and amazement. Who hadn't gone to a store to purchase shit like condoms, lube, a bag of mandarins, and a *Star* magazine, and had your cheeks burn with embarrassment because the person ringing you up looks at you like you've been running naked through the store after using lube and eating Cuties in the paper goods aisle? *Ring the fuck up my groceries, Janice. Who are you to judge me?* And that's what Harvey Parrish did to the Suttons, to the consumers of ostrich filets and wag-yoo steak, and to his "regular" customers. Because of judgy merchants like him, I had started purchasing my rubbers and lube online, *thankyouverymuch*.

"Well, Mr. Parrish"—since he hadn't invited me to call him Harvey yet—"if there's anything you know, anything at all, it's best that we talk about it now. Sort it out together."

Harvey's lips parted, but no confession tumbled out.

"If you know something, *anything*," I said, "please tell me. I don't have to mention names. I don't care about names. I just want the dog back." I paused, then added, "You think an ex-LAPD homicide detective is thrilled looking for a dog? But I'm doing this because, like you, I need money to pay for shit. The Suttons got money; I need money. I'll find the dog. You chop the sirloin and keep it pushing. Don't give them any reason to fuck up your life."

His unreadable eyes flicked to meet mine. For a moment, I glimpsed a spark of guilt or fear, maybe, but then it was gone—shuttered away with Granny's coffee cake and 70 percent ground round.

Harvey finally exhaled, then turned back to the Pacific, as though the resolution existed right off the continental shelf.

And so, I stepped back, giving Harvey space while allowing my mind to race with possibilities. Like . . . Figgy never being found. No—I wouldn't let that happen. Closing this case mattered, and I'd find another way to draw out the truth, patient and precise. After all, the stakes were high—Figgy's disappearance had shown me the fault lines I wouldn't have known existed. Political divides, class divides, what was authentic Haven, what was progress. Who got to decide the direction of a town like this—and who'd do anything to keep that progress from happening?

"I didn't steal the dog," Harvey said, his words flat. "I ain't got nothing to do with her being gone. I'm innocent."

He may not be guilty, but after reading just a speck of background on Harvey Parrish, he was far from innocent. Any man who torched cars, I knew not to fuck with. But I still appreciated the irony: Here he was, pissed that Figgy ate quality meat, and there he was, insisting that his wife died of COVID-19, even though she'd shown no signs of the disease during her video-conferenced birthday celebration a day before. I couldn't wait to find out what other shit the meat man had done in between wrapping up ground bison and smoked duck breast while scowling at his customers.

I slapped my steno pad against my thigh. "Thanks for talking with me. If you remember anything, give me a call or stop by the office. We both know this isn't over."

He gave no indication that he'd heard me, choosing instead to stare out at the ocean.

I said, "Have a good one," then backed away to the Bronco. Yeah, I wanted to see him coming if he was coming for me. There was something about Harvey Parrish and those pearly scars on his hands and those six months he spent in prison for arson and that recent arrest for possession of an unregistered firearm . . . Even if I found the dog, I'd never turn my back on a man like that—a man who'd have no problem pushing me off a cliff.

20.

I slipped into a parking space in front of the gray Victorian after dropping off that syringe, random pill, and broken chain that I'd found at Xander's death site.

When I climbed out of the Bronco, I hadn't planned to join the village tour—I had paperwork to complete—but sometimes, a girl couldn't help it.

Pastor Devon Monroe just looked too sad for me to ignore. He was as tall as Cooper but stood out because he was also dark and brooding, even wearing his white-collared black cleric's shirt. There was Cooper at the lead, talking about his grandiose vision for Haven, and there was Devon Monroe, grief draped over him like a shroud. The minister didn't speak—not one word to counter Haven's safety record, not one word to me as I fell in step beside him. He was the only tour participant not chomping Earl Grey macarons from Sweetlife or perfectly seasoned french fries from Mason's or gasping at the never-ending beauty of Seaview Way before it dropped dramatically into the Pacific Ocean. With his son dead, Devon didn't give a fuck about the view, a boutique, a gym, or a winery.

"Hey," I whispered, touching his elbow, "do you *have* to be here? They'll be fine—"

"I'm good. Thanks for checking." He tried to smile. "Distraction helps."

"Is Lori joining you?"

He shook his head. "Family's coming in tonight, so she's at home cooking. Staying busy. Again, distraction from . . ." He shrugged.

"Mind if I keep you company?" I asked. "I wanna hear this tale of New Haven."

Cooper was now talking about the meadow across from the cemetery and how it would move Haven from a sleepy seaside town to a sleek, modern destination. He paused after seeing me standing with Devon at the back of the group. The others assumed that the minister and I were together because of course we were. No one asked for introductions, and so, I didn't offer any. I assumed the woman with the wavy auburn bob and fashion-forward chunky black eyeglass frames was Tracy Louise, owner of boutiques bearing her name. The short, muscular guy with the low haircut who looked like he'd gone AWOL from the Russian army this morning had to be Reginald West. The older guy with the thick white hair and expressive wrinkles on his forehead and around his mouth was vintner Bob Lee—I'd seen him before on *House Hunters*. The three business owners had brought with them four dark-haired, Young Republican types who wore pantyhose and neckties this close to the Pacific Ocean. Each assistant carried a legal pad filled with notes and phones filled with shots of the empty lots adjacent to the cemetery.

Cooper enthusiastically gestured to the tabletop-size rendering stapled to a post beside the serene meadow. Faux Craftsman-style storefronts with blond hardwood floors, open terraces for drinking and dining, palm trees in planters, couches and lounge chairs with soft pillows. So ordered and clean, and frankly, prettier than the Haven of Today.

"I'm promising this," Cooper said, wearing perfectly distressed jeans, a cream-colored shirt with its tails peeking perfectly from his blue cardigan, and the pricey but not ostentatious Batman Rolex with its black-and-blue ceramic bezel. Studied casual. "Haven *will* become a beacon of progress for the northern part of the Bay Area. A place where safety and innovation walk hand in hand." His blue eyes flicked over to Devon and me.

Bob Lee motioned to the board. "Everything sustainable, LEED-certified?"

"Of course," Cooper said. "Here in Haven, we believe climate change will continue to alter the way we do business. The storms are getting worse everywhere, and since we suffered some erosion in that last storm system, we'll soon start retrofitting the coastline to keep it from falling into the Pacific." He laughed, and so everyone laughed.

I forced a smile as I listened to bullshit about safety and environmental sustainability. All of it made my jaw tighten, made me sad for the grieving father standing beside me.

"Pastor Monroe here," Cooper said, nodding to the man in the collar, "is also leading our clergy into coming up with language to persuade our churchgoing climate deniers. We'll then take that language and share it with communities beyond Haven. While our home is first priority, we realize that what happens fifty miles north or south of Haven also impacts our families here. From helping to keep Highway 1 healthy—we all have suffered from Big Sur being unreachable—we're playing our part to keep travelers enjoying that gorgeous drive up and down the coast. We're changing the way our fisheries and fishermen catch—serving only seafood in sustainable categories. No threatened fish or shellfish eaten here in Haven. We are one letter away from being called Heaven, but our founding fathers didn't wanna brag."

The group chuckled as their assistants scribbled and snapped pictures. They all imagined T-shirts with a graphic of an *E* in parentheses—*H(E)AVEN*.

Devon nodded with hollow agreement at each of Cooper's statements. His eyes, though, betrayed a soul torn between hope for the community and the abyss of personal loss.

"In my mind," Tracy Louise said, "Haven is like a gated community but without the gates. Like, a place where children can play freely, where families thrive without fear—"

"Without fear?" I whispered, unable to hear that and not respond, even if my response was an outraged whisper. Heat was creeping into my gaze, over my ears, into the voice of my pissed-off whisper. I knew that I was now glaring at Cooper.

Cooper withstood my glare, the epitome of detached corporate ambition. A flicker of discomfort crossed his face. Ever the shark, though, he masked it with a smile. "Without fear," he affirmed, doubling down with a confidence that bordered on arrogance. "Haven is poised to be one of the safer places in the region."

"Is that right, Pastor Monroe?" the vintner asked, squinting.

Did Bob the Wine Guy not know . . . ?

Caught off-guard, Devon took a sharp breath. "Uhh . . ."

Surges of shock at Cooper's audacity swelled through me. How *dare* he stand on this hallowed adjacent ground, less than two miles from where this man's son had been found dead, and tout safety statistics? That Devon Monroe had been expected to attend was ridiculous and mean, and forcing him to toe the line? Fucking despicable.

"'Safer' doesn't necessarily mean safe," I said now, my voice steady despite my outrage. There was my challenge, a line drawn in the sand. I'd let some shit go, but insulting this poor father was beyond the pale.

The wheels turned in Cooper's head as he weighed the impact of my observation.

Now the gym owner, boutique owner, and vintner all turned to look at me. Their eyes lit with surprise. They'd already noticed me—because I dared to talk, because I dared to not only contradict the man leading the tour but to offer something other than my mouth sucking Cooper's corporate dick.

"This is Alyson Rush," Cooper said. "She moved here from Los Angeles on Monday. If anyone knows safety, ha ha . . . Miss Rush retired from the LAPD to relocate and is now taking care of her mother who is suffering with early onset dementia." He paused, then smiled. "If a cop with a vulnerable mother moving here doesn't convince you, then I don't know what—"

But then he caught my eye and saw something there that shut him up. A look, I've been told, that could freeze boiling water.

Cooper beckoned the group to follow him back to Seaview Way. "This may sound corny, but I truly believe the safety of a place isn't measured by the height of its walls or the sophistication of its security systems but by the well-being of its people." He paused, then said, "Wouldn't you agree, Pastor Monroe?"

"Indeed, Cooper," the minister said, his voice low but firm. "Safety is a community's promise to one another—a promise we all must keep. And I'm sure, if it's ever breached, a community like Haven will move heaven and earth to find the splinter and the burr, pluck them out, and seal that gap. I've only been here since June, and while I haven't seen that kind of . . . *collective exorcism*, I'm sure it will happen. Any day now."

The group laughed. The gym owner looked dramatically at her watch, then tapped her chin as though she, too, was waiting for the Bad Thing to happen.

Momentarily chastened, Cooper cleared his throat and steered the conversation back to parking spaces, rideshares to either Silicon Valley or San Francisco, and beautiful weather.

"What about you?" Reginald West turned to ask me. "What do you do now that you've retired? Except stand around lookin' pretty. Not that anybody minds that, but I'm sure it doesn't pay that much."

"I'm thinking she came here to find a husband," the boutique owner said with a sly grin. "No ring, Reggie, *hint, hint*. Mr. Sutton lured you here, Alyson—didn't he—with promises of a luxury rideshare program?" She giggled.

"I'm a private investigator," I said, "and—"

"Let's move on," Cooper said, consulting his watch. "We have a lot to do before dinner."

"What are we having?" the vintner asked.

"Some of the best seafood you'll ever eat," Cooper said. "Wine from Bob's vines over in the Valley, and a key lime torte from Sweetlife.

Elliott and Giovanni, who you met, supply pastries and baked goods to Mason's. That's where we'll have dinner later. It's this kind of collaboration that will galvanize New Haven."

It was a little after two o'clock and the afternoon sun cast long shadows over the sidewalks. I felt the weight of the townspeople's glares either boring into my back or boiling against Cooper's forehead. Some wore expressions tight with disapproval—the anti-developers—and their lips were tight and white with discontent and anger. Others tried to appear casual as they stood in their doorways. Elliott and Giovanni were on the sidewalk with a coffeepot and cupcakes, their eyes bright with the promise of more and better.

And that's when I realized it—all the MISSING DOG flyers that had covered every space possible, they were all gone. Even the quadrant of flyers in florist Marge Henley's windows. Was a missing dog too much of a threat to the business interests of this trio?

"Riddle me this, Cooper," the gym rat said now. "If Haven is such a bastion of safety as you claim, what's the need for a private investigator?" He turned to me. "No offense." His smirk was ingratiating, an attempt to disarm me now that he realized his muscles hadn't impressed me.

My restraint frayed, but I tucked it back like a loose strand of hair behind my ear.

"Every community has secrets, Reggie," Cooper said, his tone light yet pointed. "Sonny and her boss Ivan Poole do work that ensures personal matters are discreetly managed, contributing to the peace of Haven." He smiled and shrugged. "I've personally seen to it that every bubbling effort, no matter how nascent, is popped and smothered before it spreads. Last week, I kept a guy who'd downed too many Red Bulls and vodkas from driving. He's not a local, thank goodness. Still, the bartender knows who to watch out for, in other words."

Tracy Louise rolled her eyes. "Where were you when a flash mob robbed my store?"

"You hear they're closing Macy's in San Francisco?" Bob Lee asked.

"Shoplifting has totally gotten out of hand," Tracy Louise agreed. "And no one's doing anything about it. Don't want to upset the liberals—"

"Says the liberal," the wine guy snarked.

She scowled. "Only on Tuesdays."

"Now, that's another question I have," Reginald West said, "the demographics of this town. I don't see a lot of diversity."

"I'm not complaining," Bob Lee said. "Let Haven be what it naturally is. Not everyone gets to afford this place. You have low crime rates here—I saw the stats. No murders, no rapes, no strong-arm robberies. You may pay more in real estate but low crime costs. Let those who can afford it come here. They'll have just as much stake in this community as everyone else—and they'll do anything to keep it that way, CRT be damned."

Devon Monroe scoffed and asked, "What does critical race theory have to do with—"

"Let's keep walking," Cooper said, an edge now in his voice. The proud member of the ACLU, Planned Parenthood, Human Rights Watch, and APLA clamped his jaw.

I wouldn't add to this bullshit festering beneath Haven's idyllic surface—especially now that I knew who we were dealing with. People who considered *dark underbelly* as a literal thing, those who believed all colored people are shit, except for you.

Cooper's shoulders tensed beneath his cardigan. His silence spoke volumes.

As we rounded a corner, the glares intensified from a small cluster of older locals who had gathered outside the old post office—a building rumored to be on the chopping block in the Sutton Developers' grand design. Their arms were folded defiantly across their chests, their brows furrowed in silent protest. They cherished Haven's small-town charm, the history that had seeped into every wooden beam.

But Cooper had ignored them to fill these potential business owners' imaginations with the promise of more. He fueled their excitement with word sirens like *new opportunities* and *property values*, *per capita*, and *world class*. Coming from the mouth of a man like him—obviously wealthy and thriving, the embodiment of California beauty—they'd all been drawn in. They believed in everything he said, and they—like Devon Monroe and me—had all believed him. Haven lured us here, the need for quiet and better and more orbiting like satellites around Cooper. We were all drawn in by the gravity of his promises for wealth and modernization—to exist in an environment that could foster and sustain a healthy personal and business life.

So, there it was. The signpost that told me danger ahead. With just these three business owners, Haven's coffers would grow 300 percent. It would be no good for them to discover this town had killed a Black kid who'd managed to survive in Oakland for seventeen years. I knew then that I would have to navigate the Monroe murder carefully—as well as any future case that might diminish the star of Haven, any issue that would push out people who said words like *CRT* and *woke* and *diversity*. Red-capped culties who hated immigration, yet hired crews of them to build and maintain their businesses and care for their children.

Did people know about Cooper's grandma? What conversations had he heard from being around people who'd assumed he was all the way white? Would he remain quiet forever for commerce's sake?

Was this Cooper's intention? Make Haven more Coeur d'Alene than Santa Monica? Or did he secretly agree with them while burnishing his liberal creds—and his dick—by building in the urban areas of Los Angeles and the Bay, pricing people out of their homes and their lives? Xander Monroe threatened that vision with his diamond stud and #5 tattoo—his cornrows and quick feet and brown skin. Parental panic after his false arrest had brought Xander to Haven, but any attention he received on the gridiron would bring more people, all kinds of people. Too many kinds of people.

I listened to Cooper's continued sales patter, but the excitement of gentrification had drained from him. He'd made too many promises about safety and old-fashioned this and authentic that, and the group before him had interpreted that as something else, twisting his words into something untrue.

Unless he, too, believed that America would become great again only if . . .

All skinfolk ain't kinfolk.

"Comprehensive security systems in every business," Cooper was saying, his voice faltering. "We do a robust summer here—almost a million visitors a year. And I've talked to the folks behind Coachella down in Southern California, and they're interested in something big like that here. And while Coachella Haven-style would bring in a lot of business—"

"It also brings crime," the vintner pointed out.

"But he's saying we'd have state-of-the-art surveillance at every corner," Tracy Louise said. "Nowhere is one hundred percent peaceful living."

"Yeah," Reginald West said, "I read about that guy who cut up his mother and took a picture of him holding her head. Or the boy found in that Vegas suitcase. Small towns."

"But if something like that happens here," Tracy said, "Cooper's saying it wouldn't be a problem from then on. They have, like . . . fixers? Personal security, right?" She turned back to look at me and grinned. "Like their own little police department—"

"Something better than the police," Reginald said, arms crossed. "They don't have to be nice and worry about protestors and all that shit. Sounds like they take care of the problem quickly and quietly. On the DL, right?"

I smirked at him before turning my focus to Cooper. He no longer had that twinkle in his eye. His lips had turned hard and white. A streak of red burned against his golden cheeks. He kept his sentences short. And he was about to start limiting his word count.

He deserved to be miserable.

I hoped he would never sleep through the night again.

21.

By the end of the month, after I brought the Monroes justice and found his dognapped goldendoodle, Cooper would hate me. That was certain. Because as much as he hated people like the ones in this tour group, he was a capitalist through and through. A whore and a private dancer, if that brought him wealth and influence. He'd build a tougher facade to protect that sliver of compassion that made him a guardian of liberty in any left-leaning organization in America.

Eventually, I fell farther behind, becoming lighter the less I heard Cooper's fabrications. Eventually, I could only see poor Devon Monroe trailing behind the group like the guy who swept up the horse shit in a parade.

"You think he's going to hell, too, don't you?" London Sutton had slipped in to stand beside me, a vape pen to her lips. She was shaking her head as she watched her husband sell away Haven's heart.

"Who am I to judge?" My face burned just looking at her looking at him.

"Oh, c'mon. Be honest." London's cool gaze swept from the group with Cooper to land on me. "He's such a liar but he's so *good* at it. You wanna believe everything he tells you." Her eyes hid behind a cloud of strawberry milkshake–scented smoke.

"Cooper doesn't seem to like his guests," I said, swiping away the appointment reminder text message on my phone for my therapy session tomorrow morning with Dr. Nicole Pugh.

"He can't stand them," she said, tapping the pen against her bottom lip, "but Coop knows that he can't grow Haven on vibes only." Her eyes were the color of an overcast sky, and they glinted like a paring knife—but a knife, nonetheless. Her voice was caramel and question marks, warmth and curiosity, a good night's sleep forever. Yeah, she had a carbon monoxide voice, and she smelled like a fancy candy store. "Alyson? Sonny? Which do you prefer?"

"Sonny. Thanks for asking."

As she pushed away her hair, a charm bracelet slid down her thin forearm.

I had one just like it that matched the multistone filigreed heart pendant I'd listed for $200 on The RealReal. Only worn once. Pristine condition.

"Well," she said, "since we're here and Mason's is down there and it's five o'clock somewhere . . ." She smiled at me. "Please tell me you're a wino."

A moment later, we slid into a plush leather banquette at the farthest window in the back of Mason's. Bathed in the soft glow of amber lights, London and I looked like best friends scheming to catch a cheating husband in the act. The server delivered our cocktails: a greyhound for her and a sidecar for me. "Classic drinks," the young woman said, "just like in the olden days. I love it."

"*Full House* olden days or *Dynasty* olden days?" London asked, her eyebrow arched.

"Both." The server nodded enthusiastically. "My nana watched those shows all the time."

Once the server flitted away, London said, "Did that bitch just call us old?"

I laughed, genuinely amused. "I say we tip her like it's 1988."

London lifted her chilled glass of vodka and grapefruit juice and, I lifted mine, and we toasted. After taking slow sips of our drinks, London asked, "How did you like the tour? I'm guessing not so much since you left before it was officially over."

"I wasn't officially invited," I said. "I'd wanted to talk to Pastor Monroe, so I just walked in the back as we both learned how wonderfully safe Haven is. Never did get a chance to talk to the pastor about his son found dead in this wonderfully safe village."

Heaviness hung between us, and I felt her judgment press against my face.

"Am I wrong?" I asked, my eyebrows now high.

London shrugged. She dug around in her purse, a junky Neverfull filled with tangled charging cords, scrunchies, a copper-colored perfume bottle, and random dollar bills. "You've already made a decision about who we are here." She didn't find what she'd been looking for.

"I mean . . ." I shrugged. "Someone killed Xander and—"

"Killed?" she whispered, sitting up in her seat. "I thought he took his own life."

I sipped my cocktail, wishing for more brandy. "I shouldn't have said that. His death hasn't been formally classified as a homicide. My point is . . . I've been in Haven since Monday evening, and I've talked to people about him and Figgy, and I've heard this kumbaya—*come by here and live your best life in Haven* but . . ."

"It's complicated." She took a long pull from her glass.

"Sure," I said. "Had you met Xander?"

"I did but we'd only had two appointments. I'm a clinical psychiatrist. Lori, his mother, wanted him to keep coming to me for therapy. The move from Oakland really upset him, and he'd become incredibly secretive. Great kid. Between us? I wish his parents had let him finish out his senior year up at Bishop." She sighed. "That's why I didn't blink when someone mentioned suicide. Made sense to me."

"Was he on antidepressants?" I asked, immediately regretting it.

London's eyebrows furrowed. "You know I can't divulge that."

My cheeks burned. "Apologies."

"Tell me about yourself," London said, swirling her drink around the glass. "I know you're from LA, and I know you were a detective. Who are you without a badge?"

I was no one. My badge *was* my identity. But I didn't say that to her.

"And to be honest," she continued, "when Mack told me you drove a Bronco, I couldn't picture you . . . until I saw it."

"FaB," I said, smiling. "She belonged to my dad before he gave it to me."

"And you did the restoration on . . . *FaB*?"

"Fabulous Ass Bronco," I said. "I did—well, I paid for the restoration. I'm not a mechanic type." I winced at the melting sugar on the rim of my glass—I hated sticky fingers and with oil and grime, I'd probably implode. "Let's see . . . I'm a daughter—my mother moved here with me. She's a pastry chef. Owned three shops back in LA. She's starting to experience some dementia, which is one reason I came here. And I've already realized that a new start is more complicated than changing zip codes." I told her about Mom's wandering in the forest back on Tuesday and the security system and guards on the door.

London sipped from her cocktail. "If a quiet environment kept dementia at bay, then only people living in big cities would have it—and we know that's not the case. My mother-in-law, before her death, was struggling with it."

I squeezed the bridge of my nose, then winced because now my nose was sugar sticky.

"Ex-husband?" London asked. "Children?"

"Never been married," I said, throat tight. "Don't have kids. Engaged once. Promised another time. Being in homicide meant long days and late nights at the office."

"I'm sure you had your offers," she said, wearing a conspiratorial smile. "You're very pretty, and even though we've just met, I can say that you're also interesting. Though some men find that an anathema. *Just give me a beej and grab me a PBR while you're up.*"

I snorted. *"Hey, babe. Did you buy another bag of CHEETOS or . . . ?"*

"Ha! Get out of my marriage. Coop loves CHEETOS. And PBRs. And BJs. Ha!"

There was a wistfulness in London's eyes that didn't match her picture-perfect life—a rich husband, an entrepreneurial twentysomething daughter, and—I was guessing—a house that looked straight out of *Architectural Digest.* Did she know that her marriage was just like Haven? Shiny and bright—leave your door unlocked, but once you're inside, some other lady's thong is stuffed in your husband's briefcase, and people hate you and steal your shit.

While I craved normalcy, I didn't crave her life. While I'd shared my bed with a cheater, London Sutton was the one wearing the ring. She didn't know about Cooper and me—I knew that. She wouldn't be sitting here now, splitting a giant pretzel with me if she did.

"Grass always looks greener, right?" I said. "Little do you know that grass is fake."

London laughed. "That deserves a toast."

We clinked glasses. After sipping, she said, "You've met my daughter. You've kinda met my husband. You're looking for our dog. I'm a clinical psychiatrist. The only one in town. Not true—there's Myra, but she's into reiki and astrology, and some folks in Haven can barely stand believing in eclipses. I went to Stanford, which is where I met Coop—"

A phone buzzed, and it was coming from her purse.

She muttered a curse, grabbed her bag, and dumped most of it on the table. "Sorry, but I need to clean out . . ." All those charging cables, that gorgeous perfume bottle—TOM FORD's Vanilla Sex—and scrunchies . . . and her cell phone. She grabbed it and scowled. "All that for an unknown caller."

The server returned. "Can I get you ladies something else?"

"A dirty martini," London said. "Grey Goose. Extra dirty. Three olives."

"A Tom Collins," I said. "Beefeater 24."

Once the server left us, I said, "I hear that you have political aspirations."

"Who told you—oh. *Keely.*" She rolled her eyes. "Yes. I will be mayor of Haven. I've won the game, but now, I need something more. I mean . . . It makes sense. I'm smart. Well connected. I'm honest. I'd definitely be a better mayor than *that* loser. Oops." London covered her mouth. "I'm not supposed to call her a loser since her daughter's missing." Her neck flushed with pink, and she muttered, "Whatever."

I caught London up on the search for Figgy.

She squinted at me and said, "Ask me if I'm surprised. Why should Harvey care what meat people eat? Just buy the freaking ostrich breast, Harv, and mind your fucking business."

"I've done some background on Mackenzie," I said. "Just to—"

London held up a slender hand. "She *was* stalked, and someone *did* vandalize Food Desert. We haven't opened the store since then. I know for a fact that Honor Butler—Keely's daughter—was responsible for both, which is why I also believe her mother may have taken Figgy this time. She's such a fucking gaslighter. Yes, Mack does shit for attention but not this time."

"Oh-kay." My mouth popped closed.

London's lips lifted into a weak smile. "I'm aware of what people think of my kid and sometimes . . ." She shrugged. "But Mack, despite the rich-bitch vibes she gives off, is actually kind and generous, and she can't help who her parents are. If she grew up working-class like Coop, she'd be the heroine of some romantic suspense novel or . . ." She flicked her hand and stared out the window. "Poor thing."

The server dropped off chips and artichoke dip.

Here was a woman who had everything, but appearances masked reality. *He would've never killed his wife. She would've never killed her kids. But he's the youth pastor.*

No, the grass wasn't greener. It's just that you couldn't see all the blood that had seeped into the dirt.

London swirled the skewer of olives around her glass. "It's almost time for me to formally announce my intentions to run for mayor."

"Yeah?" I said. "You prepared?"

"I will be." London was staring at me. "It's gonna get really nasty. But I'm not worried." A shadow crossed her expression before she smoothed it away with another elegant smile.

I said nothing, just arched an eyebrow. Over at the bar, ice clinked into glasses. Men cheered as someone threw a ball at someone else. First dates and an anniversary celebration and a baby screeching and somebody's dog farting beneath a table.

"I'll be coming to Ivan again for another job," she said. "Opposition research."

"Against . . . ?"

"Who do you think?" London used her teeth to pull an olive off the skewer. "And I'd like to work with you, Sonny Rush. I'll only have one opponent, and you've met her. She's awful, but people are patient with her because Honor is missing."

I made another noncommittal grunt and dragged a tortilla chip across the lake of dip.

"She'll drag my business out into the open," London said, "so I should prepare my own folio on Keely Butler. I'll pay whatever you'd be paid if we were in San Francisco."

I blinked at her. "That's a lot of money."

"I'm rich." She nodded to the place outside the window. "And I'll be richer once Coop persuades people to invest in Haven."

"Why run?" I asked. "You have everything you'd ever want."

She made a lopsided grin. "I want to change lives. I want to shape policy. I want people to look at me like they look at Michelle, Hillary, Sigourney, and Meryl and bad bitches who've captured the flag and changed the world." She shrugged. "Isn't that what we *all* want? To make the world a better place while looking incredible doing it?"

I nodded.

"None of this is a secret," London said. "Just how those badass women did it . . . *That's* the mystery. But . . ." Her storm cloud eyes thundered into mine. "I trust you, Sonny, to help me do this. To figure it out. From one future bad bitch to another, you know what you're doing—"

"I haven't found Figgy," I said, chuckling.

"Someone like you shouldn't be doing that kind of work anyway. You don't have to answer now," she said. "Think about it. Your mother's care will be expensive. Coop's mom went through the same thing, and that was before he made a lot of money. Her care nearly bankrupted him." Her face tightened. "I won't ask you to do anything illegal. But if I do, then I'd pay extra."

Would my name come up as the other woman in Keely's deep dive? The thought made a sheen of sweat pebble against my forehead.

"If you become mayor," I asked, "will you keep this required facelift tax for the businesses? The folks I've chatted with are not pleased with having to pay forty dollars a square foot and a twelve percent interest rate on loans."

She shrugged, twirled the olive skewer through the splash of martini still left in the glass. "I'm still thinking that through."

I lifted an eyebrow. "I have a feeling Keely's anti-facelift. During the tour, there were a lot of sour faces watching Cooper." I paused, then added, "Something to think about."

Hearing that made London sit up. "Keely can't become mayor. She's a liar and an awful mother—pretending that she gave a fuck about Honor. She's the worst. Thinks we all owe her because her family helped settle this place. I think the fuck not. We'll be bankrupt and corrupt before her first year ends." She sat back. "And if she wants to talk about legacy . . . My family also helped settle Haven, and we didn't do it by making moonshine deep in the redwood forest."

I choked on my drink and reached for my napkin.

London's hands steepled beneath her chin. "Fucking hillbillies. Drug smugglers. Devil worshippers." She paused, then said, "I don't believe that last one, but the other shit's true."

"But if you know all of this . . . ?"

"I need hard proof," London said. "People have always whispered about Keely's family, and now they're saying Honor ran off with some drug mule, which she's done before."

"This is the same woman who served me vegan chili a few days ago?"

"Yeah . . . I don't think Honor is missing," London's eyes roved the bar, taking in her surroundings and what everybody had in their glasses. Radiant in her effortless elegance. Warm and inviting one moment, calculating and observant the next. Honey and absinthe.

Why did I like London Sutton, MD?

Historically: her defiance against being one thing in Haven was as strong as she liked her cocktails.

Sociologically: no damsel in distress, she was complex, sexy, and independent.

Realistically: she was confident and entertaining. The Scooby-Doo villain of Haven.

What will she do to Cooper and me once she learns the truth?

I didn't know.

I *did* know, though, that she was like Harvey Parrish. She, too, was the ocean, and I wouldn't ever turn my back on her either.

Police Still Investigating Report of Robbery and Shooting at South Los Angeles McDonald's

March 2, 2022

LOS ANGELES — LAPD homicide detectives are continuing to investigate a report of a shooting and robbery that killed college student Autumn Suarez, 19, late Sunday night at a McDonald's on La Brea Boulevard.

The shooting occurred at about 9:15 p.m. at the restaurant in the 3600 block of La Brea Boulevard and

Obama Way according to an incident report released Wednesday by the LAPD.

Police said that Suarez was shot twice in the head by a female with blue braids and a green hoodie who fled the scene in a waiting gold Dodge Charger. The incident report characterized the weapon as a 9mm gun.

The female victim was rushed to Cedars-Sinai Medical Center in serious condition, but she succumbed to her injuries later that evening.

There is no word on what led to the shooting, and no arrests have been made. According to the incident report, police officers searched the area but could not find a suspect or the Dodge Charger.

Anyone with information about the incident should call . . .

22.

Saturday morning brought with it thick fog. But as I drove north on Highway 1—before I could even begin to list types of gems—the fog thinned, and sunshine spread like butter across the blacktop. And then I saw the blue sky and the gray ocean, and ahead of me, there was nothing but a straight road without one curve or bend.

This was not the devil's highway.

Why couldn't all of this highway be straight? Why was it crooked headed back to LA?

My grip loosened, and I unclenched my sphincter and rolled down the windows. I was now driving like I wasn't on my way to court-mandated therapy.

I'd save that list of gems for a true emergency.

India knew many of the health and mental care providers in Sableport. As a medical examiner, she'd performed autopsies on their clients and had shared a courtroom bench while waiting to testify on the stand. "Nikki is super sweet," she'd told me the night before. "She's also discreet. She's lived life. You'll like her."

Feeling swell in a pair of white jeans and a soft-pink lace-cuffed Henley, I glided onto Brayan Street. The glass and coral-colored two-storied office building was nestled behind a phalanx of tall palm trees. Parking in the lot was free, and there was a secret side entrance that didn't alert the world that I had come to see a shrink. I almost looked forward to talking to a stranger for forty-five minutes.

I held my breath as I walked down a pale seafoam green hallway marked every five steps with a new door to a therapist. I stopped at the end of the hallway and the door of Dr. Nicole Pugh. After several big breaths in and slow breaths out, I pushed open the door and entered a waiting room with taupe and cream light wood furniture, framed photos of the Pacific coast, and an administrative assistant who blended in with all of it. The nameplate on her desk told me that she was Gemma Strauss. She smiled her white smile and tilted her blond head and said, "Good morning."

I told her my name and smiled right back at her before plopping into the armchair that faced the door.

Gemma pushed a button to let Dr. Pugh know that her nine o'clock had arrived.

I hadn't checked out Dr. Nicole Pugh on the internet or PeopleFinder—that's because I hadn't planned to call her and schedule an appointment. Compliance, though, had caught me by surprise. India trusted her . . . Then again, India married Tyler, who'd actually cheated on his existing girlfriend when he started dating India. Sometimes, my bestie's judgment could also be shitty.

The door opened, and a white woman with dark eyes, salt-and-pepper hair, and a broad smile said, "Alyson?" She wore a white shirt with French cuffs that I immediately coveted, and her soft-pink espadrilles gave me ideas. Now that I was a private detective, I could wear espadrilles too. That made me smile.

Her corner office was just as calm as her sitting room and as comfy as those pink shoes looked. She offered me a seat on the fluffy brown couch that faced the door, and she took a seat in the adjacent armchair.

I sat on the edge of that fluffy brown couch, even though the simple gesture of turning the sofa so that I, a former cop, could see what was going on around me told me that Dr. Nicole Pugh was the real deal. But I was no longer entranced by the shirt or the soft scent of teakwood puffing from an atomizer on the credenza. I couldn't bullshit her too much.

We danced for a moment: *India is so great. India is so smart. Sableport is so beautiful; seafood here is so fresh.* Then Dr. Pugh offered me her credentials. She earned her BA from Berkeley and her MD from Stanford. She had twelve years of experience working with patients faced with post-traumatic stress disorder and specialized in first responders. She was the proud mother of a Corgi named Stan and had a wife named Lissa. "Not Alissa. Lissa," she said with a wry grin. "What brings you to my office—beyond Judge Swinton's requirement?"

"Did Dr. Molina send you my digital records?" I asked.

"She did," Dr. Pugh said.

"So, you know why I'm here, then." I sounded steady, even though a hurricane was blowing through my head. "This wasn't voluntary. And honestly? After the shooting? I broke. And now, I look forward to you helping me to repair."

Dr. Pugh nodded, her gaze flat. "Repair . . . ?"

I took a deep breath, but my throat tightened even more. "My life, post-verdict. My life post-dismissal. My life dealing with a mother with dementia. Moving to a new town. Breaking up with my boyfriend four days ago." I frowned. "Everything's happening all at once, it seems, and people think I have it together, but I don't have it together, and that makes me anxious, and all this fog brings to surface another issue that I have—that I've already talked with Dr. Molina about—and I thought I was fixed but . . ."

"You don't think you are?" Dr. Pugh said.

"No. Oh, and throw in financial turmoil," I said, squinting. "I think that's everything."

She offered a soft, supportive chuckle. "Well, Alyson—"

"Sonny," I said. "Please."

"We have a lot to get through, Sonny," she said, opening her folio, "but I think everything you mentioned can be sourced from one issue."

"Which is?"

"The reason you're here. We'll figure out the truth. The root. Okay?"

"So, until we figure out the root," I said, "I should keep pretending that I'm fine."

She studied me with a practiced eye. "Is that what you want? To pretend?"

"No," I said, "but I'm pretty good at healing beneath the mask. I'm good at playing my part. Being the good soldier even when I'm being fucked over."

Dr. Pugh waited a beat. "Even though we're not at the answer yet, I encourage you to reduce some of that pretending. I'm here to help alleviate some of your distress, Sonny, and I'm glad you're open to the idea that you *are* in distress. Many first responders think that's a ding on them if they admit that they're hurt in some way. Are you ready to lift that mask?"

"I don't have much of a choice, do I?" My gaze met Dr. Pugh's, and for a moment, my skin chilled as though I wore no clothes . . . until a wave of heat—anger—swept over me.

"Everyone has a choice," Dr. Pugh said, "even when it seems like they don't."

"I've been in therapy for almost a year now," I said, "and as you can see in my digital record, I've never missed a session. I've been trying, and I'm sincere in my efforts to . . . do whatever it is that the powers that be need me to do, to be, or see." I sat back on the couch and tried to swallow the giant burr scouring my throat. "Can you just . . . *tell* me what to do? Like . . . what *actionable* thing can I put on a checklist to actively improve that I can cross off? Like . . . say an affirmation every morning. Or list three good things that happened that day."

"You know that I can't do that." She uncapped her fountain pen and said, "I'd like to do this. At the start of every session, we create an agenda, and first, we'll talk about how you felt—physically—between sessions. Anxiety. Insomnia. Bursts of anger. Lethargy. Then we'll talk about those factors that are fostering your physical distress and why they continue. Third, we'll identify what you'll need to do outside of our time together, and then finally, there will be sessions with just you talking, telling me about what had been happening in your life before the shooting and what has happened since the shooting."

Then she did what Dr. Molina had already done—talked about trauma and its aftereffects. Avoidance. Assimilation. Undoing the event—*I should've done A instead of B.* How trauma doesn't fit with how we see ourselves, how we see others, how we see the world. Overaccommodating the trauma—*I couldn't trust myself.* "And of course," she said, "we'll look back at your childhood. Your father was also a police officer, yes?"

"Yes." My eyes already stung with tears, and I hadn't even really talked yet. "My mother wanted me to become a psychologist," I said, chuckling. "Maybe I should've . . ."

Assimilation.

I jammed my lips together. "I became a cop because I wanted to help figure out the *why*. To help families move from hopelessness to hopefulness. I wanted to be someone my community could rely on. I loved being a homicide detective, and I'd hoped to continue my track, becoming a lieutenant but still doing that thing I loved the most. Finding out the *why*.

"But I don't trust my judgment anymore. And while I'm a private detective now, while there's not an entire city looking at me and evaluating me, I still feel . . . *stuck*."

"Have you talked to anyone lately from the LAPD since leaving?" she asked. "Not as a formality but on a friendship level?"

My throat tightened, and I gave a quick headshake. "My partner, Dak—Dakota Perez—he and I would talk almost every two weeks, but now . . ." I pulled at my laced sleeve. "He got promoted to lieutenant, and the world moves on, right? His son graduated high school back in May, and I sent a gift. Dak left a voicemail. 'Thanks, Al. Bam-Bam loved it. Hope you're well.' And that was that." Tears burned my eyes, and anger bubbled in my belly—I'd got shot in the fog because Dak had stayed in the car ten seconds too long texting some cadet named Cheyenne.

"My captain," I continued, "he'd send me to conferences and to meetings with VIPs. I checked the boxes for The Future of the LAPD. I met the mayor several times—the governor of California twice. I sat in the same ballroom as the president. And then . . ."

Now.

Teardrops slipped down my cheeks, and I snatched tissues from the box on the table. "I didn't choose the solution *they* say I should've selected. But I still don't believe I'm wrong, but I must be because why, then, was I dismissed? Why was I sued? Why did I lose? And why can't I wholeheartedly say that I was wrong? And that's why I'm stuck. None of it makes sense."

I wiped my eyes and held back the sob now pulling at my throat.

Dr. Pugh wrote all of this down while saying, "We'll figure out what's keeping you stuck. In five minutes or less, tell me about one of these traumatic events. The one you think about the most."

"Seeing the body of Autumn Suarez on the tiled floor at McDonald's."

"Thank you for sharing that with me," Dr. Pugh said. "How did it feel sharing that?"

"I felt . . ." I swallowed. "Embarrassed. Stupid. Scared. Anxious."

Then she explained the difference between natural emotions and manufactured emotions.

Natural emotions dissipated with time. Like smoke from a fire dissipated after the blaze had been extinguished. Those emotions—fear, anger, sadness, and the rest—were real, and each emotion's intensity faded with time. Except I didn't want to let those emotions go—I didn't want to feel less afraid, less angry, less sad. So, I revisited those emotions and stoked them, reigniting the blaze, which resulted in them becoming manufactured emotions. Manufactured emotions were fueled with statements like, "I'm so stupid for thinking this was a good decision," or "Why did I do that—it was that dumb." Throwing twigs and kerosene on those emotions right when the fire's about to burn out.

"You keep thinking those thoughts," Dr. Pugh said, "about how stupid you are. By doing that, the emotion—anger, bitterness, fear—never dissipates. It *can't* dissipate—"

"Because I keep fueling the fire," I said, nodding.

"Which means you never recover from your trauma."

And then our time was up. Next time on *Sonny Gets a Clue*: I would write an impact statement about what it means that Autumn Suarez was killed by a woman I didn't arrest. How it changed my beliefs in myself, in others, of the world. How it affected my ideas of safety and trust, competence, intimacy.

I gathered my purse and said, "One more thing." A clock ticked as the room slipped into silence. Anxiety tightened my gut. "Maybe . . . Could you prescribe something for me?"

Dr. Pugh flipped through my chart and studied something there for a long time before looking up at me. "I don't think medication is the answer. Drugs treat symptoms not causes, and we need to get to those causes."

My jaw clenched.

"You don't need medication, Sonny."

Okay, so that's bullshit.

As she scribbled, she asked, "Are you drinking?"

I quirked a smile. "Right now?"

She blinked at me, then said, "You should probably limit your consumption of alcohol."

"Anything else?" I asked, sounding more arch than I meant.

She offered a smile. "This will be rough, but you can do it."

With nothing left to say, I forced myself to smile and say, "Yes, next week at the same time is good," before rushing out and forgetting to say goodbye to Gemma Strauss.

Once I was safely behind the wheel, I pushed out a last breath, and I turned the ignition with a shaky hand. No more fueling the fire. No more manufacturing emotions . . .

I should've arrested Royalty.

23.

I leaned against the chain-link fence that bordered Haven High's football field and watched the team run drills beneath the softening summer sky. Visually, I stood out from the parents in my bright-white jeans and expensive brown skin—and none of them came over to say hi, to ask if I was lost, to figure out if I had a kid joining the team. I also caught a few curious glances from some of the players, grimy and sweaty from practice. *What is a woman like you doing in a town like this?*

One of them, a tall kid built like a man, tucked his practice helmet beneath his arm and approached me with his sweaty blond hair stuck to his scalp. A smaller kid with close-set facial features joined him. This kid wasn't sweaty, and his clean uniform looked like football cosplay, like he had no intention of catching a ball and running up a field from boys as big as his buddy.

"You're here about Xander, right?" the blond said, a bit cocky for talking to an adult. "You his aunt or something?"

I offered a small smile. "Nope, not family. Just a concerned friend who wants answers. The real answers, not the bullshit I've heard so far." I paused, then asked, "What made you think I was his aunt or something?"

The smaller kid blushed. The bigger kid tossed me a cocky smile. "Because you're . . ." He gestured at his own face. "And I met his mom, so I know you're not her. So, I figured . . ."

"Because I'm Black I must be his aunt or something?" I asked, nodding. "That's a wild guess. No, our skin color doesn't make us related." I pointed to the blond kid and then the dark-haired kid. "You two related?"

The dark-haired kid said, "Whatever, man." He looked embarrassed and uncomfortable.

"Practice almost over?" I asked.

The afternoon sun cast long shadows across the field. The marine layer hovered close to the shore, waiting . . . waiting . . . A few more players were heading my way. All big white kids. Loud-talking. Cussing. The only obvious diversity was the flavors of Gatorade in their bottles. The team surrounded me—those towering boy-men, all eyeing me with a mix of suspicion and interest.

"She's asking about Xander," the blond said, then caught up his teammates.

A few of the mothers wearing capris and Haven High T-shirts were now standing in the bleachers, one hand on their hip and the other hand shielding their eyes as they looked to see who their sons were talking to.

"You a cop?" a red-faced redhead asked.

To the blond, I said, "Now, *that's* a question." To the redhead: "I used to be LAPD, but I live in Haven now. I'm a private investigator."

They looked blank-faced at me.

"I'm just riding around," I said, "getting to know this place. I'm also looking into Xander's death. Trying to figure out who he was on and off the field. I wanna know what you guys thought of him and what you think happened. No one's in trouble. I don't have a badge."

"Do you have a gun?" a linebacker asked.

I nodded. "Hell yeah."

"What kind?"

"My fun gun or the fuck-around-and-find-out gun?"

Laughter.

"Did you guys talk to the cops yet?" I asked.

They all said, "Nope."

"Coach called us Tuesday morning," the redheaded kid said.

"Xander could play some ball, dude," the blond kid said. "He owned the field."

"And you are . . . ?" I asked.

"Hunter," he said. "Senior class. Starting quarterback. Practiced a lot with Xan. We had to know each other more than anyone else out on the field. We're both competitive. He fuck up, I pick him up. I fuck up, he picked me up. I didn't have that before."

Those two positions—quarterback and running back—relied on trust and intuition, thinking what the other thought and understanding the meaning of every gesture. "Must have been a big change, him transferring down here to Haven," I said. "Were you guys excited about him being on the team?"

"Excited?" the redhead said. He told me his name was Ian and that he was also a senior and played cornerback. "Hell yeah! We were bottom league, and then suddenly we had this star who fucking landed in Haven. All of a sudden, Coach is like, practice every day—"

"Cuz people started to care," another player added.

"Even with just practice," Hunter said, "our running game fucking soared. Our passing game fucking picked up. Xander made it work like it was supposed to. He, like, knew when I was gonna hand it off, when I was gonna keep it. We watched some tape of his games from last season. He'd get the ball and just fuckin' . . . *explode* through brick walls."

"He was quick and strong and fucking . . . could catch the ball," Ian said. "We were finally gonna get some points up on the board."

"And scouts were gonna start showing up," Hunter said. "X was already set to sign with UCLA, but he hadn't signed officially yet. Gonzaga wanted him. Michigan wanted him. Fucking Cal Lutheran wanted him. Which meant that there was a chance some of us could get noticed too." He shrugged. "Maybe not for D-I schools but some D-II and definitely D-III."

"Fuck," Ian said, "I'd play for the Lutherans if they gave me some scholarship money."

"So, in a way," I said, "it felt like he was putting Haven on the map, then, for football."

Everyone except the small kid agreed, pride in their expressions.

"Some parents were pissed that he transferred down here." Ian nodded at the small kid. "Especially his dad. 'That kid is taking my boy's place.'" Ian narrowed his eyes. "Xander was, what? Six two, a hundred-ninety pounds?"

"And what are you, Justin?" the blond teased. "Four three and a tablespoon?"

Justin blanched, and his small features grew smaller.

The boys laughed.

"His dad acted like he was competing with Xander," Ian said. "Xan was a beast. They said he was a showboat, but I didn't see that at all. Cuz he had confidence? We all better have confidence going out on the field. I think . . ." Ian clamped his lips together.

Hunter pushed him. "If you won't say it, I will." He turned to me and said, "They called him a showboat cuz he was a Black kid who wore an earring and ran like a fucking gazelle."

"They?" I said.

"Parents," all boys except the dark-haired kid said.

"It's fucked up," the redhead said. "It was like we finally had a shot at something big, you know? Everybody was talking about the games, people were fucking pumped, man. Even kids up in Sableport and Fort Bragg were talking about Xander."

"Scouts would've seen *them* too," Hunter said. "Whoever killed X fucked us all up."

I lifted an eyebrow. "So, you think he was murdered?"

"He sure as fuck didn't kill himself," Hunter said. "We've been around suicidal kids—"

"Two last year," Ian said. "One jumped from the bridge over the waterfall. The other shot himself. They used to smile and pretend everything was good, but their eyes, man. You can tell they were faking cuz of their eyes. Now, when anybody gets that look, we tell Coach."

"X was nothing like them," Hunter said. "He was happy. A little uneasy—some of the parents said fucked-up shit about him during practice. But once he was on the field . . ."

"Not everybody on the team liked him," Ian said. "They thought he was overrated—"

"That he was stuck-up," the linebacker said.

"I heard people say 'thug' a bunch of times," Ian said. "Yeah, right. The kid whose dad is a minister, whose mom is a fucking geochemist—the kid who grew up in Oakland Hills and got an internship at JPL is a thug."

Thug had become shorthand for anyone darker than a dinner roll.

"What about drugs?" I asked. "Could he have OD'd?"

"On what? Toothpaste?" Ian said.

They all laughed. Shaking his head, Hunter said, "We gotta take pee tests every week. If drugs showed up, you get kicked off."

"Even for pain meds?" I asked, eyebrows furrowed.

"For Oxy, hell yeah," the linebacker said.

"What about the other one?" I said, bullshitting. "I can't remember . . ."

"Toradol?" Hunter said. "That one's fine. That's like taking Advil."

"I think she's talking about tramadol," the redhead said.

"Oh, hell no," Hunter said. "It's about to be on the list."

"The list?" I said. "Of shit you can't take?"

The boys said, "Yup."

"You can't take it while playing, or you can't take it *ever*?" I asked.

The boys shrugged. "Depends."

"But that's not happening until next year," Ian said.

Oxy, morphine, and growth hormones were also prohibited.

"From what I could tell," Hunter said, "X didn't use. He didn't get high or drink."

"His daddy woulda kicked his ass," the linebacker said.

"Mom woulda got that pickax," Hunter said. "Drilled that ass."

Everyone except Justin laughed.

The redhead cooed, "You didn't take natural sciences, Justin? See, geologists use pickaxes to dig into rocks and dirt and—"

"I know about geologists, asshole," Justin spat, his eyes hot.

"You got him mad," Hunter said. "Now he's gonna get his dad to kill you next."

Ian smirked. "That was a joke. Harvey is a completely rational guy." He rolled his eyes.

Harvey as in Good Pickings butcher Harvey?

"X and me?" Hunter continued. "We were supposed to drive up to Sableport on Tuesday for some K-tape and mouthguards. Girls loved that guy. They came over to say hi whenever he was around."

The other boys—even Justin—smiled.

"We weren't losers," the redhead said. "For once, people looked at the Bobcats like we were the team to beat. Some asshole fucked it up for all of us." He paused, then said, "Fucked it up even for you, Justin."

"Sounds like Xander made quite an impact in a small amount of time." I filed away each response—and nonresponse—and then nodded to the dark-haired kid. "You haven't said a word, Justin. Any thoughts?" I searched the boy's face for a glimpse of a green-eyed monster.

Justin shrugged. "He was cool with me, I guess. He was a better athlete than me, but my dad didn't care."

"Your dad's been a real asshole," Ian said. "He was before, but he was off the chart the moment Xander stepped on the turf."

Justin chewed his bottom lip, his eyes distant. He opened his mouth to speak, but he didn't get to.

"All right, enough chitchat!" their coach shouted at the gate. He had a body like Tom Brady, a face like Shrek, and a wedding band as wide as Lake Superior. "Let's get back to it!"

Before the boys trotted away, I said, "If any of you wanna tell me more, just stop by Poole Investigations on Seaview. If I'm not there, just leave a message."

The coach eyed me and said, "How are you today?"

"Great." I tossed a smile that made men grin. They stopped thinking once they started grinning. "How are you today?"

The coach nodded, that look in his eye. "Pretty good. Great day to be outside."

As the boys trotted back to the field, the coach looked back over his shoulder and smiled.

At least five of these kids respected Xander, that much was clear, and they painted a picture of a young man who lived for the game, who elevated those around him—a far cry from someone looking for an escape through death.

I needed to dig deeper, peel back the layers, talk to the coach. Maybe make eyes at him just enough that he spilled his guts before snapping out of it. He'd tell me more about the Bobcat parents—and could maybe even tell me who hated Xander enough to kill him.

Though I had a good idea of who already.

I stayed a few minutes to watch more of the football practice from my car.

Justin Parrish was not fast, couldn't handle the ball like he should've, and didn't like being hit. Like for *real* for real. No wonder Hunter and Ian couldn't wait to play that first Friday night game with an athlete as dynamic as Xander Monroe.

The Haven Bobcats football team had spoken about Xander with a mixture of reverence and sorrow—they wanted him there to help push them, to help elevate their profiles and level of play, and to help them meet decision-makers who could change their lives.

If these boys were angry, they weren't angry with Xander. No, they knew Xander's murderer had also fucked them over.

Harvey Parrish, for instance, was a zealous football dad who resented Xander's arrival in Haven. The new kid had become the starting running back as his son Justin rode the pine.

Before leaving the parking lot, I pulled my laptop to the center console and clicked around the internet.

The sizzle reel started with a still shot of Xander smiling that Hollywood smile. His GPA in white letters: *4.13*. There he was in action, shouting, "Let's go, baby!" in his black-and-gold football uniform, running out of the locker room and onto the gridiron, "California Love" by Tupac as the soundtrack. There he was again, green carat over his head like a videogame character—catching, leaping, running, scoring. All of this was intercut with shots of him in the school laboratory, conducting science shit with wires and a microscope, standing by trophies, presenting a PowerPoint slide show on atoms or something. There he was handing out care packages to homeless people, wrapping injured paws on rescues, teaching fitness to school-aged children with disabilities. There he was, back on the football field beneath those hot Friday night lights, winning.

Shit.

The video caught me off guard, and tears burned hot in my eyes and scorched trails down my cheeks.

I got you, Xander.

I closed the sizzle reel and pushed out a breath . . . then another.

I'd already searched around PeopleFinder for background information on Harvey Parrish, but that search had been cursory and not directed in any way to Xander Monroe's murder. Now that I knew that Parrish hated the new kid . . .

I wandered back to the archives of *Haven Voice*, digitally sifting through articles for any mentions of Justin and his father. Every time I clicked, more pieces of the puzzle emerged. There was Justin, beaming as he scored a touchdown in one game last season before Xander had arrived. Another article showed Harvey red-faced and yelling at the referee from the bleachers.

One click on a hyperlink—"Superstar RB Joining Bobcats Football"—led me to a *Haven Voice* article that I'd missed earlier announcing Xander's transfer. ". . . leading rusher the last two seasons at Bishop O'Dowd High School in Oakland, CA . . . 7,200 yards rushing and 82 touchdowns . . . the number one running back . . ." The article was schizophrenic in tone—from excitement about his arrival to angst about transfers like Xander Monroe hurting high school prospects overall.

> ". . . not bitter grapes but a true concern. This is about every kid getting a fair shake," high school counselor Jimmy Whitaker said. "The boys are working hard, but they aren't getting offers because the coaches are all about transfers."
>
> "What would a coach rather have?" Cooper Sutton, developer, said. "A transfer blue-chip running back who comes in ready or a mediocre high school cornerback he has to develop?"

The comments section varied—some were happy with Xander's arrival, and these fans couldn't wait to finally win a championship or even more than three games. They compared Xander's stats to Justin's, and there was no question who the better player was. Other readers called Xander Monroe "overrated" and "nothing but a thug." "DEI has found Haven."

I'd met some of those bigots already. By now, the barista at Deegan's had swapped his usual warm greeting to me for a cool nod. And then there was the redhead at the *Haven Voice* who escorted me out of the building the other day. The cashier at the supermarket didn't speak to me except to say, "Debit?" I was an intruder stirring shit up by asking questions. Someone who'd looked like me had brought violence to Haven, and here I was, spreading that shit around town with my questions and judgments.

In no *reasonable* universe, though, would Justin Parrish ever be considered a football star. In the last season, he'd earned less than one thousand rushing yards, had one rushing touchdown, and had earned the nickname Fumbles. But Harvey Parrish was the president of the

Bobcats' booster club and had personally donated thousands of dollars for travel, equipment, and improvements to the football field. All of this came, of course, with strings attached.

Harvey, the Geppetto to Haven High's Pinocchio, had been interviewed in a *Haven Voice* article and complained that he'd donated so much and said that his son had worked hard for his spot on the team. He ignored the fact that Justin ran the forty-yard dash so slow, he ran it backward. Still, for Harvey, Xander Monroe was given Justin's spot because Xander was Black. The man refused to acknowledge that the Oakland kid ran the forty-yard dash in just under five seconds and was also a straight A student with an interest in physics. After winning a championship for his old team, Xander Monroe had already helped improve his new team's passing game in the few months he'd lived in Haven. Xander had been quoted:

> "I love physics and football, which don't go together. I know what football does to your body. But I wanna take all that I've learned in physics to help make football safer, in helmets and protective gear to even diet and rest." Monroe chuckled and added, "I guess I'm my own guinea pig. Running fast keeps me from getting hit."

I clicked over to Harvey's Facebook page—grilled meats, guns, and football. "Somebody should take that Oakland kid down a peg," and "Somebody needs to show Oakland and his parents that they can't just come in and steal shit from Havenites," and "I can't say none of this because cancel culture . . ."—*blah, blah, blah woke blah, blah affirmative action.*

Yeah, if anyone in Haven hated Xander Monroe, it was Harvey Parrish.

My instincts pulled me toward the butcher-gunner-booster, and those instincts intensified as I read his comments while noticing the "WLM" and "13/90" wrist tattoos that Harvey proudly showed

Facebook world. Approaching Harvey and Justin directly could be a mistake; accusations hurled prematurely often did more harm than good. Yet I couldn't shake the feeling that my instincts were homing in on something insidious that involved Harvey Parrish—and that somehow, he held a critical key to unraveling Xander's untimely end.

PART III

A Havenite's Guide to Crime and Cronies

24.

Butchering meat was only a side hustle for Harvey Parrish. He was also the sole proprietor of Haven's only gun store—Pacific Guns & Ammo tucked away on Whispering Wind Way beside mantaRay's Auto & Bike. The gun store looked benign in its pale-blue Victorian-era clapboard. Its gold-and-black painted sign with old-timey letters conjured memories of barbershop quartets, ice cream in silver dishes, and grilled cheese sandwiches—*not* Berettas, hollow-point bullets, and serrated knives.

The bell above the door jingled as I entered Pacific Guns & Ammo. It smelled of earthy leather and slightly sweet gun oil, like every gun store I've ever visited. Rows of firearms glinted beneath the track lighting with a long wall of rifles and shotguns over there, a short wall of handguns beneath an American flag over there, and gun bags and cleaning supplies over there. Hunched behind the counter, Harvey Parrish was cleaning a handgun, his broad shoulders strained against his red-and-black flannel shirt.

"Can I help—" Once he looked up, he didn't complete his sentence.

"Hi," I said, smiling. "Didn't know you worked here too."

A lie. I knew that he owned the store, employed three other part-time employees, taught shooting classes, and that his father had paid less than a hundred thousand for this plot of land thirty years ago.

"It's my store." He placed both of his hands atop the counter. "What do you need?"

"Ammunition," I said, leaning on the glass display. I wasn't studying the knives featured in this case, even though my eyes were directed there. I was watching Harvey's face in the glass's reflection, and right now, his skin was flushed.

"What kind of ammo?" he asked.

"Nine millimeter." I told him the make and model of my gun. "I also have a service revolver, so I'd need ammo for .45s too." I paused, then asked, "And I see knives here—"

"Wanna buy one?" he asked.

"Oh, no. I already have one. A Spyderco folding G-10."

"Ambitious?"

"Resilience. I like big blades. Anyway, I wanted to know if you sharpened them here."

He blinked at me, then gave a short nod. He was thinking.

Good. He should know that I'm armed.

He turned to browse the wall of plastic clamshells of magazines before selecting one. Then he studied a wall of ammo boxes. He selected a black-and-gold box of bullets and slid it across the counter. "Anything else?"

"Nope," I said. "That's it."

He scanned my purchases. "You planning to shoot something?"

"Hope not," I said. "Just like being prepared. What good is a gun without a bullet? I'm not trying to throw the damned thing, right?"

He grunted.

"Is there a range in the back or somewhere in town?"

"Nope."

A lie. He'd had a range built in the basement of this building two years ago.

"I went over to the high school today," I said. "Spoke to a few players on the football team. They told me that Xander took your son's position on the team. Justin's a running back, right? I think he was one of the boys I talked to."

Harvey snapped his head in my direction. "You can't be interviewing minors without their parents present."

"First, it wasn't an interview. Nor was it talking to any of the boys one-on-one. And also, I'm not a cop, so that rule . . ." I shrugged and shook my head. "Doesn't apply to me."

Harvey's hands stilled, and his jaw tightened. "Football's a competitive sport. Positions should be earned and not just given to people. Boys who've put in the time and money—"

"Xander's parents *have* put in both time and money," I said, "and they're serving this town as a pastor and scientist. From what I've learned, Xander spent a lot of time to become as good as he was."

My shoulders tightened from suppressed rage, and I wondered if I still wore a poker face or if that had also been taken from me along with my badge. "I know you're a little heated about him being on the team. I heard that you were the leader in the anti-Xander group and that you even complained to the school superintendent, which . . . *Wow.* The dedication."

"Football matters to our family," he said.

"I got that," I said, nodding. "Yeah, I was told that you'd do anything to keep Xander off the team so that Justin could take his rightful place back on the field."

"Who told you that crap?" he growled, his composure cracking like thin ice beneath my probing. He grabbed a brown paper bag like it stole his last dollar.

I offered a one-shouldered shrug. "*You* did, actually. I found old articles from earlier this summer. And if you weren't being quoted in the article, you'd left comments that made clear it's what you thought about the new kid."

Nostrils flaring, he glared at me. "Hundred-five dollars."

I fished around my bag and found my debit card, taking some time for my lungs to stop pounding against my ribs.

His face shifted to an alarming shade of mauve, and his eyes narrowed into slits beneath his bushy salt-and-pepper brows. He ran the card with an angry flick. "First, you accuse me of stealing some fucking dog, and now I fucking murdered some kid from the hood?" The credit card machine beeped, and he tossed my card on the display case. "You've got some balls."

I grabbed my bag of bullets and debit card. My breathing had evened out, but my mind still raced. "I haven't accused you of anything. I'm just telling you what I read and heard—"

"You heard that I killed the boy who ruined my kid's life?" he asked, his fists clenched.

"Ruined?" I asked, eyebrow cocked. "I met Justin today, and he didn't look *ruined.* He *did* look miserable, though. His teammates don't respect him. Like . . . not at all." I needed to pull back some, but now, I saw how his purple lips had darkened to plum. This guy was *pissed.*

Harvey threw up his hands. "What did I ever do to you? You trying to ruin me too? Accusations like the ones you're makin' can destroy a man. Just because I expressed my opinion? I can't express my opinion without people trying to cancel me?"

I grimaced at him. "Cancel you? Have I accused you of anything? I can't make observations now? I can't ask questions? That's my job—asking questions. Are my questions making you a little uneasy? Why have you gone to the extreme?"

Harvey realized he was losing it and took a deep breath and unclenched his hands, spreading his fingers across the glass display case that separated us.

"Other than him allegedly taking Justin's spot," I said, "what did you think of Xander?"

"Allegedly?" he scoffed. "There's no question that he did. Coach chose some outsider instead of a native. Oakland probably pissed somebody off down here in Haven, and the bastard let him have it. That's who you need to be harassing."

"Fine. Do you have any ideas who would've let Xander have it?" I met his glare with an icy detachment that rivaled glaciers.

"Ivan sent you here?" Harvey asked. "To harass me like this?"

"I go where I go," I said, smiling slightly. "And this isn't me harassing you."

"Well, why don't you get the fuck out of my store," he demanded. "You got your bullets. Get the fuck out."

I squinted at him. "You didn't say please." My eyes never left his.

Harvey Parrish didn't scare me. Other people in Haven may have jumped when he barked, but I've never been one for jumping.

He pulled in a breath once he saw that, no, I would not be pushed around, that I wouldn't get the fuck out of his store until he either said *please* or put his hands on me. He definitely didn't wanna put his hands on me—an unknown quantity now stomping her shit-thick shoes all over his pristine town.

"Thank you for your business," he said, faux pleasant. "I have work to do. I appreciate your consideration, and I hope the bullets are to your liking. Now, leave. *Please.*"

I held up the bag of ammo and said, "Thanks." Then I turned on my heel and strode out of Pacific Guns & Ammo, aware that I now wore a target between my shoulders.

I climbed back in the Bronco, the leather seat cool against my back, and slowly exhaled. The high of being an asshole was now wearing off, and as always, I swallowed my cocktail of emotions and clenched my trembling hands around the steering wheel.

Harvey peeked out at me through the plate glass window, his head bobbing beneath that flecked gold-and-black lettering.

I pretended not to see him looking and backed out of the parking space, feeling the warmth of a new target forming over my heart.

Zeus, Aphrodite, Venus, Mars . . .

25.

The sun was lost in pearly soup again, but this time, I didn't have to drive in it.

India decided to spend her Saturday evening with Mom and me and drove down to Haven. At a little past five o'clock, she showed up with fried chicken, macaroni and cheese, collard greens, and cornbread muffins. "I know they don't have soul food in Haven," she said, looking refreshed in her black linen pants and cropped black T-shirt. But her grin was too wide—like she needed something to be true. A soft touch, it would take India drinking only two glasses of wine for me to figure out why there were shadows behind her smile, why she couldn't stop staring at her pink-polished toes.

"You need soul to cook soul food," Mom said, also a bit low energy, but she wasn't too tired to bring home a fruit torte she'd baked earlier. Her shoulders rode near her ears, and she moved food from one side of her plate to the other. She wore her favorite shiny purple tracksuit even though it was dusted with flour, even though she had clean versions in red, black, and green.

Wearing comfy sweats and treaded socks to complete my what-the-fuck-ever vibe, I brought my charm and good looks to the dinner table along with two bottles of a 2017 Bengtsson Cabernet that tasted of blackberries and was known for being a little spicy and a little toasty.

After dinner, we retreated to the deck with plates of torte. As we ate, warm air met cool water to make a dense fog that slinked around the trees and made real things into dark smudges.

"You know that's all it is, right?" India asked, seeing me grip my wineglass tighter. "Water vapor condensing—"

"I don't care," I said, the rim of the glass to my lips. "Shit's evil. Can't trust it."

Soon, Mom tottered back into the cottage to take a bath, leaving India and I huddled around the firepit. India escaped into her phone, checking in on Brooke and Sam. "He fed them McDonald's again," she said, sighing. "I don't think he's ever fed them vegetables. Not a salad. Not even tempura. What's-Her-Face is allergic to every fucking thing under the sun. Corn makes her stomach hurt. Peas make her stomach hurt. Green beans give her hives. She's good with beets, though."

"Phew," I said, wiping fake sweat from my forehead.

"Everything okay with Mom?" India asked.

I shrugged. "I'm just worried that she's pretending. Last year this time, Val Rush would've *never* worn that dirty tracksuit to dinner. And then sometimes, I forget that she forgets because she makes . . ." I wave to the torte on the platter. "Beautiful desserts."

"She feels safe in that tracksuit," India said. "It's familiar and brings her comfort."

"And that's fine," I said. "But it needs to go into the washing machine."

India didn't respond immediately—then: "Has Cooper finally sent help?" She peered at me over the flames.

I tapped my foot against the deck and tapped my fist against my lips. "No, and he was supposed to do that back on Tuesday night. He says he wants to talk again first. I go hours thinking I don't need shit from him, but then around midnight, my strength and fortitude become a pumpkin, and I'm picking up the phone to text him and say send it or else. I don't know how long I'm giving him until . . ."

"Until what?"

I shook my head. "Dunno."

The fog was now rolling lower over our heads, and I dared to reach high and drag my fingers through the clouds.

India sat up in her chair. "Oh! You'll love this." She showed me a picture of a blue Porsche Carrera.

"That's hot," I said, squinting at the picture of the two-seater sports car.

"It's Tyler's," she said.

I snorted. "No, it's not."

"And you're probably saying 'No, it's not' because he now lives in a one-bedroom apartment, even though he has two children." India humphed and sat back in the chair.

"He bought a two-seater Porsche while living in a one-bedroom apartment?" I asked, eyebrows high.

"Make it make sense," she said, shaking her phone. "Brooke sent that picture to me on my drive down. And Kimberli-with-an-*I* is *impressed*? Then again, Kimberly-with-an-*I* is happy because he owns an air fryer and a blender."

"And you had kids with that man?"

India held up two fingers and mouthed, "Two kids." She reached into her bag for a manila envelope. "I'm still waiting for a few results, but . . ."

"Is this from the pill and syringe I dropped off?" I asked, taking the envelope.

Autopsy Results—Xander Monroe

My eyes skipped around and settled on *Evaluation*.

> The body was found in the woods . . . on his right side . . .
> Leaf litter, twigs, insects (ants, rare spider, and rare beetle).
>
> All teeth, including all wisdom teeth, were present.

> Examination of the soft tissues of the neck, including strap muscles, revealed injury described above . . . The skin at anterior right aspect of the neck had a poorly defined elongated contusion measuring 0.5" x .25". Dissection of the neck revealed a small, round puncture wound in the soft tissue . . . Lateral abrasions on his back consistent with dragging . . .

I flipped the page to *Radiology Consult.*

> *Premortem skeletal fracture in the right foot.*
>
> TOXICOLOGY FINDINGS (*S*eparate report pending)
>
> HEART BLOOD, ALCOHOL—Negative
>
> HEART BLOOD, DRUG TEST—ibuprofen, tramadol, nicotine

"The tramadol and nicotine?" India said. "Extraordinarily high levels. Like instant death for that amount of nicotine. And that pill you found off the trail? Tramadol."

Tramadol—the opioid that reduced pain perception. The Haven Bobcats had mentioned that drug. Some bad shit and so addictive, it had been banned in the UK and a ban was scheduled to go into effect in the US next year.

Did Xander Monroe have a legit prescription? And if so, what was the dosage? Would a pediatrician or even an orthopedist prescribe tramadol to a seventeen-year-old?

India leaned forward. "Did you find out yet if Xander smoked?"

I shook my head. "I'm having lunch with the Monroes after service tomorrow. I'll find out a lot more then."

"There was a fucking ton of tramadol in his system," India said. "Definitely too much for an aboveboard prescription, even if the kid was built like a man."

I continued scanning the report and then stopped. "What's a turret spider?"

"Don't know anything about them," India admitted.

Back to the report.

White soil. Evergreen huckleberry. Bishop pine. Poison oak. Xander's mouth and nose had been covered in this debris. The huckleberry and pine needles had been found in his hair. Flakes of poison oak found on his mouth and nose.

I sensed the heat of India's gaze. "What?"

Her eyes bore into mine. "I know you want to solve this case. To be Superman again."

"Of course I do."

"Just remember why you have this in your hand." She leaned forward, elbows on knees. "Remember that there are people behind this report, and their boy is in one of my freezers."

That directive chilled me. Not that I had forgotten about Xander—I'd been immersed in his case all day—but investigating required you to squint a lot, and if you squinted too much, you couldn't see that dead kid nor their family. Just breadcrumbs like the ones in this report.

"You can buy liquid nicotine anywhere. Smoke shops." I nodded to myself, thinking. "Maybe he wasn't dying quick enough for someone's liking. For instance, the person he was with that morning. So, they brought that syringe I found and—"

"How would they get that close to him, though?" India asked, checking her text messages.

I closed my eyes and thought about that question. Once I knew, I looked at her. "Because she hugged him and that's when she probably stuck him in the neck."

"She?" India squinted as she thought about it. "But there are no indications it was a *she*. Could be a *he*."

"My point is," I said, "someone he was intimate with—someone he trusted—wielded a syringe full of liquid nicotine." I paused, then added, "Who would have access to tramadol?"

"Doctors, nurse practitioners, orthopedists . . ."

"Coaches anxious for their star running back to heal?" I asked, eyebrow cocked.

"That broken right ankle."

I shook my head and added Coach Wes Oakley to the list of suspects. "I know that's what you found, but I'm still gonna say that's impossible. He was running when he died. If his ankle was broken—"

"We found wads of K-tape that came off in his sock," India said. "That tape probably kept everything together. The tramadol reduced the perception of the pain he probably felt. Most likely, he wasn't as quick as he was before he broke it—"

"Like, how long ago?" I asked, looking at the notation near the diagram's right ankle.

"Maybe two months ago. How he broke it is still a question for you and Ivan. Maybe you can ask his parents tomorrow."

"A blue-chip athlete on pain meds," I said, my victim's profile filling out even more.

Xander, the new kid, a football player trying to navigate the treacherous waters of high school hierarchy and small-town politics, now a victim of something that seemed increasingly complicated—and adult. This derailed my theory about Harvey . . . unless Xander was dating a daughter of Harvey's. That wouldn't go over well with a man who had "13/90" and "WLM" tattoos.

I needed to talk to the Monroes—about Xander's injury and treatment, about his love life.

"Be careful, Sonny," India warned, her gaze steady. "Between the white supremacy tattoos and murder, shit's nutso in Haven. Remember: You don't have all the information. Remember: You're not wearing a cape anymore. They took it from you. Fly close to the ground."

I released a breath I didn't realize I'd been holding. "Kwon and McCann have everything you've given me?"

India tilted her head. "They have more."

I blinked at her. "Ah." Because I was no longer a law enforcement officer.

"But they're dragging their feet," India said. "I sense the bubbling of hot shit."

As though hot shit would stop me.

I stared at the ankle fracture on the X-ray and traced the white line with my finger. "Was it healing?"

"Maybe, but he was reinjuring it by running and not resting. Disobeying the laws of physics." She paused, then asked, "Do you think the nicotine was intentional? Whoever had it wanted to kill him? Could he have taken it himself? Or used it since liquid nicotine has benefits."

I grimaced. "Benefits?"

"Alertness. Relaxation. Reduced anxiety. Euphoria. Improved memory—"

"Don't know." I reached over to my left ear, and yeah, *physically*, I could've positioned a syringe to shoot up. I flipped back to the diagram of Xander's back. I pointed to the lines up and down his back. "These?"

"Abrasions," she said. "I didn't include the pictures of that, but you've skinned your knee before, and that's how those marks looked. But not as mean, not as bloody."

"Which confirms what we thought before," I said. "That he was dragged after he died?"

India nodded. "Most likely. His blood had coagulated by the time he was moved. And there would've been some blood but not a lot. It didn't really stain his shirt so it's not like he'd been experiencing heavy bleeding while alive."

Someone had pulled Xander's body across the trail and left him in the poison oak.

"Xander was 190 pounds," I said. "Six two. You're strong. Would you be able to drag someone that big through the forest?"

"I want to say no, but . . ." She shrugged. "Maybe there was more than one person doing the dragging."

My head ached from all of this talk of death, and as I walked India to her car, I exhaled again. My gratitude for having all of this information bucked against my new reluctance of sharing any of this with Devon and Lori Monroe. The revelation about the drugs would be a blow—families were never prepared to hear how little they knew about their children's lives.

Was I ready to step back into the hurricane of grief and anger that would come once the drug details emerged? I had to be, even though my recent past had taught me to tread carefully around sorrow. I still wore the scars from Autumn's death—scars that also reminded me why I was fighting in the first place.

To find the *why*.

26.

Never did I think, on God's green earth, that I'd *choose* to walk Seabreeze Trail in the morning fog *again* while investigating a murder. Yet, here I was for the second time, surprising myself. This time, I was armed with the holstered Glock beneath my hoodie and sheathed knife against my ankle. My boots crunched against the gravel, an even crisper sound since nothing else around me was crunching. The twisty dirt trail that disappeared into the mist—through a grove of pines, past a pygmy forest, over a bridge, and into another grove—made me tighten. My will, though, stayed loose enough to grab my gun if I needed it. So far, it was me, this fog, and this feckless Sunday morning sun.

After my first visit to this site, I had questions. Now, most of them still hadn't been answered. There were just more questions, like where, on this trail, did Xander collapse? Where had he been dragged from? What is a turret spider?

There had been light-colored dirt on his lips. I'd never seen that color soil before, even as I scanned the forest floor looking for it. Before leaving the office earlier that morning, I'd downloaded pictures of huckleberry leaves and bishop pine needles—some of the debris that the forensics team had collected from Xander's body. I walked slower than before as I checked my printouts of those leaves against the trees and shrubs.

The fog thickened the deeper into the forest I walked. The woods were awake, and invisible creatures skittered and chattered, chirped and cawed.

My neck bubbled with sweat, not from anxiety this time but from walking. I hadn't hiked since New Year's Day—I'd felt too exposed, my face too familiar to those who knew about the wrongful shooting case. Sometimes, passing hikers had given me a thumbs up. "You're one of the good ones," and "You didn't make that girl shoot her," and "They had to throw somebody under the bus. Why not the Black woman everybody liked?" Other times, a passing hiker would call me "sellout," and "baby killer," or "pig." One burst of spite was akin to a single milligram of ricin, and so, I kept my ass at home and poked open the wound that had started to heal. Just like Dr. Pugh had observed.

Oh, yeah. I need to start that assignment.

I reached Xander's death site and peered at leaves and shrubs, trees and soil. I sifted through the printouts to remind myself that instead of webs, turret spiders built small towers—*turrets*—on north-facing slopes in moist woodlands and near shady streams.

Once I reached Xander's resting place—balloons, stuffed animals, flowers, and electric candles marking the spot—I slowly rotated, searching for those non–redwood tree needles and that light-colored soil that had made it onto India's stainless steel table. Maybe Xander had cut through the forest, going off trail?

My phone vibrated with an Instagram notification. I'd asked to be alerted anytime someone posted specific hashtags, including #mendocinocoast, #mendocinocoastcyclists, #mendocinocoastline, #mendocinocoastaltrail, and #mendocinocoastseabreezetrail. Last night, I'd tried combing through every profile with these hashtags and logged off after viewing the hundredth picture of waves crashing against the shore. It was a long shot, but maybe someone who'd regularly posted had uploaded pictures of this part of the trail, capturing something or someone on the morning Xander died.

@amberwavesofgrain had posted about completing her morning run of Seabreeze Trail. But at that moment, there was no sweaty brunette wearing pink running shorts and a white Cal Poly T-shirt at my location.

> Don't stop won't stop! Haven't missed a morning yet! Ready for #baytobreakers2024! #mendocinocoastseabreezetrail

She hadn't missed a day yet. Did that include the early hours of Tuesday, August 1?

I swiped through @amberwavesofgrain's shots of the coastline and bright-blue waves, beagles on bluffs, wildflowers on bluffs, stories and recorded Live posts, and trail selfies—a post for each date.

Foggy morning shots on the morning of Tuesday, August 1.

Just like that, my knees weakened—the long shot was working so far.

The photo on August 1 was just the first of seven shots @ amberwavesofgrain had taken. A spot of low-growing trees with a trail slinking between them. The trail . . . Light-colored soil.

The trees where I stood now weren't small in size like the trees in the IG posts—I couldn't see the tops of the trees in my world. In @ amberwavesofgrain's post, there had been a span of blue sky. The sky in my world right now was obstructed by tall trees.

Where was she? Where were those short trees?

I tapped "Follow" beside @amberwavesofgrain's profile name, but then that circling circle of circling doom found me. Crap. I had just one and a half bars of reception. I'd have to wait for a more robust connection to finish swiping through @amberwavesofgrain's posts.

Back at Xander's memorial, I took pictures of poison oak, ferns, and the moss-covered log. I recorded video, slowly turning to capture my location, zooming in on spiders and creepy-crawlies on that log and in the soil. I snapped more photos and captured more video of the sky.

After recording all that I could, I bowed my head and closed my eyes. *Be with the Monroes. Comfort them. Open the minds of those who search for answers.*

I studied that picture of Xander wearing his former high school's black-and-gold football jersey. "We're looking, Xander," I whispered. "We're trying to figure it out."

After slowly exhaling, I started walking south again. The dirt never changed from dark soil to white soil. No creeks or brooks babbled nearby. I stopped in my step since Xander hadn't walked this far.

Open the minds of those who search . . .

Back in my truck, three bars popped up on my phone, and three is always better than one and a half. I tapped "Follow" beside @ amberwavesofgrain's bio and swiped to the second picture of her August 1 post: foggy—the beginnings of a growth of trees ahead, the dark-tan dirt trail beneath, the shoreline, and a ribbon of white water waves barely visible through the mist. The third picture: the trail with trees on one side and a sloping meadow on the other. The fourth was video: @amberwaves talking—*unmute, Sonny, shit.* I started over again.

"Hi guys. It's six a.m. Hardcore, right?" Her voice was high-pitched and singsong. "It's the first day of August. Woo-hoo! To date, I've run two hundred and ninety-three miles. Let's get to three hundred!"

What was that behind her?

I replayed the video, paying less attention to @amberwaves and focusing on . . . *him.*

In the background, a man had run past her.

"Shit." I started the video again and paused it the moment the figure appeared just to the right of @amberwaves.

The pausing was blurry, but I could see that the tall figure was a Black male—gold shorts, black T-shirt, black running shoes. He'd jogged from left of the screen to the right and into the grove of trees. He had to be Xander.

The next video: @amberwaves grinning, tears in her eyes. Still standing on the light-colored soil trail.

"Hey, guys. It's six thirty, and I'm just about to hit mile three hundred! I'll do a Live when I'm about to cross so you can celebrate with me!"

Another person—another runner—had now jogged in the same direction as Xander.

I tapped to replay the video. A white woman wearing a black cap. Her hair had been in a bun, so I couldn't tell the color. She'd worn orange running shoes. Age? Couldn't tell. Face, a blur. Thin. One more time, and that viewing offered no more than what I'd already observed. Where was *this* location?

I swiped to the final post for August 1. A video of the trail ahead and the bridge that crossed over the dried creek bed. @amberwaves huffing and puffing and then: "Hey, guys. It's six fifty! On the other side of this bridge? Three hundred!"

Just ahead would be that log, that poison oak, those ferns.

@amberwaves had crossed the bridge and slowed down to hold up the phone. Her face was pink and sweaty, and her eyes shone with tears.

"I can't believe it. Three hundred miles! Thanks, guys, for supporting me. I can't believe it. These are tears of happiness. I never thought I could do it. I'm gonna catch my breath."

She was breathless as she started a slow jog, passing that log, that poison oak, those ferns—getting closer and closer. *Keep walking, @amberwavesofgrain.*

"Think I'm ready to run almost eight miles for Bay to Breakers?"

Walking and huffing.

Closer . . . closer . . .

"Who's coming with me? It's not a marathon, more marathon-adjacent."

She laughed.

Closer . . . closer . . .

"Just cuz I hit three hundred doesn't mean that's it. Don't stop, won't stop. Peace."

She stopped and threw up peace fingers.

Right behind her—maybe seven paces—that poison oak, that log, those ferns. Had she run past where the memorial was now? Had she seen anything strange?

She'd crossed the bridge at 6:55 a.m. An hour and fifty-five minutes before Ace found Xander.

Had Xander already been dead and left at that log?

Besides the Black male and white female, no other joggers had passed through @amberwaves's videos.

I tapped on the posts for August 2—a chronicler like @ amberwavesofgrain would certainly mention the discovery of a body that she'd run past the day before. She'd be tearful and would probably regret not paying closer attention.

There she was, smiling. The caption:

> Hey, guys. Same time, same place. Ready to grind. This will be my last day doing this trail. I'm a little bored with . . . such beautiful and peaceful surroundings. Ha. #spoiledrotten.

No mention of the tragedy. No breathless mention of a teenager found off this trail.

So, I doubted whoever had dragged Xander to the log had crossed this bridge. Too exposed. Too unpredictable. The monster had to have dragged him through the growth on either side of the trail. How long had that taken?

Yeah, I needed to go off trail, but I hadn't dressed in protective gear. How much poison oak grew around that part of the forest? And also, I'd sure as hell get lost. The only *woods* I knew were Inglewood and Brentwood. Maybe Giovanni and Elliott could bring me back. Ivan wasn't a hiking type but maybe if the case dictated that he needed to be . . . If no one joined me, then I'd choose the nuclear option—asking Cooper. Or . . .

I tapped the message button for @amberwavesofgrain. Since she didn't follow me, my message would remain in requests. Maybe she'd check her inbox this morning before I left the trail. So, I typed a message saying that I wanted to know more about her running journey, about the morning of August 1, that I would be sitting in a slate-blue classic Ford Bronco in the parking lot at the one-mile mark. That I'd stay there for thirty minutes more.

I swiped through her posts again, replaying that video of the Black male running past her.

Vibration. A response from @amberwavesofgrain.

I charge 75$ for interviews
If your interested in talking farther
my Venmo is @@amberwavesofgrainrunning

"First of all," I said to the phone, "it's *further*, not 'farther.' *You're* not 'your.'"

Second of all, absolutely not. Paying for interviews was never a good idea, especially if this case were to reach the court. If I took the stand, I'd have to admit that I paid @amberwavesofgrain for information, which suggested that the runner would say anything for a person who paid them to cooperate.

I had to find another way to convince her. I glared past the windshield, then tapped:

I can't pay but I'll buy you coffee

Please talk with me

75$

I'm a detective

Don't make me take this FURTHER

Ellipses bubbled on the screen, then stopped, bubbled and stopped.

I returned to the post with the female jogging behind @amberwaves.

Orange running shoes, just as Jairo noted. Did she know Xander? Had she met him before? I still believed that someone he trusted had come close enough to him for that needle jab. But if she killed him, *why*? The video couldn't tell me how strong she was, but she looked athletic enough. To drag a nearly two-hundred-pound dead man, though?

I swiped back over to the messages. No response from @ amberwavesofgrain. By the time I reached the office, my inbox was still bereft of new messages.

Fine

Enjoy your secrets for now

Don't want to bust you out with what I know about you

but I will

Please talk with me

Or else.

Not cooperating would cost the would-be marathoner more than seventy-five dollars.

She didn't know me. And I knew nothing about her. *Yet.* But I had my ways.

"Don't stop, won't stop."

27.

I opened my laptop and popped into my Instagram inbox again.

Still no message from @amberwavesofgrain.

I swiped over to her profile and—

The lock icon. *This account is private.*

Since when? And did she do this because she didn't want to talk to me? If so . . .

Brava.

I now had no way of tracking her movements through her posts. Worse, I had no access to the video that she'd recorded on August 1. Pissed, I plopped into one of the waiting room's armchairs. For a Sunday, I'd already exhausted myself enough for it to be a Wednesday. Rubbing my eyes, I aimed the remote control at the television, and after clicking through, I landed on *Indiana Jones and the Temple of Doom.* Appropriate.

The bell above the front door jingled. A woman with lank dark hair and too much eyeliner crept across the threshold. Her thin lips were already downturned, her raccoon eyes already red. Her gaze darted over to the TV and then landed on me. "Are you Alyson Rush?" Before I could respond, she flicked her hand. "Stupid question. Of course, you're Alyson Rush. I'm wasting time."

I slowly pushed up from the armchair. "And you are?"

She peeped back at the door. "Can we talk away from the windows? Out of the open?" She rubbed her lips against her left shoulder.

"Sure," I said, "as soon as you tell me who you are." Her twitching made me nervous.

"Ruthie Parrish, okay? Harvey's wife. I guess."

I blinked at her. "You guess."

Ruthie clutched her battered canvas purse to her chest. "Can we—"

I grabbed my folio and laptop and led her to the loft.

She was thin—too thin—and moved like a startled bird walking the shore, surprised every time sea-foam touched her toes. Her poor fingernails had been nibbled to the quick, but she hadn't given up on that poor left thumb. Ruthie didn't want coffee. Ruthie didn't want to sit. Ruthie wanted to tell me something.

"Go ahead . . ." I flipped to a clean page in my notepad.

"Harvey wasn't home that morning," she said, her voice thick with barely contained panic. "The morning they found that dead Black kid on the trail."

"Oh?"

She rubbed that raw left thumbnail against her lips. "He lied to you and to the other detectives. But that's what Harvey does, okay? He hates people, and he lies. I should know."

I cocked my head. "Do you have an idea where he was the morning of August 1?"

She nodded. "Either fucking around on me or doing some other dastardly shit."

Dastardly shit.

"And I found this in his car." She reached into her bag and pulled out a pink dog collar.

Figgy also wore a pink dog collar.

"We don't have a dog, okay?" Ruthie said, squinting at me. "Do you understand what I'm telling you?"

I squinted back at her. "Are you saying . . . ? He stole the Suttons' dog?"

She shrugged. "I just know that something's going on with that fucker, okay, and no one believes me, and I need you to believe me because people think I'm in on his evil ways. I'm not, okay? He scares me sometimes, so I don't fight back, but that's not because I'm his evil queen. Take it."

She dropped the collar on top of my computer.

On the collar's inside, one black-inked word: FIGGY.

"I'm still looking around his man cave for hard evidence to prove what he did to that kid," Ruthie said, "but that may take me a moment, okay? Baseball's on." Before I spoke, she said, "I need to go," and hurried back down the stairs.

As I parked in front of the Monroe family's house, I was still thinking about the woman who'd dropped two stones into my lap: Harvey's false alibi and this pink dog collar. But I needed more than Ruthie's suspicions and chewed fingernails. Making a false accusation against the butcher would cost more than just my reputation and my job—it would wreck any movement toward justice for the Monroe family.

The flagstone walkway at 1 Oyster Road led to the Monroes' brown ranch-style home with newish landscape and modern windows. The air smelled of ocean and garlic, and my stomach growled.

Have I eaten today?

The Monroes' invitation to lunch had also come with an invitation to attend the next church service. But I didn't plan to, nor did I want to go to church. I'd had faith that Royalty Miller would change her ways after I'd caught her stealing. I'd had faith that I'd made the right decision to not arrest her. I'd had faith that I wouldn't possibly be blamed for Autumn Suarez's murder and that my bosses would see that I'd sought to do the right thing. I'd had faith that my previous commendations would save my job and that the powers that be wouldn't really make me turn in my badge. I'd been wrong about all of that—and my faith became irrevocably broken after making that first payment to settle Autumn Suarez's wrongful death suit. Yeah, I was on a break from church and faith. Maybe one day, my faith in people would replenish and grow to be the size of a mustard seed.

I stood in the Monroes' home—the ocean glistening a hundred feet away from the back deck—breathing air scented from fresh-baked bread and lemon furniture polish. High ceilings. Blond wood floors. An open floor plan. Pictures of their family on the mantel, every space occupied by cards and flowers from Xander's former high school and the Monroes' former congregation. Casserole dishes covered the coffee table in the living room. A Bruin teddy bear and matching blue and yellow flowers sat in the middle of the coffee table. I saw nothing obvious from Haven High School's Bobcats football team.

Lori, barefoot, wore a cornflower-blue fleece sweat suit. She looked gray and flat. Her hair was curled but didn't believe it. Though red-rimmed from crying, her eyes held both hope and caution.

"You have a lovely home, Dr. Monroe," I said.

She whispered, "Thank you. And please. Call me Lori." As she sat across from me at the table, she tried to smile, but the sparkle of gratification and pride never moved past her lips.

Pastor Monroe offered us glasses of white wine.

"Thank you, again, Pastor—"

"Devon," he said.

"Thank you, Devon, for inviting me," I said, then sipped. The wine plucked my taste buds. So good. So cold. "Sauvignon blanc?"

"Viognier," Devon said, sitting at the head of the table. "Lori's favorite."

"You must bring your mother next time," Lori said. "Warning: Church here isn't like eleven o'clock service back in Oakland. Our friends up north have been sending people to help me clean and cook, keep track of bills and everything . . . And Haven Methodist . . . Well, the congregation has been very . . . nice to us."

Over smothered chicken and rice, cabbage, and yams, we talked about everything except for Xander. I told them about my life in Los Angeles, the struggles my mother faced, our move to Haven, my connection to Ivan. Dessert was blackberry cobbler and coffee. Then there was nothing else to eat that would delay the conversation.

"The detectives emailed us an update," Lori shared, "but I couldn't understand it, and Devon couldn't understand it. We're just exhausted. So, I'm sending it to you." She forwarded the email from Detective Kwon.

Preliminary toxicology and autopsy results. I could tiptoe less now that I knew about their son's state at death.

"I went out to Seabreeze Trail twice now, including this morning," I said, "around the time Xander ran every morning. And after talking to the medical examiner . . . Umm . . ."

"Please tell us," Devon said. "I know Xan had secrets. Every kid has secrets. We'll find out everything anyway, so at least you can prepare us for that."

My eyebrows furrowed. "Your son and drugs? Did he take any?"

"Absolutely not," Lori said, shaking her head. She looked to her husband. "Right?"

"Pain relievers," Devon said. "Football injuries."

"Those aren't like *drug* drugs," Lori said, rubbing her eyebrow.

"The tests came back showing a lot of tramadol in his system," I said. "Like he'd been taking it for a very long time. Also, the autopsy showed that his right ankle was fractured."

The couple looked at each other, and Devon dropped his eyes.

"He broke his ankle earlier this summer," Lori said, "at a practice he wasn't supposed to be attending but somehow found his way there."

"Lori," Devon grumbled.

"Don't," she snapped. "He told me, and *you* told me that he was better. He told me, and *you* told me that he'd take it easy until it was time for preseason practices to really start up. You both lied to me."

Devon kept his eyes on his empty wineglass.

"Did Xander use e-cigarettes or vape?" I asked.

"No," Lori said, "unless he did, and that was also kept secret." She glared at her husband.

"He didn't smoke," Devon said.

"Liquid nicotine was found in his blood," I said.

Both parents looked at each other, eyebrows furrowed, perplexed.

"Would you mind letting me look around his room?" I asked.

A moment later, I hurried back to my truck for my evidence collection kit and returned to follow Devon down a brightly lit hallway to the first bedroom on the right. The door was open, a rare thing. Many families walled off this space—to keep something in, like the last sprays of perfume or the scent of ketchup from that last order of french fries.

Xander's room was one of the neatest boy's bedrooms I'd visited. Posters of Neil deGrasse Tyson—autographed—and Carl Sagan hung on the wall along with pictures of Marshawn Lynch and Christian McCaffrey. Ribbons, trophies, and certificates everywhere. He had enjoyed a view of that ocean.

I took pictures of all of it.

"What did the other investigators collect?" I asked, taking pictures. "His phone? Any school notebooks. Diaries?"

Devon shook his head. "They only took his iPhone."

I peered at him, keeping my face neutral even as my brain screamed at Kwon and McCann for being so fucking lazy. "Would you mind if I looked through some of his things? Take a few items if they spark a question? If the investigators need it, I'll bring it all back."

"Of course," Devon said. "They should've taken more, right?"

I pulled on latex gloves, not wanting to ding the investigators but *goddamn*. "I'll be sure to make a list."

Boys rarely kept diaries, choosing, though, to write rap lyrics or spoken word poems in notebooks. Now, in Xander's desk drawers, I found notebooks filled with comic book panels, scratched-out origin stories for a character called PhizX in neat handwriting that sometimes became slanted, hurried, and cramped.

I opened his closet—a neat walk-in, the clothes and shoes organized by color. Hanging near the back of the closet: his knapsack and gym bag.

I didn't know what I was looking for, but whatever it was would most likely be in one of those bags.

The backpack smelled of Starbursts and pencil shavings. A half-eaten bag of Flamin' Hot CHEETOS, phone cords, dried-out pens and . . . *a condom*. Lambskin with spermicide typically cost ten dollars each. Who had he bought expensive rubbers for? There was no sign of a girlfriend in this room, though. No coupled-up pictures of him and a girl at a school dance or an amusement park. No withered roses. No teddy bears.

I grabbed the practice bag from the closet hook and held my breath, preparing for the olfactory horrors of a man's gym bag. Sweaty, musky, cheesy . . .

Yeah, there was that, but there was also a baggie of yellow-and-green capsules with *T50* imprinted on each. I took pictures of the baggie and close-ups of the pills themselves. Then I dipped my hand back into the bag and . . . A black flip burner phone. A burner still charged at 12 percent. Why would he need it when he had an iPhone? Dealing drugs? Maybe talking to someone he shouldn't be calling? Like the female on the other end of that lambskin spermicide-lubricated ten-dollar condom?

I opened the phone and scrolled through Recent Calls. None of these numbers meant anything to me, but there was a pattern. Only four phone numbers had been called or received. I searched the bag but couldn't find a charger. "Kwon should've found this," I whispered, frustrated.

"Everything okay?" Lori now stood in the doorway, sipping from a glass of red wine.

"Did you know that he had . . . ?" I held up the phone and the baggie of capsules.

Her eyes widened but then softened. She shook her head.

"Did Xander have a girlfriend?" I asked.

Lori narrowed her gaze. "There was a girl . . . He said he wasn't ready for us to meet her yet. They were just hanging out, he said. I knew she was Mackenzie Sutton, who's like, what, four years older than him. Why are you asking?"

Hands shaking, I showed her the condom. I didn't expect to hear Mackenzie's name in this house nor in this bedroom.

Devon joined Lori at the door. He held a thin folder with a clear cover, the kind used for book reports and "What I Did for the Summer" essays. Lori caught him up—on the burner phone, the condom, and the drugs. His shoulders sank with each revelation.

I placed each item into paper bags and marked them with my Sharpie. "Who may have had a beef with Xander?"

Lori and Devon exhaled a sigh of relief. "No one's asked us that yet," Devon said. "We have a list but the detectives . . . They're not interested. Said it's too soon to look at suspects."

Why were Kwon and McCann dragging their feet?

"This is for you." The pastor handed me the folder. There was a table of contents and then pages of headshots, bios, and addresses. Each headshot ended with a *Reasons Why They'd Kill Our Son* page.

1. Harvey Parrish—football, competition, angry white supremacist
2. Justin Parrish—football, competition
3. Cooper Sutton—Mackenzie and X in secret relationship
4. Mackenzie Sutton—secret relationship, embarrassment
5. ??

Suspect Three could be the supplier of Xander's stash of tramadol.

My hands shook seeing Cooper's name. Would he really kill Xander just because Mackenzie was secretly dating a high school kid? Would Mackenzie kill Xander because she'd secretly been dating a high school kid?

Back to the gym bag. "May I keep emptying everything out? Do you have a trash bag?"

Devon returned to the bedroom moments later with a white trash bag. "Use this."

I dumped the rest of the gym bag's contents into the trash bag.

Fine white sand. A shard of colored glass. A hairbrush.

"Yours?" I asked Lori, pointing at the brush even though long, light-colored strands were tangled in the bristles.

Devon and Lori exchanged glances, an entire conversation happening in silence. His eyes darkened, and his hands clasped tightly over his head, physically holding back the anger simmering beneath the surface. Lori folded her arms and dipped her chin to her chest, her grief squeezing her and leaving her breathless.

A final item fluttered from the gym bag like an afterthought, a PS to this sordid affair: a paper receipt from a Sephora in Sableport for TOM FORDS's Vanilla Sex Parfum, before tax, $395.

Who the hell was Xander—

My phone vibrated.

A text message with only three words:

I KNOW EVERYTHING.

28.

An evening breeze blew around me, shoving me and my evidence bags from the quiet home of Lori and Devon Monroe back to the mean streets of downtown Haven. No one looked my way. On one side of the street, a couple walking a schnauzer stood with another couple walking a dalmatian. On my side of the street, in the bakery, Mom and Elliott were frosting tomorrow's cupcakes and chatting about *Vanderpump Rules*. He'd drive her home afterward.

I couldn't stop looking at my phone.

I KNOW EVERYTHING.

"Everything" as in Xander's death? Figgy's disappearance? About my former life with the LAPD? Or "everything" as in my relationship with Cooper Sutton?

Whatever its meaning, those three words were a sucker punch, and my head ached from the sudden blow.

How would I respond?

That was my singular thought as I locked up Xander's belongings in the office and then walked down to the office of *Haven Voice*. Should I sound tough—*Say it to my face, bitch*? Should I seem worried—*Who are you?* Should I respond at all?

I still didn't have an answer by the time I stepped into the newspaper's lobby. The newsroom smelled of bacon and the whispered breaths of the three people now peering at me. My smirk grew into a smile—I was enjoying this annoying detective cosplay.

Tanner Orr greeted me at the front desk and whispered, "Play along." Louder, he said, "What now?"

A week ago, I would've thought him to be paranoid. But in a week, I'd already received my first pseudotext–message threat. Yeah, Haven had proved to be a goddamned delight.

Playing Columbo, I grinned at the news team as the redhead, Faith, sat at her desk with copy for some nonthreatening story of the week. She scowled at me, and so did her boss.

"I'd just like a second of your time," I said to Tanner.

Faith said, "He doesn't have—"

"I'm not talking to you," I interrupted, not even meeting her eyes. "Thanks, Tanner. It won't take long."

Faith's nostrils flared as her hands balled into fists.

Tanner sighed and turned to the glaring redhead. "Come get me in five minutes." To me: "Five minutes, Miss Rush."

I finally acknowledged Faith as I strode past her. "Girl, it's Sunday, and this is *Haven Voice*. Go squeeze some sand between your toes."

I followed Tanner into his dimly lit office, the only illumination coming from the banker's desk lamp. He closed the door, plopped into his chair, and said loudly, "Please call ahead next time." He gave me a clandestine thumbs up and then he held up his phone and announced, "Set an alarm for five minutes," loud enough for eavesdroppers.

Tanner cleared a space for his notepad, pushing aside the chaotic blend of newspaper clippings, sticky notes, and copy paper. He rested his cell phone up against the stack of notepads so that I could see it as well as anyone else interested in our conversation. Twenty seconds had already been lost. "What's happened?"

"Tell me what you know about Ruthie Parrish," I said, my voice sounding more assured than my queasy belly.

"Harvey's wife?" Tanner sat back and twisted in his chair. "Well . . . If I had to save either her or Harvey from a volcano, I'd jump into the volcano instead. They're awful people."

"I saw his tattoos," I said, pointing at my wrists. "Is there a community of white supremacists living in Haven?"

"A community?" Tanner waggled his head. "There were a few idiots who set up compounds farther inland. Marijuana farms, trafficking, those sorts of things.

"It was easy for the town leaders back then to shut his whole operation down," Tanner continued, "and they gave him a choice: either stop the white supremacist shit and stay in Haven or go whole hog and take your wife and kid with you. That's when he opened up Pacific Guns and took on the meat department at Good Pickings. Made him feel tough."

I tapped my pen against my lips. "Ruthie visited me this afternoon. Told me that Harvey lied about where he was on the morning Xander died."

Tanner cocked an eyebrow. "That family is going through some things, and Xander taking Justin's spot on the Bobcats just threw kerosene on an already out-of-control fire. Ruthie wants a divorce. Harvey doesn't want another divorce, especially now that he needs her."

"'Going through some things,'" I said, scribbling in my notepad. "Like . . . ?"

"Not too long ago, we published an article on DNA familial testing," Tanner said. "You know, people finding out that they're seventh cousins of Alexander Graham Bell or something like that. Harvey and Ruthie insisted on being one of the couples featured to prove that they were pure-blooded white people."

I cocked an eyebrow. "And?"

"Ruthie's great-great-grandmother was a Mayan woman who'd been raped by a white man from Pennsylvania, and Harvey's great-great-grandfather was a sharecropper from Mississippi." He paused, then added, "A *Black* sharecropper from Mississippi."

"I'm guessing they didn't want to be featured in the article anymore."

Tanner made gun fingers at me. His phone vibrated from a banner text message now bright over the countdown clock:

How about clam linguine for dinner?

Tanner's chair squeaked as he continued to twist back and forth. His hands were shaky, and he tried to hide that by rubbing his stubbled cheek. He sure as hell hadn't planned on coming to Haven and being scared shitless, worried that the wrong person would see him cooperating with the new detective—interested in digging up bones and asking why.

The alarm on his phone signaled. Just like that, someone rapped on the door, which opened before Tanner responded. It was the redhead.

"Oh my lord." I turned around in my seat. "Did I run over your dog or something?"

Her lips pursed. "I hate people who think that they're better—"

"Think?" I said, tongue poking my cheek.

"Almost done, Faith," Tanner said, rubbing his temples.

"But I need you to look at the new masthead," she said. "The printer needs it *now*."

Tanner sighed and stood from his desk. To me, he said, "This won't take long." He followed the young woman back to her desk.

As I waited for the editor to return, I decided to send a bold response to the threatening "I KNOW EVERYTHING" text message.

If this is an offer, then make it

If this is a threat, then kiss my ass

I could handle an offer and a threat. Blackmail, though—

Tanner's cell phone vibrated from its place against the notebooks, and a text message sat at the top of his phone screen:

If this is an offer, then make it

If this is a threat, then kiss my ass

What the fuck?

My underarms burned as the breath from my nose rolled over my top lip. I took a quick picture of Tanner's screen, then placed the phone face down beside the stack of pads. Tanner couldn't suspect that I'd seen my response on his phone.

We hadn't known each other long, but the editor's betrayal still stung.

Tanner knocked on the doorjamb, and said, "Miss Rush, I need to cut this short. We *are* a daily paper, and I have lots to do. Next time, I'd appreciate a warning. We're very busy here."

Yep. Burying more bones for me to dig up.

What did Tanner want from me? As a journalist, what he wanted could be anything. If he was pretending to be a jerk to me for his staff, who was he pretending to be for me?

Worry twisted my stomach, and once again, I felt like the world was watching me and that the sun was beating too hard on the back of my neck.

Back at the office, I found Justin Parrish, wearing a red Bobcats hoodie and matching track pants, sitting across from Ivan, who was now talking on the phone. "She just walked in. Thanks, Elliott." Ivan ended the call, and said, "I've been trying to reach you."

I shrugged. "You weren't trying very hard, then. I was over at the paper." I smiled at Justin and said, "Nice seeing you again."

Ivan glowered at me. "Oh. So, does Justin know where Figgy is?"

My smile dimmed as I leaned against a file cabinet. "Maybe?" I paused, then said, "How can we help you, Justin?"

The boy's eyes skipped from me to Ivan and back to me. "Mr. Poole probably already knows this but . . . My dad isn't a good guy."

My skin prickled, and my eyes flicked to Ivan before settling back on Justin. "What do you mean by that?"

The boy dipped his head. "Dad was pissed because he'd bought all our uniforms and paid for travel and fees, and that Coach pushed him aside for some . . . N-words. He hated Xander and his family. Called them the N-word a couple of times." His cheeks reddened, and he whispered to me, "Sorry."

My throat scratched like I'd swallowed rusty nails. "Anything else?"

Justin pushed his hands through his hair. "He got back at people who wronged him."

"But Xander and his parents didn't wrong him," Ivan pointed out. "They didn't even know Harvey existed."

Justin shrugged. "That's what my Mom told him, but Dad wouldn't hear it. He just screamed and yelled about things being 'woke' in Haven and that people like Xander were taking over the team—"

"Is there another person of color on the squad other than Xander?" I asked, squinting.

Justin shook his head.

"There were twenty-four other people on that team," I said, "with one Black kid, but *Xander* was taking the spot?"

Justin folded his arms and slumped in the chair. "Dad said that he wouldn't pay another dime to help out if this was the direction Coach Wes was taking. He also said he'd get Coach fired. Dad promised that I'd start at the first game, that he'd personally see to it. He even called a few college recruiters and begged them to come see me play."

I raised my eyebrows. "How did he plan to keep that promise of you starting? Which meant Xander *wouldn't* start?" When Justin didn't respond, I said, "Do you have anything other than your words to support this? Text messages, emails, recorded conversations?"

Hint, hint for the future, kid.

Justin shrugged. "Maybe? We have our camera doorbell's security footage. It shows that he left the house at five last Tuesday morning."

The Tuesday morning Xander was murdered.

The boy added, "And Dad didn't come back home until ten o'clock that night."

It was possible that Harvey had found Xander on the trail and killed him. He could have stayed away as the police and forensics teams combed the area for clues. Then the coroner's office had arrived to take Xander's body, and the investigators combed Xander's resting place for more clues. Harvey would have had to keep hiding lest he be caught on the scene.

"What does your mother think?" I asked Justin.

"That he did something to Xander and that he took Mackenzie's dog."

Ivan leaned forward and narrowed his eyes. "Why did he take the dog?"

Justin bit his lip and said, "He didn't approve of interracial relationships."

"Do you know where Figgy is?" I asked.

Justin shook his head. "I haven't seen her since Wednesday night. Mom asked Dad if he'd left the dog in the forest, but he wouldn't answer her."

My blood turned to icy slush, and my racing mind slowed as I tried to think this through.

Ivan made notes on his steno pad. "I'll see if there are cameras operating around the trail. The sheriff's investigators may have something."

Were we looking at one man for both crimes? According to his son, yes, we were. Which meant these cases *were* related.

"Would you mind sending us that footage from the camera?" Ivan asked.

Justin pulled his phone from his pocket. "I could do that right now."

Beep-bop-boop, my phone and Ivan's vibrated from receiving the time-stamped video that voided Harvey's alibi. And the pink collar—Figgy's collar—now sat in a paper bag in my locked file cabinet.

"My dad's dangerous," Justin said, his eyes hot as we led him back to the lobby, "and he has a bad temper, and he scares me and my mom all the time. He's hurt people before, and he's gotten away with it, and I'm scared what he's gonna do next. So, be careful around him."

The boy met my gaze. "Especially you, Miss Rush."

29.

I kinda liked driving up to Sableport. Didn't have to worry about curves or logging trucks, steep roadsides, or deer. This morning, I rolled down the windows of my Bronco, turned up the volume to vintage Mary J. Blige, and used only one hand to steer, enjoying the push and pull of the ocean breeze against the truck. If only the driver flirting with me in the convertible Bimmer in the next lane knew how much my life was fucked up on this Monday morning . . .

I KNOW EVERYTHING.

Glad Tanner Orr did because I sure as hell didn't.

After giving my name to the security guard at the gate, I followed a sinewy road down a hill. The closer I rolled toward the Pacific Ocean and to that dull roar of crashing waves, the more my chest tightened, and the longer I held my breath. I pulled into a vacant parking space outside a sand-colored condominium complex that sat closest to the shores of the Pacific and the salty sea air. Trees lined the walkway to the unit, separating one home from the next.

Cooper leaned casually against the door of unit 7A. He straightened when he saw me and removed his sunglasses, managing a smile that almost reached his eyes. The sleeves of his blue shirt were rolled to his elbows, and his hands were tucked in the pockets of his camel-colored trousers. "Hey."

I said, "Yep." Anxiety frothed in my belly like the water at the shoreline. Just ten minutes ago, I'd had all my windows down, letting my hair whoosh all over my head, and now here I was, a mummy cocooned in a jacket with my arms crossed tightly over my chest.

He studied me for a moment, then stuck a key into the lock of 7A. He pushed open the door. He stepped aside to let me enter. "After you."

The condo was modern and sterile, with stark white walls and floor-to-ceiling windows that framed the blue waters beyond.

"As you saw," he said, "the property is gated with twenty-four-hour patrols." Cooper walked me from empty room to empty room—new teak plank flooring throughout, marble island in the designer kitchen, wood-burning fireplace, two large bedrooms upstairs with en suite bathrooms and walk-in closets. I trailed behind him, trying to ignore the scent of his cologne, trying to ignore that heavy sadness I'd been trying to push away, trying to keep my head up.

"You're quiet," he said.

I let my hand drift along the counter. "What do you want me to say?"

He watched me wander deeper into the living room. "Anything, to be honest."

"It's beautiful," I said, "and it's peaceful and clean. No helicopters or sirens. The rooms are filled with light and the view—"

"All the features you like the best," he said, his head cocked. "But if you prefer a one-story since your mom would be visiting you and she shouldn't be—"

"Going up and down stairs," I said, nodding. "Maybe that would be best. But then again . . . I think I passed the memory-care facility on my drive. Bright-yellow building? A park on all sides?"

"Yep," he said.

According to the website, Sunset Park Senior Living had flat-screen televisions in each room, in-room sensors that alerted caregivers since dementia patients may be unable to use the call button. There was a restaurant-style dining room, a spa, and a salon. All this could be Mom's for just six thousand dollars a month. A perfect place for people like my mother, who were losing pieces of themselves to time's cruel erosion. It was a logical and practical solution, a free solution even, but my pride shackled me to the notion that I'd be abandoning her—that I should handle it all, even though I couldn't afford any of it. Cooper would pay—he promised he would—but then he'd promised me so much more.

Sunset Park promised safety and access to professionals trained to navigate the foggy corridors of dementia. Alarms sounded if a door opened without authorization. On Tuesdays, they did tai chi. Putting her there wasn't defeat. No, it was acknowledgment that the woman who had once been my rock now needed sheltering herself.

"I'm not sure about that place," I said, my voice sounding distant and hollow.

"Thinking about the cost?" Cooper asked.

"What if we didn't choose the trained chef?" I asked. "Would that drop the price down to, like, two thousand?"

"We'll figure something out," he said.

I motioned to the space surrounding us. "And how much for the condo?"

"For you? Nothing." He cocked an eyebrow. "I know the guy who owns this whole complex. He can be nice sometimes. He has great hair."

"Regardless," I said, shaking my head. "I need to pay something, Coop. And don't say utilities and shit. Those aren't real bills."

He snorted. "You must not have lived in fancy Northern California." He paused, then said, "Pay HOA fees, then."

"How much are those?" I asked, wandering over to the floor-to-ceiling windows.

"Eight-forty a month."

"American?" I asked, wide eyed.

"Bottlecaps," he said, grinning—a reference to the videogame he'd watched me play sometimes because I loved that game. *And I love watching you do anything you love,* he'd said.

But that was then, and this was now, and *now* was an expensive time to be alive.

"What the *fuck*, Coop?" I said. "And people *pay* that? On top of their mortgage?"

He stood beside me, silent for a moment. "Alyson . . ." He exhaled, then reached for the handle of the patio door and pulled it open. He'd changed his mind.

The sound of the waves rolled toward us as we both stepped out onto the private patio.

Cooper pointed at the grass. "A small yard. Unobstructed, panoramic views. Two-car garage, large storage area, and . . ." He paused, then added, "It's far enough from Haven, gives you . . . *us* . . . some space."

Tears burned in my eyes, and I looked over at him, at his clenched jaw, at his dark hair. "I hate you," I whispered. "You know that, right?"

He didn't speak for a long time, then: "Yeah." He added. "India hates me too. She called me and told me how fucked up I was. I apologized to her too. I miss her friendship."

I backed away from him and returned to the living room. I closed my eyes and rubbed my temples, willing my headache to hold back for a moment more.

I wanted to ask him about Mackenzie and Xander—about their friendship, about their secrets. But no one knew I was here at this condo. If I asked and Cooper reacted violently . . .

He wouldn't. You know him.

Did I?

Cooper closed the patio door, dunking the condo back into silence. "Sonny, I—"

"You were supposed to make a deposit into my account," I interrupted.

His Adam's apple bobbed until he nodded and pulled out his phone.

"You reneging?" I asked, eyebrow high.

"Of course not," he said, swiping the screen. "That look wasn't about money. It was about . . ." He tapped here and there. "It's just . . . Life wasn't supposed to happen like this. You and me . . . We were supposed to be—"

My phone chimed: an alert from my bank. "Oh, look. You sent me enough to pay down the settlement by seventy-five percent." I paused, then added, "Which is less than one hundred percent."

"We need to talk about some things, first," he said, a new chill in his tone.

"Believe it or not, I didn't come here to argue, to plead, or to ask you why." I stared at the teak plank floor that cost more than my former salary. "I didn't even come here to look at this beautiful cage you're offering me."

He sighed. "It's not a—"

"Will you listen for a moment? Here." I handed him my phone.

"What?" When I didn't respond, he looked down and saw the text message. His lips turned into a tight slash, and his face drained of the only color he'd inherited from his maternal ancestors. He kept his eyes on that screen, as though it would take him a year to finish reading it. "'I know everything,'" he said, meeting my gaze, his nostrils flared. "Who the fuck sent this?"

"I'm not telling you that yet—"

"Who sent it, Sonny?" His eyes darkened.

"Why? So you can kill them?"

He paced, read the text message again, then paced some more. "Is this person possibly telling the truth? Or is this some fucked-up extortion scheme?"

"Yes and maybe."

"And I see your response," he said, holding up my phone. "But they haven't responded."

I shook my head. "Since murder ain't an option—"

He lifted his chin in defiance. "Says you—"

"What do you wanna do?" I asked.

"I don't know." He ran a hand through his hair, a rare display of vulnerability. "This person tell you what they wanted?"

I shook my head. "Not yet."

"This could possibly ruin everything, huh?"

"Yes and maybe," I whispered, wandering back to the patio door to gaze out at the eternal span of blue beyond. "Lately, I've wished that I could just erase the past. I've wished that I arrested Royalty. That my mother's brain was still working. I've wished that I became a detective sergeant, that I never fell in love with you. That all of this would just disappear." I watched his reflection in the clean glass.

He covered his eyes with his hand. "I have more wishes than the grains of sand out there on the beach."

I envied him—my breaths were coming out as short, ragged gasps. I retreated over to the kitchen and laid my palms against the cool marble island. The chill relieved the scratchy heat in my hands. "Does the water work?"

He nodded. "Yeah—"

I staggered over to the sink, turned the cold tap, and thrust my wrists beneath the freezing water.

He hurried over to touch my shoulder. "Sonny, it's gonna be okay."

I splashed my face with water and gasped at the sudden chill.

"It's gonna be okay," he repeated. "I swear—"

"Cooper," I said, *this close* to dunking my head beneath the cold water, "if this gets out—that we were in a relationship up until a week ago—then it's no longer just about us anymore."

He turned off the water and leaned back against the counter, his posture rigid. "I know." His eyes, usually so confident and commanding, now held a glint of fear.

"London is running for mayor," I said, "and she's planning to hire me to do opposition research. What if Keely Butler hires someone too? They'll dig up everything, Cooper, including everything about you and me."

Neither of us spoke. The silence was disturbed by the drips of water from my wrists and chin into the stainless steel sink.

"Fuck," he muttered.

His marriage and life with London, her campaign—it would all come crashing down.

I wrapped my wet arms around myself, feeling more in control than before. "We'll figure something out. Or we'll just rip off the bandage. Neuter the threat."

He rubbed the bridge of his nose. "Not an option. At least, not right now." He looked over at me. "Who sent it?" he asked again.

"I'm not telling you," I repeated, shaking my head. "At least, not right now."

We stood there, eyes locked, ensnared by the gravity of our situation. I'd come out okay—no one gave a fuck about me in Haven—but Cooper and his family . . . I shouldn't have cared so much, not after he'd lied to me, after he'd led me to believe that he wanted to spend his life with me, but I liked London, and I wanted Mackenzie to find her dog, and I wanted him to make Haven better and I . . . I . . . wanted . . . *something*. I didn't know what it was—or at least, I didn't want to accept what I wanted.

"Cooper," I said, regretting the question now forming on my tongue. "Did Mackenzie know Xander?"

His eyebrows furrowed. "No. Why?"

I searched his expression, looking for a tell, a flinch, an averted gaze. But he'd already proven to be a masterful liar. So, I shrugged. "He was involved with someone, and so I have to consider everyone who'd be in his circle."

He chuckled. "She's too old for him."

"Sure," I said, not so sure. "Yeah."

No.

That pang in my belly spread. This extortion scheme . . . Tanner Orr didn't understand just how much danger he was in by sending that text message. If Cooper found out from some source other than me, I could talk him back to reason. If London found out, jeopardizing her hopes of becoming Meryl Streep Obama, then Tanner Orr wouldn't see Christmas. Knowing that . . . satisfied me some.

No one should splash around in water where you can't see the bottom. You never know what's about to eat you alive.

"You should warn whoever this is," Cooper said, nodding now. "You should tell this asshole that I will personally destroy them, and then I'll destroy members of their family and any friends standing in the fucking splash zone." He stood up straight, all six feet four inches.

"I'm not taking the condo," I said. "Not right now. I have shit to finish first."

He gazed back at me, and something in my expression made him grin. "You'll handle it, then? If you won't, you know I will."

I dried my face with his shirtsleeve. "For to me it seemed that no one could possibly be happy under any evil."

"Oh, fuck, she's quoting Cicero," he said, smiling.

"Was he right, though?"

He took in a deep breath and slowly released. "He was right."

"Give me a few days," I said.

"Thursday," he said, "and then . . ."

Our eyes met, and in that moment, we understood each other perfectly. Any day now, a bomb was going to blast our lives apart.

I'd handle it. How? Didn't know that yet, but I would. Because that's what women did.

Handled shit.

Ugh . . .

I fucking hated Haven.

30.

Light showers greeted me as I returned to the village of Haven feeling $40,000 lighter. Back in the office of Poole Investigations, I leaned against the desk that had been mine for a week now and stared out at bleak Seaview Way through a rain-pebbled window. Haven clung to its fog and clouds just like its residents held on to their—and someone else's—secrets. I now had my own to keep. I was adapting.

Keely Butler—she was not my problem. *Yet.*

Tanner Orr, though. What would I do about the editor who claimed to know everything?

I brushed away my bangs, and for the six hundredth time today, I pushed out a frustrated breath. Nothing was ever simple here. Despite Cooper's belief, Mackenzie may have been sleeping with Xander Monroe, and now Xander was dead. I had not wanted to ask Cooper about this—though I still didn't believe he'd freak out and kill a kid. He'd ick out over the age difference but certainly not because Xander was Black.

He wasn't *that* committed to passing.

The bell above the front door jingled, snapping me from my reverie.

Speak of the devil.

Mackenzie Sutton, wearing a vintage pink Adidas jacket and flip-flops, tottered in, red-eyed, red-nosed, and trembling. The young woman clutched a crumpled piece of paper in one hand and her Stanley mug in the other. She filled the room with anxious electricity, the kind that never galvanized but exhausted every resource in that space.

"I tried calling first," Mackenzie said, her voice hoarse, "and then I stopped by, but you didn't pick up, and the door was locked." She thrust the crumpled paper at me. "Someone left this on my windshield."

"Good afternoon to you too," I said, smirking.

Once she muttered, "Good morning," I indicated that she should place the note on the coffee table.

"Don't want to get my prints on it just in case . . ."

> Dear Mackenzie:
> Do you miss Figgy yet? We now know what we want. And if you go to the cops, you will never see your dog again. We're watching you.
>
> First, take out $20,000 from the bank, IN CASH. No dye packs, no marked bills, no tracking devices. We see any of that, Figgy's on her way to doggie heaven.
>
> Then let us know that you have the money by wearing a Golden State Warriors T-shirt. We see you wearing that shirt, we'll tell you what to do next. You have 24 hours. At hour 25, you'll never see your dog again. Tell your daddy to give you the keys to the vault or else.

The demand was printed on regular white copy paper with a twelve-point Courier font. No misspellings. No wonky sentences. Clear in its directive. Whoever wrote this ransom letter certainly sounded assured and cocky that they'd get what they'd asked for.

Even though she already had her oat milk matcha taro latte tea, I led Mackenzie up to the loft, stopping first in my office for latex gloves, a new paper bag, and the bag with Figgy's collar. "The dog thief told you not to go to the cops and yet—"

"I haven't," Mackenzie said, plopping onto the couch. "You're not a cop."

Oh. Yeah. How about that?

I sat in the armchair, pulled on the gloves, and took a few pictures of the note. "You found this on your windshield. Was it in an envelope?"

"No. It was just the note."

"Was it wet? Did you find it on your windshield last night and the fog and rain—"

"No." She dropped her chin down to her knees. "It was damp but not overnight damp."

Which meant the person slipped the note onto the windshield early this morning.

"See anything strange last night?" I asked. "Anyone you've never seen before?"

She whispered, "No," then took a long sip from the travel mug. "And I haven't seen anyone by my car—"

"Which was parked where?"

"At home. What if my dad won't take out the money?"

"Let's not focus on that right now."

I passed her the brown bag. "Someone gave this to me yesterday."

Mackenzie shook the bag, and the pink dog collar clanked onto the table. "Who?"

"I can't tell you who," I said, "but let's just say that they may know who took your dog."

"Nuh-uh," Mackenzie said, her eyes narrowed. "Whoever told you that is lying. This isn't Figgy's collar. It's not even the same pink. And it's Versace with gold studs, remember? I gave you a picture last week. This doesn't even have gold letters on the inside." She rubbed FIGGY and black ink transferred from the leather to her fingers. "This—"

She pushed away the collar. "This is some generic pet store crap." She cocked her head. "You didn't *detect* that, *Detective*?"

My face burned with embarrassment as I compared the collar on the coffee table with the collar in the missing poster. *Really, Sonny? Not paying attention. Wanting to move on to something more exciting. Not taking my time to make sure shit was tight. Fucking up by having my mind in the clouds. Again.*

Did Ruthie Parrish really find this collar in Harvey's car? Who wrote Figgy's name in black marker? Was she fucking with me? Was she working with Harvey to hide the dog and made me look this way instead of that? Was she trying to scare her husband, all *You cheated on me, and now I'm gonna frame you*? Was I in the middle of some married-people bullshit?

With the familiar itch of anger under my skin, I clenched my jaw as Mackenzie wept. I glared at the dog collar, convinced now that Ruthie Parrish wasn't an angel. Angels didn't marry men with white supremacist tattoos. Angels didn't allow their husbands to bully coaches and parents—and kids. She may have been truthful in one thing—Harvey was doing some "dastardly shit"—but it probably wasn't related to this dog collar.

Now that I looked at it, the collar hadn't even been worn. No old dog hair was caught in the buckle. There wasn't any real dirt on the leather—still stiff and vivid pink. Someone was playing a game, and I was being played like a pawn. I needed to reclaim my queen status—moving across the entire board, powerful and deadly.

To do that, though, I needed to get my shit together. Queens noticed black ink.

I leaned back in the armchair, my skin burning, anger pushing against my chest. I needed to treat this case like I'd treated my cases back in Los Angeles—with binders, forms, a corkboard, and a whiteboard. Pins and yarn and transcripts—everything in one place. I couldn't keep the lies and misdirection—the similarities and cross sections, who I'd talked to, who had threatened me, what was true and what was not—all in my head. I needed a box to hold paper bags of evidence, like this note and this fake dog collar, because even if it wasn't Figgy's, I'd been bamboozled for a reason. After this conversation with Mackenzie, I planned to organize and find all the materials that I needed to conduct a proper investigation.

Mackenzie eventually stopped crying and plucked tissues from the box on the coffee table. "Can you tell me what to do next?"

Coming out of my funk, I leaned forward and said, "Your family have a home security system? Cameras on your doors and all that?"

Mackenzie's eyes bugged as she nodded, relieved. "I have an app, and our system has a proximity setting. Anybody who comes onto our property gets recorded." She searched in the Neverfull and found her cell phone.

Awesome. But how close would someone have to get to trigger the system?

"A quick question," I said, "which may or may not relate to Figgy. Did you date—"

The bell above the front door tinkled again, and footsteps tapped against the waiting room floor and down the hallway. "Mackie? You here?" It was London.

Shit.

London popped up the stairs, a study in quiet elegance with her off-shouldered sweatshirt and buttery leggings that cost more than a Benjamin. Her hair was as sleek and shiny as her icy gaze. "Why didn't you wait for me?" London asked her daughter.

Mackenzie glared at her mother with tear-filled eyes. "Why do you care more about your routine than you do about me or Figgy?"

London dropped her bag onto the floor and strode over to the coffee maker. "I swear, you're being such a fucking drama queen."

"Good afternoon," I said, pointedly.

Like daughter, like mother.

London popped a pod into the maker and pressed "Brew." Then she looked at me over her shoulder. "Did she show you the note?"

Wildfire blazed across every bare space on my body.

She must've seen my anger flare because she swallowed, shrank back, and said, "Sorry. Hello. I'm just . . . We're just . . ." She rubbed her cheeks until they darkened into eraser pink. She pointed at the dog collar. "What's that?"

"Intentional misdirection or a simple mistake," I said.

London scrunched her eyebrows. "I don't understand—"

Mackenzie held up her phone. "Found it."

"Found what?" London sat beside Mackenzie and wrapped her arm around her daughter's shoulders.

Mackenzie scowled and shrugged out of London's hold.

"Why are you looking at the security camera video?" London asked.

"To see the person who left that note," I said.

"Any more questions?" Mackenzie asked, eyebrow high. When London didn't speak, she turned back to the phone. "This is the first clip after midnight . . ."

The perimeter lights of the security system had kicked on because a deer from the neighboring forest had come down for a midnight walk. He had clicked up the flagstone walkway like he had been invited, his magnificent antlers ready to shred the first fool who opened the door without looking. But this buck didn't leave the note. He had no thumbs.

Next.

4:40 am. Haven still lay shrouded in slumber.

Still dark out . . . until a dark-colored sedan that was too close to determine the make or model pulled behind Mackenzie's BMW. The driver climbed out of that mysterious sedan wearing baggy dark clothes, a dark hat, and a mask. The person's build couldn't be determined because of the shapeless outfit. Whoever it was moved with purpose, leaving behind the ransom note like a calling card before disappearing just as quickly as they'd arrived. They reversed the sedan, preventing the security camera from capturing a clearer view of the make and model.

"Again, please," I asked Mackenzie.

We watched the phantom place the ransom note beneath the blade two more times. Even as the video played on Mackenzie's phone, the video also played in my mind. A hooded ghost before the break of dawn, posing more questions than providing any answers.

Did other security cameras possibly capture that car reversing past their homes? Cameras that captured a license plate—something traceable?

"Does this person look familiar to you?" I asked.

"Are you seriously asking that question?" London scowled and sipped coffee.

"I am." I turned back to Mackenzie. "Anything familiar? The hoodie? The small part of the car?"

The young woman shook her head, disappointment creeping back into her expression.

My phone vibrated on my desk—Mackenzie had forwarded the video. "Well, the thief knows your car," I offered. "And other houses in your neighborhood may have security cameras that I can—"

"Other houses?" London said, chuckling. "Guess you haven't been to our home. You'd see that we're all pretty spread out up there. It's not like a . . . *regular* neighborhood."

My cheeks burned, and I said, "Ah," then turned back to the video.

The phantom wasn't tall—their head barely passed above the car roof. Harvey Parrish was a tall guy, who remained tall even if he stooped.

"Do we withdraw money from the bank?" Mackenzie whispered.

"Ugh. We seem to be bleeding money lately," London said, rubbing her temples.

And I was now a part of that bleed—from Cooper paying down my settlement to potentially paying for Mom's place at Sunset Park. How much money did he have?

"Withdraw it, and wear the stupid shirt," I advised. "But you won't be giving it to them. We need to know what they want you to do once they see you have it."

"Who would do this?" London wondered, her breath shaky.

Was Tanner Orr behind this threat too?

31.

Ivan hired me to be a private investigator.

I shouldn't have felt bad for doing my job.

Ivan gave me a key to the file room.

I shouldn't have felt bad for searching for answers there.

So, why couldn't my fingers stop trembling long enough to guide the key into the lock? How was this any different from combing the official LAPD database for priors? I never entered a trap house in Hyde Park or a modern-day brothel in Holmby Hills without knowing as much as I could about the players on the other side of that door. Here in Haven, a town no bigger than Holmby Hills or Hyde Park, players were just as dangerous. I couldn't just wander the village hoping for the best, trusting that the good folks of Mayberry by the Sea wouldn't actually *kill* me. But then again, even the Mayberry of television had a jail.

Perfection didn't exist, not even in the golden age of television.

The lock to the file room clicked and the knob turned and the smell of metal file cabinets and paper enveloped me. The flickering fluorescent light cast shadows from the dead flies and spiders stuck in its long tubes. I whispered, "Okay," and stepped into the room of secrets—out of necessity, not nosiness. I consulted the list on my notepad.

Ruthie and Harvey Parrish

Coach Wes Oakley

Keely Butler

Cooper Sutton

I closed the door—didn't want a client walking in and discovering this room. My breath hitched as I pulled open the *P* drawer, half expecting alarms to sound or traps to spring. But there was just the soft roll of an opening cabinet—unlike the screechy roll of drawers found in church basements or in the office of an independent CPA who also sells aloe vera juice in between tax seasons. Preparing for disappointment, I held my breath as my fingers flipped through the *P*s: *Page, Palmer, Parker . . . Parrish (Harvey), Parrish (Ruth)*. No folder on their son Justin, yet.

I pulled out both Parrishes' folders—his file was thicker than hers. I opened to the first document in Harvey's dossier.

Subject: Harvey G. Parrish

Date of Birth: June 14, 1965

Current Address: 1244 Seahorse Way, Haven, CA

Occupation: Butcher, Good Pickings

Owner, Pacific Guns & Ammo

Background:

Harvey G. Parrish is a Caucasian male with a history of white supremacist affiliations. Born and raised in Springfield, Texas, Parrish inherited the family business, Pacific Guns & Ammo Market, from his father Jonathan in 1990. In recent years, he has catered to a clientele in Haven and surrounding towns with a pro-gun stance.

Criminal Record:

- 1998: Arrested for assault and battery after a bar fight. Charges were dropped due to lack of evidence.

- 2005: Convicted of a hate crime for assaulting an African American man outside Good Pickings. Served six months in prison.

- 2010: Investigated for suspected arson at a mosque near Humboldt. No evidence found to link him to the crime.

- 2015: Arrested for possession of an illegal firearm. Case dismissed due to a technicality.

Associates:

- Peter Parrish: Brother of Harvey, known to share his family's extremist views.

- Ruthie Parrish: Wife of Harvey, keeps a low profile. Extramarital Activity: Sidney Santos*, Bryson Maddow*, Gia Wu†

What did the asterisks stand for? The dagger typically meant deceased. Did it here? Ivan had cataloged page after page of *Recent Events*—too many for a brief scan—so I stuck to the most recent.

Recent Events:

On the evening of September 10, 2017, 13-year-old football player Marcus Green. Marcus was a star player for the Springfield Tigers and had a heated rivalry with Haven Middle School Bobcats, specifically, Justin Parrish. The rivalry escalated during the championship game when Marcus scored the winning touchdown, leading to a physical altercation between Harvey and Darryl Green (father of Marcus). The next week, Marcus was found beaten and left in the forest off Highway 1.

Suspicions:

Given Harvey's history of violence and extremist beliefs, there is a strong possibility that he may have been involved in Marcus Green's assault. The motive could be revenge for his son's perceived humiliation during the championship game. However, there is insufficient evidence to make an arrest.

Recommended Action:

Continue surveillance on Harvey and his associates. Interview witnesses and gather any additional evidence linking him to the crime. Exercise caution, as Harvey is known to be armed and dangerous.

Confidential:

Son, Nasir Little (DOB 1/5/04), with Fuchsia Little, AA woman in San Jose. Ongoing.

3 month sentence for SA, Coeur d'Alene, ID, 1/20/2021–3/13/2021

"Dastardly shit."

I found a mugshot of Harvey Parrish taken by law enforcement in Idaho. *So, Harvey was a rapist and caught two years ago.* Somehow, that didn't surprise me. I flipped past more pages and found photographs of Harvey at a beach embracing a Black woman with goddess braids and a great ass. Now *that* surprised me. My jaw dropped as I read about his second home, his Friday night family dinners, and the bouquets of flowers he brought for Fuchsia Little.

Ruthie Parrish was right—Harvey *was* fucking around on her.

The man with racist tattoos was having a decades-long affair with a Black woman? And he had a Black son? Nasir of all names? And he was still with her? Did she know he was a married white supremacist?

His white power buddies couldn't have known this—Harvey was still alive. But if the butcher ever got out of line, Ivan knew something no one else did.

As I grabbed the files, I noted folder tabs with the names of Haven's residents. Seven Kemp, that barista who didn't like me, had a gambling addiction. Viv Blankenship, the surly checkout clerk at Good Pickings, was embezzling. Skyler Sweeny, the twenty-something son of the mayor, had a diaper fetish. No folders on the Monroes, yet.

A shiver ran down my spine. Was this leverage? Blackmail material? The thought made my stomach twist. These were my neighbors, people I had begun to know—but not necessarily like—whose sins were now blurbs and bullet points in Ivan's files.

Holy fucking cow.

The room closed in on me, and the air became thick and hard to breathe. But I wasn't done. I needed to find one more folder, and I didn't want to. I didn't *have* to. All was fair, though, and open game.

My fingers flicked to the *R* divider. No file.on me. I exhaled, relieved. My fingers flicked to the *S* divider, and near the end of the section, I found *Sutton (Cooper)*, *Sutton (London)*, and *Sutton (Mackenzie)*.

I needed to leave this room without windows, to take deep breaths again. I gathered the files into one arm and used my free hand to open the door—

The knob didn't budge.

My hands were shaky coming into this space, and now they were shaking and sweaty trying to go out. Simply turning a doorknob had become akin to rappelling off the face of Mount Rainer. I swiped my clammy hand against my jeans and turned the doorknob again.

Nope.

My gaze fell on the unused doorstop wedge that Ivan had shown me on the first day.

Shit.

Panic surged through my arms, and I fought it back with assurances: *Of course I'm not locked in*, and *It's just a little stuck*. And so, I kept turning a knob that wouldn't turn, and my mind started to race.

I placed the folders back on the small table and wiped my hands again against my denim-clad thighs. Dry, I turned the knob again.

Nope.

It was faint, but the bell over the front door chimed.

Excitement and hope rolled through me, and I pounded on the door and shouted, "Ivan, you out there?"

No shout back.

The intercom!

I pressed the "Talk" button and said, "Ivan, you there? The door won't open."

No response. He wasn't out there—he was out gathering secrets to feed these drawers.

Pistachio, macadamia, walnut, chestnut, pecan, filbert, peanut, cashew . . .

"It's gonna be okay." I patted my back pocket for my phone. The same phone that I'd left on my office desk.

"Fuck me." I pushed my hair from my forehead and studied the door. Couldn't kick it down because it opened in. Hinges—I could disconnect the hinges and take off the door. Using what, though?

Almond, hazel, Brazil, pine . . .

A cup filled with pens and pencils back on the desk also held a metal letter opener. Would that work? It had to work. I grabbed the letter opener and aimed its sharp tip over the screw . . . *Damn it.* Too thick to work as a screwdriver.

Kola, hickory, coconut . . .

Frustrated, I kicked the door. How the hell was I getting out of here? I paced as my eyes scanned the room for something, *anything*, that would free me. Finally, I stopped pacing, took a deep breath, and slowly released it through pursed lips.

"One more time." I wiped my sweaty hands on my jeans again and grasped the doorknob, praying *please open, please open*. Slowly, I turned the knob—turning, turning, and turning until . . . clack. The sound of freedom. I pulled open the door. If freedom had a body, I would've kissed it.

Gasping for air as though I'd been underwater, I emerged from that prison, files in hand. Berating myself—*use the doorstop next time, genius*—I shuffled down the hallway on weak legs and back to my desk. *And prop the door open too. Just like Ivan told you to do a week ago.*

My steps faltered as my gaze swept around the office. There was my phone. There was my unopened sparkling water. There was my laptop. Even though I knew better . . . Had someone come in and stolen . . . ?

What did they steal, though?

I pawed through my purse. Wallet, car keys, diamond studs with one missing the back . . .

Everything was here.

Who came in?

The doorbell had *tinkled . . .*

Right?

32.

Ivan, seated at his desk, removed the Slim Jim from between his teeth and leaned forward in his chair. "What the hell's wrong with *you*?"

With files in my arms, I dropped into one of his guest chairs. "I went into the file room to start doing background on both Figgy's and Xander's—"

"Xander?" he said, angry brows meeting together.

"Yes, Xander, because there's a link," I said, "so fucking relax and listen because I have questions about Harvey and a kid found on the side of the road—Marcus Green—and the Black babymomma. Anyway, I'm in the file room, and I either get locked in or . . ."

The big man folded his arms. "Or what?"

I folded *my* arms. "Or someone locked me in."

"Why would someone lock you in?" he asked. "And why didn't you use the—"

"I forgot to use the doorstop wedge, okay?" I interrupted, hopping up from the chair. "And when I was freed—either by physics or my captor—"

"Captor?"

"Someone came in."

"Who?"

I shrugged. "They came in—I heard the bell—but didn't leave. The bell would've tinkled."

Ivan blinked at me. "So . . . nothing happened. Except you locked yourself in the file room." He waited a beat, then said, "That is impossible. I can't believe it—"

"Stop."

He grinned at me, then took a bite of the Slim Jim.

"I didn't imagine this."

"*Which* this?" Ivan asked, twisting in his chair. "That you were locked in the file room or that someone entered a business and left when they saw no one here? Maybe they kept the door open, which then prevented the bell from ringing again?"

"I want to see the video from our security system," I said, straightening.

Ivan chuckled. "Okay. First, though, you gotta install it."

I gaped at him. "We don't have a system?"

He spread his hands. "Don't see a need. No one's ever broken into this office."

I muttered, "Unbelievable," and pushed my hair back from my face.

Ivan pointed at the guest chair I'd just abandoned. "Sit down."

"I don't wanna sit," I said, my voice steady despite the tempest swirling through me. "I want you to believe me. I'll prove it to you—"

He waved his hand. "Whatever. Why were you in the file room in the first place?"

I cocked my head. "What does *that* mean?"

"Hon, will you relax and sit down? Please?" He rubbed his stubbled cheek with one hand and squeezed the bridge of his nose with the other. "You're driving me nutso, Sonny. Geez."

I dropped the manila folders I'd taken from the file cabinets onto his desk and asked, "What *is* all this?"

"Intelligence," Ivan said, leaning back, his fingers intertwined behind his silver head. "Insurance, Alyson. For both of us." He squinted at me, then added, "We're not the LAPD, kid. This is meaner and sometimes a little . . . I don't know what to call it."

"You're spying on everyone in Haven," I said.

"Yeah. And? What the fuck do you think we do for a living?" He laughed. "What part of *investigations* don't you get?"

I stared at him. Good question. Gathering information—a.k.a. investigating, a.k.a. spying. "It just feels different. It seems more *proactive* than what I did at home."

"Because it is," Ivan said. "I don't go out and stick my head in people's bedrooms. A lot of that"—he pointed toward the file room—"is passive collection—shit I've discovered while investigating something else. And it's helpful since I don't have to always start at the very beginning of who so-and-so is. I know that they have a history of shoplifting or that they've slept with everything that ain't nailed down. Sometimes, the information just sits, and I'll never use it, and I'll never look at that person's file again. Lately, I've been adding a lot to it."

He pointed to the files on his desk. "Harvey Parrish is an asshole who enlisted people to beat that poor kid up—but some of the people who did it also wore badges—and Fuchsia Little doesn't know about Ruthie or Justin—"

"I didn't see one, but do you have a file on me?"

"No." He tilted his head. "I know you, and for the most part, you're clean."

I startled. "'For the most part'?"

Ivan's gaze was unflinching as we sat there, silent. "You and Cooper. Your affair could make you vulnerable. I need to ensure that no one leverages that information to threaten either of you—or me, for that matter. And for those who think they can? I have shit in my files to keep their mouths shut."

I felt a chill, the kind that didn't melt beneath a summer sun. Here I thought my secret was safe, buried beneath my silence and Cooper's discretion. Yet here it was. "Uncle Ivan, I didn't know he was still, like, *actively* married. He was supposed to be divorced two weeks ago. I only found out that he wasn't when London and Mackenzie sat . . ." My cheeks burned with embarrassment as hot tears swelled in my eyes. A teardrop tumbled down my cheek, and I swiped it away. "Does Coop know that you know?"

Ivan leaned forward. "Sableport is pretty nice," he said, his voice cutting through my fog. "A seaside condo. A safe place for Val. I could get you a job with the sheriff's office or if you want, help you start your own agency."

Mom's aging face burned in my mind. The way her eyes could clear for a moment—sunlight breaking through clouds—and offer a glimpse of the woman she used to be. The Sunset Park Senior Living village was state-of-the-art, promising compassionate care and a community of support.

Ivan said, "It's a good offer, Alyson."

"Cooper's offer is none of your business," I snapped.

The truth was this: surrendering to Cooper's gilded cage scared me just as much as it enticed me.

"It becomes my business when it concerns someone I love," Ivan said, his voice softening slightly. "You're a resourceful woman, Sonny. Brave, intelligent. But even you can't deny the appeal of stability, especially for Val's sake."

"Don't," I shouted, pointing at him. "Do *not* use my mother against me."

Ivan blushed and his focus shifted to the desk.

I let my hand drop back to my side. "And being a kept woman isn't stability," I added, though a seed of doubt had already been planted.

Mom needed care I couldn't afford, and Cooper's offer solved that problem.

Survival required compromise. Career advancement forsaken to be a full-time parent. Doing all the emotional labor in a romantic relationship to avoid conflict. Neglecting self-care to care for others. Trading the uncertainty of freedom—life in Haven—with peace of mind in Sableport.

"And if he reneges or gets squirrely," Ivan said, "trust me—he'll change his mind immediately and do as he promised."

Because he had the goods on Cooper Sutton.

Which worked in my favor . . . until it didn't. Ivan had just become an unknown quantity in this equation, a joker in a deck of cards that weren't mine.

I winced as my nails dug into my palms. The office walls felt too close—this place of secrets making me breathless. I needed air—a moment to think, to figure out which road I needed to take.

"Take the night, Sonny. Consider all your options," Ivan said, searching his desk drawer for another Slim Jim. "Whatever you decide, I'll support you. I know folks up in Sableport who need good PIs. They'd be thrilled to hire you, and you could charge more since there's more money in—"

"Wait a minute." I stood from the chair and paced in front of Ivan's desk, my boots scuffing the gray Berber carpet with each step. "You're trying to fire me, aren't you?"

He smiled as he found another beef stick. "Many powerful people in this town want me to fire you. You're interfering with the balance of things, and that's my fault for even encouraging you to move up here—"

"Who says I'm interfering with the balance?" I asked, frowning. "Who have I offended? Cooper? Keely Butler? The mayor? The barista at Deegan's?" I stopped in my step and glared at him. "One person knowing their secrets is already bad. Two people . . . it's a janky, wartime H-bomb waiting to explode, and I'm the janky, wartime H-bomb." I chuckled. "These people who want me gone, are they the same people you're basically blackmailing with those files back there? Or is it that *you* want me gone, which is why you're holding Cooper over my head? Remember, though. *He's* the adulterer, not me."

Ivan's lips curled into a humorless smile. "*Blackmail* is such an ugly word, Alyson. I prefer to think of it as *leveraging information.*" He walked over to a side table, where an antique decanter sat atop a plastic tray. "As for how I gather secrets," he continued, pouring bourbon into two glasses. "Let's just say Haven's residents are more forthcoming than they'd like to admit. A favor here, a promise there—it's all about trust, and they trust me."

"Because they have no choice." I took one of the glasses, and we toasted.

"Maybe," Ivan said, taking a sip from his glass. "And I'm not firing you. I get it. You're not listening to me when I ask you to focus on your own case because you think you're better than a dog case, right? Or you think you're smarter than me—that I'm too old to make a connection between the dog and the kid." He took his drink over to the desk and sat back down.

"It's not any of those things." I sipped, narrowing my eyes as the liquor burned my throat, trying to figure out the motive behind his sudden acceptance that there could be a connection that he'd failed to make between Figgy and Xander. Ivan presented ideas and interests as though they were gifts. In truth, they were often traps.

IVAN: *So you were in love with someone else, which happens, right? And you didn't have a lot of money to pay alimony and all that shit. Understandable. To move past all this and live your life the way you wanted, you had to get rid of obstacles. Your wife. Or maybe you two just had an explosive confrontation.*

BAD GUY: *Neither of those things . . . that wasn't it.*

IVAN: *If the reasons I stated weren't the reasons you killed Jenn, then what were the reasons you killed her?*

Because to have a *that* you had to have a *this*. And I knew this game well enough by now. Something else was more at play than just Ivan being interested in what I'd learned.

"I'm not ready to say it aloud yet," I said, my resolve hardening, "because I'm still researching. That's why I was in the file room. Trying to solidify those links. I wasn't flipping out. I'm prone to anxiety, not delusions."

"Well, whenever you solidify that link, let me know." Ivan's tone was smooth, almost condescending. "I don't want to retrace something you've already sketched out. You're valuable to me, Sonny. To Haven, even if some people here think that you're an asshole." He tapped the table, then pointed at me. "Keep your nose clean—even if it implicates your boyfriend."

That last sentence hung between us, a reminder that he knew and that I'd stay the course because once upon a time—just last week—Cooper Sutton meant so much to me, and despite my anger, I wouldn't want his life destroyed.

Now I understood the rules of engagement, the dance around the unsaid and unseen.

And I intended to play by said rules . . . until I no longer wanted to.

Even with Ivan—the man that I'd known all my life, my second father—I could no longer take anything he said at face value. This was Haven, after all. Secrets were currency here, which made him the richest man in Haven—and as dangerous as the fog rolling in from the sea.

33.

Mom and I squeezed into the last two folding chairs at the back of Haven's community center, a space that could either accommodate the local book club or host pickup games between retirees who couldn't run an entire court. It smelled like every community center in the world—the musty scent of old wood, the ripe, round odor of basketball shoes, the aroma of freshly brewed coffee from a table near the entrance. Even in Los Angeles, community centers smelled like this. Sometimes, there was also the scent of smoke from wildfires, but it was the same smell, the same white noise, and the same impersonal chatter.

"This is cozy," Mom whispered, her eyes scanning the room. Wearing the red version of her favorite tracksuit, she clutched a pink box of fresh-baked pastries that she didn't want to share without someone noticing. I, too, was tasked as guardian of pastries, and my own box was filled with coffee cake and oatmeal raisin cookies, glazed doughnuts, and something gluten-free. Just give me a cup of hot coffee . . . But Val Rush had no intentions of parting with these boxes or any of the goodies inside without acknowledgment or awe.

"This is cozy," she repeated.

"Charming," I said, tucking a strand of hair behind my ear. I checked my watch—it was an hour before the deadline given to Mackenzie by the dog thief. My attention skipped from one face to the next—I didn't see her in the room. Did she withdraw the money? Was she wearing a Golden State Warriors jersey?

So much drama in just this eyeful of Havenites. There was Faith—the pick-me bitch at the *Haven Voice*—now wearing a diamond crucifix around her neck. No Keely Butler or Audrey Lujan in the seats. Over there, closest to the stage, were the swingers who threw the key parties. The moonshiner hovered over at the drink station. Beside him stood White Power Harvey. And there I sat, pink box on my lap filled with sweet things, hiding my own secret.

And there was one of my skeletons right now, walking up to the podium wearing a brown corduroy jacket, a white shirt, and jeans.

A hush fell over the center as Cooper's dark hair caught the golden light of the overhead projector, the halo effect almost deliberate. He cleared his throat, like a conductor before his orchestra. Yeah, he was about to play this room.

"Good evening, Havenites," he began, his voice deep and resonant. "Welcome to 'New Haven: The Next Phase.' I hope you've enjoyed pizza, courtesy of Nick's Pizza People, pastries from Sweetlife, and for those of you with kids, childcare provided by Haven Help Us."

Applause for the donations of time and yummy food.

"As you know," Cooper continued, "Sutton Developers has been spearheading the redevelopment efforts for our beloved town."

Some folks grumbled. Most folks grinned and clapped. Nearly all looked up to the podium and at Cooper with reverence and cultlike love—or hate—for their handsome leader. No one blinked as Cooper spoke of progress, of the potential influx of businesses that aimed to plant roots in Haven. With each point he made—more jobs, improved access, increased property values—the residents' reactions sharpened. Either more scowls and narrowed eyes or more nodding and smiling and quicker note-taking.

At the double doors, Harvey Parrish leaned against the check-in tables, his tattoos covered by a green flannel and his *large* beefy hands. His face showed no emotion—pro-development or anti-gentrification, he wasn't telling.

"Change can be daunting," Cooper continued, casting a look of acknowledgment that swept the center. "But change also represents opportunity. A new chance for growth and prosperity for every person in this room."

Fidgeting, Mom leaned over and whispered, "Does that man look like Cooper to you?"

I whispered, "It is Cooper, and I'll explain everything after this, but right now, pretend you don't know him, okay?"

Eyebrow cocked, her expression soured—an unspoken, *What did you do now?*

I turned away from her and resumed listening to Cooper's spiel about progress and prosperity, about the Haven dream folded into the American dream like cookies into ice cream.

Cooper reminded the room of his experience turning small towns into destinations, dreams into reality. He spoke slowly and with conviction, not acknowledging the undercurrents of tension threading through the room, the unspoken fears and hopes tangled like fishing lines.

He was right. I'd also come to Haven for another whack at the piñata of good fortune. Making enough money to start over with a good career that allowed me to care for my mother and, before knowing the truth, starting my own family with the man now extolling the virtues of better schools, higher-quality health care, and opportunities for children like his daughter and the other daughters of Haven and sons too.

"I'm not saying there won't be challenges," Cooper said, "but there will be *better*—we just have to do it. We just have to 'Build Back Better.'" He smiled as some clapped at the motto; then he nodded to Tanner Orr, Pick-Me Faith, and then to me. "Like it or not, you're all now a part of Haven's new story."

Whatever, Coop.

As for Tanner, he pretended that he didn't see me even as I stared at him. *"I KNOW EVERTHING."* He hadn't answered my response to his threat. Even if I'd freaked him out and he'd changed his mind, I still needed to burn him down and salt that earth—kill his urge to spark up and grow balls again. That made me reach for my phone and tap out another message to him.

Well?

Out of the corner of my eye, I watched him look at his phone and flush.

After an update on the renderings and a quick click-through of the reimagined pier and the added pedestrian-only walkways, Cooper's aide—a tall, thin man who reminded me of vanilla soft-swirl ice cream—clicked off the projector.

Cooper said, "Questions?"

Hands shot up all around the community center.

Cooper pointed to Milton, an older man who ran the hardware store and, according to Ivan's files, regularly slept with his mother-in-law. "More of a comment than a question. I've run my business here for thirty years," Milton said, his voice like gravel. "Haven's charm is what brings people from all over. This redevelopment might just be the fresh coat of paint we need. I'm all for it. Sign me up." He sat down to a smattering of applause.

Pam, the helmet-haired woman wearing a nylon tracksuit who ran Haven's only dance studio, agreed with Milton. "I've taught everyone in this town tap dance, salsa, or hip-hop. I need more clients." She touched her neck and smiled at Cooper. "Thank you, Coop, for thinking about this town's future and for caring about the people who make Haven great." Yeah, given the chance, she'd have Cooper naked and tied down in her basement with a gag in his mouth.

A woman rose, her frame rigid with indignation. I didn't recognize her, so I didn't know her secret. *Yet.* "Fresh coat of paint?" she spat. "More like stripping away everything that makes Haven unique!" Her words carried the weight of conviction, cutting up the room's newfound optimism with precision. "We don't need big-city ideas. We need to preserve our town's heart. And you all act like change comes free. Nothing's free." She scowled at Cooper. "Tell them the truth, Cooper. That none of this is free and that you're only giving certain people loans with reasonable interest rates."

Others grumbled with her.

Why isn't the mayor here?

Why haven't you distributed a written plan?

Why do you keep calling it "New Haven"?

Why are you trying to erase us?

Cooper's eyes turned shark-dark even as he continued smiling and shaking his head with patience and great understanding, even as tension thickened like fog rolling over the bay.

Mom shifted uncomfortably beside me. "This ain't good," she whispered, her fingers tapping the top of the pink pastry box. She leaned over. "What did he lie about?"

I widened my eyes—*Will you shut up?*—and shook my head.

She chuckled, clearly enjoying my discomfort.

Before voices rose too much, before Cooper's temper had a chance to annihilate everyone in the room, Pastor Devon Monroe stood from his seat in the first row. He asked everyone to stand, bow their heads, and pray. His wife Lori wasn't here—she'd kept Xander alive in Oakland for seventeen years. Haven had him for nearly two months and had taken him away. She couldn't give a damn about Old or New Haven.

Yeah. This town needed prayer.

The meeting adjourned, and Tanner Orr bolted as soon as folks murmured, "Amen." Mom took both pink boxes of pastries and headed to the table, ready to be the belle of the ball with her fresh-baked cakes and cookies. That meant I was alone to drift around the community center, pretending to be okay with drifting alone. As I made my way to the side of the room, though, London headed in my direction. Wearing a slender-cut red pantsuit that I'd kill to own, she held a can of Diet Coke in one hand and Cooper's hand in the other.

"Sonny," London said, brushing her cheek against mine. "I'd like for you to officially meet my husband, Cooper." Her bright smile was supposed to bridge the gap between Cooper and me. I wanted to push him off that bridge.

"We've actually met, babe," he said with a thin smile. "Over at Sweetlife. Her mother Val makes those lemon bars—"

London fiddled with her earring. "Ah. Yes. The legendary lemon bars."

"She brought a few bars for the meeting, actually," I said.

London sucked in her cheeks. "I'm addicted." She turned to Cooper. "Sweetlife is one of the best investments you've made." She smiled at me. "Elliott and Giovanni are so lovely. Wait, so you're their new tenants, then? You're renting their cute little cottage?"

My smile faltered. "I am. How is Mackenzie? And the whole . . . ?"

"The whole . . . *what*?" London asked.

Cooper kept his gaze on me, sharp-eyed and cold but with enough warmth to fool any stranger into believing that he was enjoying this encounter.

Something was off. Were they not taking the threat of Figgy's doom seriously or . . . ?

"So, Sonny, what did you think of the presentation?" London asked, clutching Cooper's arm. "Are you pro-development or . . . ?"

"Uh . . ." I shrugged. "I just got here. And so far, Haven's . . ." I bit my bottom lip.

London stared at me. "Ah. Yes. The . . . Yeah. Xander. I guess you don't see us in the most positive light right now." She nudged Cooper's cheek with her nose. "There's a leadership vacuum that has allowed something as violent as murder to blossom in this town."

Cooper rolled his eyes.

London giggled. "Don't worry. I'm not about to launch into a stump speech."

Neither Cooper nor I spoke as London prattled on about Haven being either a chessboard or a sanctuary, depending on the player and the game. New Haven would value a small-town bakery like Sweetlife while also leading innovation and ideas that nurtured family and faith.

I nodded when needed and smiled when encouraged. I asked questions: *How do you ensure the environment remains protected? How do you keep the cost of living reasonable? What about traffic?* Probing yet polite questions. Sometimes London answered. Sometimes Cooper. But beneath my collective calm, a prickling sensation crept along my spine. My focus shifted from the Suttons to the folks around the room.

Mackenzie still wasn't here nor did I spot her beyond the open doors of the center.

There was Harvey Parrish, though, snarfing crullers with his ex and current wife Ruthie. There was Devon Monroe, his eyes flat and swollen, nursing a cup of coffee while listening to a cadre of old men talk about something he couldn't care less about. No one was looking my way—and I didn't believe that for a minute.

"We can't afford to stagnate," London was saying, "but we also can't lose what makes us . . . *unique*." London turned to a couple with kind, round faces and name tags that read *Oscar* and *Tommie*.

Mom, with her warm smile and pink-box energy, no longer lorded over the baked goods tables on the other side of the hall. She'd been standing there near the draped American flag, fielding questions about the cakes and her prices but now . . .

She no longer stood beside that flag or near the refreshments tables.

My eyes sped over the faces—all pale faces, not one toffee-colored face, not one face belonging to my mother.

Nearly choking on my breath, I spun away from the Suttons. "Shit, shit, shit."

Behind me, London said, "I'm not sure you know our newest resident. Sonny, this is—"

Where was my mother?

I said, "If you'll excuse me, I have to—"

A woman with vibrant silver hair and a broad grin blocked my way. "You're the one helping out at Sweetlife, aren't you? Those cinnamon rolls . . ."

"Yes, thank you," I said, feigning interest. I edged toward the door, trying to explain away my panic, trying to reason that she couldn't have just . . . *left*. That I didn't lose my mother while she'd stood less than fifty yards away from me.

"Are you okay?" Cooper was now standing beside me.

I gulped air; I wanted to confide in him, to ask for his help, but doing so could mean exposing something beyond us pretending to be acquaintances.

"Looking for my mother," I managed, charging toward the exit.

"She was just here," he said.

I didn't stop moving. If I stopped, I'd lose control and unravel. If I stopped, I'd sink in quicksand, and I'd be trapped, and I'd never find her.

Why wasn't I watching her? Why did I stop to talk to London and pretend that Cooper and I . . . ?

"Excuse me," I kept repeating as my mind screamed and pleaded, *Please be outside. Please be near the truck. Please be somewhere I can see you.* I forced my way through the crowd. Breaking free, I pushed through the double doors and emerged into the cool evening.

My mother wasn't outside near my truck. She was nowhere that I could see.

She was gone.

34.

My chest heaved as I raced away from the community center and down the gravel sidewalk, my boots crunching the powdery dirt with desperate urgency. The overcast evening sky did little to cool the heat flushing my face or slow the frantic pounding of my heart. The marine layer rolling in from the sea did little to keep my eyes from darting across gloomy downtown Haven, scanning for any sign of my mother, whose mind had once again become a maze of fading memories.

"Mom!" I shouted, my voice tinged with panic. I moved swiftly, weaving through the crowd, my tunnel vision blurring any face that didn't resemble my mother's. Each passing moment of not seeing my mother weighed down on me, forcing me back in time when my life's path—Mom's life path—seemed clearer, cleaner, simpler.

If only I'd chosen differently.

If only Mom had chosen differently.

I reached the edge of downtown, stopping once I stood across from the old cemetery. "Mom!" I shouted, my voice cracking but strong enough that she'd hear me if she was wandering between the headstones and memorials. The sun was close to disappearing altogether, bringing about a twilight that promised to swallow my mother whole.

I'd never find her again.

Not an option. I had to find her.

Backing away from the cemetery, I sprinted back toward the community center, panting. My eyes, now burning with unshed tears,

I continued to scan the dwindling crowd for any sign of my mother. The salty sea breeze whipped through my dark hair and prickled my scalp—now tense and tender from worry.

The sun sank behind thunderheads, and that unsettled sky swirled above me—not sweet and far from nostalgic—breaking the promise of perfection. Tourists cast worried looks at the incoming storm as they walked their bikes back to their inns and rented cottages. Dogs barked and gulls shrieked as children screeched on a beach now being pounded by the violent crash of waves. A car alarm wailed in the distance, a perfect soundtrack for the peril I now felt.

I rounded the corner of the pizza joint and headed down the stairs that led to a firepit and picnic tables boasting views of the ocean. Families tossed me curious glances before digging back into their pies and mozzarella sticks and conversations about football season and new episodes of *The Bachelor*. At the edge of the patio, I stared out over the vista down to that sandy beach. No luck.

"Did you see an older Black woman passing through moments ago?" I asked one family.

They shook their heads and consulted each other before shaking their heads again.

I backed away from the ledge, dashed up the stairs, and headed in the opposite direction—my gaze scouring the walkways and shop fronts for any sign. We couldn't keep doing this—me looking away for a moment, my mother disappearing in that split second, me racing around town scared to death only to find her chilling at a fence or in the pasta aisle in a grocery store. Me whispering yet another prayer, asking God to pull us out of the fire one more time. When would our luck, our blessings, run out? When would a Silver Alert be announced because I couldn't find my mother and hours passed without resolution? When would I be called to the coroner's office to identify a body that could be hers?

My phone buzzed in my jacket pocket, jarring me from my spiraling thoughts.

A text message from Cooper.

Is everything okay?

My thumb hovered over the keyboard, but I didn't tap a response. I couldn't form the words. Not yes or no. Neither was true. I slipped the device back into my pocket, leaving him on "Read." I pushed down the cry dislodging from my throat and quickened my step.

"Damn it, where are you?" I muttered.

She hadn't returned to work at Sweetlife nor was she seated in my Bronco, which I passed twice more in my search.

AirTag!

"That's right. That's right," I whispered, swiping over to the app.

There she was! Her dot bubbled before the vast blue shade representing the ocean.

I raced past Mason's, my eyes flicking back to the app and then straight ahead, the dot looming larger as I hurried past the sounds of clinking cutlery and chatting diners. Soon, silence surrounded me, and I could hear only the sound of lapping waves and . . . a woman talking.

Down the pier's wooden steps, right at the pier's end, I found my mother—her red tracksuit bright against the gray sky. Beside her stood a Latino male—balding, muscular, a young Pitbull-type if Pitbull had given up reggaeton for a life moving crates from one spot to another. The man smiled at Mom as she talked and kept his hands tucked into the pockets of his jean jacket, toeing the worn planks with his black Dr. Martens boots. Any other time, I might have passed him on the street without a second glance. But there, at that moment, he was an anomaly—a wolf and snake moments away from swiping at my mother and wrapping around her neck to steal her life.

"Mom," I called, breathless. I eyed the man warily.

He did the same to me.

I asked, "Who are you?"

His eyes sparked—my brusqueness had caught him off guard. "Just a concerned citizen, standing here and chatting with this wonderful lady." He smiled and his tone sounded light, as though we were discussing the final game of the national curling championship. "Drove up from LA and was just passing through Haven—stopped for a bite and saw Miss Val here looking out at the water."

Los Angeles?

"Have we met before?" I asked, squinting at him.

He smiled and shrugged. "Have we?"

My mind raced as I tried to place Concerned Pitbull's face. When I couldn't . . .

Was he related somehow to Autumn Suarez?

He nodded at Mom. "This your mother?"

"Yes," I said, my instincts prickling as I stepped closer to her.

Mom smirked. "You were supposed to meet me here three hours ago," she complained.

I quickly met the gaze of the stranger. I almost started to shake my head and explain that she was mistaken—that she'd been faced with memory problems, that I hadn't been neglectful—but none of that mattered. I didn't, though. Didn't want to argue.

"You should be more careful," he said, more to me than my mother. "Storm's about to come in, and there ain't a rail to keep folks from falling over into the ocean." He paused, then added, "I know a little something about losing loved ones."

My throat tightened, and I whispered, "Thank you for keeping her company."

With a noncommittal shrug, the man excused himself, walking past me without a word. Until: "Have a good night, Detective Rush."

His steps had faded by the time I turned around to watch him go. Once he ducked into the pizza place, I released the breath I'd been holding since rushing out of the community center.

Was he a member of the Suarez family? Had they found me here in Haven?

"Come on, Alyson," Mom said, taking my arm. "Let's get you home." She guided me away from the pier as though I was the one in need of an anchor.

Maybe I was.

The drive home was silent, punctuated by the hum of the Ford's engine and the occasional rumble of my cell phone bright with text messages. My mind raced, replaying the moments before now. All of it had been wrong but this last part with the stranger . . .

"Frances, why are you so tense?" Mom asked, her words shards of broken glass through my thoughts. "I just took a walk, and Yurem kept me company."

Who was Yurem? Hell, who the fuck was Frances?

"Mom, it's me, Sonny," I corrected softly, a lump forming in my throat.

"I'm not an idiot," Mom snapped. "I know who you are. If anyone's an idiot, it's you, believing that he wanted to marry you. I told you about white men. And I don't care what his grand-mère or whoever was. He act how he act. But did you listen? Did you think? No, and now look at you."

I gripped the steering wheel tighter, knuckles whitening as I slowly rolled down the small road to the cottage, the short drive longer than ever.

Alabama, Arkansas, Alabama, Alaska . . . Alabama . . .

As the Bronco took us farther back in the woods, deeper into the fog, my mind churned. Who was the stranger at the pier? Was he related to Autumn? Or was he just a random I'd arrested once upon a time? I had no evidence that he would do something to me except for that cold, gnawing instinct warning me that something wasn't right.

"Is he home yet?" Mom asked.

"Is *who* home?"

"Your father. He said he'd pick up Sassy from ballet today," she said, digging through her purse.

Sassy, our German shepherd, had died twenty years ago. And Sassy hadn't taken ballet. *I'd* taken ballet for a month before settling into martial arts.

I didn't say any of this but only unclenched my hands from the steering wheel.

She pushed her bag to the floorboard, and said, "I think your father took my keys again."

He'd had a habit of grabbing his keys, getting distracted—forgetting that he'd picked up his keys already—and taking Mom's.

She grabbed her purse again and resumed searching. "I'm tired of this. He knows you gotta be at the dojo in ten minutes. Chasing behind fucking Ivan." Scowling, she pointed at me. "You need to start speaking up. I'm tired of being the bad guy. A thousand dollars here—you said she needed a new gi and tournament fees. Six hundred there—you said she needed toe shoes." She huffed, her nostrils wide. "And you think I'm being a bitch." She closed her eyes and squeezed the bridge of her nose. "I can't handle this anymore."

I slowed as the Bronco neared Summer Way. The weight of Mom's confusion and frustration added to my own mounting stress.

"Chasing behind fucking Ivan." I'm sure he'd heard by now that I'd run around Haven like a madwoman in search of a missing woman. And where was he, anyway?

My phone buzzed from the cup holder with an incoming call.

"If that's him," Mom whispered, "tell him that I changed my mind."

I answered the call without looking to see who was calling. "Hello?" My voice sounded hoarse, like I'd been crying all night.

No response on the other end.

Was this an innocently dropped call or something more nefarious? Now that I knew Haven and its players . . .

I pulled into the cottage's carport, stopping once the hanging tennis ball touched the windshield of the Bronco. Mom hopped out of the car, humming Tina Turner's "What's Love Got to Do With It," as though nothing strange had happened today.

Delaware, Florida, Georgia . . .

My phone's new vibration jolted me from my thoughts.

The phone screen had brightened—this time with a text message from Cooper.

Did you find your mother?

I hesitated for a moment but then tapped my response.

Yes.

Is everything okay?

My mother had reached the end of the coast of California and had been kept company by someone who knew me as "Detective Rush."

My boyfriend was another woman's husband.

A dog was missing.

A boy was dead.

Was everything okay?

Had it ever been?

35.

The violent crack of shattering glass yanked me from sleep. "What the hell?" I whispered, pushing the comforter from my legs. The bright-white perimeter lights popped on, making shadows and keeping me blind. I grabbed my gun from the bedside table, slipped my phone into my sweatshorts pocket, and shoved my feet into my slides. I checked on Mom first before leaving the cottage.

She lay in bed, asleep—lightly breathing, oblivious.

Glock ready, I peeked past the living room curtains and out into the woods. No fog. I didn't see anyone loitering, and for a moment, I wondered if I'd dreamed the sound of the breaking glass.

Only one way to find out.

I unlocked the front door and flipped over the security bar that kept Mom from wandering. My pulse slowed—five minutes in this stance with this gun made me less anxious than thirty minutes with a therapist. The Glock's grip rubbing the callus beneath my right pinkie felt like holding an old friend's hand.

One, two . . .

I yanked open the door.

The smells of late-night forest—redwood and moss, mushrooms and rot—rolled over me. I took a small gulp and stepped onto the porch.

The moon cast an eerie glow over the driveway that led to the carport. In the carport, the tennis ball on a string that acted as a proximity guide swung over the windshield—or what remained of the windshield. That glass was now a spiderweb—and the driver's side mirror a limp petal against a door now marked with silver scratches. One side of the Bronco sat higher than the other—the two passenger-side tires had been slit.

Too astonished to cry, I gaped at the vandal's angry handiwork. Lightheaded, I squeezed shut my eyes, took a deep breath, and held it.

This was a nightmare. In all my years living in Los Angeles, my car had never been attacked—and I'd grown up in a neighborhood that had perfected rim-stealing.

This was no random act. *Who was up at 2:10 on a Tuesday morning?* Whoever it was now demanded that I pay attention.

I let my gun hand drift down to my side and ran my left hand across my mouth. My phone buzzed in my pocket and I yelped, startled.

A text message and an attached video.

Since you want to fuck around

As the video loaded, I nibbled my thumbnail and peeped at the cracked windshield and the—*No!*—broken driver's side taillight.

The video was ready.

Silent footage of a cinder block sailing through Sweetlife's plate glass window, leaving a jagged hole beneath the painted letters. Shards of glass sparkled against the pavement like diamonds.

No! My locking knees almost dropped me to the ground.

Since you want to fuck around

"Who are you?" I whispered to the video, squinting at the grainy human-shaped pixels. "Why are you doing this?"

My gun—I wouldn't walk around without it, not anymore.

I'd encourage Giovanni and Elliott to hire security guards too. I was sure Cooper would help with that—Sweetlife was one of his pet projects. If he wanted people to build businesses here, he needed to protect the businesses that were Instagram- and LGBTQ+-friendly. I scoured the video for any clues, but the harder I looked, the blurrier the images became.

I backed away from the Bronco, my slides crunching glass.

These were not mere acts of delinquency and vandalism. No, this destruction was a massive threat. This was also personal—a targeted strike meant to rattle me. And it worked. They—the Suarez family, the Parrishes, maybe even total strangers—had reached into my world and kicked down the life I was trying to build and the stability I was trying to provide my mother. Vulnerable—that's what I was now, and that openness clawed at me.

"Sonny?"

Giovanni stood on the porch of their house. Elliott, taller, stood behind him, his hands on Giovanni's shoulders.

"What happened?" Giovanni asked, eyebrows knitted.

Elliott's eyes bulged, and the veins in his forehead pushed against his flushed skin. "Who did this?"

The video did not come from Tanner Orr's phone number. Whoever was behind this wanted me gone, and they were willing to tear apart my world—and the worlds of those who supported me—to make that happen.

"I fucking hate this place," Giovanni muttered.

"Can we not?" Elliott said. "Haven didn't do this."

Giovanni trudged down the porch steps, his face hard. "You good?" he asked me. "Physically, not . . ." He flung his arm at the car.

I shrugged.

From the porch, Elliott said, "I'm calling the police."

After he disappeared back into the cabin, Giovanni released a deep long sigh. "I never wanted to come here."

I swallowed and said, "I can tell."

"For shit like this and hearing people say shit that I'd ignore back in San Jose. Racist, homophobic bullshit hits different in the middle of the forest, in a place that's supposedly 'a letter away from Heaven.' He promised it would be better. *Cooper* promised it would be better. I'm just not feeling it."

I rubbed my eyes and said, "Yeah."

Giovanni squinted at me. "And how are they just rolling along when Xander . . . ? Like none of that matters. Like . . . ? I've seen strangers in San Jose care more about each other than the people here. The Monroes should be thigh-high in tuna casserole and moments of silence and ribbons tied around trees and shit."

He shook his head and ran his hand through his hair as his eyes scanned the redwoods. "I don't know if we're gonna make it here."

"We" as in the bakery? Or "we" as in him and Elliott?

The video on my phone of Sweetlife's destruction would help him make that determination. I stood there, though, reluctant to show my landlords the video of their bakery being vandalized, but I had to—and held my breath the entire time.

Elliott's knees buckled, and he sank onto the porch, his hands hiding his face.

Giovanni glared at the phone screen and chuckled, not surprised.

"I'm so sorry," I kept saying, shrinking every time those words tumbled from my lips.

Neither man looked at me. Nor did they look at each other.

Would Mom and me be homeless at the end of the day?

Since you want to fuck around

After Baldie's Tow & Go came to take away the Bronco to the garage, Giovanni tossed me the keys to his black Nissan Sentra. I hadn't driven a sedan this small in ages—Mom used to drive a yellow minivan that had carried all of her pastries around Los Angeles County. The Sentra was clean and smelled of real pine and fake lemons, and I felt so small and vulnerable in that cloth seat, so low to the ground. But I no longer stood out in my big truck with its big engine. No, I blended more into Haven's small-town tapestry.

By the time I parked the Sentra in front of Sweetlife, the bakery's busted picture window had already been boarded up. I held my breath as Mom and I stepped into the bakery. Like I had earlier this morning, I apologized profusely to Giovanni and Elliott, but they slapped my words away.

"*You* didn't throw the cinder block into our window," Elliott said.

"And who's to say, Sonny, that this had anything to do with you?" Giovanni added, shrugging now that he'd once again repressed the anger that had finally burst through his chest as the morning sun lifted over the horizon. He'd launched curses in both English and Spanish—at the gods of Haven's forests and seas—stomping from the porch of their house to the pool of glass that had been my windshield. He'd pointed at my phone, then he'd pointed at Elliott, whose lips had become a hard slash.

"What do you want me to say?" Elliott had kept asking.

Giovanni had surrendered then, dropping onto his haunches and holding on to his knees.

And, Giovanni reminded me, "We've been attacked before. This may not be related to you nosing around—"

"Honey," Elliott snapped.

Mom laughed. "Well, she *is* nosing around."

"Not that I'm not grateful," Giovanni said. "There's something sick about this town—"

"Oh my lord, will you shut up?" Elliott said.

Giovanni turned to me. "He feels it too. That's why he's freaking out."

Elliott kept sweeping up glass with the push broom.

"Whew. Y'all got me stressed out." Mom ambled to the kitchen, shaking her head, over the shenanigans—preferring instead to prepare the morning orders of coffee cake and cinnamon rolls. This was more than she'd said all morning; she'd only grunted after I told her why I was now driving Giovanni's car.

Before grabbing another broom, my phone rang from my pocket.

Unknown Caller.

I pressed the device to my ear and, with a steady yet cautious voice, said, "Hello?"

Silence followed by a click. Disconnected. The third call like this.

I frowned and slipped the phone back into my pocket.

On the fifth call, my patience frayed, I shouted, "What?"

I kept answering these calls just in case I heard something—a train whistle or a school playground or any aural clue that would key me into the caller's location. This fifth time . . .

Barking—the ruff of big dogs and the yap of small ones.

A clanging gate . . .

Then a click. Then nothing. No barking. No clanging.

Disconnected.

"Is there an animal shelter somewhere close?" I asked Giovanni.

He cocked his head as he thought, then said, "Sableport but that's kinda far."

Did Unknown Caller live or work up in Sableport?

According to the maps app, Shoreview Shelter was twenty minutes away.

After sweeping some more, I slid behind the wheel of the Sentra and backed out of the space, slamming the brakes as a white Suburban with blacked-out windows cut behind me, not wanting to wait. The man behind the wheel: Concerned Pitbull, the person who'd stood with my mother yesterday at the end of the pier.

So he wasn't just passing through like he'd said.

Adrenaline surged through my veins, and I followed the Suburban, hanging back some so that he wouldn't realize I was now following him. But why was I following him?

The truck wove through downtown Haven and roared toward the intersection at Highway 1, where it blew through the yellow light to make a left.

I didn't run the red—just watched the truck race north until the green light. Then I turned left and sped ahead.

The truck turned right onto Hollister Road, a street with overgrown shrubs and redwoods.

I hung back as the big white Suburban slowed halfway down the block. I parked at the curb since I could see well from there. The stranger hopped out from the driver's side, opened the liftgate of the truck, and pulled out a plastic shopping bag and a big bag of dog food. His steps were measured and unhurried as he disappeared behind the hedges of a neat Victorian with flaking gray paint and dingy pink eaves. The house looked sad—from the weed-choked lawn to the wind chimes hanging still.

Who lived there?

Was this a short-term rental?

How did the stranger know me?

I snapped a few pictures with my phone and took pictures of the white Suburban, including its license plate. I U-turned and parked in front of a house with an overgrown lawn and an ancient Datsun 280Z on its axles.

Such a strange little neighborhood. A world away from the sleek street of the Monroes with its environmentally friendly lavender and sage yards, and double-paned windows. This neighborhood, with its lack of light and professional landscaping, would be one of the first shoved into the crevasse of Old Haven to make way for New Haven.

Where would these people go?

Did Haven's leadership care?

Or was this the plan?

36.

After returning to Sweetlife and helping more with cleanup, my fingers were caked with dirt. White dust smudged my face. My brow dripped with sweat. Too far from home, I walked to the office and immediately hurried upstairs to slip beneath the hot water in the shower. Last Tuesday morning, little did I know as Ivan walked me around Poole Investigations for the first time that I'd be using this bathroom after spending my day sweeping up glass and debris both at the cottage and the bakery.

I had poured every ounce of courage and determination I possessed into this new start. Yet here I was, filthy and anxious—more diminished over these last seven days than I'd been in Los Angeles over this last year. My life had become unrecognizable, distorted by a new strain of chaos that had somehow germinated with my original brand.

After pulling on a pair of gray leggings and a black T-shirt I found smashed at the bottom of my bag, I tugged a brush through my wild hair. As soon as I scooped gel onto my fingers, my phone buzzed from the sink with a text message. "No more," I whispered, focused on taming the flyaways into a smooth ponytail. I was done—for now—listening to threatening silences.

But what if something had happened to Mom?

Annoyed, I rinsed off my sticky fingers and checked the text message.

YOU WILL PAY FOR YOUR SINS

Fine.

The text came with another attached video, and even before I could tap "Play," my stomach lurched. There was Cooper and me—unmistakable, even in the grainy nighttime footage—clenching each other naked on the balcony of some distant Cabo San Lucas hideaway.

Pay for my sins?

Fuck that.

We'd taken that trip to Cabo three months after we'd started dating. Who'd been following me? Or had they been following Cooper?

I propped open the file room door with both a chair *and* the doorstop wedge. The free-flowing air did nothing to lessen an atmosphere still thick with secrets. What was I looking for? No clue. I just needed to know . . . *something*, and I prayed that it showed itself without much prodding from me.

A manila folder sat on the desk. A blue sticky note had been slapped on its front with a message written in black marker by Ivan.

READ THIS

I squinted at the file label—MACKENZIE SUTTON—and flipped open the folder.

Photographs tumbled out first: images of Mackenzie in various states of disarray—eyes glassy, makeup smeared, chin wet with vomit or whipped cream. Passed out. Hyped-up. Shots. Picklebacks. In Haven. In Vegas. Beneath the redwoods. On the beach. Brightly colored tabs on her tongue. White powder on her nose. Tendrils of smoke from blunts curled around her head.

Then police reports and hospital records, prescription information . . .

The young woman's drug problem leaped from the documents, stark and undeniable.

"That there is a treasure trove." Ivan's baritone sliced through the silence.

I shuddered before whirling around to face him.

Ivan leaned against the doorframe, his hands shoved in his pockets. "It's your ace, sweetheart. Cooper and London would move mountains to keep this shit out of the spotlight."

I closed the folder and shook my head. "Why would I need this?"

He chuckled. "You tell me."

My phone vibrated from the desktop, and my blood turned icy. For a moment, I imagined it could be someone reaching out, offering a lifeline. But when I saw the screen, I immediately recognized that this text was no message of support or solidarity.

LEAVE HAVEN
OR WE WILL EXPOSE EVERYONE YOU LOVE

I showed Ivan the text messages.

He glared at the screen. "Oh, hell no."

"I'm fine," I said. "I've experienced worse—"

"In a city of four million people." He waggled the phone at me. "I'm not fuckin' with whoever the hell this is. Not here. Not in Haven. Not while I'm breathing."

I plucked my phone from his hand. "It's an anonymous caller."

"Then I'll burn down the fucking forest—"

"Killing everyone—"

"Including the bastard threatening my kid." Ivan muttered more curses and slipped his hand over his mouth. "You're a good person, Sonny. You fuck up but *that*?" He pointed at my phone and shook his head. "They're taking it too far now."

"Who is 'they'?"

"You tell me."

I thought of the Mexican getaway sex video. "I don't know."

"You don't, or are you bullshitting me right now?" He kept his steady gaze on mine.

I opened my mouth to snap, "I don't bullshit," but my mind didn't believe that. Only one person had asked me to leave Haven—and now I had pictures of his daughter lost in a haze of drugs. "I'm not using this," I said, tapping Mackenzie's dossier, my mouth tasting like bile.

"Someone's out to get you, Alyson," he shouted. "Slicing your tires. Breaking windows. Who'd do that? Who wants you to leave Haven? Who has the most to lose right now? Who—"

"Cooper and London," I shouted back.

"I know you love him," Ivan said, "but obviously, you two are done. And now you're gonna have to fight fire with fire."

"Again, what does fire do?" I asked, arms out to my side. "It burns everything—"

"Are you listening to me?" he shouted. "Are you listening to yourself? These fuckers have thrown down the gauntlet. You need leverage to stop them, to protect yourself. To protect Val. Your father would do everything he could to—"

"You know and I know," I said, "that I'm not some weak bitch who plans to run away from a fight. I have two flavors of gangs in my fucking blood, Ivan. I want safety and stability. Not an endless war with crazy motherfuckers who are willing to . . . to . . . No."

I'd seen enough lives scorched by deceit and retaliation to understand that flames only consumed. No matter how tempting it was to wield Mackenzie Sutton's secrets as a weapon, I didn't want to add more fuel to the blaze already threatening to engulf me.

Ivan's eyes were cold. "Don't make me kill somebody to protect you. I told Al that I'd do everything I could to keep you and Val safe, and I'll do it."

"I want my truck back," I muttered. "I want my breath back. I want my badge back."

Ivan sighed. "I know."

I rubbed my face, then looked out at the world. "Do you know someone named Frances? Mom called me Frances yesterday."

Ivan grunted and said, "An old family friend. She was married to one of our sergeants back in the day."

"What about Yurem?"

Ivan rolled out his bottom lip and said, "Nope."

I waited for more but Ivan didn't offer any additional information.

"You gave me a deadline," I said. "I'm not starting my own firm in Sableport."

I'd become the keeper of others' vulnerabilities yet stood naked against my own. I blinked at Ivan before looking back to the folder of Mackenzie Sutton's substance abuse problem. "There has to be another way."

He shrugged. "Maybe there is. While you're looking for it—" He pointed to my phone. "Let that fucker know that I'm waiting, and I'm ready to burn their shit down."

37.

India's office had windows, but each had been covered by iron grates—a visitor would never know the Pacific Ocean sat a mile away. Today, it smelled of tangerine, rosemary, and jasmine. Even with the dead yards away, her space smelled like . . . *summer*.

Seated on the other side of her desk in a cramped metal guest chair, I slid a single sheet of paper to my best friend seated across from me. "My signed ten ninety-nine."

She held my gaze for a moment before taking the paper. "Everything is now a part of the record. You've been established as a contractor with the Mendocino County—"

"Yay!"

"Anything else you need from me?"

"Whatever's in there," I said, pointing to the big binder. "And also the names of the prominent drug dealers in the county."

"You know I don't have that." Her eyebrows lifted in a mix of curiosity and suspicion.

"But can you get it?"

She blinked at me.

"Xander had drugs in his system," I said.

"Last time I checked, liquid nicotine doesn't come from a drug dealer." She twisted a loose dreadlock into her bun.

"Tramadol could," I said. "Once upon a time, Oxy didn't come from drug dealers. Ketamine, fentanyl, morphine all came from doctors, too, once upon a time. But guess what's happened in the last sixty years?"

India nodded in concession. "What makes you think a drug dealer provided Xander with the tramadol?"

"Because—" I held up a finger. "No legit doctor would give a kid something that will be banned in the US next year and has already been banned in the UK." I held up a second finger. "Because no legit doctor would let a kid play on a broken ankle and feed him drugs to keep him running. Should I keep going?"

She leaned forward in her chair and studied me.

"And yes," I said, "I know liquid nicotine can be purchased at any smoke shop in the county, but I talked to Xander's parents on Sunday, and the kid didn't smoke or vape."

"And you know this—"

"Because it was obvious when Kwon and McCann searched his room and his belongings. Oh, wait. They didn't search his room because if they did, they would've found the baggie of drugs, the lambskin condom, the burner phone, and the blond hair tangled in the hairbrush."

India's eyebrows shot up. "What? They didn't . . . ? This is worse than I thought."

"The case or the cops?"

She groaned. "A damn shame either way."

"Someone is Haven's candy man," I said. "Xander wasn't the only minor in Haven popping prescriptions. So, I'll ask again: I'd like a list of suspected drug dealers in the area. Could you get me *that*?"

Just a glance of the drugs in those pictures of Mackenzie under the influence . . . None of those substances were available at the neighborhood CVS.

India leaned back in her chair, the leather creaking under her weight. She steepled her fingers. "I'll see what I can do."

"I'm not just asking as a civilian. I'm asking as a . . . *contractor*. The same contractor who found a syringe at the death scene. The one who found the—"

"I'll see what I can do," she repeated. "A lot of active investigations are going on right now, and I don't want them blowing up because of a *contractor*."

I gave her a thin smile. "I'd never blow shit up." At least, *intentionally*.

It was almost seven in the evening when I ducked back into the file room. The dossiers on Cooper and Mackenzie weighed more in my mind than they did in my hand. I slid both files into my bag and stepped out of the office and into the banks of fog cloaking Seaview Way. I'd waited too long to leave Sableport after having dinner with India, so all the parking spaces closest to Poole Investigations were occupied by tourists eating dinner. As a result, I had to park farther away from the bustling part of Seaview Way. The streetlights were now mere bulbs of light in this sea of white. I could barely see beyond a few feet—the mist thickened with every step I took toward the borrowed Sentra. The chill of the night seeped through my jacket and wrapped around my bones, making me pull the collar closer to my neck. There was something about the fog—how it muffled sound, how it obscured sight, how it made the familiar feel foreign. My footsteps crunched over the wet gravel, and it sounded louder than the waves crashing against the shore.

I exhaled with relief as my fingers brushed against the Nissan's metal door handle.

A sudden rush of air and a low grunt broke the silence.

My instincts kicked in—I whirled around, but the fog betrayed me and cloaked my attacker. Before I could cry out, a rough hand clasped over my mouth, and another snaked around my waist, pulling me backward.

"Shut up," a man's gruff voice spat into my ear, the stench of cigarettes on his breath.

Adrenaline surged through my veins and fire burned in my stomach. I jabbed my elbow back with force, connecting with a soft, thick torso.

The man grunted.

I bit the hand over my mouth, tasting blood.

He cursed, and his grip loosened for a split second.

I stumbled forward and reached for the gun at my hip.

Bright-white pain exploded across my cheek, and stars burst behind my eyes. I tasted iron as I hit the ground. My bag flew off my shoulder. Files—including Cooper's and Mackenzie's—spilled out onto the gravel.

His shadow loomed over me.

I tried to push up from the ground.

His boot came down on my wrist, pinning it to the wet ground.

I twisted and kicked upward, aiming for the shadow's knee.

There was a satisfying crunch and a howl of pain.

I grabbed for the shadow's ankles, but he'd already retreated.

Panting, I crawled around the gravel trying to grab the spilled files. My cheek throbbed in time with my pulse. Teetering and lightheaded, I ran my hand over the gravel and found my phone, and I whispered into the speaker, "Call Ivan," and then . . .

PART IV

Foul Play at Haven's Bay

What Have I Become

#2

—

Page 1:

Panel 1: The hospital room is dark. Xander sits up in his bed wearing a wrinkled hospital gown. He holds his head in his hands.

Caption: How long will they keep me trapped in here?

Panel 2: Close-up of Xander's shadowed face, his eyes are bright and wide with fear.

Caption: Where is here?

—

Page 2:

Panel 1: Xander stands at the open window in his hospital room, his body hidden in shadow. A blue light softly glows in his middle.

Caption: I've changed, but the world hasn't.

Panel 2: The door to the hospital room cracks open. A slice of light shines into the darkness.

Caption: Who knows I'm here?

Panel 3: The door opens wider. The shadow standing there is curvy and female. Her face is hidden by darkness.

Caption: I know you're here.

—

Page 3:

Panel 1: Xander turns around to face the visitor. That blue glow is creeping out to his arms and down his thighs. His face twists with anger.

Caption: I should kill you.

Panel 2: Xander's entire body glows blue. Sweat pours down his cheeks. The veins in his eyes bulge.

Caption: Whatever this is . . .

Panel 3: Xander's eyes squeeze close. He grips both sides of his head.

Caption: Make it stop!

—

Page 4:

Panel 1: Darkness. Xander's back in his hospital bed, but his face is still twisted in agony.

Caption: This pain will never end, will it?

Panel 2: The shadowy female stands beside the bed. A glint of light around her neck shines in the darkness.

Caption: You wanted to be great and that's what you're becoming. My PhizX.

Panel 3: The shadowy female brushes her lips against Xander's cheek. His eyes narrow.

Caption: We can't do this—they'll catch you.

—

Page 5:

Panel 1: The shadowy female's lips lift into a smile.

Caption: I belong here, my love.

Panel 2: Xander and the shadowy female hug. Only a slash of the back of her blond hair is visible.

Caption: You will be the death of me.

Panel 3: The shadowy female stands at the door to the room, the glint of light around her neck shines brighter.

Caption: I know.

38.

My eyelids flickered open to the sterile glare of hospital lights. My head pounded as I tried to piece together the blurred edges of my memory. The beeping of monitors kept a steady rhythm as I tapped the bandage over the bridge of my nose and stroked the tender band of skin across my neck. My cropped T-shirt, ripped even more than I was, smelled of dirt and peroxide. My leggings clung to my lower half, sticky and heavy—no longer powdery-soft.

"Miss Rush? Did you hear me?" The uniformed deputy's voice cut through the buzzing in my head. He had a hatchet face and an Eagle Scout haircut.

"Y-yeah," I croaked.

His pen floated over his notebook. "Sorry, but I had to ask."

Ask what? And what had been my answer? I pushed down the wave of nausea that threatened to overwhelm me like it had before. I was used to being on the other side of interrogations, not the one spilling her guts. But now, vulnerable and exposed beneath the harsh hospital lights, this gnawing unease numbed my hands and face. Someone had targeted me, and my mind couldn't stop racing long enough to connect the dots that had led me here.

Behind me, someone knocked on the door.

"Hey, kid." It was Ivan. "I have all your stuff, including your gun. Ready to roll?"

The morning had come during my brief stay at Sableport Community Hospital, and the drive home was a blur with moody gray clouds bumbling across the tops of the redwoods—the ocean's dull color matching their mood. Ivan didn't speak as he drove us south on Highway 1. His truck smelled of fresh gun oil and gunpowder, which had dirtied the beds of his fingernails. Preparing for war.

I gripped the vomit tub like a lover—the smell of guns didn't help my nausea. A new box of Tylenol was stashed in my bag as well as doctor's orders to take it easy for a few days. Even though Ivan wasn't talking, I knew what he was thinking. He knew that my to-do list didn't include taking it easy. If I didn't find out who kicked my ass off of Seaview Way, Ivan would. Then, together, we'd dangle that fucker off the coast of California, real easy-like.

On the cottage's porch, someone had placed a blue Sweetlife pastry box on the steps. A white greeting card envelope had been taped to the side but barely clung there now since that side of the box—and most of the cupcakes *in* the box—had been ripped apart.

"Did your mom leave these?" Ivan asked.

Creeping toward the steps, I squinted at the words written on the envelope's face.

GET WELL SONNY

The only intact cake of the six looked like Sweetlife's sea-salt caramel drizzle cupcakes.

"Raccoons," Ivan said, chuckling.

With a cautious curiosity, we followed the trail of crumbs and frosting smears from across the cottage's wooden planks down to the side yard.

The trail ended abruptly at the small, still form of a raccoon. Its paw was submerged in the remains of a cupcake, its body frozen and unnaturally stiff.

"Oh my . . ." I knelt beside the dead creature, my investigator's instinct kicking in despite the throbbing in my skull. No flies buzzed around the scene—no, they were also dead in the grass and stuck in the frosting along with dead ants, a mosquito, and a butterfly. "Ivan?" I whispered, a mix of pity and alarm swirling within me.

"What the hell?" Ivan whispered, leaning forward.

"Am I being paranoid or did someone . . . ?" I swallowed, not wanting to say it aloud.

Someone had gone to great lengths to ensure that these cupcakes reached me—cupcakes that weren't meant to aid in my recovery. The sender didn't just want to simply hurt me; they wanted me dead. Thanks to a greedy raccoon, I'd narrowly avoided taking the bait.

"This . . . this is . . ." Ivan scanned the forest with slitted eyes.

My phone vibrated and my fingers shook as I fished my phone from my jacket pocket.

A text message lit up the screen.

DID YOU ENJOY YOUR YUMMY SNACK?

Together, Ivan and I stood silent as the technicians finished collecting their things. I peered at the eaves of my cottage and the eaves of Elliott's house—there were no security cameras aimed at the porch.

Lacy, a member of the sheriff's department forensics team, performed bedside tests on the raccoon, taking urine from the dead creature's urethra and placing drops of it on wood pulp and newspaper. The poison didn't turn the pulp chocolate- or coffee-colored, which would have indicated nitrate poisoning. The portable blood analyzer offered a limited panel of rapid tests, like antifreeze poisoning, but accuracy in the field was meh.

And now she closed her poison identification field kit and offered me a quiet *sorry* smile. "No results yet. We'll need to do more testing."

So many choices: ricin, arsenic, cyanide, radiator fluid, fentanyl, lead . . .

Lacy nodded at Ivan. "Anything else?"

"We're good for now," Ivan said. "I'll check in later this afternoon. Thanks, again."

Once we were alone again, Ivan said, "Are you surprised?"

"That someone is trying to kill me, or that the techs all have no idea what kind of poison is in these cupcakes?"

He said, "Both?"

"Yes. No."

"That phone number is the same number that's been texting you threats?" he asked.

"Yep."

He scratched his forehead. "Test results should come back soon. Mendo County has one of the largest databases of chemicals since we're in the Emerald Triangle—"

"This isn't cannabis, though," I said.

Could be DDT, cocaine, snake venom, dart frogs, sodium nitrate . . .

I kept my gaze on the dead raccoon's resting place, the trampled-upon patch where the grass had been cut up and sent to the big city for testing.

I wrapped my arms around my middle, trying to block the shivers that weren't just from the cool evening air. This was no time for weakness; I had cases to solve—pieces of the puzzle to put together. But first, I needed to recover and regain my strength. I mean . . . I'd just left the hospital after being jumped. The bandages hadn't even tried to fall off yet, and here I was . . .

My eyes scanned the woods, looking for whoever was watching me—someone hating that they'd failed yet again to swipe the queen off the board.

Ivan kissed my forehead and headed back to his truck. "If you need anything, just give me a call. Doesn't matter if it's ten minutes from now or six hours from now. I'll call you as soon as the results come back. Watch your back, yeah? You're no good to Val if you're dead."

The assault had cracked my armor, and the cupcakes had knocked me to my ass. Ivan was right, though. Yes, I had to live for me, yeah—but I needed to live for my mother.

Would she be safer, though, if I wasn't here? Would they *leave her alone then, satisfied that I was no longer being that asshole peeking beneath Haven's bed?*

This cottage in Haven was supposed to be my sanctuary, yet now it felt like another battleground. I needed to either surrender or steel myself for whatever lay ahead. I would fight, but first I would patch up my wounds, then open a bottle of Bengtsson Cabernet and a bag of CHEETOS, take a hot bath, and have a good night's sleep. Tomorrow, I'd confront the dangers head-on with clear eyes and a full heart. There was no other way.

"But who'd want you dead?" Elliott's flip-flops smacked against his heels as he bustled back to the kitchen table with tea balls and cups for both Mom and me. "You've lived in Haven for a week now."

I shrugged and popped three Tylenol. "I'm an overachiever."

Mom stared at her hands, silent. She wore her hair pulled into a bun and a purple silk floral housedress she'd bought in Fiji twenty years ago—a housedress I hadn't seen since Dad's death. "The cupcakes," she said, her voice scratchy. "That was our box."

Elliott froze. "What are you saying?" he asked. "That *we* made poisonous cupcakes?"

She shook her head. "Those weren't our cupcakes, but that *was* our box."

Elliott and I both looked at each other as he poured hot water into the mugs.

"How can you tell those weren't your cupcakes?" I asked.

"You take pictures?" she asked me.

"Ivan did. He sent them to me." I found the pictures on my phone.

Mom enlarged the photos of the two surviving cupcakes. "Look at the icing work."

Sand-colored icing over caramel-colored cake.

I shrugged. "Looks fine to me."

Elliott squinted at the picture. "Ohhh."

"What?" I said. "What's 'ohhh'?"

Elliott shook his head. "We'd never ice a cupcake so thin that you'd know that the cake was lemon or chocolate or red velvet."

"Look at the edges," Mom said.

Uneven and sloppy edges, if you cared about shit like that—and the two bakers seated with me cared about shit like that. "Whoever it was took one of your boxes but replaced them with their own cupcakes?"

Mom and Elliott nodded.

"And—" Mom continued, pointing at the box. "We didn't start using these boxes until almost closing time."

Elliott tapped his chin, thinking. "Because we ran out of the regular pink boxes."

"The store closes at six," I said.

Mom turned to Elliott. "We have a security camera, right?"

Elliott said, "Yep."

"I'll get my laptop to see better." I stood, but my legs buckled, and I fell back into the seat.

Elliott and Mom both hopped up from their chairs. "Not until you get rest," she said. "You can't even stand up straight, Alyson."

I nudged at the throbbing pain above my eyebrows. No matter how much I wanted to protest, I didn't have the bandwidth to rebut.

Elliott helped me walk back to my bedroom, where Mom waited with my laptop. "Someone used our boxes to kill our trash panda? I just can't . . ."

He pulled a chair on the other side of my bed, and together, the three of us pored over the bakery's Activities video feed. Customers entered and exited, but none yet carried the distinctive Tiffany-blue box that had been used to hold the poisoned treats until five o'clock. A few times, I caught my reflection in the mirror across the room. My face looked like the meatloaf and cornbread stuffing Mom had prepared tonight for dinner.

What a fucking day.

We watched patrons move in and out of Sweetlife, most of whom were people we all knew, who would never want me dead . . .

Unless they did.

And who'd want me dead?

Cooper, with his smile masking his manipulations; Harvey, with his anger and tats; Keely Butler was simply angry because she needed to be. London—well, I'd been sleeping with her husband. Right when I was about to close the laptop and send Elliott home, a familiar/unfamiliar figure wearing tan jeans and a white T-shirt filled the laptop's screen.

It was Concerned Pitbull, the man who'd stood beside my mother on the pier, the man behind the wheel of the Suburban. He'd come into the bakery—one of the last customers—and purchased cupcakes. He paced as a bakery assistant filled the box, trying to not look at the camera over his shoulder but failing. The assistant had used one of the special Tiffany-blue boxes, just like the box that had housed the cupcakes meant for my demise.

"Him," I said. "Who is this guy?"

"Ugh." Elliott scowled. "Ohmigod, he's back in town?"

"Who is he?" Mom asked.

Elliott said, "Duncan What's-His-Face. Mackenzie Sutton's ex-boyfriend. They chased this asshole—pardon my speech, Miss

Val—chased him out of Haven. What snake's den has he been squatting in? You ask him about Figgy?"

I shook my head. "Didn't know who he was. Other than meeting him at the pier back on Monday night, I haven't talked to him. He knew me, though. Called me 'Detective Rush.'"

Elliott squinted at me. "Because you, like, arrested him before or . . . ?"

I bit my bottom lip and shrugged. "Don't know."

Mom tapped her chin, thinking. Did she remember standing beside him back on Monday? "When are they calling with the poison results?" she asked.

I said, "As soon as they come in."

"And do those tests pick up everything? Like even random things?"

"They'd look for most typical poisons," I said. "Like arsenic, cyanide, lead . . ."

She tapped her chin again. "Would a raccoon eat something that tasted disgusting?"

"They eat everything," Elliott said. "But if it's bitter or, like, really, really spoiled, then no—not even a trash panda."

Mom wandered over to the window and opened the shades. "Whoever poisoned the cupcakes needed you to keep eating the cupcake so the poison could work, right? Otherwise, you'd stop eating it if you tasted something bitter or off, right? Especially since you're a cop, someone who won't even sit with her back facing the door."

I nodded. "Okay. So . . . ?"

"What if they used something that wouldn't typically be tested?" Mom asked.

I blinked at her. "Like?"

She didn't speak for a long time. Then: "Mad honey."

Both Elliott and I said, "Pardon?"

Mom turned to face us. "Mad honey. Himalayan honey. Comes from rhododendrons. If you eat too much, you can die from the toxins in the nectar and pollen from the rhododendrons."

I blinked at her, then turned to Elliott, whose jaw had dropped.

An internet search brought me pictures of a yellow-flowered rhododendron that resembled honeysuckle and azalea. *Mad honey.*

Mom nodded. "I tasted it once on a trip to Turkey. It fucked me up but in a . . ." She shrugged. "Good way? Euphoria. Lightheaded. Like a trip, you know?"

Elliott gasped. "Miss Valerie!"

I said, "Mother!"

"When in Turkey. . . ," she said, grinning. "It's not as sweet as regular honey, but if you're making both a cake and icing and you're using other sweeteners, you wouldn't be able to pinpoint anything less sweet."

"Can anyone purchase it?" I asked.

Mom shrugged. "I've never tried to buy it. That's for you to figure out."

Was it possible that Duncan What's-His-Face tried to poison me? That he'd used the box but made his own batch of cupcakes using mad honey in the mixture? Again, why would he target me? I didn't know him.

Mom checked in on me before going to bed. "I saw your boyfriend in the frozen food section at Good Pickings."

I stopped fluffing my pillow. "Uh-huh . . . ?"

"He wasn't happy to see me," she continued. "Acted a little brusque. You two arguing?"

"Yeah," I said, "we're arguing."

She squinted at me. "What's going on?"

"Well . . ." I opened the nightstand drawer—my Glock was still nestled in its holster.

"Tell me, or don't tell me," she said, "but if he's being an asshole to me, I can't imagine how he's treating you. And I can't imagine you letting him treat you like that. Not my Sonny."

Frowning, my hands clenched into fists. "What did he say to you?"

Mom's head waggled. "'Hi. Good to see you. The lemon bars are just as great here.' Usually, we talk about where he's taking you for a getaway next and how his folks down in Baton Rouge are doing." She paused, then added, "Guess he couldn't really engage. Not with his *wife* there."

Silence settled across the bedroom.

I swallowed hard, melting under my mother's hot eyes.

"Did you know that man was still married?" she asked.

I shook my head and whispered, "No."

"What happened with the divorce?"

I shrugged.

"When did you find out?"

I dabbed my eyes with the pillowcase. Tears started to fall without warning. "My first day at Ivan's. He asked me to leave Haven. Told me that he'd help us relocate to Sableport."

"Yet, here we are." Mom sat on the edge of my bed. "You two still together?"

"Absolutely not," I said.

"I haven't dated anyone else since 1972," she said, taking my hands, "but I *did* know my worth back then, and I know my worth now. No one keeps me from shining. It's like trying to stop the sun." She squeezed my hands, then kissed the backs of both. "Power is even in your name. Know your worth."

With that, she kissed me good night and said, "We'll catch whoever the hell fucked with sweets in the devil's name. I've been forgetting a lot of shit lately, but I won't ever forget that someone tried to take my baby out of my arms."

39.

I gulped water and tried to push against the hand wrapped around my neck. Water bubbled from my nose, and I couldn't see anything past the darkness. I opened my mouth to scream, but cold, slimy water filled my lungs, and the world went dark . . . darker . . . My breath hitched, and I drew in one last sharp breath and—

My eyes banged open, and my throat burned from labored breathing.

A nightmare.

Sweat clung to my forehead, and my T-shirt stuck to my damp skin. The only light in the dark came from the nearly muted television. On this episode of *Cheers*, Sam and Diane bickered about the way he'd proposed marriage.

I sat up in bed, plucking the T-shirt to cool myself, to push away the sensations of drowning. I threw off the tangled sheets and willed my racing heart to slow. I smelled iodine and rubbing alcohol. Felt the sting of ghostly cold hands wrapped around my neck . . .

It wasn't that I was out looking for him; Duncan What's-His-Face literally crossed the intersection in front of me just as I'd returned from Sableport for a follow-up doctor's appointment. And just like that, I yanked the steering wheel to turn right and followed the white

Suburban to Highway 1. The key to conducting surveillance and tailing someone was blending in. I couldn't get any more blended than I was right then—behind the wheel of a black Japanese import. With my free hand, I took pictures of Duncan's white Suburban, my hands shaking from the sudden shock of adrenaline.

He drove slouched in the seat with one elbow out the window. He hadn't noticed me yet—I was three cars behind him—and he was talking to someone on his phone, too focused on his conversation to look in the rearview mirror. I followed him, trailing far enough behind to avoid detection but close enough to not lose sight.

Duncan made a right onto Hollister Road.

I lingered before making the same right.

Like before, he stopped to park midblock at the gray Victorian with the dingy pink eaves. Still talking on the phone, he hurried up the walkway. I sped past the house and made a U-turn farther down the street. I parked in front of the house with the broken-down Datsun 280Z.

The other houses surrounding the Victorian glimmered in different states of lived-in: a lopsided Victorian with a weird addition that didn't fit the architecture, an abandoned Victorian with overgrown hedges and grass, and a corner cracker-box house that didn't belong.

On my laptop, I opened PeopleFinder and typed, *96 Hollister* into the search bar to find the homeowner's name.

R&G, Inc.

None of these homes had driveways—just lawns. Other than by the curb and on cinder blocks, where did residents park their cars? A Hyundai Sonata pulled out of a driveway behind the cracker-box house. *Ah.* Does an alley run along the rear of the block?

The windows in Giovanni's Sentra were steaming up from my tense breathing. I tapped "Record" on my phone and focused on the gray Victorian. Minutes passed without any action. I glanced at the pouch of salted sunflower seeds poking from my bag on the passenger seat. My go-to snack during long drives back in Los Angeles, I wanted to pop a few salty shells, but I wouldn't. Salty seeds required water, and water meant peeing, and I refused to use that portable urine device built for women.

A blue Mazda sedan sped past me and parked nose-to-nose with Duncan's Suburban. The Mazda's driver's side door swung open, and Keely Butler climbed out from behind the steering wheel. She wore a blue pantsuit, and her hair was pulled back into a tight bun. She yanked out a big bag of dog food from the back passenger seat and flung it over her shoulder. After closing the trunk with the heel of her hand, she hurried to the front door.

A tornado ripped through my stomach.

Were Keely and Duncan involved? Lovers? Siblings? Roommates?

Keely entered the dark house and almost immediately exited with Duncan walking behind her, both of them smiling. She wore that blue suit. He wore denim shorts and checkerboard Vans. Were they going to the same place?

I thought about my parents: Mom in her JCPenney collection, Dad wearing Dickies and his tactical shoes. Her vintage Coach purse. His Kmart wallet.

Wait a minute . . .

R&G, Inc.

Could that stand for *Rise & Grind*, Keely's vegan café?

Keely slipped back behind the steering wheel of the Mazda, gunned the ignition, and sped down the block. Duncan climbed into the truck and U-turned, following Keely's car.

I reached to turn the ignition.

The lights in the gray Victorian popped on.

Was someone else in there? Or did the house have a timer?

I sat and watched the house for another five minutes—barely moving, waiting for the Mazda and Suburban to return because maybe Keely or Duncan forgot something. But no cars drove down the block. No one in the neighborhood was out walking the dog or jogging. I started the Sentra, but I didn't pull out to drive in front of the Victorian—there could be security cameras that would capture me. Me driving past 96 Hollister could be a coincidence. Driving twice past 96 Hollister? Planned. Instead, I U-turned and drove over to the alley that led to the back of the houses.

The garage door of the gray Victorian was open.

Maybe I should be a good neighbor and close it.

Didn't want ne'er-do-wells entering without permission.

I was a ne'er-do-well.

I tapped my hip holster as assurance.

A ne'er-do-well with a Glock.

I parked in a spot that had no houses on either side of the alley—just giant garbage bins and cardboard boxes—and exited the Nissan, my legs tingling from sitting too long.

I took my phone out just in case I needed to pretend that I was trying to reach my client but she wasn't answering . . . *and when I saw the lifted garage door, I got scared and thought that she was in trouble and so I went in to check . . .*

In the darkness of the garage, I spotted bicycles, a folded trampoline, camping gear, and KEELY BUTLER FOR MAYOR yard signs. I stepped toward the cracked door that led into the house. I looked up to see the alarm sensor. The door had been left ajar enough that the sensor would've already beeped if it had been turned on.

Hesitant, I stepped onto the service porch and snuck past the washer and dryer—creeping until I stood in the kitchen. *Trespassing.* Whoever was living here had the right to shoot me.

Big bags of cheap dog food sat on the kitchen counter. On the dining room table: three KONGs and a spray can of cheese, tennis balls, bully sticks, packages of flea treatments, and bags of treats for small-, medium-, and giant-size dogs.

I took a deep whiff of air.

Dogs smelled. Even the cute ones.

But I was smelling rosewater, laundry sheets, and burned toast.

I scanned the floors.

No clouds of dog hair. No fallen nuggets of dog food. No water bowls. Dog supplies may have been here but Figgy wasn't. *No* animal lived here. *Where was she keeping—*

"I won't take long." *Keely!* She was on the other side of the front door.

Shit, shit, shit.

I searched for a spot to hide.

Fuck, fuck, fuck.

The circular dining room table was covered with a fall leaves–patterned tablecloth sewn for a rectangular table.

I ducked beneath the dining room table, hidden by the oversize tablecloth.

Keys jangled in the front lock. A lock clicked and the front door creaked open.

"I'm serious," Keely said as she disarmed the alarm system. Boop-boop-beep. Disarmed.

Who was she talking to?

I bit my hand to keep from breathing heavy.

Keely's footsteps echoed across the hardwood floor and sounded closer . . . louder . . .

My heart roared like a rocket launch.

Keely stopped right beside the dining room table. She spat, "What the *hell*?"

Fuck, fuck, fuck.

"Oh, shit," Keely shouted.

The floor vibrated with Keely's quickened steps.

"I left the garage door open this morning," she whined.

"That's the second time this week." The caller was a loud-talking woman on the other side of the call. She sounded familiar.

"Chasing after Duncan's ass," Keely said, farther away from me.

"You need to slow down," the woman said.

"I *can't*," Keely countered. "The filing deadline is around the corner and I'm—"

The garage door rumbled. Then the kitchen door closed, opened, and closed again. A sensor beeped.

"What's the point of having a security system if I keep leaving the doors—" Keely sounded closer now. "Other than me doing dumb shit, everything's happening the way—*oh!* Guess what? Ivan—"

The woman on the other line groaned.

"Maybe you shouldn't have fucked him, Renee," Keely snarked.

Renee? As in postal carrier Renee?

"He wasn't very good," Renee said, "but good enough. He paid for dinner. Bought me roses—and he didn't need Viagra, so thank the goddesses for that."

Keely laughed.

"You meet the new girl working for him?" Renee asked. "This one's actually working."

Keely snorted. "A sucker born every minute. Is she sleeping with him too?"

A plastic bag rustled in the kitchen.

"No—she's like his niece. His old partner's daughter."

"I met her," Keely said. "She's an uppity bitch. Think she's better than us hicks—"

Renee laughed. "She is."

Something dropped to the floor and landed an inch from my hand.

Keely stooped to pick it up but paused and eeked.

My stomach clenched.

"What?" Renee asked.

"I just thought of something," Keely said, the bag rustling again.

Outside, a car horn blew.

"I'm coming, damn, hold your horses," Keely muttered. "Let me call you back. He sees me on the phone, alone in the house, he's gonna think I'm calling the cops."

The other woman laughed. "Hey. Choices."

"I know, I know." Keely moved away from the table. "Gotta go. Love you."

Beeping, then, "Alarm *armed*," followed by three more beeps. "Exit *now*."

Keely's footsteps quickened.

The front door opened.

"Exit *now*."

The front door closed. The lock clicked.

"Armed." A beep, then . . . silence.

I hid beneath the table for another five minutes in case Keely forgot something else. My sweaty shirt clung to my skin like I'd stood beneath a showerhead on full blast.

Just like when I woke up from my dream this morning.

So, every door and window had sensors. If I opened any, the alarm would sound, the security company (or worse, deputies) would come, and I'd be charged with breaking and entering. That would mean Figgy would never be found, and Laurel and Hardy in the sheriff's office would fumble the ball on Xander's case, and the bad guy would go free.

Ugh.

I crawled from under the table and stood there in the dark. My pulse couldn't slow—that would mean I was in control. And I wasn't in control.

How am I getting out of here?

Not through the front door. Not through the kitchen door. None of these windows—there were sensors on all of them. I crept over to the dim hallway, my eyes pecking for any overlooked exit. The house breathed with an eerie silence, every creak and groan magnified by my fraught nerves. Maybe, in all her hurrying, Keely had left a bedroom or bathroom window open.

I edged along the hallway, mindful of floorboards that could announce my presence.

There was a bedroom to my right.

The window was secured.

In the hallway bathroom, the only window was closed and too small anyway for my big ass. My bladder wobbled as it sensed a nearby toilet. I'd just have to wait.

I crept farther down the hall.

The office window. Closed.

I trudged ahead to the last doorway, prepared to be fully disappointed. A night-light glowed lavender from the outlet closest to the door.

I kept my eye on that light as I edged closer . . . closer . . .

Pink-and-white striped wallpaper covered with posters of Taylor Swift and Beyoncé. The windows were draped with nubby pink fabric curtains. Above the white bed's headboard were five cubes that spelled HONOR. There was a nicked white bureau, its surface crowded with perfumes and makeup, hairbrushes and hair products. The mirror was clear of lipstick and ribbons and all the effects a girl would hang there.

And right in the center of the room: a Peloton stationary bike.

In front of the closet door: a Peloton treadmill.

On the bed: piles of laundry.

My gaze swept over the room and landed back on that bureau. Amid the chaos, a photo frame lay face down. I picked it up—a snapshot of Honor, bright eyed and smiling, arm in arm with Duncan What's-His-Face. Standing together like that, their age difference was . . . *horrific*.

I took a picture of the photo. Time was running out. Keely or Duncan could return at any moment, and I couldn't be found here.

My eyes skipped around the bedroom and landed on the three-drawer bureau. First drawer held underwear and a jewelry box. Age-appropriate skivvies rolled one after the other. Second drawer: pajamas, leggings, and dingy T-shirts. The bottom drawer held all the items that girls acquired during these years: lip gloss tubes, hair pins, bra pad inserts, tampons.

I crept over to the window and peered at the frame.

The dirty residue left by an adhesive. *Yes!* The sensor was gone. Had Honor pried it off in a moment of rebellion?

The window looked out to the postage-stamp-size backyard.

My fingers trembled as I tested the latch. *Unlocked.* A surge of relief washed over me, but it was quickly tempered by caution—any wrong move could trigger the alarm.

Carefully . . . carefully . . . I lifted the window, higher . . . higher . . . No beeping or blaring alarms or sirens. Night-blooming jasmine and ocean-scented air washed over me.

I sat on the sill and swung my legs out. I dropped to the ground below, sending a jarring shock through my still-battered body. A new headache cracked my skull, but at least I was out of the house. I dreamed of popping four Tylenol as I hurried down the alley and back to the Sentra. Maybe I'd finish that bag of sunflower seeds after all.

40.

I'd just showered and popped the night's dosage of Tylenol when my cell phone vibrated from the couch cushion. Mom had already climbed into bed, and the cottage was silent. *The Golden Palace* streamed on my TV and would continue to go unwatched. Intending to ignore the incoming call, I left the screen facing down and sat on the floor cross-legged with the Suttons' files spread like a fan before me. From what I could tell, nothing was missing after I'd dropped all of them in the street as someone was beating me up. Then again, I hadn't had a chance to read through any of the documents Ivan had collected.

The cell phone stopped vibrating—and started again. I grabbed the phone and said, "Yeah?"

"Where are you?" India asked.

"Home. Just showered and now I'm trying out 'taking it easy.'" I tenderly pushed my left cheekbone. Puffy and swollen.

She whispered, "You alone?"

I laughed. "Do I have someone to canoodle? Do you know something that I don't?"

She said, "Some of the DNA results from the Monroe case are back."

That made me grab my pad and pen. "Is it definitive? Is there a name or . . . ?"

"No name," India said. "Whoever it is isn't in the system—"

"Which means this person probably isn't a felon."

"But this is still more information than what you had before."

I shrugged, my excitement diminishing. "Who does the DNA belong to?"

"A white woman."

"Blond?" I asked. "Brunette? Redhead?"

The hairs in that brush I'd found in Xander's backpack had been blond.

"The tests can't give a definitive answer—"

"I know," I said, nodding. "Genetic factors and environmental factors and likelihood, la-la-la. I know—I took the class."

She took a deep breath. "There's a high chance that the hair is light brown."

"Like . . . how light of a brown?" I chuckled. "Don't answer that." I flipped back to my pages of notes.

Light brown . . . Neither Mackenzie nor Honor had light-brown hair. Both were proud brunettes. Had I even talked to a woman with light-brown hair?

"Anything else from the DNA?"

"She's a biological-born female of Scandinavian descent on the maternal side."

I cocked my head, brows scrunched. "So, the last person with Xander was . . . a white woman with light-brown hair whose momma was from Sweden or Norway or somewhere?"

"Yup." She paused, then added, "Helpful but . . . *not*. There are still the nuclear DNA tests being done, so we're not totally assed out yet."

I nodded and watched as Betty White shared a scene with Bobcat Goldthwait.

On the other side of my bedroom window, rain smacked the glass pane and wind made the redwoods surrounding the cottage groan and creak.

"Anything else?" I asked.

"This may be helpful," India said. "It may be just noise but . . . whoever was with Xander last Tuesday transferred another kind of hair on his shirt."

"Okay . . . ," I said, squinting at my pad, ready to write. "Tell me."

And so, she did.

Animal hair.

Dog hair.

Mixed breed.

Golden retriever and . . .

Poodle.

41.

A goldendoodle.

Figgy Sutton couldn't have been the only goldendoodle in town . . . *right*?

Before I backed out of the cottage's driveway, I texted Lori Monroe.

Does your family have a dog?

An ellipsis immediately bubbled on my screen as Xander Monroe's mother typed.

I hadn't seen a dog during my visit, but the pup could've been boarded after everything that had happened.

We've been fostering
Don't know if I'm ready to give her back
After all of this
Guess I need somebody to love lol
Call later? At funeral home

What kind of dog?

"Please answer," I whispered, hoping for one last response.

No ellipsis—she needed to focus on the burial of her son.

I kept my gaze skipping from the phone to the road ahead, hoping for more information before my next meeting—an unplanned Thursday-morning visit with the only family I knew who owned a goldendoodle. My mind was churning. Mackenzie knew Xander. She was just a few years older than him, and she owned a missing goldendoodle. But she didn't have light-brown hair . . . unless she'd recently dyed it chestnut.

The Suttons' modern estate sat on a bluff with views of the Pacific Ocean, the redwood forests, and the far-off city of San Francisco. Even though 1 Pearl Way was less than two miles from my cottage, this . . . *masterpiece* was a world away from even Elliott's lovely home. The single-story beauty's exterior was a smooth brown slatted metal and had lots of windows. Japanese-inspired looks here and American-inspired looks there, the Sutton house was all clean lines and manicured hedges and trees. Terraces—this place had freaking *terraces*. London's black Maserati sat before the garage, its shiny black paint pebbled with rain.

There were other beautiful houses around it, but 1 Pearl Way was the beauty queen of the beauty queens with its Four Seasons vibe and relaxed, subtle luxury.

As I sat behind the wheel of my borrowed Nissan Sentra, I glared at this piece of real estate shivering with rage—pissed that I no longer lived in the city that I loved, pissed that I sat there nervous because I was about to enter the home of my boyfriend's family.

Mackenzie wasn't home.

London was, though, and she invited me in.

No maids or helpers buzzed around the house as London showed me around in red biker shorts and a white sweatshirt with a warm, strained smile. She had workout face—flushed and dewy—with her hair held back by a headband. "My personal trainer just left," she told me. "You should talk to her. Maya is a Yoga Sculpt beast. She had me doing burpees, overhead triceps extensions, and horse squats with five-pound dumbbells for sixty minutes." She giggled. "I hurt so much right now."

"But what a nice ass you have," I said, wincing and laughing. "Yoga Sculpt. I hate Maya already. Send me her number."

London's eyes pecked at my blue silk shirt, white jeans, and blue-and-white Adidas sneakers. Her gaze lingered on my neck, as though she could sense somehow that something used to dangle there.

She was right—and oh, how I missed Cooper's pendant.

There was a glass deck out that way and a vaulted ceiling above me. Hardwood floors that probably warmed your feet in the winter and sliding glass walls that opened to cool you in the summer. Pictures of the Sutton family—their wedding, the birth of Mackenzie, her graduation, and Figgy—sat on mantels and hung on walls. A wedding portrait—a moody black-and-white photo of London and Cooper's first dance—hung above the smooth marble fireplace.

"This room is spectacular," I said, my gaze sliding from the picture of the happy couple to the glass wall that looked out to the ocean. "Stunning."

No lie.

"Coop picked out this spot fifteen years ago," she said, smiling. "Wanted our home to look like the Moldstad home on Bainbridge Island." She peeked at her watch. "Mackie is finishing up errands. At least, that's what she told me. You know kids. Nothing's a hundred percent true." She squinted at me with concern. "You look like shit."

I touched my still-swollen cheekbone. "Late-night makeover courtesy of the Haven Welcoming Committee."

Her eyes widened. "You got *jumped*? *Here?*"

"Yep. On Tuesday night."

She clasped her hands to her chest and shook her head. "I'm so, so sorry. Another reason why this stupid little town needs new leadership." She peered closer at the wound on the bridge of my nose. "They take you to Presbyterian up in Sableport?"

"No. Community. I've been doped up on Tylenol ever since."

"Mind if I tell Cooper?" London asked. "He should know. He'll *want* to know so that he can stop it before someone else is assaulted."

I shrugged. "Sure, but I don't know who jumped me. Ivan's on the hunt, though."

"Whoever it is better hope the cops find them before Ivan does. That man should team up with Maya. They'd scare the fuck out of the devil himself." She offered me coffee, tea, or wine.

I declined all of it, then followed her to the great room.

She sat in an armchair.

I perched on the love seat and eased my folio from my bag, flipping to the last page. "Do you know if there are goldendoodles in Haven other than Figgy?" When she didn't respond, I looked over to her. "In case we need to do DNA tests to prove that Figgy . . . is Figgy."

She tilted her head as she thought. "I . . . don't think so? But you may be better off asking our vet, Zinnia Lipstatz, up in Sableport—" Her phone chimed from the coffee table. "One sec." She grabbed the phone and said, "Hey, Coop."

I whispered, "Sorry, but may I use your restroom?"

She pointed ahead. "Down the hall, next to the laundry room." As I made my way down the hallway, she said, "Yeah, Alyson Rush is here . . . About Figgy . . ."

I found the guest bathroom and locked the door behind me.

The guest bathroom featured glass, brown wood, and marble and silver. How fancy were the en suites?

Out the window, there was a green lawn, backyard furniture, and a casita. The glass sliding door to the casita was open, and I could see a treadmill, an elliptical machine, a bike, and a punching bag.

I flushed the toilet—even though I hadn't used it—then turned the taps to wash my hands. I resisted opening the bathroom cabinet—people always suspected guests of snooping, and residents sometimes made traps to confirm this by coating the knob with honey or ink, or Tetris-ing the pill vials so they would tumble out if the door opened. I resisted the temptation and left the bathroom.

Family pictures lined the hallway walls: Cooper in ski gear, Mackenzie missing a tooth, London wearing a sun hat and drinking wine the same color as the rose gold pendant on her neck.

To my right, the laundry room had a long, cluttered shelf and two baskets of dirty clothes. The washer and dryer sat on one side of the space, and on the other, a shoe cubby filled with sandals, sneakers, and—

My breath snagged. A pair of bright-orange Nikes.

Shit.

The sole witness, Jairo, had told me that the female on the trail with Xander wore orange Nikes. They were unique. Expensive.

Shit, shit, shit.

I returned to the great room, forcing a smile onto my face, ready to fake the funk with London Sutton.

The lady of the house posed in the armchair, but now a glass of blush-colored wine sat before her on the coffee table and another glass sat waiting for my return.

"I know it's only ten in the morning, but I needed wine," London said, reaching for the glass. "Rosé. Filled with resveratrol. Lowers blood pressure. Prevents obesity and a bunch of other stuff that I've cared about since turning forty-five in April."

"Taurus or Aries?" I reached for the glass.

"Take a guess," she said, smirking. "My birth flower may be a daisy—"

"But you sure as hell don't . . ." *Shit.* "Wilt."

That pendant in London's hallway photograph—a rose gold daisy.

London raised her glass for a toast. "Here's to truth and justice."

Truth—did Mackenzie kill Xander Monroe?

Justice—will she receive three hots and a cot once I prove that she did? Or will her parents' wealth buy her the best defense attorney west of the Mississippi?

Now it was my time to look at my watch. "I don't want to take any more of your time—"

"No worries," London said, flicking her hand. "I don't have patients until later today."

I took a sip of rosé. Passion fruit. Peaches. "Delicious."

"From my family's vineyards over the hill. Bengtsson Vineyards."

My eyebrows raised. "Really? That's . . ." Cooper had sent me cases of Bengtsson-branded wines over the last year.

She smiled. "Yeah, I'm *rich* rich." She took another sip. "Guess you didn't know that."

I shook my head. "No reason that I should. Unless you think your competitors stole Mackenzie's dog. Like that Bob Lee guy who went on the tour last week."

"Nope." She swirled the wine around in the glass. "I thought Cooper would've told you about my family."

I frowned and shook my head. "Why would he share that—"

"I know, Alyson." She slowly pulled up her eyes to meet mine.

My natural inclination was to ask, "You know . . . *what*?" My heart knew, though, and it revved in my chest like it had been dunked into caffeine. I held London's gaze with my own, steady but not defiant. There was no point in denying it or making weak excuses. This wasn't a confession; it was an acknowledgment to the second queen on the other side of the chessboard.

My phone twinkled with Cooper's name and face bright on the screen.

I'd forgotten to delete him from my Favorites and change his ringtone.

"He's calling you," London said, peering at the wine in her glass. "Go ahead and answer. Don't let me stop you. Me being his wife hasn't stopped you before."

"I'm sorry for all of this. Sincerely." I set my glass down, wondering for a brief moment if she'd poisoned my pour. Too late if she had. "You don't have to believe me, but I'm being truthful when I say that I didn't know who you were until you and Mackenzie walked into my office last week. I was told you were divorced and were relocating to San Francisco—"

She sucked her teeth. "Let's not lie."

"I have no reason to lie—"

"Let me be clear," London said, each word measured. "I've worked too long and too hard to build this fucking town. I *will* become mayor of Haven, and I refuse to let anyone—or anything—jeopardize that. Especially Cooper's . . . cock."

The threat in her words was as bright as the wine in my glass. London Sutton was no longer my new girlfriend. There'd be no more bonding over aging and the ridiculous things we had to do to maintain muscle mass and flexibility. Her words were now icy shivs, and she'd kill me, and I'd lay there as her weapons melted, leaving me in a puddle and the world assuming it had rained overnight.

"I understand," I said, though my understanding wasn't the same as compliance. Not that I'd fuck her husband again just to piss her off. "Again, I'm sorry—"

"I don't want your pity."

"I'm not offering any," I said, shaking my head.

London stiffened, the facade of the perfect hostess cracking ever so slightly. "Cooper told me everything last night. He claimed that you two were done."

"We *are* done," I said. "I broke up with him last week as soon as I found out. I'm not interested in taking someone's husband."

"But you *will* take my money," she said.

"Your . . . ?"

"His money is my money. My money is my money." She cocked an eyebrow. "And he's using my money to pay off his whore's debts, to keep her in our condo complex and his whore's mother in a memory-care facility."

Whore? Shit. Yeah. She absolutely hated me.

"Like I said," she continued, "you're not fucking him anymore, but you're still fucking my wallet. Do you want me to do this? To destroy you?"

"Destroy me? Hmm." My ears crackled with rage—hers and mine. But I couldn't lose control even though she was starting to unravel. Instead, I took a breath and held up a finger. "First of all, he's your husband—not mine—who had a good time over the last year in my bed. I didn't force him there. I didn't force him to buy me things. And destroy me? If anyone's gonna be destroyed . . ."

I reached into my bag and pulled out pictures of Mackenzie, then slipped them onto the coffee table. "What are you gonna do about that? Sex? That shit's boring when it comes to mayoral campaigns which feature *you* talking about keeping *the elements* out of Mayberry by the Sea. But this . . ." I tapped my finger against the shot of the blue tab melting against her daughter's tongue. "Sounds like she's struggling with substance abuse. Sounds like *she's* the connect for Haven. The . . . *element*."

My body sagged as I finally exhaled. Not only had I pulled the pin on the grenade, but I'd also pushed this slick woman across from me on top of it.

London stiffened. "Mackenzie is going to rehab."

"*Again*, Dr. Sutton? How many times will that be?"

"My daughter's well-being is my priority," London growled, "and I won't have her dragged through the mud because of idle town gossip."

"Threatening me isn't necessary, London," I said. "I'm not in the business of exposing vulnerable people, and Mackenzie is vulnerable people. I only showed you these pictures to let you know that I've known about the drugs and the arrests, and I've said nothing about it, not even to your competitor who also wants to be mayor." I paused, then added, "You're welcome."

Her mouth tightened. "No wonder you got your ass kicked."

"No wonder." I slid the pictures from the table and back into my bag. "Let me do my job—that's all I'm saying. Back the fuck away and no one's secrets become fodder for the paper."

She rolled her eyes. "No one reads the fucking *Haven Voice*."

"But they do read the *East Bay Times*, *San Francisco Chronicle*, *Mercury News*, *San Francisco* magazine . . ."

London Sutton told me to get the fuck up out her house. She didn't see me to the door.

I hurried past the terraced gardens and speedwalked toward the Sentra with my phone vibrating and twinkling. I felt eyes on my back. London's, yes, but another pair.

"Miss Rush?" The older woman's voice calling out to me sounded familiar.

Audrey Lujan waved at me from a garden of another stunner down the block, a three-story home with wood siding—a taller sibling of Elliott's home on the other side of Highway 1. What was she doing over here? She lived several blocks away, across the street from the dog park.

I hurried to meet the bookstore owner, who stood up from the flower bed and knocked dirt from the knees of her jeans.

"I'm doing some gardening for my—" Her eyes widened as she noticed the bruises and cuts across my face. Her hand covered her mouth, and she gasped.

"Looks better today than yesterday," I said, touching an abrasion on my forehead.

The book lady swallowed, and said, "Sorry to shout at you, but I saw you go into the Suttons' and had to make sure that we talked before . . ."

"Before . . . what?" I asked.

Audrey's lips twitched into a smile that couldn't reach her eyes. Worry was etched on her face, and she anxiously slapped at her thighs with a pair of garden gloves. "I hate saying this but . . ." She moved toward the rosebushes and forced herself to smile while pointing to a lavender-colored bloom. Pantomiming. "It's about Mackenzie Sutton," Audrey said, glancing at me with those worried eyes and pasted-on smile. "I wanted to mention it when we talked last week, but . . . It's been weighing on my mind and now . . . Well . . . my friend who lives here—"

She motioned to the house. "Her granddaughter Pressley used to be thick as thieves with Mackenzie. They were inseparable until . . ." She plucked out her garden shears from her smock pocket. "Until the drugs got the better of them."

The mention of drugs threaded a connection in my mind, a tie to the silent plea in London's eyes—*don't tell*—moments ago.

"Press had never even taken a vitamin," Audrey continued, "but all of a sudden, she's taking Molly and mushrooms and going to those daisy festivals where they hand out drugs like paper clips." Audrey faked another smile, and this time, she touched a gray rose.

I nodded and gave her a big smile, pointing at the flower, pretending to be entranced.

"Mackie called Pressley one night," Audrey said, "and Pressley walked out the house and climbed into a car with Mackenzie and two boys, and that was it. We haven't seen her since. It's been weeks and no one's heard from her. Sandra, Pressley's poor mom, doesn't know if she's dead or alive."

Like Honor Butler.

"Sandra found all these pills," Audrey continued, "and she found all these pictures on the computer of Mackenzie and Pressley doing all kinds of . . ." The older woman blushed and dropped her eyes to the soil. "Mackenzie Sutton is troubled, and she's gotten away with murder all of her life."

Really. Those orange Nikes. The goldendoodle hair. The drugs. The dead kid.

Audrey shook her head, and her eyes filled with tears, even as she sniffed the roses. "Mackenzie knew Honor Butler too," Audrey said, nodding, "and the same thing happened to her. No one knows where she is. If Mackenzie really wants to find Figgy, she needs to come clean about what happened to Pressley and even Honor. And she needs to do that before London disappears her into some rehab retreat again where no one can touch her."

42.

Genesis, Exodus, Leviticus, Numbers . . .

I couldn't feel the leather steering wheel of the Sentra beneath my numb palms as I raced from the Suttons' neighborhood. My eyes burned from the thin shards of sunlight cutting through the overcast sky and I glared at it, wishing that it would either rain or grow the hell up and shine. This morning's anxiety hadn't come from fog. No, it came from angry wives, spoiled daughters, lying husbands, and the dead and missing of Haven, California. Since August 1, I'd lost so much. Each time I crossed Highway 1—heading toward the ocean in the morning and crossing it again going back home to the forest—I lost one more part of me.

My boyfriend, my trust in humanity, my Bronco, my perfect nose, and now . . .

This was a slow death, and if I crossed one too many times, that would be that. I'd never be me again. No more rides upon the River Styx. No more banks. No ferryman to make sure I stayed upright and navigated from one hell to the next. I wouldn't know when he'd collect his last coin and blow up the exit. That last trip . . . that's what I feared. When the truth of what—and who—Haven was shimmied in all her wicked glory.

The man who helped paint the picture of a Haven as heaven pulled into his parking spot in front of *Haven Voice*. Tanner Orr balanced his coffee cup, briefcase, and Sweetlife pastry bag as he also tried to lock the car door. I parked beside him—always willing to help.

Seeing me, his eyes widened behind his glasses, and his cheeks turned radish pink.

"Just be thankful that I didn't run you over." I plucked the hot cup of joe from his hand. "You need to answer a few questions."

He nodded over to the closed office door. "Inside—"

"No," I said, eyeing the darkened windows. "Here, right in the open. A novel idea in a town where everything's done in shadow and secret." I didn't know who was hiding in that office, ready to finally tear my last ticket in half.

"How can I help?" Tanner asked, his focus on the hot cup of coffee that could easily scald him. He smelled of men's pine-scented deodorant and flop sweat.

"How much is she paying you?" I asked.

The editor looked up, startled, his face pale and moist. "Miss Rush, I don't know what you're talking—"

"Cut the crap," I snapped. "I know you sent that text—*I know everything*—and I also know London Sutton is paying you to provide more than your keen editorial skills in reporting—*and controlling*—the news around this town."

Tanner's gaze darted around from the coffee cup to the front door of *Haven Voice* before settling back on me. A bead of sweat slipped down his temple and disappeared beneath his chin.

"So, what do you know, Tanner?" I asked.

He chuckled and shook his head.

"What do you know?" I removed the top of his coffee and steam wafted from the hot brown brew. "Admit this truth, and the coffee stays in the cup and not on your neck."

He swallowed hard, the Adam's apple bobbing in his throat. "I don't know—she wouldn't tell me. I sent the text and that's it. As far as the paper's concerned . . . Cooper's pulling the strings of the paper. He decides what goes in and what stays out."

"What about the owner of the paper?" I asked. "What does Boomer Levy think of this?"

He shrank, then dropped his head.

I peered at him as a thought popped in my head. "There is no owner of the paper named Boomer Levy, right? The Suttons are Boomer Levy."

"She needed . . . obstacles," the editor said now. "She knows that she's had an easy life, no challenges, and that no regular voter can relate to that. London wanted a big emotional and rash reaction from you so that she could have another adversary. And 'I KNOW EVERYTHING' . . . I didn't have to know what it meant for you personally. Everyone has secrets."

"She's trying to blackmail me," I said. "And she's blackmailing . . . *her*." I paused, then added, "She had you put the ransom note under Mackenzie's windshield wiper, didn't she?"

"Yes."

I swirled the coffee in the cup. "Why?"

He didn't speak. Just stared at the coffee cup.

I swirled too hard just for him and a little of the brew spilled over the rim and onto the toe of his shoe. "Oops. It's a little hot. Sorry about that." I stared at him without moving. "Why?"

"Figgy *is* really missing. That's the unfortunate truth. London thought she could capitalize on that—make it worse and more dangerous with that note."

I squinted at him. "Does Cooper know?"

Tanner shook his head. "Plausible deniability."

"Then what strings is he pulling and why?"

If he wasn't doing all this for London, then . . . ?

"We have a lot riding on this election," Tanner said. "The future of Haven. If we're going to be the next Jackson Hole or Pismo Beach, visitors gotta feel safe. Residents gotta feel safe. We can't announce every awful thing that happens here—"

"Even if reporting those awful things will ultimately help residents and visitors feel safer," I said. "You pull something into the light, it loses power."

He scoffed. "Tell that to New Orleans. Tell that to Portland."

Ivan hadn't come into the office yet, and I kept the lights off and blinds closed as I trudged past the waiting room and into my dark office. My face ached, and even if I had successfully hidden my bruises, they were pushing against the liquid foundation like steam against a closed vent. Tanner let me keep the coffee, and even though I liked mine filled with cream and sugar, this morning, I chose to keep it black.

I didn't want to do anything else today, and despite the hot shot of caffeine from the pink cup, I just wanted to close my eyes and sleep.

Cooper . . . He wanted everyone else to act right, and yet, he was the adulterer, the liar, the sorcerer. Last year this time, we'd been together at a winery in Santa Barbara talking about *Elden Ring* and the 2024 election. Now I swiped through my phone's digital photo album to study those pictures of Cooper and me doing shit only people in love did.

There we were watching a sunset while splitting a milkshake.

There we were hiking at Kenneth Hahn Park.

And now here I was, a grain of sand in the irritated eyes of Haven.

Numbers, Deuteronomy . . .

I leaned back in my chair, the books of the Bible slipping from the front of my mind and my thoughts caught up in a whirlwind of doubt. I needed to move forward. Suspicion and fear—I couldn't let it paralyze me. I couldn't let the unknown send me flying into the void bloody and bruised without a plan. At least, not yet. I needed to do some shit first. Cross off a few items from my growing list. Uncover the truth, no matter how many of my bones and breaths would be broken in the uncovering.

My hands trembled as I held my phone and keyed in the numbers on the crumpled scrap of paper I'd found hidden in Xander's bag. As the phone rang on the other end, a knot tightened in my chest.

"Hello?" A woman's voice as smooth as polished silver. "This is Sonny, right?"

I cleared my throat.

Psalms, Proverbs . . .

"Yeah." My grip tightened around the phone. "This is Sonny."

Mackenzie chuckled. "I knew you'd call." There was a pause, a breath held then released. "I know who killed Xander, just like I said in that text I sent you. And I told you to watch your back, and you kinda failed at that too. But we need to meet in person."

"Can't you just tell me now?" I asked, though I already knew the answer.

She either planned to kill me or plead for me to protect her. If I took a bullet first, she'd have time to run.

"Not possible," she said. "Especially since you pissed me off by fucking my father."

Shit. "Mackenzie, I didn't—"

"And I'm packing right now, and he's here, and Mom and him are shouting at each other, and . . . I'm hanging up now."

My ears burned. "Don't. I wanna help you—"

"Either you do it my way, or you chase your tail as I get the fuck out of Haven tonight. Because I *am* leaving tonight. Which is it?" Her tone was laced with urgency and fear.

"Fine. Where?"

"The vista point over Glass Beach. Eight o'clock tonight."

Before I could even speak, the line went dead, leaving me squeezing a silent phone.

Why so late? What was she doing now? How was she preparing to leave?

I grabbed my bag and darted to the car. Maybe I'd catch her leaving the neighborhood.

But I didn't see the black BMW in downtown Haven, so I turned onto Highway 1—

There!

A black Bimmer!

The sedan turned onto Church Road, a block over from the gray Victorian on Hollister.

I turned onto Church Road and—

This was not Mackenzie Sutton's BMW. The *My Child Is a Cal Bear* bumper sticker was the biggest clue.

Farther ahead, though, a family stepped out onto the porch of a tan Craftsman bungalow, their golden hair catching sunlight that was barely shining past those clouds, their laughter spilling through the trees. The child—a girl—looked to be about eight years old and her parents—Jen probably and Jack possibly—looked like too-young-to-be parents from J.Crew ads.

The girl—Hazel probably or Wrenley possibly, looking at the patchwork jumper and matching Converse—held a silver leash connected to a dog.

A dog with a shiny golden coat.

A goldendoodle.

Hazel-Wrenley led the dog down the porch and over to a minivan. Jack and Jen followed behind her—holding hands, smiling. Jack helped his daughter and family pet into the car as Jen slid behind the steering wheel.

I'd stopped breathing while watching something so ordinary and yet so crazy.

The family's car—a mud-caked minivan—pulled away from the Craftsman.

I counted to ten and raced down the road—the poor Nissan had never been pushed so much in her life in Haven. Gravel kicked against the fenders and windshield as I gained on the minivan. As soon as we all reached the end of the block, I swerved ahead of the Dodge Caravan and slammed my brakes.

Jen couldn't go anywhere unless she planned to roll over the Sentra.

I hopped out of the car.

Jack hopped out of the car and shouted, "What the fuck?"

Jen stayed put behind the wheel, confusion bright on her face.

In the back seat, Hazel-Wrenley and the goldendoodle snuggled, both of their tongues lolling with joy, unaware of the confrontation on Church Street.

From my spot, I saw the fig-colored birthmark on the dog's rump. I shouted, "Figgy."

The dog paused, then smiled at me, and her tail wagged fast and then faster.

"That dog," I said, pointing into the car. "She belongs to someone else."

"Who the hell are you?" Jack demanded.

"We've paid almost a thousand dollars," Jen screamed, "and you want us to what? Give her to you? Some random thug?"

"Move. Now," Jack shouted.

The little girl in the back seat was now listening. "Mommy, we can't give Lucy away. She's my dog now."

The woman reached back to her daughter and patted her head, then scratched Figgy's ear. "Noa, hon, no worries. Lucy is our forever dog."

Jack rushed over to my side. "Step the fuck back."

"She isn't for sale," I said, not stepping the fuck anywhere. I shouted, "Figgy! Come!"

The goldendoodle's ears flicked, and she bounded from the back seat up to Jen at the steering wheel.

Jack stepped in front of the window, blocking the dog from view. "She's ours. Someone found her wandering the streets a month ago. No collar, no chip."

"You're a fucking liar," I said. "You're receiving stolen property. My client has been looking for her dog—"

"Move away." This was Jen, and she held a .22 trained now at my center.

"Wow." I whipped back the tail of my shirt to show my holstered Glock. "Mine is bigger, babe. And I know how to pull quicker than you can swallow."

The gun waggled in her hand.

"Put it away," I said. "I don't want you un-aliving yourself in front of your daughter and innocent, stolen Figgy."

"Jen," he said. "Don't."

The little girl in the back started to weep. "She's mine. Lucy is mine."

"It's not hers," I whispered to her parents. "This dog has a home and a family and—"

"You can't stop us from leaving," Jen said. "Lincoln, get in the car."

"Jennifer," he said.

"Now," she shouted, near tears. "She can't stop us from leaving. She won't shoot us. Not over a dog. Not in front of a child."

Lincoln swallowed, colored, and backed away.

I chuckled. No, I wouldn't shoot them—not over a dog. But she had no place to go, the minivan stuck now between my Sentra and a telephone pole.

Once Lincoln climbed into the passenger seat, once Jennifer shoved Figgy—never Lucy—off her lap, Jennifer put the Caravan into reverse and—

Bam!

She backed into the phone pole.

She threw it into drive and—

BAM!

Right into the Sentra, pushing it away from her front bumper.

I shouted, "What the fuck?" but no one could hear me over the crunch of one car against the other.

Once more, in reverse.

Bam!

Once more, forward.

Bam!

Lincoln's eyes widened with panic. The girl's wails became shriller. Figgy started howling and barking.

I stepped back——too late to move the Sentra out of the way.

Jennifer eventually made enough room to maneuver out of the position, clipping the Nissan one last time before roaring down Church.

I'd chase her, but the Sentra was not in the best shape to chase anything. Instead, I watched the minivan storm down the road, with my phone zooming onto the license plate for my 911 call to report a theft, a hit-and-run, and—hell, why not—attempted murder.

43.

As I left a message on Ivan's voicemail, my pitch sounded tinny and thin. "She was a complete asshole, and I promise, if I see that woman in life ever again . . ." I let out a long breath. "Anyway, let me know who that minivan belongs to. In addition to taking stolen property and hitting my car and running, whoever they are fucked up. I'll let you know if I hear anything on my end." I ended the call, disappointed that he hadn't picked up.

How was I supposed to tell Giovanni that I had demolished his car?

Keeping the lights off, I paced my dark office, replaying in my head the violent scene with that family in the minivan and Figgy. The bangs, crunches, and creaks of twisting metal. The squeal and stink of screeching tires. How little Noa Minivan screamed as Figgy barked and howled. How Lincoln Minivan gripped one hand on the headrest and the other on the dashboard. How Jennifer Minivan just pulled a gun on me and then kept hitting everything around her. Parents of the year.

I needed to tell London about all that had happened—word would get out that a minivan-driving dog thief nearly killed her private investigator.

The medical office of therapist London Sutton, MD, was located on Sea Rose Way, a block away from Poole Investigations. I'd passed by this ecru-and-white-trim converted Craftsman-style clinic nearly every day not realizing that my ex-boyfriend's wife practiced here. The waiting room had beige walls and chairs upholstered in brown fabric with space for about seven people. The check-in desk was crowded with staff and a mom corralling three small children. The clinic smelled of potpourri and ambition, and framed photographs of famous athletes hung on the walls—from soccer star Carli Lloyd to football great Tom Brady—which had to be more of an artistic statement than a representation of the patient population.

Most patients looked high school age and wore various types of braces, tapes, and crutches. Justin Parrish, main competitor against Xander Monroe, sat near the window tapping on his phone. He saw me and offered a flash of a grin.

"She's pretty booked today." The receptionist was a dark-haired pixie wearing a *FATIMA* name tag.

"It won't take long," I whispered, "I'm doing contract work for her, and I have an update on her family's dog."

Fatima sighed and clicked through the schedule again.

Eyes burned my back as I stood there, but I didn't want to turn my attention away from the gatekeeper with the schedule.

"Maybe she can see you in about . . . two hours?" Fatima looked up at me with hard eyes that burned with *you shall not pass* energy.

I placed my hands on my hips and clicked my teeth. Fine, it wasn't *my* dog, and I couldn't force this woman to let me in.

After leaving the building, I stood in the vestibule, squinting into the light, squinting at the battered MISSING DOG flyer with Figgy's picture on the community corkboard—not wanting to walk back to the office, not wanting to make that call to Giovanni about his car, not wanting to check in on my vandalized Bronco, not wanting to figure out how I'd reach Glass Beach without driving that curvy highway at nighttime.

"Mrs. Rush."

Even though I was far from a Mrs., I still looked over my shoulder.

Justin Parrish stood in the breezeway, hidden in shadow. "Have you found whoever killed Xander?" he whispered. The darkness made his tear-filled eyes lycanthropic.

My stomach twisted. "I haven't." I crept toward him, not wanting the kid to freak out and back into me or beat me with his crutches. "But we're still looking."

With those sad, silver eyes, he looked toward the door.

I tilted my head. "You okay?"

He shrugged, shook his head, shrugged again. "I wish I would've been able to play with him. He deserved that spot. I'm . . . too slow. I got hit at practice this morning, and it felt like every bone in my leg just . . ." He made an explosion sound.

I frowned. "Why aren't you at the hospital?"

He smirked. "That's a twenty-minute drive that my father would never let me take."

I squinted. "Because . . . ?"

"That's admitting failure. His only son can't be a failure."

Oh, Justin. You aren't Harvey's only son. He has a Black one down in San Jose.

The young man's eyes shifted away from mine and down to his knee. "I'm taped up like a mummy under here."

"In pain?"

"Yeah, but Doc can take care of that, at least, for a little while."

The door to the waiting room opened, and Fatima said, "Justin, Dr. Sutton's ready to see you."

He limped away from me. "I'm gonna get what I want out of this, but I'll probably never walk straight again. That's what happens, though, when you get greedy, right?"

Twenty minutes later, Winter, a cross-country runner sweaty from running and pain, followed a nurse into an exam room. A pair of school-aged twin boys wearing soccer gear bustled past me and exploded into the waiting room. Their weary-looking mother smiled at me and said, "Maybe she can give them all something to sleep, ha."

I said, "Ha," and returned my focus to the phone. Two hours had passed and London still hadn't made time to see me. My phone was dying and needed to charge. My abrasions stung from dirt and perspiration. I needed to pee. I couldn't maintain this state if I planned to see Mackenzie tonight.

Inside the clinic, one of the twins knocked the framed picture of Michael Phelps from the wall. Weary Mom held her hands to her face, on the verge of tears. Maybe London could give *her* something to sleep—

Wait.

Justin Parrish . . . He complained about his leg and said that his father wouldn't let him visit the hospital and that Dr. Sutton would prescribe him something.

London could write prescriptions, including drugs for sports injuries.

Drugs like Toradol.

Drugs like tramadol.

Had Mackenzie stolen a prescription pad from her mother to write scrips?

Half a league, half a league,

Half a league onward . . .

Maybe reciting "The Charge of the Light Brigade" could help shake the sense of unease coiling in my gut—listing fruits hadn't. The fog had rolled in thick because of course it had. Glass Beach was ten miles from Haven, and the mist made this twilight drive feel like I was traveling through a clouded dream.

All in the valley of Death

Rode the six hundred . . .

If I didn't breathe soon, I'd pass out. And if I passed out, then the Sentra would careen off the highway, crash through the redwood grove and Dukes of Hazzard off the bluffs and into the craggy part of the California coast.

But Highway 1 didn't believe in letting drivers of this road breathe.

I sipped air as I clutched the steering wheel, the dark, twisted highway snaking before me. Each pinhead curve took my breath away, and I gripped the wheel even tighter. The sun dipped lower, a sliver riding the Pacific. The light from the Sentra's lopsided headlight no longer worked thanks to dog thief Jennifer Minivan. The one remaining light was too weak to completely obliterate the shadowy murkiness around me.

Why the hell did I agree to meet Mackenzie Sutton down there?

Because you didn't think it would be this bad.

I was breathing too hard—the windshield was fogging, and the Sentra's defroster had already been dying even before someone drove over it. I swiped my hand across the glass . . . only for it to ghost around the edges of the windshield and turn all white again.

"Forward, the Light Brigade!"

Beads of sweat popped along my hairline.

Never again.

That's what I said when I drove here from Los Angeles more than a week ago. I used to be a rational person, not one to give in to hysterics or hyperbole. But this road . . . This road was scarier than getting jumped. And then the eerie sense of being alone on such a dark highway . . . Anxiety sat on my chest and grinned down at me like the meanest drag queen in the world.

This could be a trap.

Of course it could—but I'd also been assaulted a mile from my home. Ivan knew where I was headed, and if I didn't check in at ten minutes after eight, he'd leave the office and head to Glass Beach.

Knowing that he had my back didn't quell my anxiety right now, though.

"Charge for the guns!" he said.

Into the valley of Death

Rode the six hundred.

I glanced in the rearview mirror—still no other car behind me.

Two miles to go.

I rounded another curve.

A green highway sign:

GLASS BEACH
NEXT EXIT

My hands loosened their grip.

Someone had blundered

Theirs not to make reply

Mackenzie knew that I knew that she knew more about Xander than what she'd claimed days ago. Her phone number had been found in his call history—incoming and outgoing, just hours before the kid was found dead on that trail.

She knew who killed Xander Monroe.

Would this be a confession?

I reached the turnoff to Glass Beach, and I let out a long breath of relief as I exited and drove straight for the first time in almost thirty minutes. God did not make straight lines. Neither did the men who built this highway.

A former dumpsite, Glass Beach looked like its name. Covered in small, smooth pieces of colored glass flattened by the pounding waves of the ocean. People called it The Dumps once upon a time because they'd thrown their fridges, glass, and old Honda Civics over the cliffs.

Mackenzie's car was parked at the end of the paved lot just where she said she'd be.

I pulled into a spot behind her and grabbed my phone to text her.

One bar of cell phone reception . . . *barely*.

I announced my arrival the old-fashioned way: I flashed my one working headlight.

Mackenzie didn't leave the car.

I climbed out of the Sentra.

The thermostat on my watch said it was sixty degrees out. Any heavenly bodies hidden above me were now behind the rolling sea of fog.

Mackenzie sat in the driver's seat, her head against the headrest, sleeping as she waited for me to creep down Pacific Coast Highway—a drive twenty-five minutes longer with me behind the wheel.

But I was here now, and that was the most important thing. Relief washed over me like a cool wave . . . until icy dread replaced it.

Because something was off.

I reached for my gun, my eyes still on the Bimmer but also skipping to the cliffs up ahead and the public bathroom to my right.

The crash of the waves below drowned out my heavy breathing. Chilled ocean spray speckled my face.

"Mackenzie," I shouted, creeping toward the car, "it's Sonny Rush!"

No answer.

The windshield of the sedan was white from her breath, almost hiding her.

"Mackenzie?" I tapped the rear window.

Her head didn't move.

Swallowing hard, I stepped to the driver's side window and peeked through the glass.

There she was, sleeping.

I knocked on the glass again, tossed one last look around before I bent to peer at the young woman.

Yeah. Something was wrong.

I reached for the door handle—and stopped.

If something was off, then . . .

With no latex gloves in the Sentra, I used my shirttail to pull the door handle.

Please let the door be unlocked . . .

I took a breath and pulled the handle. It gave but I didn't exhale, not yet.

The door swung open.

Mackenzie's lifeless eyes stared ahead as foam dried on her lips.

Pills were scattered across her lap and the passenger-side seat.

Shit!

My hands shook as I grabbed her wrist.

No pulse.

"Shit," I shouted again, then tapped "Emergency."

Nothing happened. One bar of cell phone reception.

I closed the car door and ran up the road that led back to the highway, hoping to flag someone down. I paced as I waited, but the dark became darkest dark, and no car headlights shone in the distance.

My eyes blurred with tears, and I swiped them away on my shoulder. Once more, with slippery and shaky fingers, I tapped "Emergency."

NO SERVICE.

I tried Ivan's number anyway.

NO SERVICE.

I tried Cooper's number and prayed for a miracle.

NO SERVICE.

"Come on, please come on," I whispered, pleading for a ringtone that would never come, not in this part of California.

I stood frozen beside that guardrail, the metallic taste of fear tweaking my tongue. I looked behind me and down to the BMW, left like a discarded soda can at the bottom of a ravine.

The wind picked up, and my hair whipped around my face, hard, stinging. I shivered—from the cold, from my sense of helplessness, from my mind blanking when I needed it to work.

Zero reception wouldn't suddenly turn into 70 percent no matter how long I stood here. Bile bubbled up my throat as I glanced at the Sentra parked behind Mackenzie's BMW.

Okay.

An idea formed in the gap of silence between crashing waves:

Drive back toward Haven until I find a cell phone signal. Pull to the side of the road and call 911. Tell the dispatcher my location and Mackenzie's. Tell them of the overdose. Hurry back to Mackenzie and wait.

Yes. That would work.

With renewed determination, I ran back to the Sentra and slid behind the wheel. "I'll be back, Mackie," I said, as though she could still hear me.

I pulled onto the road, onto Highway 1, going north now, with a new hazard: my attention divided between the curves and peeking at my phone for at least three bars.

Please, please, please.

Ten minutes into the drive, the universe took pity on me, and one bar appeared on my screen and then . . . *four!* I pulled to the side of the road and tapped "Emergency."

The line rang . . . rang . . .

Theirs not to reason why,

Theirs but to do and die.

Into the valley of Death

Rode the six hundred.

I tapped Ivan's number.

He picked up. "I was about to hop in the—"

"Ivan!"

"What happened?" he asked, calmer than me but still on alert.

I told him that I'd found Mackenzie Sutton dead in her car—pills everywhere—that I couldn't call 911 because of the lack of coverage.

"You still armed?"

"Yep," I said, feeling the pinch of the holster against my kidneys.

"Drive back to her," he said. "I'll call 911. I'm on my way down."

I whispered, "Okay," then ended the call. I pushed out another breath, willing my hands to stop shaking. To return to Glass Beach and Mackenzie's car, I needed to drive farther north on the highway to exit, get back on the highway, and drive south. How far away was Ivan? How far away were first responders? How would I explain all of this?

I reached the road leading to Glass Beach. Farther ahead, I could see that the parking lot was still dark and no other car's headlights pierced the darkness. Right before I turned into the lot, my phone rang.

"Where are you right now?" India asked, her voice filled with icy fear.

"You wouldn't believe me if I told you," I said. "I'm driving—"

"Pull over right now," she said. "London Sutton."

"What about her?" I asked.

"Her fingerprint was found on Xander's earbuds. Looks like she was in AFIS after a DUI twelve years ago. I thought maybe it was just a coincidence, but . . ."

I rubbed the bridge of my nose. "India, Mackenzie is dead."

"What?" she shouted.

I told my friend all that had happened tonight. "Ivan's on his way down with the police."

"Why?" India asked. "I don't understand."

Then I remembered that the expensive perfume that had tumbled out of London's bag at Mason's during happy hour on last Friday—TOM FORD's Vanilla Sex—was the same perfume listed on the Sephora receipt found in Xander's gym bag. She could prescribe opioids, including tramadol. That pendant found in Xander's mouth had been a rose gold daisy pendant—like the pendant in that picture I saw in the hallway at the Sutton house. Like the . . . I gasped.

The comic book panels in the notebook I'd found in Xander's bedroom. PhizX in his dark hospital room. The shadowy female visitor with that light glinting around her neck. *"I belong here."* That's what she'd said. At the hospital. Because she was a doctor.

And that glinting light . . . The pendant. I'd found its broken chain on Seabreeze Trail.

Those orange Nikes . . . Did they belong to London too?

Cold fury bubbled inside of me. The thought of a forty-five-year-old woman taking advantage of a kid looking for healing, a kid flattered by the attention of an older, beautiful woman.

"You'll be the death of me." That's what PhizX had lamented.

This bitch deserved to burn.

Adrenaline shot through my veins, and I was no longer scared of the curves or the darkness. Moonlight peeked between the gaps in the redwoods and the racing clouds, but now I no longer needed light. My anger was a light unto my path and lamp unto the wheels of this janky Nissan Sentra.

I continued my drive toward the parking lot.

Mackenzie's car was still parked in its space and I—

BAM!

The Sentra swerved and careened wildly, its tires screeching against the pavement as everything exploded all around me—the deafening crunch of metal against metal for the second time today. This time, the car's airbags deployed, jolting me back against the seat and obscuring my vision with a cloud of dust and smoke. That violent force kept me from gripping the steering wheel and turning out of my skid, just as I'd been taught to do at police academy.

My head banged back against the seat, and I saw white again. My heart pounded in my chest as my car came to a stop. I could already feel bruises forming on my skin from the impact. My head throbbed, and I tried to get my bearings, my senses reeling from the collision.

Everything was silent for a moment. My ears rang as I struggled to regain my senses, the taste of metal and adrenaline thick in my mouth. The smoky smell of burned rubber and gasoline seeped through the vents, and as the air cleared, I could make out the crumpled hood of the Sentra. I fumbled for my seat belt with shaking hands. It finally clicked open, and I pushed the door. As I staggered out of the wreckage, every muscle in my body screamed.

Two accidents in one day wasn't just bad luck; it was destiny.

Beyond the smoke and powder from the airbags, I saw a black Maserati. London was stalking toward me, a Beretta pointed out in front of her. She wore a white sweatshirt, blue jeans, and a Bengtsson Vineyards baseball cap. She was screaming, her mouth twisted.

The high-pitched ringing in my ears drowned out all sounds until her voice cut through the chaos. "Put your hands up," she shouted, pointing the gun at me with a trembling hand.

London's grip was unsteady. She held the Beretta with one hand—like a Nerf Blaster—her thumb placed beneath the gun's beavertail instead of on the side. She obviously had no experience with weapons, which made her even more dangerous.

Dizzy and sick to my stomach, I stood before her, refusing to raise my hands in surrender. Another wave of fear washed over me. This was where I might take my last breath.

A beautiful place to die.

London sneered at me. "You should be scared," she taunted, her voice distant and cold.

I said, "Okay."

"You don't think I'll shoot you?" she asked, her eyebrows furrowed in disbelief.

I shrugged, trying to remain calm, even though terror was bubbling inside of me. "I don't know what to think anymore." I paused, then asked, "Why Xander? He was a good kid."

She shook her head, a flicker of regret passing over her face. "It wasn't supposed to go this far. We were friends . . . until he started acting differently. He needed my help. He was struggling, and I wanted him to be his best and . . ."

Her grip on the gun loosened slightly, her arms growing tired from holding it up for so long. "He instigated everything. Complimenting me. Buying me perfume. Being interesting. He wanted to show me his football workout, and we started running together and . . .

"He was going to tell—about us. He thought I was taking advantage of him one day; he thought he was too good for me the next. He felt guilty on Tuesday; and then, on Friday, he was blowing up my phone."

"Because he was a *child*," I said. "He didn't know what the hell he wanted. That's where you, the grown-ass woman, who shouldn't have even *been* in that space with him, should've—"

"*You* are the arbiter of morality?" she asked, gaping at me. "The woman sleeping with my husband?"

"Your husband is an adult," I said, shaking my head, "and I'm not a statutory—"

"Don't," she warned, her finger on the trigger. "You will not call me that."

I clamped my lips together.

"I told him not to say anything," London said, the gun drifting back to her side. "I *begged* him. I even told him that I'd tell UCLA and all the other schools that he was injured and that he'd been hiding his injury with drugs. If he wanted to destroy my future, I'd destroy his. He didn't believe me." She shook her head, tightened her grip on the gun and leveled it at me again. "I wanted him to believe me."

My fists clenched at my sides as anger rose inside me. "So, you killed him? Destroyed his future because yours was at risk?"

London's arms dropped again. "I didn't mean for it to happen like this," she whispered. "I loved him. He cared for me. He saw me as someone deserving space and attention and love, even though I had everything in the world. But I couldn't let him ruin my life. People already resented me. No one ever felt sorry for me. This . . . And with him . . ."

I stood frozen, unsure of what to do or say. *A beautiful place to die.* All because of jealousy and selfishness. And then: "Mackenzie . . ."

London's eyes widened, the whites almost entirely eclipsing her irises. "She knew about Xander. And she was holding it over me. She was blackmailing her own mother! Just like she was blackmailing Cooper after she'd followed him to LA and saw him with you. At first, she didn't believe it, but then she saw you in Cabo, and she took that picture . . . She didn't know we were already in divorce proceedings."

I glanced over at that BMW now a tomb holding Mackenzie's lifeless body.

"Cooper wasn't lying to you," she said, her voice trembling with emotion. "I was supposed to move to San Francisco, and you were supposed to move here. But Mackie told him that he couldn't. She didn't want a family like her friends', and she didn't want some Black woman from LA as a stepmother and a cop on top of that. She threatened to tell the world what a cheater he was and that she'd go to his competitor with his plans and the financials so that they could underbid us for all of these redevelopment deals.

"I was the one who asked her to follow him around and come back and tell me if he was cheating—but I wanted proof because of *money*, not love. I could give a fuck who he fucked, but I refused to let you or anyone take my shit. Mackie, though, she just . . . She let it go to her head."

My hands balled into fists at my sides again as I struggled to contain my anger.

London's shoulders slumped in defeat as the weight of everything finally hit her.

"Did you kill your daughter?" I asked.

The question hung in the air, heavy and suffocating.

The woman standing before me snorted. "Does it matter?"

My jaw tightened in response. "Everyone and everything matters. Every choice, every action has consequences." I tilted my head, studying her carefully.

She stood here surrounded by twisted metal, shattered glass, and death that she had caused. None of this would be here if she truly cared about anything or anyone. Yeah, nothing truly mattered to London Sutton—except for her and her feelings.

She shook her head. "She listened to me for the first time. Everything she's done up until now . . . Her life was over anyway, and she knew it, and she finally listened. Rehab wasn't going to fix any of this." She looked at me, tears streaming down her cheeks.

A twinge of sympathy sparked in my heart for this broken woman.

But then she grinned at me, her expression almost manic. "Did I force her to stuff her mouth with pills today? Yesterday? Three years ago?" A sad smile tugged at the corners, and she waggled her head. "Xander caused his own death."

"*What?*" I shook my head. "No. *You* caused Xander's death. Your fingerprints were on Xander's earbuds. Your pendant was in his mouth. And you'll spend the rest of your life in jail."

She gaped at me. Tears tumbled down her cheeks, and with an angry hand, she slapped them away. "Well, they'll have to find me first." She lifted the gun and pointed it at me.

Without hesitation, I reached for my gun and fired a shot at her foot before she could pull the trigger. She dropped the weapon and crumpled to the ground. I kicked the gun out of her reach, twisted her arm behind her back, and placed my knee on her ass, pinning her down on the pavement with all my strength despite my sore muscles and exhaustion.

"Kill me," she whispered, tears streaming freely down her face. "I can't face them. Please. Kill me."

My muscles burned as I kept her in this position, as she begged for death, as blood spilled from her sneaker and onto the asphalt, onto the cuffs of my white jeans. It took all of Ivan's strength to pry me off of London Sutton, the worst Haven had to offer.

44.

I could feel India's eyes on me as I gulped another bottle of water. We stood in silence, watching a closed-circuit television as a female deputy escorted London Sutton—limping and wearing her new orange jumpsuit—to a jail cell that would be cold and stark, with nothing but a small, narrow bed and a metal toilet. Had Cooper been notified that his wife had been arrested and that his daughter was gone forever? As I watched London's hands, now stained black from the booking process, I couldn't shake off the guilt and turmoil inside of me.

Xander was gone. Mackenzie was gone. Figgy was still gone.

Did London Sutton deserve this ending? Should she be upright and alive right now? Should I have shot her at center mass and ended her right then and there?

Anger and helplessness washed over me, and I wanted to sink to the floor and cry.

Once London had disappeared into the bowels of lockup, I glanced back at my laptop and the grainy footage taken from Deegan's diner, across the street from where I'd been attacked.

India kept pausing and replaying the video, trying to find some clue or answer, but all I felt was a sense of unease and confusion. "One last time and I'll stop." She hit the "Back" button and played the video again.

"Wait," I said, standing straight. "Pause it. Go back."

India hit "Back" again.

"Stop. The build of my assaulter is too wide to be Cooper."

I zoomed in on the man's wrist. "The numbers on his watch are digital and white," I said, staring at its black face.

"Can't be sure," India said, "but it looks like one of those tactical watches."

I swiped the screen up and pointed to the man's shoes. "And those."

"What about them?" India said, squinting. "A few of the guys around here wear shoes like that."

"They're cop shoes," I whispered.

India shrugged, but then she tilted her head.

"And the house on Church Street?" I asked, eyes still on the frozen video. "The house where that family picked up Figgy. Whose name was on the lease?"

"Not an individual. It was a company . . ." India grabbed her notepad and dragged her fingers across the page. "The title says the house belongs to . . . Jingle Belles, LLC. *B-E-L-L-E.*"

No one at that house had come outside to watch Jennifer Minivan monster truck over Giovanni's Sentra. No curiosity? No running out of the house bug-eyed and shouting, *What the hell?*

"No." My eyes burned with tears as I took a step back from the desk.

"What's wrong?" India asked.

I met her gaze, then turned away. "Jingle as in jingle dress. Belle as in Anabelle."

"I don't understand." She shook her head, then ran a thumb along my forehead. "You're pale. Maybe I should drive you to the hospital."

I whispered, "Ivan's wife was a member of the Chumash tribe."

"Yeah. So?"

"There's a picture on his desk of her wearing a jingle dress at a celebration," I said.

"I don't—" She gasped and covered her mouth with her hand. "Belle. Jingle . . . Belle's."

Ivan owned the house that the Minivans had visited to pick up Figgy.

Ivan owned a tactical watch and shoes matching the person in this video of my assault.

Ivan—my father's best friend, my play uncle—had jumped me.

Why would he hurt me, though?

What would I do about any of this? *What if I was wrong? Who was—*

"Hey," India said, softly, "they have a proposition for you."

"They?"

"The powers that be. We need a seasoned homicide detective. Someone like you."

Her offer broke through the noise in my head.

A job as a homicide detective would be an anchor, a lifeline in the storm that was threatening to pull me under. It meant a chance to rebuild, to fight back against the uncertain tides of Haven.

"Part of me wants you to say no," India said. "For personal reasons, of course. Danger. Emerald Triangle. Long hours. A larger part wants you to say yes. Shit. What you'd be able to accomplish with a badge . . ." She grinned. "It would be a fresh start for you and a win for me."

My phone vibrated with a text.

Cooper.

Alyson

I slipped my phone into my sticky back pocket. "I'll think about it," I said, my thoughts already racing ahead to the day I'd be sworn in.

India nodded and stood straight. "Let me drive you home."

My head nearly cracked open three times in the last forty-eight hours. Giovanni's Sentra was on its way to the car graveyard. I didn't know what I'd do about his car, my car, or my future.

And there was nothing I loved more than figuring out *why*.

Mom sat on the couch, cocooned in a vibrant crocheted blanket. The soft glow of the TV shone across her tired face as she watched an episode of *Murder, She Wrote*. A plate of freshly baked lemon cupcakes sat on the coffee table, their sweet scent filling the room. Her eyes were bloodshot and weary from a restless night of worry and prayer. "Boring day?" she asked, shifting over to make space for me on the couch.

"Yep," I said. "Nothing exciting ever happens to me."

My phone vibrated with a text message.

Lori Monroe.

Is it true?

Yes

I got her

My eyes blurred with tears.

"You okay?" Mom squeezed my wrist.

"Mm-hm." I nodded and swiped my wet cheek against my shoulder. "Just finishing up."

One more wrist squeeze, then Mom released me.

I looked at my email inbox one last time for the night—a few of my luxury baubles that I'd listed on Poshmark had sold and a $1,200 deposit would soon be made into my account.

"Those pants," Mom said, her eyebrows crumpling at my filthy white jeans. "You know you can't wear them past Labor Day. Might as well burn 'em now."

"Might as well." Smiling, I grabbed a cupcake and sank into the couch cushions, allowing myself to be enveloped by the familiar sounds of late-night TV.

For now, I'd let the warmth of the room and the company of my mother soothe my frayed nerves. Tomorrow, I'd return to my job as store manager of Fucked Up Things and face the reality of Ivan's betrayal and consider the job offer with the sheriff's department that could change everything. Tonight, though, there was solace in the electric-blue glow of the television and the simple act of sitting beside my mother.

A sharp rapping sound jolted me awake. The television now played an infomercial for wrinkle cream. My eyes burned with exhaustion, and my heart raced from the jarring noise. I sat there, alone on the couch, the crocheted blanket spread across my shoulders.

Another knock.

I glanced at the clock on my phone.

Fifteen minutes past two in the morning.

Nothing good ever happened after two in the morning.

That's why I slipped my gun from its holster and crept over to the door. I peeked through the peephole.

A young woman with matted brown hair wearing a dirty rumpled T-shirt and jeans stood on the porch.

She knocked again.

I reached for the door and paused, my hand hovering over the doorknob.

"Yes?" I asked, my tone even.

"Can I talk to Alyson Rush, please?" A teardrop tumbled down her gaunt cheek.

I unlocked the door and pulled it open. I let her see the Glock in my hand.

Her eyes widened—yeah, she saw it—then returned to meet my gaze. "You don't know me," she said, "but—" Her voice broke and she bit her lip, glancing back into the darkness as though someone was lurking there.

"Who are you?" I asked, now lifting my gun.

She took a deep breath and closed her eyes as that breath drifted from her nose. She found my gaze again and said, "I'm . . . I'm Honor Butler."

Acknowledgments

Welcome to Haven, y'all!

I want to thank you, dear reader, for picking up this story. So many of you loved my Detective Lou Norton stories and kept asking me, "When is Lou coming back?" Lou's not back, but someone who could be her cousin is, and I'm falling in love with her just like I fell in love with Lou. I hope you do too! Your support means so much to me, and I can't wait to share more Sonny stories!

Thank you, Jill Marsal, for continuing to be the agent of my dreams.

Thank you, Jessica Tribble Wells and Clarence Haynes, for being extraordinary editors and friends.

Thank you, Gracie Doyle and the Thomas & Mercer team. I love bragging about y'all.

To folks at the Mendocino Coast Writers Conference, thank you for answering questions about your beautiful town. Mendocino Coast is nowhere near as murder-y as fictional Haven, and it is one of the most stunning places I've ever visited. The highways to get there, though . . .

Thank you, Crystal Patriarche, Grace Fell, Taylor Brightwell, and the entire BookSparks team for helping readers find my stories. We've promoted so many books together now. Does that mean we're going steady, lol?

My writing community continues to offer incredible support, and I want to say thanks, especially, to Jess Lourey, Kellye Garrett, Yasmin

Angoe, Shawn Cosby, Alex Segura, and Naomi Hirahara. I'm also lucky to have lifelong friends who show up for me and for each other. I love you, Gigi, Ema, Richard, Karlton, Daniel, and Duania. Here's to more wine tastings, taco nights, hugs, and long text strings that I need to mute sometimes.

Family matters, and I'm blessed to have a loving one in my life. My mother, Jacqueline, has always been so excited to see my writing life grow. Thank you, Mom, for nurturing my love of books and words way back then. Thank you to my siblings, Terry, Gretchen, and Jason, for just being cool, interesting people with wild-ass stories. I love you, Rowdy and Brilliant Howzells.

Maya and David, you both have my heart, and I love you, and I love our life together. Looking forward to experiencing new adventures at home and abroad . . . especially abroad.

About the Author

Photo © 2023 Andre Ellis

Rachel Howzell Hall is the *New York Times* bestselling author of *The Last One*; *What Never Happened*; *We Lie Here*; *These Toxic Things*; *And Now She's Gone*; *They All Fall Down*; and, with James Patterson, *The Good Sister*, which was included in Patterson's collection *The Family Lawyer*. A two-time *Los Angeles Times* Book Prize finalist as well as an Anthony, Edgar, International Thriller Writers, and Lefty Award nominee, Rachel is also the author of *Land of Shadows*, *Skies of Ash*, *Trail of Echoes*, and *City of Saviors* in the Detective Elouise Norton series. A past member of the board of directors for Mystery Writers of America, Rachel has been a featured writer on NPR's acclaimed *Crime in the City* series and the National Endowment for the Arts weekly podcast; she has also served as a mentor in Pitch Wars and the Association of Writers & Writing Programs. Rachel lives in Los Angeles with her husband and daughter. For more information, visit www.rachelhowzell.com.